# ASSAULTMISTRESS
# KIDAHIN

A Hunter's Universe Novel by David Michael Martin

For information contact:

 Bent Briar Publishing L.L.L.P.
Denver CO 80226
www.bentbriarbooks.com

978-1-942665-16-8    SC
978-1-942665-18-2    eBook

10 9 8 7 6 5 4 3 2 1

**Dedication**

This book is dedicated to all female combatants everywhere, whether they are women in single combat or in combat units. Embrace your inner Hunter, Warrior or Comari.

**Acknowledgments**

I want to thank my agent Laura Kathleen Sutton for the hours of work she spent in getting *Assaultmistress Kidahin* published. I also thank BetteRose Ryan and everyone at Bent Briar Publishing for their time and efforts. Their work is greatly appreciated.

**Author Updates**

For more information regarding Mr. Martin, the Hunter's Universe Saga, and his works in progress visit davidmichaelmartin.com.

**Other Titles by David Michael Martin**

*Hunter's Moon*
*Honor and Obligation*
*WARPACT!*

# 1

## UNION WITH THE MALE, THE HEART IS A LONELY HUNTER, SEEING TRAPS, SNARES, AND POISONS...

"Team-Two assaultmistress," Kidahin trilled in musical counterpoint to the shaking and banging the stealth insertion vehicle made as he fell through rough turbulence far above the coastal jungle. The title sounded clumsy in her twitching ears. It reminded her of a Warrior female crashing through dense rainforest undergrowth with all the supple grace of a heavy tank.

Her trilling rose to a self-deprecating insolent pitch. A Hunter female herself, Kidahin thought all Warrior females were noisier and clumsier than Hunters.

"Maybe you should not have accepted assaultmistress duties without first giving the security duty offers more than a passing glance," Jassalin growled from the bulkhead behind the pilot seat.

"Melkorka pushed the assaultmistress assignment on me as a sign of her confidence. That confidence was well deserved because we succeeded on our first combat mission beyond all expectations," Kidahin sang.

But past success did nothing to silence her doubts. Those whispering doubts had lately found fertile soil in memories of the scent-linked empathic visions she saw during her adulthood ceremony some forty months ago. Her family females used their pheromones to wrap her in scent-linked empathy and sent her mind into the Oyya Web of the spirits. During that pheromonal vision quest the spirits told her that she held the high ground for a singing male who fought for all Eyloni on the low ground. Soon after the ceremony she had opted for warship duty and four weeks later her warleader was dead. In her role of huluhar she picked another male for her warship society to choose as Warleader, a most remarkable male.

In her arrogance Kidahin thought this Warleader was the singing male the spirits had revealed. Then a Comari female chose him as the one male she was going to guard and protect forever. Rare male and rarer

Comari together meant the Warleader could not be the singing male on the low ground in her adulthood visions.

Yet those keening doubts were singing dire warnings now. What if the Comari could not reach him in time? Impossible, for a Comari never left her chosen bondmale for more than an hour and even less if she was uncertain of his safety. Doubt was driving Kidahin to backtrail and loop along the same line of thought as she tailchased explanations for those doubts. For her to fight alongside the Warleader she had to prowl with him and not with Assault Team-Two on surface or boarding missions.

Why did she not take the warleader special security assignment? Only Hunter females worked at those security posts. Serious, dour, and deadly, warleader special security Huntresses were respected, even feared.

Those Hunters possessed a steadfast mental attitude, an attitude like Aplilin.

Aplilin was one deadly Huntress, and yet it was Tialdrin and Kyralin who served in security during Battle Status aboard their warship. They were also potential warleader special security recruits. A twinge of envy crept its way down Kidahin's long, beautiful tail.

Choices, life came down to making the right choices. Did she make the right choice?

"Doubt kills, my Kidahin," Aplilin trilled. "You made the right choice and now you have us."

Kidahin sent loving affection through her pheromones to her lover as she banked the SIV into a spiraling descent over the sprawling Ah'vou'ree Clan rainforest. She landed the SIV in a tight clearing above and within sight of the coastline. Ah'vou'ree Clan territory sat on the southwestern La'huaset Tribal continent and only a few degrees latitude north of the equator. Occasional groups of orange and red elleiu trees, hometrees, towered well above the more modest arberi trees growing up to the elleiu tree shade perimeters.

Those arberi trees with their orange trunks covered with orange and red leaves striped with yellows grew flowers from bulbous galls on their branches. Each flower was an orange, yellow, and red catkin nearly the length of her tail. The catkins gave the galls ocher auras. Their perfume, strong and pleasant, repelled insects. Arberi trees loved the coastal sandy soil mixed with the inland clay found here.

Kidahin realized she was staring through the clear SIV canopy at nothing and snapped her tail against the pilot seat and scolded herself for leafchasing the time away.

"Everybody out," she sang as she began the mission briefing. "We will insert here in the arberi trees at this elevation. Up ahead the Ah'vou'ree Peninsula coastline plunges nearly vertically into Ah'vou'ree Bay and continues down into the cold waters of the farside abyssal ocean."

Kidahin hesitated, feeling edgy. Her large amber eyes followed the landing zone perimeter. Bare slopes marked recent landslides. The rusty-brown soil did not have even a hint of new growth. Slick with wet clay, the bare slopes were impassable. Piles of mangled trees clawing at the sky surrounded the clearing in a staggered semicircle ahead. Hours of climbing up the landslide was the only way to reach their first watch point. Fallen trees and interlocking branches rested against the steep ground ahead of them. Underneath the landslide greasy red clay waited for the right trigger to slide the unstable smashed forest into the surf far below.

Kidahin flicked her ears at Jassalin. "What do you think?" she sang.

"We should get back into the SIV and fly over these tortured boles," Jassalin snapped.

"We cannot. This is our assigned landing zone. We must begin our ascent if we are to reach our watch point before the Warleader begins his battle song drumming."

Jassalin spun her tail in slow circles while weighing Kidahin's words. "You should have demanded a higher elevation insertion point. These trees are twisted up in vines and lianas. We can climb them if we are careful. The landslide mutilated them, the branches, and the boles. Some of the lianas are likely not attached to their trees anymore. Even those still attached may not take our weight."

Kidahin twisted an ear at her second-in-leadership. Jassalin was, well, not only an inventive and rational leader, a brave and mild risk-taker, but was also skeptical and argumentative. Skepticism made her a reactive strategist. She adopted whatever advance plan sounded good to her at the time. She was the oldest Team-Two Huntress in both chronological and adulthood age. She also held the highest hierarchy rank among them. Jassalin tended to do things her way, which was causing some friction between them lately.

Kidahin, the youngest of the twenty Team-Two Huntresses but having superior military rank, set the proper mood by leading the climb. Climbing in itself meant nothing to her. Eyloni lived in trees regardless of their advanced technology. Hunter females enjoyed the greater share of rhythmic aerobatic and acrobatic skills than either Warrior or Comara females or even the rare and beloved males all females watched over with protective zeal.

Climbing through twisted and torn branches upset Kidahin's sense of normalcy. The twisted branches, shattered trunks, and interlocking smaller trees a hundred ells deep—one hundred tail-lengths deep—mocked her. Scaling the landslide was like climbing overgrown jungle growing up the steep side of a summit. Climbing this was nothing like climbing though healthy trees and leaping from branch to branch and tree to tree.

* * *

Hours later Team-Two gazed from a rainforest-overgrown plateau down and through a panoramic view of sea and yellow sandy beaches along a crescent cove half-overgrown with pale-yellow grasses. A solitary elleiu tree some few thousand ells south of them grew well above their low plateau. The hometree belonged to one of the Ah'vou'ree Clan extended families. The family group living there formed the territorial watch for the immediate area.

Around them tiers of rainforest painted the hillsides in faded warm pastels. The scent of damp leaf mold in the air invigorated Kidahin and fortified her sense of purpose. She led her team to a nearby stump over a hundred ells across. Its tree, once a sentinel standing on the plateau above the landslide was now a part of the tormented timber twisted below them.

Tyreniioroneo rose from behind the distant, towering, eroded, eons-old, hemisphere-encompassing impact crater rim. A huge crescent sliver, he turned the white clouds near the highest peaks an electric blue. The clouds nearest him gleamed bluely in the days-long evening dusk, reminding Kidahin of blue waves slapping against rocky shores.

She perked her ears at the gibbous gas giant. His name meant "the Hunter females' tails-entwined celestial companion." Singing, trilling, or keening the name at different pitches and tempos varied word meaning, but the meaning most important to her was the singing pitch and tempo rendering the meaning as "the Hunter's Moon," which was also the name honoring the warship she served.

By the time Tyreniioroneo cleared the distant relic Team-Two was settling into ritual places around the wide, flat stump. They sat with tails touching the thighs of neighbors in a semicircular branching pattern. Far-distant rhythmic drumbeats began to echo across the sprawling rainforest. The drum, a slice of hollow log covered on both ends with an elleiu tree leaf, was pounded on by their Warleader. He was encouraging them with a strong bass beat that sang alongside a Hunter's heartbeat. It sang to them, "I am he; I am he; I am he."

Hunters, and all females for that matter, considered their hearts male. The drumming resonated with their own personal piece of male and whipped Team-Two into deadly aggression.

Alfara, the Gracious Mistress of the Singing People for Assault Team-Two's social society, sang first. A piercing soprano, she sang about victory and honor. The remaining Hunters joined her in melodic accompaniment.

The drummer, as though invigorated by their singing, settled into a stentorian martial beat. The Hunters rocked back and forth on the stump in sympathy with the beat. They reached out hands and touched neighboring shoulders as they rocked. They often reached over their heads and shook cupped fingers in the air. The headstrong power of female might took form and life through shared empathy and by their natural fascination with anything male. The ritual cadence continued for a few hours before they began singing the first of the ancient songs. The pheromonal metamind summoned by the empathy they shared pulled them into the Oyya Web of the spirits.

A few hours later Kidahin, in her Youngest Hunter ritual role, formally ended the Rite of Female Might. Although she was their assaultmistress, in ritual matters she ranked last. Only her military rank gave her the leadership of an assault team in which half ranked her in either social or hierarchical standing.

Rank was a touchy subject. Females were picky rank-observers. Social rank reflected civil standing in the community and flowed from memberships in the several societies common in Eyloni life. Hierarchies governed female moral conduct and were exclusively female. They formed all world-unifying social institutions. Impugning the civility of a ranking social female risked a social debt but impugning the morality of a ranking hierarchy female risked an honor point offense, a criminal matter.

Kidahin's military rank was a tail she could snap to manage Team-Two Hunters having superior hierarchical and social rank. Still, dealing with rank was always a twisting tail of peril.

"Huntresses, check your 'minders for the mission briefing materials downloaded into them. We are splitting into two combat hands. I will lead mine and Jassalin will led hers. Jassalin and I have separate prowling objectives. Our orders declare weapon use forbidden. Do not take any weapon with you, and do not use your adulthood knives."

"But Kidahin," Alfara trilled. "This is a combat mission. Whoever heard of combat prowling without weapons?"

"No weapons, Alfara! No knives, no swords, no spears, no bows and arrows, period. You hoard knives. You probably have ten knives stuffed into that combat harness right now. Leave them behind. That goes for all of you. Even you, Aplilin."

"I do not need a weapon," Aplilin trilled as she flexed her muscular arm. "My unarmed combat skills are sufficient to gain me the victory."

Kidahin gave Aplilin an affectionate tail snap on the thigh. "You are not a Warrior female. Besides, are you not more comfortable using personal heavy weapons during combat?"

*"Vi e'ta ka nabi!"* Aplilin trilled in challenge.

"We will not be 'parting the branches' today. We are splitting up to secure two watch points and wait for the Mistress of Battle to update our objectives. Jassalin, take your ten and advance to your first watch point."

"Affirm, acting!" Jassalin sang.

Kidahin sighed. The Ah'vou'ree Clan equatorial coastal rainforest looked and felt quite different from their far northern subpolar Uahua'asee'a Clan rainforests. Ah'vou'ree territory straddled the western terminator and the much cooler farside hemisphere. The meeting air currents and their temperature differences churned up storms, some of which were quite violent. It rained often. The rain and the equatorial heat made the jungle undergrowth far denser and taller than it was in the north. The sky was hazy from blue-tinted isoprene gas given off by the plants. The saturating humidity added even more haze. She did not miss the salt-seeking insects that normally buzzed through the humid air.

"Kidahin? We ought to change our stalking strategy. It takes too much effort to backtrail and loop around impassable undergrowth. Look at how dense the ground cover is here. We should climb into the trees and avoid both the heavy undergrowth and the sweltering ground temperatures," Merkrida sang.

Kidahin listened to her suggestion, something a good assaultmistress should do. Merkrida was unlike anyone when it came to consensus-seeking. Consensus was key to female "we are all equal" social problem solving. Yet Merkrida often put to consensus matters too trivial or too obvious to need a group action. Naturally proactive, she took well-reasoned risks. She was prone to anger and when provoked gave everyone attitude.

"Everyone up into the trees. Continue prowling at the same rate and bearing," Kidahin trilled.

They climbed into the nearest trees, leaping from bole to bole, from branch to branch, climbing up and down yellow lianas and swinging from green vines, pushing through the equatorial rainforest upper canopy.

Kidahin took the lead. Team-Two jumped, climbed, and squeezed between seed pods, clumps of deep-orange epiphyte plants, and tangles upon tangles of crimson symbiotic and green parasitic vines. The sweet pungency of the flowering multitudes blooming in large swaths and in small tufts between the smallest branches and the largest boughs. Billowing catkins and blooming lianas saturated the humid air with exotic and heady smells.

Kidahin loved the long trek through the canopy. It was a fabulous walk in the hours-long lengthening evening. The jungle unfolded before them in breathtaking beauty. Above them, the brightest stars began to shine through the paling blue sky, bright enough to penetrate the diaphanous pastel leaves.

They had been prowling for thirty-three Elleio Standard Time hours. It was time to get some sleep. Kidahin trilled a contact call and four Hunters immediately surrounded her.

"Are we ever going to stop?" Seliaha keened.

Kidahin twitched her ears at Seliaha and twisted her crimson and yellow striped, orange ringleted tail tuft, her pons, in slow tight circles at the other three Hunters. The youngest, not counting Kidahin herself, Seliaha exuded respect, deference, and envy. A brilliant strategist, she avoided risk and gave everyone the impression she was socially awkward.

Kidahin watched her but spoke to them all. "Make this our sleep tree. We will remain here for about twenty hours."

Kidahin smelled their relief. Well, they had been prowling a long time.

Twenty hours later Merkrida stirred and sang the call-to-action melody at no-threat tempo.

Kidahin, startled awake, gazed into the overhead canopy. More stars were out now. In another three days Ah'vou'ree Clan territory would sunset into the long night and remain in darkness for the next twenty-three EST days.

Merkrida smelled the time reference on Kidahin's scent and asked, "Did anyone tell you what to expect on mission duration?"

Kidahin gave a pheromonal shrug before adding, "Rarely does a mission timetable remain intact once teams are in the field."

They resumed their prowling and continued at the same pace for another thirty hours. Kidahin was having second thoughts about the rainforest. Their prowling was no longer a fabulous walk but exhausting work. For all the beauty surrounding them, prowling at combat stalking rhythm up, down, and through the canopy turned their sector sweep into a hike equal to a prowl across all the Uahua'asee'a Clan territory.

Kidahin reflected on her choice of vehicle. She should have chosen a troop transport over the stealth insertion vehicle. The transport hold could carry a light armored vehicle. An LAV looked like an eleven-legged mechanical insect. Merkrida was an expert LAV driver. She was sensitive to every incipient skid on unstable clay, determined when rocks barred the way, and cool in choosing her course through ruts and ravines. Merkrida often ordered Hunters out to scout the ground ahead just to keep the LAV navigation scanners offline to maintain emission silence.

Kidahin scowled down on the coastline. The view was perfect, too perfect, and that perfection gave voice to the false perception that only one in-tune with nature could distinguish.

She shook her head. The coast bent into a little cove guarded by granite points, a little fringing reef, and a shallow lagoon. The lagoon, itself thatched with yellow and amber-yellow grass and a wandering row of deep-red palms with large black flowers facing the sea.

That view should look farther away.

Kidahin led her hand uphill through treetops looking for another watch point. The telltale rumble of fast-approaching storms boomed in the distance. The thunder sounded especially violent. What looked like nearby promising, comforting and comfortable emergent layer rainforest rapidly deteriorated into a treacherous and windswept nightmare. Rain fell in thumb-sized drops, forcing them back on the ground. There, a carelessly placed bare heel slipped on slick clay and, tail or no tail, Kidahin plunged downhill at an ever-increasing speed that swept her far beyond her Hunters.

They ran after her, came face-to-face with another impassible bare slope, unstable rocks, slick red clay, and thorny scrub. By the time they skidded down to Kidahin, all bruised, scratched, and muddy, they had all but reached the limits of their endurance.

Kidahin ordered them to continue eastward through driving rain. They prowled along the rainforest floor now a maze of entangling saturated undergrowth piling up and falling over jagged overgrown landslides. The path twisted into rolling curves alongside a cascading river running parallel to a rough trail on the opposite bank.

"I hate Ah'vou'ree Clan territory," Kidahin keened. "It is nothing like home. All I see are multitudes of spindly interlaced white tree trunks. At least I can see the same twilight sky and distant mountains."

"It is not as if we are staying here," Einstika trilled in sympathy.

Kidahin perked her ears and smiled, wondering how hard Einstika's habitual diplomatic deference was wrestling with the frustrated anger she felt about the equatorial jungle.

"How are you holding up?" Kidahin trilled softly.

"Me? Oh, well enough. I love being together," Einstika sang.

Her scent revealed the truth in the simple statement. Kidahin smelled the intoxicating power of the love Einstika felt for her teammates.

Among the trees Kidahin and her Hunters paused to share in pheromonal empathy by dancing around one another in graceful rhythmic, ritual dance. They danced and sang for an hour before settling into the well-practiced routine of setting up another watch point. She glared at a distant thunderhead looming blue-black above the jungle, but thankfully it did not rain on them.

Distant singing echoed through the rainforest. Kidahin perked her ears, her tail swaying slightly behind her. Jassalin had reached her watch point and was singing her check-in song to let them know. Kidahin, then Merkrida, followed by Hollfara, Einstika, and Seliaha lifted their voices in the warbling keen of reply. Then they sang their welcoming song, beginning with four notes in descending trills, each note about a third from the one before.

They sang a duet, with Kidahin and her Hunters singing the first three notes and Jassalin with her Hunters singing the last, lowest notes of each arpeggio. But then Kidahin paused as Jassalin replied antiphonally, the wrong tone to take with teammates and allies. Kidahin's hand, enraged, took back the melody and added variants, three of ten voices in overlapping confusion. Jassalin and her Hunters replied in defiant dissonance, an insolent challenging keen.

* * *

Hunters glared at Jassalin with murderous fury.

"What have you done?" Aplilin keened, livid. She held the highest social rank in Team-Two, was their most aggressive Hunter, and possessed a sense of valor more in common with Warrior females. She also supported and defended Kidahin to the point of obsession, as only a lover could.

"The Mistress of Battle has ordered us to drive Kidahin from the field. Her continued presence in this mission is a clear and present danger to our Warleader," Jassalin keened.

Kyralin, the most devious Hunter in Team-Two and the youngest in Jassalin's hand at thirteen years and twenty-four months, growled. Her youthful male hyperprotective urges churning away at the idea of any threat to their Warleader. Tialdrin, the social sophisticate and moral theorist, a month Kyralin's senior, snarled in pheromonal empathy.

Only Alfara, the honor-driven proactive moral force in Jassalin's hand shook her head, her tail swaying lazily side-to-side, a sign of doubt. Her ears remained pricked forward above her bright red hair, while the others had already folded theirs flat against their short, brilliant orange ringlets.

"How does driving Kidahin from the field of battle keep our Warleader safe?" she sang.

"I do not know," Jassalin admitted. "The spirits know males need minders, but sometimes the Warleader needs our special attention." That in itself was sufficient to trigger their overprotective zeal, she thought. And it did not help matters that she and everyone else was coming into mating season. Male pheromones were male pheromones and although human-weak, his sent notice to them that a male was available to mate.

"What did the Mistress of Battle say about this, Jassalin? Kidahin chose him. She cannot be a danger to him. If she were a danger, Lo'sutra'est anni would have stomped through the jungle on a mission to kill Kidahin herself," Aplilin sang.

Jassalin pushed ideas of mating aside. "I do not know what to think. You have a point. All females go out of their way to protect males, but Lo'sutra'est anni would never tolerate a risk near him. His self-appointed guardian for life, she would take preemptive reactionary action and kill anyone she felt a threat to him. Both tribal law and social custom excuse any killing a Comari commits and has done so for centuries."

Jassalin hesitated, then shook her head and continued. "No, Nynava is Mistress of Battle for a reason. She knows something," she trilled at descant scale. The cultural and evolutionary drive to protect male life trilled in her ears. "It does not matter," she added.

Kyralin and Tialdrin, tails whipping now, agreed. Their youthful male protective natures triggered, they came to the same conclusion. Safeguarding male life superseded every other moral duty. They were stealthmistresses and were impatient to kill any threat to male life, especially the life of their Warleader.

Jassalin's breasts heaved beneath flimsy neckwear beads. Her Hunters faced an impasse. Aplilin and Alfara voiced doubt, and although she was their leader, she could not order them because they were not in battle. They had to reach a consensus on how to proceed.

All ten discussed the matter as equals regardless of rank.

Four hours later, consensus reached, Jassalin led her hand cautiously across a huge lavaka field. Lavaka, erosion gullies in red clay, formed easily here. The soil baked hard in the sun but the ground beneath was soft. When rain came it gouged out huge gullies in the side of hills as pieces of baked crust fell into the crevasses below. Some lavaka were clearly stabilized by orange grassy vegetation growing in the reddish gashes, but no Hunter in her right mind trusted in the stability the grass seemed to offer.

Rain fell, this time in slow-motion jungle mist, in tiny droplets finding purchase in Jassalin's frizzy, ringleted, fluorescent-orange hair. Her beaded neckwear and tie-dyed, rank-embroidered loincloth channeled droplets down her breasts and hips as she prowled through the dripping, heavy cover. She paused often, peering up into the leafy sky, with its gray-white clouds above and their faces full of rain.

Jassalin eyed the burning oranges and flaming reds rising toward the cresting ridge ahead with suspicion. A stand of arberi trees filled the foothills, their branches rustling in the breezes gave the look of flames caressing the mountains.

<<This is ideal defensive territory, and Kidahin will recognize it as such,>> Jassalin signed in battle language.

More blended pastel-ochers cloaked the rainforest downward slope beyond. Twisted white trunks towered above them.

<<This is also ideal ambush territory. Beware!>> Jassalin signed.

She stopped to get a good feel for the surrounding trees. Subdued yellow and russet leaves, themselves bigger than the area her stretching body could cover, fluttered on stiff breezes loud enough to mask an errant, noisy footfall. Trees in a nimbus of fluorescent oranges flowered all around her.

Advantage: Kidahin.

<<This is ideal camouflage ready to deceive the unwary. Scatter into your forward prowling positions and head into the gorge ahead. Hug the folded treeline as you prowl,>> she signed.

Below, a white river hurled from boulder to boulder. Jassalin and her Hunters swung across the churning rapids and climbed down the face of one monolithic granite cliff and then climbed hand-over-hand up another, pausing often to gaze at the cuts in the hillside below and behind them. Finger-deep forest topsoil exposed two-ell-deep arberi roots, and solid red clay fell from there on down and out of sight.

But of Kidahin and her Hunters, they saw no sign of them.

The sky turned dusky-pale blue when the rain clouds moved on, allowing the long late evening waning light to reveal the rainforest, its charm, and the richness of its flora. The mid-elevation forest, not having large trees with high canopies but for a scattered few elleiu trees made prowling hard with ground covered with layer upon layer of braided undergrowth.

Jassalin smiled as she thought about their Warleader. "He thinks arberi trees are tall," she sang softly.

"Yes," Aplilin sang. "Earth must have very small trees. No wonder he feels safe alone."

Jassalin growled at the weaponmistress's comment. "Kidahin said that Earth trees have tiny *green* leaves."

"And they are not parasitic or dead?" Aplilin trilled, astonished and a bit intimidated.

Jassalin trilled in awe herself. "Green means death, red means health. Males are strange."

"Simple and plain," Aplilin sang.

Little by little the clouds lifted, exposing their approach to enemy territory, bathing it in a rich golden tone, like sunset at noon. The folds of the surrounding hills, covered in deep crimson, vermilion, and gold, resembled a male's muscular back. The forest began to steam. Wisps of mist rose from valleys and hovered above the jungle understory branches, a white gauze veil over deep red velvet trees.

Jassalin could not help but think of her Warleader. Eyloni were female-dominant, and yet they gave males privileged autonomy and wide latitude in Eyloni social life. Male births were rare, one in forty, and all females loved males and were fiercely protective of them. Females almost never let a male go anywhere alone for more than a double-handful of minutes, and they never let him face a danger they could not face for him.

Jassalin smirked. Contrary to Eyloni nature, their Warleader, for some unknown reason, actually enjoyed being alone for up to several hours at a time! So they let him think he was alone when he prowled the rainforest. Several females took turns stalking him out of his sight and therefore out of his mind. After all, females without exception considered a male alone obscene.

And dangerous. Away from female pheromonal empathy males became paranoid and violent.

Singsong arguments intruded into Jassalin's leafchasing thoughts. Kyralin and Tialdrin were at it again. Tialdrin was obsessive and pushy. Kyralin was honor-driven but had a devious streak. The youngest two in her hand, their minds would be the most preoccupied with mating season. She would have to watch them as they were the most likely to land lethal blows in hand-to-hand combat.

Jassalin felt the need to mate herself. In ancient times armies of females defended their own immediate and extended families and clan territories. A well-held territory was a long-term buffer against the hardest years and seasons. Most importantly, females who managed to hold their territory passed it on to their daughters.

Today clans and the tribes they formed were the results of successful descendants over generations. Indeed, before the Be'atika Senge outlawed war among clans and between tribes, females fought to expand their territory. The prosperous clan had males. Females went out of their way to make their territory attractive to them. That meant long-term ownership and not just year-to-year occupancy.

Even in ancient times males possessed autonomy and could change clan affiliation when they matured and at any time thereafter. Having males in families meant not only family and clan survival but species survival as well. The obvious biological need to reproduce was not the only reason females sought males. Male births were so rare that evolutionary biology made the genders interdependent upon one another. A male must be present during a female birth to form what was called the near-daughter pheromonal empathic bond. Without it the newborn female died within hours of birth.

Jassalin searched for Aplilin in the canopy above her. She had advanced two trees ahead of her. No doubt Aplilin was still arguing with herself. Her relationship with Kidahin, Nynava's orders, their favorite male, and the tug of mating season were likely fighting a war of attrition in her head.

On Jassalin's left flank and opposite Kyralin and Tialdrin prowled Alfara. She and Tialdrin were natural allies. Alfara hoarded weapons, particularly knives. Leaving them behind was probably killing her.

* * *

"Kidahin, Zalzadrin. Comm check," the Mistress of Arms sang over Kidahin's discrete commlink.

"Mistress?" Kidahin sang.

"For the safety of our Warleader you must secure and hold your territory. Mistress of the Watch Phelindra has declared Jassalin and her hand ni'zakhon, outlaws. You will subdue them by any means necessary including lethal force, but you may not use weapons but what the body provides."

"Entiki," Kidahin sang as she touched her left breast and then the curving adulthood knife strapped there.

She turned and locked eyes with Merkrida, then Hollfara, then Einstika, and finally Seliaha. "Zalzadrin has confirmed Jassalin's challenge call. We are told to hold this place for our Warleader. You may use whatever level of force necessary, but you must give your honored word not to use any weapon. Unarmed combat only."

"Entiki," they vowed, likewise caressing their left breasts and adulthood knives.

Her words angered them. Her own pheromonal male-in-danger scent goaded them, made them edgy and deadly dangerous. Jassalin led, in the Society of Assault Team-Two, the subordinate combat hand, ten Huntresses. To survive, she had to eliminate Kidahin or the blemish of ni'zakhon would tarnish her honor forever.

"Everyone, scatter into the trees. Use silent-stalking and combat-prowling skills to reach your watch points," Kidahin sang at combat-imminent tempo.

"Affirm," Merkrida sang. She flicked her ears at the remaining three Hunters, and they melted into the trees.

Hollfara held Einstika back. "We must approach this problem with superior strategy. See Jassalin and the others high in the heavy branches of those arberi trees? They plan to run head-on into our stalkers," she lectured. "Do you know why?"

Einstika frowned, her deep respect for the higher-ranking female vying with a natural frustration-driven anger. She held her breath and watched the trees giving Jassalin's hand cover. The arberi trees had just started to turn spring-crimson. Their mighty leaves bent gently in the breeze, giving glimpses of new delicate pink leaves emerging. In the full dark of the coming long night arberi leaves grew so fast they could be seen and heard growing.

"What of it, Hollfara? It is too late to seek consensus now. Maybe you should have suggested a strategy to Kidahin," Einstika trilled.

"I do not mean a strategic strategy for our hand but a tactical one for us. You help take out Tialdrin. She is young and inexperienced. See Merkrida? Join her and double-team Tialdrin. I will engage Alfara."

Einstika watched as combatants came through the precarious forest canopy head-on, leaping from anchored lianas to arberi boughs. Their point stalkers converging on one another with murderous fury, just as Hollfara predicted. They overran a dense arberi overgrown with lianas, vines, and twisting epiphytes. It was a treacherous place for misstep or miscalculation.

"Affirm," Einstika trilled. She jumped from the branch and fell for eleven seconds before landing between and just behind Kidahin and Merkrida.

Kidahin and her Hunters scattered at that moment. Merkrida and Einstika closed on Tialdrin. Anger drove Einstika to keep abreast of Merkrida and together they sped past Tialdrin, one on each side, and landed hammer blows to her head and nearly tearing her right ear off and gashing her scalp open. The wound did not go to the bone because she could still twitch her ear, but Einstika could see a red thumb-length of flayed skin and muscle exposed. Tialdrin whirled on them, one ear vertical, the other out flat.

"Where is Aplilin?" Merkrida trilled.

"Below us," Kidahin sang. "She is heading for you!"

That made sense, Kidahin thought. Merkrida, proactive and passive-aggressive, did not fly into rages. She used anger, turned it into a finely honed blade, a good counter to Aplilin's naked aggression. Merkrida always planned alternative strategies, whereas the reactive and stubborn Aplilin excelled at single-minded, charge-and-overbear tactics.

"Remember to hold the high ground, Merkrida. Do not let Aplilin get above you. Keep climbing until you must face her off," Kidahin keened.

"Affirm," Merkrida sang.

"Has anyone seen Jassalin?" Hollfara trilled from her overhead clump of lianas.

Kidahin scanned the tree and its over-arching emergent layer. "I have not," she sang, "but Jassalin is a natural leader. She will have a backup plan if this frontal assault fails."

"Of course she will," Hollfara agreed.

"Who is left?" Seliaha trilled.

"Alfara and Tialdrin."

"Kidahin!" Merkrida sang from the high branches. "Tialdrin has gone missing. I lost track of her in the leaves for only a few seconds!"

Loud trills came from Jassalin and her Hunters, screaming war cries signifying an imminent charge. Kidahin managed to catch a glimpse of Tialdrin in profile, her vermilion, crimson, and yellow skin hard to find against the deep orange, red, and yellow variegated leaves.

"Spirits! Tialdrin has lost an ear!" Kidahin trilled. She bit her tongue and frowned, spitting furiously. *This is too easy.*

"Tialdrin is backtrailing and looping, beware!" Kidahin keened.

Seliaha, heedless, grabbed a liana and climbed into the tree, skipping branches sideways as she angled toward the Tialdrin sighting. As she climbed, she caught glimpses of arms and hands wriggling and clutching, leaping through trees, and then pausing to clutch at anything they could grab.

What she saw made no sense. She thought she saw Kyralin, but Tialdrin and Kyralin were allies. They could not be fighting one another.

Seliaha settled into camouflaging leaves near the branch tip. She watched, uncertain, as Hollfara and Alfara crashed through tangling branches locked in a tumbling embrace. Merkrida and Einstika broke through nearby heavy leaves at the same time, silent-stalking, and smashed into a distracted Aplilin. Einstika landed a sweeping heel strike to a surprised Aplilin, bruising her knee. Aplilin jumped aside as Seliaha grabbed her by the tail and ran into a clump of aerial roots and braced herself. She yanked Aplilin by the tail, hard. Aplilin tried to recoil from

Merkrida's hammer blows but found herself fouled by her snagged tail. Merkrida rained yellow-streaked orange fists down on Aplilin.

Distracted, Merkrida forgot about Tialdrin and her, to this point, missing constant companion, Kyralin. Pain-enraged, Tialdrin leaped from the canopy and dropped thirty ells, slamming a knee into Merkrida, and shattering her jaw from chin to left jaw hinge and knocking teeth from her open mouth. Seconds later Kyralin dropped onto Seliaha's back, smashing her into the branch.

Seliaha dropped Aplilin's tail, rolled free before Kyralin could grapple her, and charged Tialdrin. Aplilin, her knee swelling, braced herself and snapped her tail, tripping Seliaha into Tialdrin, who shoved her off the branch.

Seliaha, several hundred ells above ground, writhed desperately into the path of several branches, smacking into leaves one by one, each easily twice her size, breaking her fall and pitching her flat on her back across a wide branch.

Kidahin glared at the canopy around her. Hollfara and Einstika were together again, watching...what?

Where had their attackers gone? They had withdrawn!

Kidahin cursed. Eyloni war theory said to force the enemy to respond to you and note their weaknesses. War theory also said to always fight a territorial war and not one of attrition. She needed numbers to hold her territory, so Jassalin had pushed this attack, probed for weaknesses, and then withdrew her hand more or less intact.

Kidahin spotted movement in the cover of an adjacent tree. It was Jassalin and Tialdrin climbing into low ground. Why? What were they up to now? War theory said that fighting on low ground was foolhardy if the high ground was not secured first. She watched Tialdrin hesitate, draw herself to her full height, and scent the air in Kidahin's direction. She canted her ears as if she had never smelled Kidahin's scent before. Jassalin did the same.

As Kidahin watched, they leaped down branches, leaving her feeling frustrated. Several seconds later, Tialdrin returned.

Alone.

She glanced up, her tail drooping almost to the ground, her posture reflecting profound sadness. Then she glanced after a fleeing Jassalin and listened.

Jassalin was moving into the rainforest, likely heading for some prearranged rallying point. There, they would recoup their strength and save their energy for another sortie. Tialdrin keened a contact call to her departing fellows and followed them into the deepening red shadows.

Several hours later Jassalin led her hand in a full-frontal assault.

"Attack!" she sang at assault tempo, sending her Hunters against Kidahin's arberi refuge. Aplilin took point. Alfara and Tialdrin followed close behind. Jassalin held back to watch. Two of Kidahin's most aggressive females, Merkrida and Einstika, came at them. In the last charge she had Tialdrin and Alfara flank them and fall back in feints, trying to lure Merkrida or Kidahin into ceding territory. She, Aplilin, and Kyralin had pressed the advance then.

But this time she put Tialdrin in the front rank with Alfara only a little behind her.

Kidahin pointed out the tactic, not surprised. "See? War theory in operation," she sang to her hand. "Never fight a war of attrition. Tialdrin's injury will put her out of action in the long run. Jassalin can no longer afford delaying tactics or probing assaults."

"I saw this confrontation coming," Hollfara lectured. "Tialdrin has no reason to take care, and Aplilin is always the aggressor in wargame scenarios. Jassalin must press the attack now or risk losing Tialdrin to a concussion and perhaps Aplilin to a broken kneecap."

"Recall to me. We will make our stand here," Kidahin keened. They crouched, caressing one another, tails wrapped around the small branch as they waited, a branch scarcely wider than their torsos. It was a stupid strategy if Jassalin was using bows or spears. But unarmed combat was a tail of a different color. Ten set opponents could easily resist charging and overbearing maneuvers. Kidahin and her Hunters looked like the picture of togetherness as they sang a sweet soprano challenge and sat ready to repel the assault.

Jassalin did not give them any more time. She jumped into the tree, driving the attack forward. "Aplilin, take the lead. Knock them off that branch. Everyone else, overbear and grapple them."

Hands, feet, and tails flew as Hunters spun over one another on the narrow branch as they broke tail grips to face new opponents. They parried and feinted, grappled and broke too quickly to reach each other with more than glancing blows. Almost always two or three females in a hand did the actual lunging for them all. But in this extraordinary moment Jassalin and her hand attacked as one.

They ground Kidahin's defenses to a halt.

The combatants broke away and glared at each other. Kidahin and Merkrida held the line while Hollfara, Einstika, and Seliaha tried to flank Jassalin. Aplilin saw them and jumped to the branch above her and drove them back to Kidahin. Aplilin then drove them all from the arberi tree, allowing Jassalin to take possession of the territory.

Kidahin and her hand whirled to face them from the neighboring tree and feinted as though they were attacking. Jassalin and her Hunters, glaring from their tree with teeth bared gave Kidahin pause. Tialdrin stood there with her torn ear. Aplilin launched herself from the branch above and landed on Kidahin.

It was too much. Warrior strong and big for a Hunter female, Aplilin forced Kidahin to back off, literally back off, without turning away. Only when they reached a safe distance did Kidahin and her hand stalk down the tree and into the low ground, the ritual sign of surrender. Aplilin, Jassalin, Tialdrin, Alfara, and Kyralin, with due caution, advanced into the upper canopy and occupied the high ground in ritual acknowledgment of victory.

An hour later Jassalin led her hand down and out of the tree and reported to her assaultmistress.

"Kidahin," Jassalin sang, her pricking ears conveying her deep respect.

"Well done, Jassalin. You know, when I saw Tialdrin backtrailing and looping, I wondered if I should have..."

"Do not think you have done well!" Mistress Zalzadrin trilled through the thick orange undergrowth. The Hunter Mistress of Arms, normally an insufferable joker, continued, "We are going to discuss this miserable failure here and now!"

"Yes!" Warrior Mistress of Battle Nynava trilled at imperative tempo. "I expected more injuries than a bent ear, a bump on the knee, and a few broken teeth!"

"So much," Zalzadrin keened, livid, "for any concern you pretend to have for our Warleader!"

"Zalzadrin!" Nynava trilled in astonishment and froze, bare feet flat on the ground, four-jointed toes and opposable big toes gripping surface roots. Kidahin's ears dipped in fury, triggering Nynava's reflexive jump backwards. Any female guilty of being incautious with male lives received the death penalty from any one of the thousands of hierarchies governing female social life on Elleio. Zalzadrin's insult was too serious to convey mere shame and was never sang in polite company.

Nynava felt a vibration as an enraged Team-Two pounced on Zalzadrin and drove her into the trembling ground. Kidahin's Hunters were strong, but twenty-one Hunters overbearing another Hunter could not make the ground vibrate no matter how far they fell.

The rainforest heaved and shook around them with the force of an earthquake. Nynava, her tail twisting in panic, ordered everyone to immediate readiness as the low setting sun flickered and died. The trees around them warped and shimmied, not in time with the shaking ground, bled into smears of red, yellows, and oranges, and abruptly vanished.

*"Battle Status!"* Warleader Delwyn bellowed over the combat address system. "Shields up. Melkorka, damage report. Hlinlodyn, tactical scan. What in the hell did we just jump into?"

Silence followed. The combat address system tracked and transmitted every sound the Warleader uttered throughout their warship, but it did not transmit the voices of those he spoke with. His presence, his need for female defenders, and the focus and moral boost they gained from him made his voice absolutely essential.

Twenty-two females stared in shock at the sculpted high-relief wide weaving pathways of the combat deployment bay laid bare without the home option force field sculpted holographic jungle flora.

"Merkrida and Tialdrin, report to Health Center for healer attention. Everyone else report to Battle Status stations!" Nynava sang.

Merkrida, her jaw a shattered wreck, growled a high-pitched negative and rushed to her secondary weapon systems damage control station.

Tialdrin, not bothering to give even an insolent reply, sprinted to her warship security team Battle Status duty station.

# 2

## THE SONG OF THE WILD MALE, SHARED SECRETS, THE FERAL FEMALE...

Kidahin ran through the pale yellow-green, sculpted, high-relief, and utterly barren combat staging area. The environmental system giving *Hunter's Moon* his shipwide rainforest interior was offline in this part of the command hull. When the Ah'vou'ree Clan combat training jungle terrain was not in use, the system defaulted to its routine landscape settings for the staging area and adjacent deployment bay. The staging area should be filled with seaside jungle all the way to the bay, where bright yellow sand and seaside beaches continued out to gentle breaking coastal waves on a horizon concealing the airlock bulkhead and bay door.

Rows of troop transports, light tanks, medium tanks, heavy tanks, hovertanks, light armored vehicles, armored personnel carriers, and self-propelled infantry weapons rested in bare service alcoves on bare deck plating and not on yellow sand in niches hidden within concealing yellow dunes.

Kidahin sprinted deeper into the unnaturally open staging area, dipping and weaving over the rough pathway of a jungle trail stripped of its ocher undergrowth, golden lianas, and magnificent crimson and vermilion trees.

A greenish-yellow glow gave the combat staging area an eerie pall meant to drive home that an emergency existed. Battle Status in and of itself did not require killing the shipwide rainforest landscapes. Indeed, jungle terrain gave the crew background cover their leaf-patterned bare skin easily blended into.

"Forget the environmental options," Delwyn's deep reassuring voice boomed over the combat address system. "Only life support matters right now. Trebithia, all stop. Hold position here and scan local space. Hlinlodyn, tactical analysis."

Kidahin twisted down a wide denuded hillside pathway leading from the staging area and deeper into the lower command hull and its bare paths and trails. Several Warrior security watch triads and solitary Hunter stalkers on their alert prowls gave her passing glances as they prowled their sweeps.

She jumped into a side path and ran down another bleak, gloomy trail. It narrowed into a tunnel and dipped and straightened back out before opening into a gently climbing rise.

A Hunter darted across her path on the way to her own duty station. She was dripping wet and naked but for the adulthood knife strapped to her left breast and her military rank earring. She likely came from one of the command hull hygiene centers.

Kidahin jumped onto a narrow maintenance trail, twisted on nimble bare feet, and climbed through another level up a nearly vertical access path. She reached its end and slipped onto a wide pathway heading aft.

Up ahead the auxiliary command center blast door glowed greenly. That door and its surrounding bulkhead was normally hidden by jungle scenery, but now it looked starkly utilitarian and wrong. The door recognized her as authorized personnel and rolled aside.

Kidahin glided around several Hunters and Warriors attending their stations. She sat down at the auxiliary navigation console. Cursing her lateness, she logged into and activated the Battle Status auxiliary navigation system.

The navigation console reported command center primary helm and navigation systems online with no damage and attended to by Mistress of Pathwalking Trebithia and helmsmistress Tulloraha.

"Mistress Trebithia, Kidahin," she sang from her console commlink. "Auxiliary navigation is attended to and ready."

"You are late. We will discuss this later. Navigation scans show no natural or artificial objects within our defensive perimeter. I can find no collision debris. Mistress of Sails Anailiatha reports widespread environmental option holographic and force field emitter power failures but does not know why. You will scan our jump point exit and surrounding local space for navigation hazards."

"Affirm, Mistress Trebithia," Kidahin sang. "Mistress? Is Delwyn well?"

"Delwyn is fine and busy managing a furious Melkorka. Do as I ask and make those navigation scans," Trebithia trilled.

"Affirm, acting," Kidahin sang.

* * *

Kyralin and Tialdrin ran down deforested command hull pathways. Their Battle Status duties included warship internal security. They constantly prowled throughout the ship during Battle Status looking for anything suspicious. But first they had to find Phelindra, the Eldest Huntress of the Ship and Mistress of the Watch. She was Delwyn's

Protectress and was always with him. They would soon see for themselves and know their Warleader was safe.

"Does it hurt? Your ear?" Kyralin trilled.

"No. It tickles. It only hurts when hearing stupid questions. What do you think?" Tialdrin hissed.

Kyralin glanced sideways at Tialdrin. Her ear flopped up and down as they ran. The filleted skin was scabbed over and the blood running from the wound had dried in long streaks down her beautiful yellow-variegated, red, and mellow-orange skin.

"What do you think Phelindra will have us do?" Kyralin sang.

"I do not know," Tialdrin admitted. "In the handful of months we have been aboard Phelindra has taken us on prowls throughout the ship several hundred times and introduced us to the warleader special security Huntmistress and Lo'sutra'est anni. I expect Phelindra will tell us to make stalking sweeps throughout the command hull."

Kyralin shuddered on hearing the Comari's name. "All Comara with bondmales are known by this phrase. A title and a name, it means, 'acting from a physical joining and living relationship in compelling moral duty I endure this bond to him forever more'."

"Easier just to say, 'his own ward,' which is the battle language translation," Tialdrin sang. Spirits but Lo'sutra'est anni was a scary female. Comara skin was uniform pale yellow. Their straight hair was pale and hung to the waist. They had no tail, were thin, petite, mute, and sterile. Although frozen in perpetual adolescence, they were strong and easy to offend. Lo'sutra'est anni, like all Comara, wandered into and out of mental awareness of the world around them. They seemed to wander along the metaphysical threads of the Oyya Web of the spirits. Tialdrin thought only a danger to Delwyn would snap Lo'sutra'est anni back into day-to-day awareness and kill everyone near him she considered a threat.

The two Hunters twisted down a ravine cut into the sculpted deck, sprinted along its length, jumped onto a ledge, and scaled a steep cliff up through several decks.

Kyralin smiled at a memory as she climbed. Kidahin once told them about a visit to a human warship. Humans apparently loved narrow parallel corridors on flat decks, stairs and ladders, and lifts. How could anyone prowl down a smooth, straight path? Why put up with stairs and lifts? Lifts were for moving heavy equipment and ordnance, not people. People climbed up and down boles and through aerial roots to reach pathways and trails on other decks. Eyloni climbed their elleiu trees all the time, so what was the problem humans had with climbing?

Kyralin dwelled on human preferences as they climbed onto the path leading to the command center blast door. It rolled open and they ran around Mistress of the Ship Melkorka and up to Phelindra.

She stood behind Delwyn and to one side. Lo'sutra'est anni stood next to him, just within his one-ell radius personal space. Warleader and Comari, both tailless, made a unique and jarring display.

"Mistress Phelindra, we are ready for stealth prowling duties," they sang.

Phelindra flicked her ears at them but said nothing. She kept eyes on Delwyn.

He was doing something with his console. From his station on the Warleader's Watch he could override any console in the command center. He was hard at work, for drops of water beaded on his forehead.

Eyloni did not perspire, they panted. Mistress of Healers Allohindra told them humans dripped water when hot or under stress. Kyralin thought he was frustrated. He was linking his console with the combat analysis station attended to by Mistress of Tactics Hlinlodyn.

Phelindra smelled blood, jumped aside, and whirled on them, her left hand reaching for the curved adulthood knife strapped around and under her left breast, and froze.

"What happened to your ear?" she trilled.

"Unarmed combat training, I got double-teamed," Tialdrin sang.

"Take care of it later. I want you both prowling our warship. That means combat hull, forestation, command hull, left and right outrigger hulls, aftstation, and the engineering hull. Go now!"

"Affirm, acting," they sang, paused, and gave Delwyn longing looks and trilled their need.

Delwyn, hearing the two young Hunters trill, stood and turned. He walked to them and touched them, caressed them, and sang a greeting to them. They entwined their tails around his waist and pulled him into their shared embrace, a tolerant Lo'sutra'est anni watching closely.

"Tialdrin, you need Allohindra to fix your ear, but not now. Once we have environmental systems online, report to Health Center and have her regenerate it."

"By your command," Tialdrin sang huskily.

Phelindra ground her teeth, impatient. Although Melkorka was Mistress of the Ship, Phelindra held the highest military rank aboard. The two young Hunters should have jumped with a "yes, Mistress" and fled but for one fact of Eyloni life. No female could impede another's access to her warleader for any reason whatsoever.

Delwyn, sensitive to Phelindra's mood, gave the two a final caress down their bare, muscular, velour-soft shoulders and sent them on their way.

Tialdrin, pain temporarily wiped away by the natural pheromonal empathic reaction to his smell and touch, twisted her tail around a reluctant Kyralin and led her from the command center.

"Where to first?" Tialdrin trilled.

"The combat hull? Start there and prowl aft?" Kyralin sang.

Tialdrin twisted her orange-ringleted tail tip, her pons, and twitched her good ear in agreement. "To the combat hull, then," she sang.

***

Seliaha and Aplilin followed Nynava and Zalzadrin through the spacious combat staging area and into the deployment bay and its rows of combat equipment waiting in their service alcoves.

"Aplilin, you will help the bay mistress secure these vehicles. Since you are a heavy weapons weaponmistress, I want you to sign out a heavy plasma cannon and conceal yourself in the overhead bay tractor pod. From there you can cover the combat staging area and the deployment bay airlock door. But verify vehicle status first," Nynava sang.

"Affirm, acting," Aplilin sang. She turned to the fiery redheaded Mistress of Arms. "Mistress Zalzadrin, you need to authorize release of the infantry plasma cannon."

"I have already done so. I know how much you love that weapon. Go to the arsenal charging rack and sing to the locker for weapon release when you are ready," Zalzadrin trilled.

"Affirm!" Aplilin trilled. "Mistress Nynava, where are you assigning prowler units?" she trilled as she jerked her tail at the Warrior infantry and skirmisher teams rushing into the combat staging area.

"Here. Zalzadrin, you should release the small arms and personal weapon caches," Nynava sang.

"I know this!" Zalzadrin snapped.

"Aplilin, remember that not only do the caches contain knives, swords, bows and arrows, spears, bucklers, shields, and other traditional personal weapons, but they also contain thumpers in their inventories. A thumper will burn out any moderately shielded device in range. That means a close enough or powerful enough one could overcome your favorite cannon's shielding and it will die. You should grab a bow, bow quiver, and a few cases of arrows for use as backup," Nynava trilled.

"Yes, Mistress. I know this," Aplilin trilled dryly. She, like all Eyloni, preferred hand-to-hand combat or traditional weapon combat. The plasma cannon was meant for assaulting mechanized ground forces and not individual enemy combatants. To use the weapon against individual combatants was to label oneself a coward.

"I am sure you do. Seliaha, come with me," Zalzadrin sang.

"Yes, Mistress."

Zalzadrin wrapped her tail around Seliaha's waist and pulled her toward the waiting Warrior forces. "Help the small arms weaponmistresses sign out weapons to these skirmisher teams and security triads."

"Yes, Mistress Zalzadrin," Seliaha trilled. Hundreds of Warrior females were forming up in groups. Several prowler triads waited impatiently for weapons. Their tails whipped and snapped behind them, their ears set wide apart in listening posture, and their eartips were dipping, a sure sign of pent-up anger. Groups of thirty, combat skirmishers, likewise waited as inventory control weaponmistresses passed weapons to them.

Seliaha flicked her ears in acceptance, nodded respectfully to Zalzadrin, and headed off to one of the caches. She sang to it for weapon release authorization and began handing weapons to the grim Warriors.

***

Merkrida, Hollfara, Einstika, Alfara, and Jassalin sprinted up a vertical ascent path. They rushed toward the aftstation, the interface decks bridging the command hull and the engineering hull. They hurried. During Battle Status all techmistresses reported to Power Systems and Propulsion in the engineering hull. Anailiatha, the Mistress of Sails, needed them to help her locate the damage and repair the fault.

They ran down a broad, weaving, pale pathway toward a greenly glowing, heavily shielded blast door and the Warrior watch triad standing before it.

"Purpose?" Aheila trilled as they stopped.

"Propulsion and Power Systems maintenance and damage control techmistresses mustering in the engineering command center," Jassalin trilled at insistence tempo.

Aheila nodded to her two Warriors and twitched an ear to activate the discrete commlink attached there.

"Watchmistress Cailindreda? Hunter techmistresses requesting aftstation passage into the engineering hull," Aheila sang.

"Admit them," Cailindreda sang.

The blast door rolled aside to reveal a small sally port sealed at the other end by a second blast door. The Hunters stepped in and the door rolled closed behind them.

"Wait until I receive confirmation of your movement from Nynava," Mistress of the Aftstation Thiodnuma sang over the combat address system.

"Affirm," Jassalin trilled. To her companions, she sang, "Always take care in the aftstation. This is a restricted area attended to by Warriors only. They have their own security, their own techmistresses, and their own gunners who fire the secondary weapon systems ringing the aftstation outer hull."

"Jassalin, you and your techmistresses may enter the aftstation," Thiodnuma sang.

"Affirm," Jassalin sang respectfully.

The blast door rolled open and they walked through and on into the aftstation proper, a self-contained fortress of narrow trails and pathways.

The missing jungle landscape normally covering the area in heavy undergrowth would have given the tight, random-seeming featureless bulkheads the look of impenetrable undergrowth. It looked like a maze of high-relief bulkheads and lacked its jungle charm now. Watch triads prowled everywhere, and Jassalin tugged her Hunters toward a third blast door, blocked by yet another watch triad.

"Mistress Thiodnuma allows you entry into the engineering hull sally port, but you may not exit if Anailiatha refuses you entry," the Warrior sang.

Jassalin flicked her ears in reply and the security triad stepped aside.

The ten Hunters glided into the sally port, approached the final blast door, and waited several minutes before it rolled aside.

Once in the engineering hull they ran recklessly for Power Systems and Propulsion, the FTL drive, sublight engines, and main power distribution spaces, and almost rammed into the Mistress of Sails herself in their haste as they entered the engineering command center.

"Merkrida, join the secondary weapons damage control techmistresses. I have inoperative diagnostic systems and no idea if the secondary weapons are online or not. You will help them visually confirm secondary weapon system status. Go!" Anailiatha sang.

<<Affirm, acting!>> a mute and suffering Merkrida signed in battle language before turning and running after the damage control techmistresses.

"Einstika, Jassalin, and Alfara will join the power systems techmistresses. Help them trace the power loss. Power system self-checking networks are offline. That means a lot of manual testing. Go!" Anailiatha snapped.

"Affirm," they trilled.

"Hollfara, come with me," Anailiatha trilled.

"Yes, Mistress," she sang and then paused. "Mistress? Where are we going?"

"You are a spaceframe design techmistress, are you not?" Anailiatha sang.

"Yes, Mistress," Hollfara trilled, dread filling her.

"I am leading a team of structural techmistresses to sound the ship. Do you know what this entails?"

"Yes, Mistress. To sound the ship is to make a hull survey. Hull integrity is necessary for successful FTL jump translations. Has the hull been compromised?" Hollfara trilled, her dread turning icy.

"I do not know. Not obviously so, anyway. Something applied a wrenching torque to our warship during jump completion. I do not know how such a thing is even possible. Saying so does not mean it is not so. I need to find out if the keel has been torqued enough to skew jump point geometry. Obvious signs are buckled decking and hull plates, outgassing from microscopic breaches, and the like," Anailiatha trilled.

***

"Ship status?" Delwyn asked his Mistress of the Ship.

Melkorka unwrapped her tail from the odd, curved sword Delwyn had given her upon becoming Warleader, picked it up from its resting place across her thighs just above her knees, stood, and glided from her command chair forward into the Warleader's Watch.

*Uh-oh.* Delwyn watched as the fluorescent-orange-haired Warrior approached him, her nearly two-meter-long tail whipped madly behind her. She hated the unknown and possessed a frightful temper.

"Major power failures are confined largely to holographic projectors and force field emitters. This is why the rainforest environmental options are offline. Having no force field systems also means no internal local fields as well," she growled.

Delwyn nodded. The force fields sculpted the jungle flora, making it yielding but solid. The holographic systems painted the force fields, giving grass and tree fields the look and feel of real grass and trees. The internal local field emitters were a potentially more serious problem. Phelindra used them to close sections of the ship during security alerts and Anailiatha used them to seal hull breaches and reinforce battle-damaged decks.

"Weapon systems? Shields?" Delwyn demanded.

Melkorka shook her head and flicked her ears forward. "No apparent damage to any weapon system. Navigation, anti-EMP, radiological, and particle shields show nominal red status. The only force field derivative technology is the tractor field emitters and, before you ask, yes they are offline, too."

"I'd say we got lucky," he muttered.

"Do not go thanking the spirits just yet," Melkorka trilled in warning. "Anailiatha is sending damage control and maintenance techmistresses out to check all affected systems. So far, they have found no damage. Nothing! The power just stops."

"Stops? The affected systems draw no power at all?" he asked.

"They draw power," Melkorka corrected. "Yet the power does not reach the emitters."

"Mobius fracture," Delwyn muttered.

"What?" Melkorka trilled at interrogative pitch. His pheromones gave her scent-linked empathic mind the mental image of a frayed twisted elastic band.

Delwyn caught the change in her pitch and the interrogative note. Learning to identify the difference between sung words, trilled words, and keened words took time. Tempo added a level of seriousness to the word, and pitch increased that seriousness. Tempo and pitch conveyed modes, such as interrogative, imperative, insolent, and other emotional modes.

The words didn't change so much as how they were sung, at what tempo they were sung, and at what pitch they were sung. It was so easy to add the wrong level of seriousness and emotional mode to even the simplest statement.

"Delwyn?" Melkorka trilled.

"Hmmm? Oh, I was just thinking. Coalition hyperdrive technology opens a wormhole by creating two mobius manifolds and joining them to form a klein bottle. When the two mobius bands fail to join, the wormhole fractures into billions and billions of cosmic strings with diameters a proton or less. The strings leech subatomic particles, particularly electrons. Mobius fracture would explain why electrical power seems to evaporate away, but the effect isn't selective. It siphons electrons from all sources and not just from force field emitters and holographic projectors alone."

Tense, Melkorka's anger ticked up another notch. "Can this effect be weaponized?"

"I don't see how. Anailiatha might know," Delwyn confessed.

Melkorka punched the Warleader's Watch commlink. "Anailiatha, did you hear..,"

"...What Delwyn said about cosmic strings?" Anailiatha trilled in typical, dry Warrior humor. "Of course I did. The combat address system works, so obviously everyone can hear our Warleader."

"What do you think?" Melkorka keened.

"Give me some time to gather reports from my techmistresses, Mistress. I lack more than a basic theoretical understanding of human hyperdrive physics."

"Delwyn can help...," Melkorka sang, but Anailiatha cut her off again.

"Delwyn is no techmistress and you remember the last time he tried to act like one."

"Act like a techmistress? Delwyn? When did he...?" Melkorka trilled before pausing a moment as the memory surfaced. He had once ordered Battle Status full power to all repaired but untested power systems. Anailiatha's spluttering fit at the time had lasted for several days.

Melkorka gazed lovingly at their clueless Delwyn and sighed.

"I remember. Then again, he and Hlinlodyn are chasing something down a trail for the last hour or so. Do not discount any ideas they may come up with."

Anailiatha trilled an irritated but exaggerated growl. "I will not, but I will not let him blindly turn systems on and off again, either," she snapped.

As Melkorka watched her favorite male the exasperated scowl on her dark, reddish-black lips gradually faded into a fond smile. She agreed in principle with the Mistress of Sails. Delwyn enjoyed sharing risks with them, but everyone else aboard knew better. Females kept males safe, and the best way to keep Delwyn safe was to keep him occupied here in the command center.

* * *

Anailiatha wrapped her tail around Hollfara and pulled her down a wide, featureless pathway.

"A mobius fracture?" Hollfara sang at interrogative pitch.

"Whatever that means," Anailiatha snarled. "It may be important, but we must sound the ship first. If the jump point geometry has changed we cannot use the jump drive without destroying ourselves. Come. Sounding the ship is a slow and tedious process. Staring at our tails and leafchasing the time away will not get them to do the work for us."

"Affirm," Hollfara sang.

"Mistress Anailiatha?" a techmistress sang over the combat address system. "Over-pressure tests are completed. No outgassing was detected."

"Well done. Resume normal life support damage control and maintenance readiness," Anailiatha sang.

"That means no damaged airlocks, vents, hatches, or hull plates, yes?" an anxious Hollfara trilled.

Anailiatha nodded, her ears canting sideways in a posture of relaxed pleasure. "And no buckled decks or hull plates. Come, we must take another hull axial profile scan."

"Yes, Mistress," Hollfara sighed in sibilant surrender. What she, the techmistresses, and Anailiatha were doing now amounted to looking at their warship from eleven key angles to see if he was bent or twisted. The task sounded simple and trivial.

It was neither. Their warship was 3,124 ells long and 1,043 ells at his broadest beam. Each series of transversal scans viewed his profile from a single key angle and compared them with the axial profile scans taken by Kem Basinga Clan after warship final assembly.

They could not rely on internal sensors for profile scanning. Sounding the ship meant wrestling heavy and unwieldy equipment to several key triangulation points located within the ship. They had to wait several hours for each transversal scan to complete before moving the equipment to the next triangulation point for another scan.

The entire process was repeated for the next key profile scan.

Each profile angle had its own set of triangulation points. They could not scan multiple profiles from the same triangulation point. They were nowhere near completing the longitudinal axis profile, the easiest of the eleven key angles to scan.

* * *

"I see no damage here," Alfara trilled in complaint after scanning another power distribution node. "What am I doing here, anyway? There is no damage to control!" she trilled.

Jassalin and Einstika flicked sympathetic ears in Alfara's direction but continued with their own tasks.

"Ready to reset?" Jassalin sang.

"Ready," Einstika confirmed. "Self-checking network enabled. Power distribution shutdown crowbar is ready to disengage."

"Resetting...now!" Jassalin trilled at imperative pitch as she cringed and silently begged the spirits to please not let the distribution node explode.

"Node 24,231 online. Full power available. Self-checking network detects no fault," Alfara sang in disgust.

"Still no power to local force field emitters," Einstika sang back from the strangely bare maintenance trail.

"A'pea!" Jassalin trilled.

"You sound like Anailiatha," Alfara sang. "Are you using her favorite curse to gain her favor?"

"What? That is the stupidest thing you have ever said!" Jassalin trilled, her anger rising. "This should not be happening. Electricity has to go somewhere."

"Delwyn said...," Einstika began.

"I know what Delwyn said. We heard him. Everyone heard him," Jassalin growled.

"But what do you think, Jassalin? Do you think he found something?" Einstika pressed.

"I am a techmistress, not a physicist. Anailiatha knows more about such things than I do."

"Delwyn knows something. He recognizes similarities between what is happening here and what happens to a defective Coalition hyperdrive," Einstika trilled from the maintenance trail.

Jassalin and Alfara paused as they smiled in vague but certain relief. The universal female maxim said *males were strange*, but the phrase was as much a loving, indulgent tail-tug as it was a true reflection of what females thought about males and their vexing behavior.

"Anailiatha should listen to him," Alfara sang.

"And we do not?" Jassalin trilled rhetorically.

"It is in our nature to listen to males," Einstika sang with some heat. "Why would you, a Hunter, suggest only Warrior Anailiatha listen to him when we all... Oh! I get it. You mean..."

"I know what I meant!" Jassalin hissed. "We listen to Delwyn, but Anailiatha should follow up on his suspicions." She closed her eyes and counted slowly to ten.

*Males did this!* Something was wrong, and the danger to him could not be overstated or underestimated. The female drive to safeguard male lives, even at the expense of their own lives or the lives of their infants, raged within her. The instinct came upon her even stronger now than it had during the combat training scenario in the combat staging area.

Alfara caught Jassalin's scent and her empathic mind translated its pheromonal content into a long rambling scent-sentence filled with mental pictures and emotional overtones.

"Why are you dwelling so much on Nynava and Zalzadrin's test? And what about Delwyn? What do you think they had in mind?" Alfara trilled.

"Emotional control," Einstika sang as she retraced her path back from the maintenance trail. "You remember what the Ah'vou'ree Clan Combat Training Center mistress of battle did to Kidahin while we trained there?"

"I do," Jassalin growled. "She told Kidahin over the commlink that Delwyn was dead. Kidahin broke comm silence in shock to ask how he died."

Einstika flattened her ears in fury. "It is the same here. They laid a false trail for us, rubbed our awareness of Delwyn in our noses, and goaded us on with his drumming. They then concocted an implied threat to him."

"To what end?" Alfara demanded. "Nynava authorized the use of unarmed lethal force. It was a real possibility for one of us to kill a fellow Team-Two Huntress."

"Discipline," Jassalin sang. "A male in danger triggers female violence. We cannot help it, but we can be rational about our actions. How can we protect our Warleader, or any male, if we go leafchasing after irrational strategies?"

"But we did not," Einstika trilled at discordant pitch.

"And we won!" Jassalin snarled. "We drove Kidahin from her tree."

Alfara emphatically shook her head, a recently learned habit thanks to Delwyn. His poor nose caused him to miss the pheromonal equivalent to simple gestures.

"I do not think we were meant to act on the orders Nynava and Zalzadrin gave us. I think we should have sung for consensus and discussed the matter. How was Delwyn threatened by the charges leveled against both Team-Two hands? I think we were supposed to reach a Major Consensus."

"A Major Consensus? Do you really think we could have reached even a minor consensus, a simple majority, holding their orders unreasonable? You know that no minority can exist in a Major Consensus and only a Major Consensus can be adopted by a group of females in resolution to a conflict between them," Jassalin sang.

Einstika twisted her tail in lazy circles, plugged her test equipment into the next power distribution node, and gave a mental shrug evident to the others through her scent.

"Ready to reset?" she sang.

Jassalin nodded then froze and swore. "I am nodding, sending body posture cues as though I am speaking on the commlink and not in person. We met Delwyn only a few months ago and I am already picking up his in-person body cues."

"The effect males have on us," Alfara sang, "simple and plain."

"I am not complaining," Jassalin trilled. "It shows how much I care for him, which also explains our reaction to Nynava..."

Jassalin paused. Globes of tiny yellow sparks had surrounded them.

"Look! *Ta'na!*" she sang in delight.

Einstika glanced up and frowned at the hovering, glowing night-insect colony. "I thought the environmental systems did not simulate jungle fauna," she sang.

They watched the sparks fade to dull orange and open into hundreds of thumb-sized funnels.

"Not ta'na!" Jassalin keened. She spread her arms wide and jumped into Einstika and Alfara. Around her the power distribution chase faded to a dull violet briefly as the three Hunters landed on soft, tall, bronze jungle grasses.

Jassalin stared at the grass in stupefied astonishment. The rainforest simulation was online again. The high-relief deck plates and pathway were covered in foliage and followed the terrain of a narrow trail wandering through northern La'huaset temperate rainforest.

Einstika spent several seconds groping through tangling grasses searching for her test equipment. She found it seemingly plugged into an old stump.

"Mistress Anailiatha? Jassalin. We are in the Forward Combat Operations Center auxiliary power chase. Home environmental options are now working in this section of the combat hull, but we did nothing to restore power," she sang over the commlink.

"Reports are coming in throughout the ship confirming home options are online. My damage control diagnostics console shows all power now available at nominal levels," Anailiatha sang.

"Mistress, just before the options came online we saw what looked like ta'na colonies sparkling around the distribution network," Jassalin trilled.

"Ta'na? You know the rainforest simulations do not include fauna. We certainly would not carry living insects with us because they would foul my equipment," Anailiatha snapped.

"I know this, Mistress," Jassalin trilled. "These look like sparks that expanded as they faded away."

"Sparks? As in electrical shorts?" Anailiatha keened.

"No, Mistress. As they faded away they bathed the chase momentarily in dim violet light. It happened so fast I thought I was imagining it."

"Violet? This is probably an out-of-focus holographic projector painting incomplete force field flora. I will run a spectral analysis on holographic interference patterns verses field diffraction and refraction parameters when I have time. Return to the engineering command center, I have other tasks waiting for you," Anailiatha sang.

"Yes, Mistress," Jassalin sang and curled a length of tail around her fellow techmistresses. "You heard her. Disconnect your gear and let us go."

"Affirm," Einstika and Alfara replied. Together they retrieved their equipment, hoisted carry sacks over shoulders, and prowled tails-entwined down peaceful and relaxing jungle trails.

***

Merkrida crawled along a narrow rift. Above her a superconductor power conduit cut an angle from the compartment ahead through the ceiling bulkhead. She was glaring at the ugly mechanical eyesore when it began shimmering.

Startled, she tripped on forest floor vines forming across her path. She stumbled into the heavy jungle undergrowth bursting into being around her. The undergrowth instantly changed the rift into a vine-enshrouded ravine with one end of a log leaning against a tree and the other end buried into the ledge above.

Caught flatfooted, Merkrida stumbled again, this time over exposed tree roots. She fell flat on her face.

Her shattered jaw exploded anew in blinding pain, and she keened in agony.

"There you are!" Allohindra growled in suppressed fury. "The outrigger secondary weapon gun crews called me in Health Center the minute you left."

Merkrida shouted a pheromonal *no!* through her scent at the Mistress of Healers. Unable to speak, she changed to battle language.

<<No, Mistress. I am fine. I need to cross over to the left outrigger and confirm secondary weapon status.>>

"No, you do not. I cannot regenerate this injury like any simple break or flesh wound. Your head must remain stable, and that cannot be done here. Come with me, healers orders."

Merkrida objected by varying her scent but otherwise gave up further argument. She prowled alongside the primary physician, content. She concentrated on trying to enjoy the Warrior's company, the restored rainforest trail, and the distractions both gave her from the pain. Health Center occupied the lower forward command hull, no short walk from where they were now. The sun burned bright above them in partly cloudy blue sky. Glowing pale yellow light shined down through crimson, vermilion, and golden leaves. The warm ocher blend fell on the reds of lesser trees before reaching the faded yellow, pale orange, and light red jungle ground plants.

The trail narrowed, twisting between boles and through heavy undergrowth. Several minutes later it widened again into a pathway leading to a massive elleiu tree aerial root shroud. They passed through the natural ragged opening and turned into a maze of fused, twisted orange roots that ascended into the outer layers until they reached a bole opening onto a branch wide enough for a light armored vehicle to crawl down.

Allohindra led Merkrida to a fork in the branch. Reaching its narrowest point, she jumped onto a neighboring branch and waited for Merkrida to follow. Together they sprinted down the branch to its wide base and the open bole waiting there.

Once through the bole threshold their feet touched forest floor rather than the wood of a hollow branch several hundred ells above ground.

Merkrida sighed, relieved. They were on the same deck as Health Center. The broad pathway flanked by heavy jungle growth led into a winding grassy meadow. At its far end stood another elleiu tree, the Health Center complex.

Allohindra and Merkrida stepped into the tree's surrounding fused root layers. Inside, faux aerial roots formed intricate yellow-orange wooden mazes. Built into and wrapping around the heart trunk was the trauma center. Circling the trauma center and soaring above it were individual examination boles, intensive care abodes, pharmacies, autopsy theaters, quarantine abodes, laboratories, and convalescence abodes. They filled out the simulated lower tree aerial root shrouds and trunk. Above them, the upper trunk and main branches reaching into the crown supported staff abodes for everyone dedicated to the healing arts.

"Come, Merkrida," Allohindra trilled, gliding into one of the hollow branch examination abodes. "Sit here and put your chin on the rest."

Allohindra glanced at a shelf, grabbed a device, and returned to Merkrida's side.

"Comfortable?" Allohindra trilled.

Her healer-rhetorical question annoyed Merkrida, and she sent Allohindra a nasty empathic *No!* through her scent.

Allohindra locked her patient's head into the facial reconstruction halo and programmed it for jawbone regeneration. Too bad she could not use simpler bone accelerated healing methods here. This was no minor break or fracture. The bone was shattered and teeth were missing. The jaw had to fully regenerate. Growing a new jawbone and teeth took much longer than mending a simple broken bone. Regenerating bone was painless and took pain away. Merkrida signaled profound relief through pheromonal empathy to Allohindra.

"Enjoy this while you can," Allohindra trilled. "Dental regeneration means growing new dental nerves for all the teeth first and then encapsulating them in mineralized tissue to form enamel. It is painful, so I am giving you a sedative. Try to relax."

* * *

"Are you not finished?" Aplilin trilled.

"Almost," Seliaha sang. She paused then added, "All small arms are assigned. Inventory checklist confirms weapons distributed by control number and verified by person receiving the weapon and me."

"And the thumpers?" Aplilin pressed.

"Thumpers? They are not traditional weapons. They are technology-based devices. Um, they are not even weapons," Seliaha trilled.

"*Dou'tu'tay*, Seliaha!" Aplilin keened. "Everything is a weapon if it can be used as one. We use electromagnetic pulse thumpers to burn out Ni'zakhonii powered personal and light infantry weapons. The EMP also burns out battlefield scanners, commlinks, and other moderately shielded electronic devices. What do you think a Ni'zakhonii can do with a thumper?"

"Not much," Seliaha sang. "We fight with traditional weapons, unpowered devices."

"*A'pea!*" Aplilin keened. "Use your head. A thumper can kill our commlinks, kill local force field emitters, kill local holographic jungle cover, and kill local combat address speakers. With a thumper a Ni'zakhonii can deprive us of comms and talkback telemetry among ourselves, with Nynava or with Zalzadrin. They can kill camouflaging cover, kill pathway isolation and breach-arresting force fields, and," Aplilin paused for effect, "kill Delwyn's voice in any local area!"

Seliaha's large amber eyes widened in shock. Depriving females of the male voice during any crisis event in itself made a missing thumper a potentially dire weapon indeed.

"I see your point," Seliaha trilled in admission. "Aplilin?"

"Now what?" Aplilin sang, bored. She was a demolitions expert and heavy weapon weaponmistress. Securing combat vehicles that nobody was driving down warship trails and pathways anyway wasted her skills. Nynava had not even authorized the release of mobile infantry platforms most Warriors routinely used and very few Hunters bothered to learn.

Except her. Aplilin was qualified in plasma cannons, the lightest infantry platform weapon in inventory. In Assault Team-Two she used the weapon for covering fire while her fellow Hunters advanced. She sang an access code to the hidden arsenal and pulled one of the cannons from its charging rack in the weapon cache.

Zalzadrin did not release the self-propelled infantry platforms. Only she could order weapon release, just as only Nynava could authorize combat vehicle access, including the self-propelled platforms. Not even Warleader Delwyn or Mistress of the Ship Melkorka could order weapon or vehicle release directly. Only the Mistress of Battle and the Mistress of Arms could do so.

That line of thought snagged a vine in Aplilin's literal mind.

"Stupid," she trilled aloud.

"What?" Seliaha sang. "I already conceded your point."

"Not you," Aplilin trilled. "Nynava's training choice makes no sense to me."

"Now you make clear sense," Seliaha trilled. "She told each hand the other was a danger to Delwyn. What point did she have but to make us feel his danger?"

Aplilin slammed the brush-concealed heavy weapon locker shut and locked the cache. She spun on her companion. "Our current mission," she sang with certainty. "She knows some danger to Delwyn, and she wanted to prepare us."

"And what better way to prepare us than to declare him in danger," Seliaha finished, doubt filling her scent. "It seems awfully extreme to me."

"Wrong-headed," the stubborn Aplilin trilled in agreement. "Zalzadrin and Nynava pitted me against Kidahin knowing she and I are tails-entwined partners. And they did it anyway! And Delwyn! He likes going off on his own. I know males are strange, but solitary behavior from any Eyloni not suffering from amusia is stranger than strange. Yet, I tell you this quality of his is attractive to me because I enjoy solitary stalking."

"That is just the mating urge singing to you," Seliaha sang.

Aplilin paused, her pupils dilating until her amber irises vanished into deep black pools. She shook herself to clear the image of her favorite male from her head.

"No, I do not think so. I think Nynava and Zalzadrin suspect he might try to..."

"Do what, exactly?" Seliaha trilled. "Males stay with females for protection. He would never strike out on his own away from female support."

"Kalinn, our ship's previous warleader, did," Aplilin sang.

"I learned the same ship history songs from Mistress Mirrahindrallin as you did. Delwyn is not Kalinn!" Seliaha snapped angrily.

"Still," Aplilin trilled, not used to deep thinking. "The mission may present unique problems, problems specific to Delwyn. The combat drill was meant to prepare us for some contingency."

"If you think so, then I will keep it in mind," Seliaha sang.

Aplilin twisted her tail tightly around her companion's waist and led her down the trail back to the combat staging area.

***

"Warriors are such pains in the a'pea," Kyralin trilled in complaint. "They think my humor is insulting? Then they never crossed Zalzadrin's sharp wit."

"You are lucky none of the forestation watchmistresses or the Mistress of the Forestation herself bothered to press an honor point offense against you," Tialdrin trilled. "You always take social and honor issues right up to the edge of offense. Warriors control both the forestation and the aftstation, and they take those two areas and their duties there seriously. I suspect the only reason they did not report you to their hierarchy representatives is that, on some level, they agreed with your sentiment if not the time or place or your way of saying it. I do not think Warriors are all that funny, and your turns of phrase are just as dry as most Warrior humor."

"I was not being insulting," Kyralin keened.

"You told them they should leave the forestation so we, *we,* could do a security sweep for them. No matter how phlegmatic your phrasing, you should have known you were yanking their tails. Every Warrior female in the forestation has more social, hierarchy, and military rank than you and I combined," Tialdrin trilled in complaint.

"I am glad the rainforest simulations are back," Kyralin sang, changing the subject.

"What? Oh, yes. Me, too. The forest undergrowth provides excellent cover for stalking, and I prefer it to bare, high-relief deck plates on pathways and trails. They were too open for my tastes and had no convenient trees, lianas, or branches to climb from level to level," Tialdrin sang.

"You think they fixed the problem?" Kyralin sang.

"Does it not now resemble La'huaset rainforest all around you?" Tialdrin sang. Beautiful as it was, she had Health Center and her ripped ear most in mind at the moment.

"That does not mean Anailiatha fixed it...," Kyralin trilled to silence. She listened as Delwyn's deep mellow voice sang from the combat address system. The mesmerizing male voice tantalized and enthralled her. She stood straight, pricked her ears forward, set her tail curving up behind her until it looped above her head and curved back down, her pons twitching.

"His voice sounds so...intriguing. I could listen to him all...*ungh!* Tialdrin...!"

"Run!" Tialdrin keened and slammed into Kyralin again, this time looping her tail around Kyralin's waist and pulling her head-first into the undergrowth seconds before it and all the pastel jungle foliage bled around them like an exploding rainbow.

Tialdrin watched the jungle trail revert to sculpted high-relief deck plating surrounded by swarms of sparkling ta'na.

"Mistress Melkorka, Tialdrin. I am in the forward central combat hull just below the nutrition center. Kyralin and I are surrounded by swarms of what look like ta'na. I do not..."

"Tialdrin, Kyralin, and everyone near apparent ta'na swarms. Evacuate the area immediately!" Delwyn sang over the combat address system.

* * *

Kidahin sat at the navigation console in the auxiliary command center scanning local space when she heard Delwyn's shipwide evacuation order.

Two things followed almost immediately. The sky-high tree house rendering of the auxiliary command center vanished, giving her a momentary sense of vertigo as her senses adjusted from being in a tree far above ground to a sudden appearance on the deck in a broad bay bathed in greenish-yellow emergency lighting.

Her navigation console flashed an alert at the same time. A dimensional anomaly several million ells deep into the star system ahead had triggered a navigation hazard warning.

"Mistress Trebithia, Kidahin at auxiliary navigation. I am detecting trillions of subatomic discontinuities radiating from a point within the system. My scans have pinpointed what appears as debris from an artificial object."

"Affirm, Kidahin. I am transferring your console scans to primary navigation. Hlinlodyn, open an FTL scanning window to auxiliary navigation scan coordinates."

"Affirm, Trebithia," Kidahin heard Hlinlodyn sing over the commlink.

The navigation suite gave Kidahin full access to the augmented data the Mistress of Tactics was retrieving from the FTL navigation scans. An extensive dust ring left over from the system's genesis orbited the star. Shattered and smashed in that junk a ship drifted, one of neither Compact nor Ni'zakhonii origin.

"Scan that object," Kidahin heard Delwyn sing over the combat address system.

She watched as images from the sensor sweeps played across her three-dimensional navigation display. The scan shifted pickup several times. It looked like a ship of some kind.

The scan centered on the shipwreck's bow. Along his left side Kidahin read a line of partially obliterated and ungainly human text.

CECS *Londiwe Khoza*.

"Damn," Delwyn whispered over the combat address system.

# 3
## THE DUAL NATURE OF FEMALES, LINKED MINDS, THE DEVALUED LIFE...

*"Londiwe Khoza* is the source of the gravitational anomalies," Kidahin reported from her station in the auxiliary command center.

"Your observation is obvious," Mistress of Pathwalking Trebithia trilled. "Delwyn? Is this what a mobius fracture looks like?" Kidahin heard Trebithia ask over the open console commlink.

"No, not quite, at least not from what I can remember," Delwyn's voice replied. "Mobius fracture happens when the hyperdrive coils fire out of sequence. Hlinlodyn, scan the *Khoza's* hyperdrive coils."

"By your command. I am reading twenty distinct powerful energy surges firing in random order. Reactor and power plant emissions show full power is available to at least the coils."

Kidahin twitched her ears in amusement. Twenty power surges. Delwyn often forgot that Eyloni counted limbs—legs, arms, and tail—as the base of their number system. He counted his fingers and thumbs as a basis for his number system. Why he did not count his toes as well was confusing. She asked him about it once, but he ignored the question and asked why she did not consider the head a limb.

Kidahin exited the command center tactical scan file and opened a new one. She wanted to pursue her own analysis. She was good at solving navigation problems. Her adolescent years spent training in wet navy three-dimensional underwater submersible navigation problems gave her skills that attracted Trebithia to her when she approached Melkorka and the command mistresses during their search for crew replacements.

She studied the data coming over her navigation scanners. An interesting problem presented itself. Could they even navigate around or through whatever it was the Coalition warship was spitting at them?

"Kidahin? What are you doing?" Trebithia trilled over the console commlink.

"I am making a detailed map of local space between us and the shipwreck. I see a pattern in the data. It resembles the pattern those tiny vortices looking like ta'na swarms make when they appear. There is some form of dark energy surging from a thirty-one vertex, thirteen cube, forty-four square, one hundred twelve edged, and thirteen hyperplane-bound four-dimensional cube near the Coalition warship."

"A four-dimensional cube is called a tesseract," Delwyn added.

"Meaning what, exactly?" Melkorka's voice trilled over the open commlink.

"I don't know," Delwyn confessed. "That's all I remember about it. I don't think a tesseract has anything to do with hyperspace geometry."

Kidahin growled in frustration. She knew next to nothing about how her warship jump drive worked and knew even less about how a Coalition warship jumped into and out of a hyperdimension.

It did not matter. She was responsible for auxiliary navigation, but while her console was linked into main navigation she could also access Hlinlodyn's tactical station data at will. And according to those scans the Coalition ship had not taken fire and the damage was not consistent with an attack. She suspected a collision accident.

"Mistress Trebithia? Could *Londiwe Khoza* have jumped into the dust ring orbiting this star?" she asked over the commlink.

"Possibly," Trebithia sang. "His navigation scans should have identified an asteroid field this dense. It would trigger a gravitational anomaly on their sensors and...wait, Kidahin."

"Yes, Mistress," Kidahin sang. Hlinlodyn must need Trebithia for some helm or navigation data. She waited and checked her navigation console. Nothing so far. It was still working on the problem she set it to analyze.

She needed more data, but interrupting Hlinlodyn was a bad idea. The Mistress of Tactics was a prickly Warrior when bothered. Kidahin downloaded the latest tactical data from Hlinlodyn's console. So far, her tactical analysis found inconclusive life signs.

Kidahin downloaded the tactical scans of the Coalition shipwreck as well. The bow and amidships sections were smashed in several places, but the aft quarter was stretched and compressed somehow. His stern looked as if it had been melted and drawn away from the rest of the ship. It reminded Kidahin of a blob of molten glass teased to a long-tapered tip by a skilled glassblower.

Kidahin decided to risk Hlinlodyn's wrath and tapped her station commlink. "Mistress? What caused the aft sections to compress and elongate?"

"Spaghettification," Delwyn's voice muttered over the combat address system.

"What does this word mean?" Kidahin trilled.

"When a Coalition ship jumps from hyperspace into normal space or from normal space into hyperspace within a star's hyperlimit, the wormhole connecting normal space and hyperspace distorts as its event horizon contracts, causing it to shrink down to a few meters across. In theory it can shrink down to the diameter of a cosmic string. The contracting wormhole compresses and elongates a ship's mass into a stream of wreckage several thousand meters long."

"Oh. Why do you not call it longitudinal elongation? What does spaghettification mean?" Kidahin sang.

"Spaghetti is a long, thin, round pasta, a noodle. Used in this context, it means a reduction of a mass to the likeness of a string of spaghetti," he explained to Kidahin and everyone else listening to the combat address system.

"Are we near the star's hyperlimit?" Kidahin trilled.

"No. In fact we are far from it. I don't see how..."

"Kidahin! Why are you bothering the Warleader with nonsense questions?" Hlinlodyn trilled at imperative pitch. "He is helping me frame a theoretical question for the Mistress of Sails. Trebithia, tell Kidahin to do something useful!"

"Kidahin? Trebithia. Use only the navigation sensors and tell me what you can about the Coalition warship."

"Yes, Mistress. Switching to high-resolution navigation sweeps and scanning. The ship lies on his right side up against an asteroid roughly eleven times his length. External scans show apparent kinetic impacts not caused by ordnance. From this data I am confident the Coalition ship exited hyperspace at high sublight velocity and rammed the edge of the dust ring. His navigation shields absorbed and redirected kinetic impacts as the ship decelerated before they burned out. The crew apparently raised the combat kinetic shields while the ship decelerated, and they absorbed more asteroid impacts until they burned out as well. The ship's reactive armor and hull plating took further battering as he collided with the asteroid he lies on."

"Give me some hull damage details," Trebithia sang.

"I found several crush points, crumpled areas, and hull breaches. Several of them look wide enough for combat EVA suited prowler and stalker teams to pass through. I am scanning amidships now. Mistress! There are..."

"Kidahin?" Trebithia sang at interrogative tempo. "What did you find?"

"Mistress, the warship took a huge left side broadside impact, one that gouges through both exterior and interior hulls and into several decks of the ship. It is nearly as wide as the left side of the ship and is several compartments long. There is a lot of drifting wreckage, loose equipment, personal effects, and...bodies. Mistress, male bodies, fists and fists of male bodies...all those male deaths. I...," Kidahin keened.

"Kidahin," Trebithia trilled. "Kidahin, I am with you. Move on and keep busy or you will succumb to empathic shock. Focus now. What can you tell me about the interior decks?"

Kidahin shook as a remnant of the juvenile fascination with anything male threatened to overwhelm her. There were dead males here, human males but males, nevertheless. There were human female bodies as well, but instinct drove her attention back to the males. She could do nothing for them. She could not save them. Unbalancing rage seethed through her.

"Kidahin, I need you to scan those exposed decks now!" Trebithia sang at imperative tempo.

"Affirm, acting!" Kidahin sang. "I am continuing my scans. I found inconclusive life signs. I see heavy internal damage. The decks and compartments look like he was dropped from a great height causing inertia-driven collapse of the hull. It reminds me of when you drop a ripe... Mistress, I found decks and compartments having minimal but stable life support!"

"One moment, Kidahin. Confirmed. Delwyn!" Trebithia keened.

Kidahin's auxiliary navigation console displayed a breathtaking data pattern meant to alert her that it had a solution to the navigation problem she posed to it. The data told Kidahin that *Hunter's Moon* could not navigate through local space without intersecting increasingly powerful ta'na events. A small proxy vessel such as a troop transport might successfully navigate through the area without suffering power losses. What to do about the ta'na effect itself was beyond her.

"Mistress Trebithia?" Kidahin sang to the commlink. "My navigation analysis confirms we are not free to navigate in this space, but a troop transport can if he proceeds with care."

"Understood. Hlinlodyn? You heard?" Trebithia sang.

"If a troop transport or a stealth insertion vehicle can reach that ship, then so can kinetic ordnance. I say we destroy him," Hlinlodyn sang insistently.

"No. Not yet. Not without knowing if survivors remain aboard," Delwyn's voice boomed from the combat address system.

***

Globs of glowing ta'na erupted out of thin air above several high-relief, sculptured deck places. Pale yellow-green emergency light took on a hint of violet mere seconds before Tialdrin saw her bare feet suddenly stepping on rusty jungle trail. Partly cloudy blue sky framed the sun. Bright yellow sunlight beamed through the reds, oranges, and yellows of rainforest leaves as far as she could see.

"Finally," she grumbled. Her ear hurt. Her split scalp hurt, too. The wound was scabbed over and swelling. The swelling stretched and split the scab. The swelling and torn scab made what little control she had over her ear even less. The nearly immobile ear not only mangled her acute stereoscopic hearing, but it also ruined proper social cues signaled by ear motion.

"I doubt Anailiatha fixed the problem," Kyralin grumbled.

"I doubt it, too," Tialdrin growled. "But right now I do not care. Our duty is to prowl our warship. We will reach Health Center soon. Once my ear is healed I will feel better about all the scenery abruptly changing."

Kyralin pricked her ears forward, flipped them wide, and then pricked them forward again.

"Movement ahead," she sang at a whisper.

Tialdrin cocked her head to pitch her bad ear forward.

"I hear it, them," she trilled. "A noisy Warrior watch triad."

"Aheila," Kyralin sang. "I smell her scent on the breeze."

Tialdrin caught the identifying pheromonal flavor of the young Warrior and flicked her ears in agreement. "I thought they were guarding the forward aftstation blast door."

Kyralin twitched her ears in negation. "They are not aftstation security under Thiodnuma. They answer to Phelindra just as we do in all security matters. Do you want to stalk them and see what they are up to?"

"Did your experience in the forestation not teach you anything? You really do have a devious tail," Tialdrin trilled in soft laughter. Normally she would do just what Kyralin suggested. Hunters and Warriors carried on a rivalry of sorts. But their warship was at Battle Status and Warriors really did have a dour sense of humor.

And besides, her ear was reminding her not only of her responsibilities as a warship security stealthmistress but also that their prowling loop took them to Health Center.

"Aheila!" Tialdrin sang in greeting.

"Tialdrin!" Aheila sang back from under forest cover. "Do you have any news?"

"None," Tialdrin sang. "Do you?"

Aheila and her two Warrior teammates crashed through tall amber grasses nearly as tall as they. "No," Aheila sang. She gave one curt nod to Tialdrin and spun on Kyralin.

"You are barred from the forestation for one week because of your disrespect!" Aheila hissed.

Kyralin flicked insolent ears at Aheila. "See what I mean about Warrior humor?" she sang to Tialdrin.

Aheila whipped her tail back and forth, agitated. "This is not a question of humor," she sang, "but a question of respect while in another's territory. You are getting off easy. I am a Warrior female, but I am not an aftstation Warrior. If I ever suggested doing a security sweep for them, they would not just bar my passage through the aftstation. They would probably hand me my own tail!"

Tialdrin gave Kyralin a meaningful glare before asking, "Where are you prowling to now?"

"We," Aheila sang, including her teammates with a brush of her tail, "are prowling main pathways through the command hull until we reach the forestation aft blast door. Once there, we have sentry duty until we rotate back through the command hull to the aftstation forward blast door. Do you have anything you wish conveyed to the Mistress of the Forestation?"

"Like what?" Kyralin sang innocently.

"Kyralin!" Tialdrin trilled, in pain and impatient with her fellow Hunter. "We may be at Battle Status for some time. When not on an Assault Team-Two mission we are security stalkers. You cannot serve as an effective security Huntress if you cannot prowl the command hull. And you cannot gain access to the combat hull without passing through the forestation."

Kyralin clenched the rusty ground with her bare feet, her four-jointed toes grasping at soil that was not real soil.

"Tell the Mistress of the Forestation I apologize for my disrespectful behavior. In keeping with the Rite of Forgiveness I seek her pardon and ask her to set my offense aside, withhold punishment, forget my offense, and abandon my social debt."

"I call upon all here to bear witness. On your honor do you apologize?" Aheila sang formally.

"Entiki," Kyralin sang as she brushed flimsy beaded neckwear strands aside, cupped her bare left breast, and caressed her adulthood knife.

Aheila perked her ears forward, caressed her teammates with her pons, and flicked her ears at the two Hunters. "Good stalking to you, Tialdrin and Kyralin. Kyralin, do not attempt passage into the forestation until the Mistress of the Forestation sends a message to your 'minder."

Kyralin pricked her ears at Aheila.

Tialdrin waited until the Warrior triad was a few minutes up the trail before turning her attention on her teammate.

"Lucky you," she sang.

"Aheila and I are occasional nest-mates. We twine tails often," Kyralin trilled.

"That is why I say lucky you."

"Yes, I am," Kyralin sang, and the pheromones in her scent told Tialdrin she meant it.

Several hours of prowling and eleven more environmental system failures later they prowled into sight of Health Center. But without the home environmental landscapes Health Center looked like the multi-tiered, terraced, roughly circular and ascending maze of bays, tunnels, and abodes built into the compartments and bulkheads of a warship that it was and not the mighty elleiu tree they were accustomed to seeing.

The lack of jungle beauty did not distract Tialdrin from the certain knowledge relief was soon at hand. Her long, now-inflexible ear was swollen to twice its normal thickness. The left side of her swollen face from tightly curled ringlets to cheekbone pulled the skin taut enough to affect her vision.

Kyralin wrapped her tail securely around Tialdrin's waist and led her down the bare trail. Her footing was becoming careless and abrupt changes in scenery tended to catch her by surprise. Kyralin pulled her onto a branching path, took three steps, and immediately found herself surrounded by warleader special security.

They stood in three groups of three around her and Tialdrin, fourteen in total. A single strand of green thread woven through the multicolor webs of the Hunters' rank earrings identified them and the duties they shared on behalf of Delwyn. He called the rank earring 'dreamcatchers,' but nobody ever dreamed fondly about warleader special security Huntresses. They were almost as dangerous as Comara and almost as dry in humor as Warriors.

"Tialdrin and Kyralin," the Huntmistress trilled. "Mistress of the Watch Phelindra tells me you both have skills helpful to warleader special security. Is this true?"

"Yes, Huntmistress," Tialdrin and Kyralin sang.

The Huntmistress snapped her tail, flicked her ears forward, and nodded. "Phelindra has concerns, therefore we have concerns."

"What has Delwyn done now?" Kyralin trilled softly.

"Most perceptive, Kyralin," the Huntmistress sang approvingly. "We do not know what causes these ta'na swarms and the unknown is a danger. We are the Hunters who meet danger before Delwyn ever sees it. Phelindra, Melkorka, and Lo'sutra'est anni want Delwyn safely surrounded in the command center."

"He is at his Watch. I saw him there myself," Tialdrin objected. "He is busy working with Hlinlodyn. His place is there, he sings comfort and courage to us from there, and he is in the most shielded and protected part of our warship."

"What you say is true," the Huntmistress admitted. "Yet Delwyn can sing from anywhere and the combat address system will send his voice throughout the ship. As Warleader, he can go anywhere he wants anytime he wants. Delwyn is also peculiar, even for a male. He stalks the rainforest terrain alone for hours at a time."

Tialdrin heard the frustrated admiration in the Huntmistress's musical voice, could smell it on her pheromones. "So?" she trilled. "He is not prowling now. As I told you, he is busy with Hlinlodyn."

Kyralin wrapped her long tail around Tialdrin's arm and gave her a gentle tug. "Remember what Kidahin told us about him?" she sang softly.

"Kidahin told us the same thing," the Huntmistress trilled ominously.

"What Kidahin told us about Delwyn? She told us many things about him," Tialdrin sang. She paused, her eyes glazing, her pupils contracting as memories of Kidahin's stories engulfed her. Delwyn once led elite combat teams for the Coalition of Earth Colonies. He went on solitary prowls like a Hunter was wont to do. Melkorka declared him *sire cairn*, battle leader, and as sire cairn he led female combat teams at Nikkiolo. He, alone, boarded a Ni'zakhonii light attack craft and evaded the crew while rescuing forty-two females. They in turn captured the ship for him. Kidahin made it clear to Team-Two that Delwyn thought nothing wrong about stalking alone or leading assault forces.

The Huntmistress stood patiently, tail swinging side to side, her red-ringleted pons twisting slow circles as she scented Tialdrin's pheromones. The scent-linked empathy resonating between them allowed her to feel Tialdrin's emotions and see emotional pictures of the events Kidahin had described to her, images of Delwyn in Ibeetu forests, images of him aboard the Ni'zakhonii ship, images of him alone.

"You understand the problem?" the Huntmistress trilled at a discordant pitch.

"No, I do not," Tialdrin snapped angrily, frustrated at being pulled away from emotional stories about her favorite male. "He is in the command center. He has no reason to go wandering throughout our warship alone during Battle Status. There are no female forces gone missing for him to strike off on his own and rescue."

The Huntmistress twitched her ears wide and snapped her tail in rising impatience.

"Mistress Phelindra has concerns. The shipwreck in the dust ring is a human warship. Trebithia deems it dangerous to approach him while these ta'na events are occurring. Hlinlodyn tells me we are beyond translation range of the wrecked ship, so we cannot send Warrior skirmisher teams directly from here to there. Kidahin thinks a troop transport can reach the shipwreck, but she is uncertain whether a transport can dock with him."

"Humans say warships are females," Kyralin trilled abruptly.

"What does that have to do with anything?" Tialdrin sang.

"Well," Kyralin trilled and then paused, squirming uncomfortably under the withering gaze of every warleader security Huntress. "The male voice," Kyralin sang tremulously, "is the song of reason when we fight on their behalf. He may feel the need to rescue *Londiwe Khoza* because he sees him as a female."

The Huntmistress gaped at Kyralin in respectful astonishment. "You make sense, Kyralin. This is exactly the worry Phelindra has. She feels Delwyn will attempt to board the shipwreck by insisting he lead an assault team."

"After Warleader Kalinn led a boarding assault force into a Ni'zakhonii destroyer and got them and himself killed? Our society will never allow it!" Tialdrin keened, livid.

"We will not, indeed," the Huntmistress sang. "But Delwyn is resourceful and lacks the normal Eyloni male need to surround himself in female protection. What we believe no sane male would consider doing or would consider prudent, Delwyn may attempt."

"So, what does Phelindra want? You nor your Huntresses would be wasting time with us unless you have some security assignment for us," Tialdrin trilled.

"Yes, about that," the Huntmistress sang. "I convey to you upon my honor that Phelindra suggests after you leave Health Center, you both return to the command center and remain near the Warleader's Watch and keep Delwyn in sight no matter where he goes. Lo'sutra'est anni knows you are joining her in this effort. Your success in this task will go far in advancing you into consideration for warleader special security duties."

"Affirm, acting," Tialdrin and Kyralin sang in duet.

Kyralin watched the Huntmistress and her Huntresses sprint down the bare pale pathway until they rounded a bend and dropped out of sight. "We have a priority security assignment," she sang in delight.

Tialdrin stared longingly at the nearby Health Center complex for another minute before joining her companion. "An assignment near our Warleader fills me with joy but prowling within killing range of a Comari fills me with dread," she trilled.

***

"Aplilin? What do you know about our mission?" Seliaha sang.

"What?" Aplilin trilled, roused from her simmering fury. She missed Kidahin, wanted nothing more than to twine tails with her on the sleeping nest in her abode, cuddle, talk, and sleep. "Why? What did Zalzadrin say to you?"

"Nothing really," Seliaha sang. "Just that this star is on the pons of Ni'zakhonii territory. The A'tayotan asked the Be'atika Senge for a stealth mission here. They, seating as the Compact Counsel for the Ten Tribes of Elleio, approved it. All I know is that this system has a single gas giant wandering into and out of the star's habitable zone. The planet has one large moon similar to Elleio in size but only marginally habitable. Zalzadrin wanted me to begin readying combat EVA suits once we finished the training scenario with Kidahin in the staging and deployment bay."

"Nynava told me something similar," Aplilin sang. "She said that Team-Two would deploy for a prowling and stalking sweep and that I could bring my cannon," she sang happily as she patted the heavy infantry weapon. "Nynava also told me demolitions were needed and that I should ready my demolitions gear, too."

They stepped into open space where several pathways converged. In jungle cover the area resembled a grassy clearing having wide trails surrounded in heavy undergrowth. Now, without the rainforest simulation the high-relief deck plates and weaving tunnels bathed in pale green were depressing. Depression made Aplilin think of Kidahin.

"You are a demolitions and heavy weapons weaponmistress. You have special clearance. Did Nynava say why a demolitions Huntress was needed?" Seliaha trilled.

"Nynava mentioned something about a slight chance of finding a Ni'zakhonii bunker, but she did not say much else other than I may need to do a lot of blasting."

"That is not saying much," Seliaha growled.

"What did you expect? She was not giving me a mission briefing. She was giving me advance notice so I can plan for a demolitions mission. It was nice of her to give me some up-front information. I do not have to worry about last-minute guessing. Guessing is the wrong way to plan a combat operation," Aplilin growled.

"That is a Delwyn saying," Seliaha trilled happily.

"A what? Oh, yes. Kidahin told me several examples of his combat doctrine. I wish he was coming with us on this mission," Aplilin trilled wistfully.

"Really?" Seliaha keened in surprise. "We would be too busy protecting him and not paying attention to the mission. It would put his life at risk."

"I know this," Aplilin snapped. "I want him to watch me fight."

"Why?" Seliaha sang, certain she already knew.

"I want to mate with him," Aplilin sang sensuously.

"And you think I do not?" Seliaha trilled.

"Of course not," Aplilin reassured her. "Everyone having their immediate family's permission to mate this cycle will want to mate with him."

"Like it matters," Seliaha keened. "Kidahin is not even sure Delwyn can mate with us. He has no tail and cannot twine tails to achieve pleasure. He is not a scent-linked empath and cannot share mating pleasure. His reproductive organ is all wrong. And we are different species, so conception cannot succeed."

"But not for want of trying," Aplilin sang in gruff reassurance. "We twine tails with other females all the time to experience pleasure. We will experience pleasure twining tails with Delwyn, too. Mating with him will not bring us infants, but having our favorite male to ourselves is more than enough for me," Aplilin trilled comfort to Seliaha.

Seliaha impulsively twisted her tail twice around the muscular Hunter's waist and then twisted her pons around hers as well, sharing close intimate contact as they stepped out of a tunnel and through the forward bulkhead and into the deserted combat staging area.

"We did not expect others here, remember?" Aplilin sang to her. "All the Hunter prowler and Warrior triads are already armed and at their watch points or are stalking their security sweeps."

"Should you not get a bow and get to your watch point?" Seliaha sang reluctantly.

"Like it will do any good," Aplilin growled.

"A backup weapon is always good to have."

Aplilin curved her tail until her pons was only a thumb-length from Seliaha's nose. She slowly spun her pons in a tight circle in what Delwyn called their 'rolling the eyes' tail sign.

"We do not use nontraditional weapons against individual enemies. The reason Nynava wants me in the tractor pilot pod is to repel any vehicle assault against the deployment bay airlock, bulkhead and door. Since the other side of the airlock is vacuum, an arrow, even explosive antipersonnel arrows, are useless against a mechanized breaching assault," Aplilin trilled.

"Oh, so you do not want the added encumbrance?"

"I do not want the encumbrance, but Nynava did order me to carry a bow as a backup weapon. Even without her order, I planned to get a bow and a case of antipersonnel arrows. Mechanized breaching vehicles must disgorge their forces sooner or later."

Seliaha nodded, opened a weapon cache, and pulled a bow and bow quiver from the rack and handed them to Aplilin.

"One or two boxes?" Seliaha sang.

"Give me one case of antipersonnel arrows and one case of standard sheaf arrows. If they have, or gain access to, a thumper, then the AP arrows are useless."

Seliaha scowled, remembering their earlier EMP discussion. "Here, take one case of AP and one case of sheaf arrows."

"My thanks, Seliaha," Aplilin sang and turned toward the deployment bay tractor pod climbing frame.

Seliaha stood and watched Aplilin walk away and felt abandoned.

Aplilin smelled Seliaha's scent and the emotional loss she felt. She turned sideways.

"Go find Zalzadrin," Aplilin trilled. "She may have need of you. When we return from Battle Status to Action Ready Status you will be busy for hours recovering weapons, logging returned weapons to their caches, looking for lost and damaged weapons, and making requests for repair and replacement of weapons. If she has no immediate need of you, come back and keep me company."

"*Me nako nabi,*" Seliaha whispered: I wish you well and hope to meet you again.

"*Meh nati ka meh,*" Aplilin sang: you go with the spirits.

* * *

Merkrida, probably the most altruistic Hunter aboard the Compact warship *Hunter's Moon,* felt far from altruistic at the moment. Despite the sedative she long ago reached the limits of her good-natured patience.

"Easy, Merkrida," Mistress of Healers Allohindra trilled. "Take courage, for you are almost halfway through dental nerve regeneration."

<<You are an a'pea!>> Merkrida signed though pain-riddled fury. <<Dou'tu'tay, Allohindra. Go shove your tail up your a'pea!>>

Allohindra snarled at the vile, disgusting curse and fought to restrain her own healthy Warrior anger.

"Maybe you should consider what dental regeneration feels like without the sedative?" she snarled hotly. "Do not give me attitude. You do not have the rank to counter any formal challenge I might make. But, pointing out the obvious, I know from experience what you are feeling. You pride yourself on consensus-seeking but not everything revolves around consensus. You had the right to refuse medical treatment and you did not. I know your outburst is not you. I can smell it on your scent, too."

<<I am trying to be respectful, Mistress. But it really does hurt!>> Merkrida signed.

"What you need is a distraction, and I think I have one suited to your disposition. But first, I have a question. How do you feel about Tialdrin?"

<<She is my teammate and I love her. We occasionally twine tails with Kidahin,>> Merkrida signed and added a pheromonal shrug.

"So you hold no grudge against her for shattering your jaw and forcing you to endure jawbone and dental regeneration?" Allohindra pressed.

<<Spirits, no! How can you even think such a thing? We were all told that Jassalin's hand was a danger to Delwyn. Jassalin was told we were a danger to him as well. Tialdrin had his interests in her heart. I would have done the same thing had I the chance to strike first.>>

Allohindra twitched her ears in agreement. Merkrida was forgiving to a fault, more forgiving than most Hunters and certainly more forgiving than the average Warrior.

<< I did not anticipate Tialdrin's leap. I knew she was above me but discounted her as a threat because I saw her only as a stealth prowler and not a hand-to-hand combatant. This injury taught me not to make stupid, unfounded assumptions.>>

"Yes indeed, you will remember your folly. Now, about the problem I have."

<<Something is wrong with the bone regeneration?>> Merkrida signed in alarm.

"What? Oh, no. You are healing well. The jawbone is perfect and soon your teeth will erupt through the gums. You should be done in just over a Delwyn hour," Allohindra trilled in reassurance.

Merkrida trilled a snicker, painful as it was to do. A 'Delwyn hour' was an hour in the human time standard and was just over two hours Elleio Standard Time, the Eyloni female standard. It was also about two and a half hours in Tyreniioroneo Standard Time, the Eyloni male standard. Custom held, but for traditionally gender-associated events, males used TST and females used EST. Each gender naturally converted to the other standard when, say, a male told a female to wait for an hour. He meant a TST hour. If she told him to wait another hour, she meant an EST hour. Delwyn often forgot and reverted to the human time standard.

<<What is the problem?>> Merkrida signed. <<Are there casualties on the human warship? >>

"Not that I know of," Allohindra trilled. "But casualties may become a problem. Human warships have nearly equal numbers of males and females aboard them. Delwyn told me this once and added that it was normal practice for them. I guess they do this because human male births are not rare. Their females never evolved the binding gender interdependence we did."

<<So their females do not care if males face danger?>> Merkrida signed as shock laced her scent.

"Not like we do. I think this is why Delwyn enjoys prowling through the command hull rainforest alone as much as he does. It also explains why he gets annoyed when he finds himself being stalked."

Merkrida growled through her restrained jaw. <<Phelindra made us stalk Delwyn once. Kidahin told us he would catch us at it, but we did not believe her. We were told humans cannot empathize with scent and cannot smell pheromones at all. And yet he caught me stalking him. I was forty ells into heavy undergrowth and downwind from him. Every time I moved he turned and followed my silent-stalking prowl as I flanked him. It was as if the spirits were pointing me out to him. I do not see how he did it. Even after Kidahin told us he was an elite ground forces combat specialist who empathized with his surroundings, I still do not see how he found me,>> she signed, her pheromonal awe overpowering her scent.

Allohindra, caught up in pheromonal empathy with her patient, shared through her own pheromones the emotions she felt for their odd, intriguing, and lovable favorite male.

<<You are worried about human males? Why? Delwyn certainly will not join them.>>

"No, it is not Delwyn, but human males I do worry about. What if there are human male survivors aboard the wrecked destroyer?" Allohindra trilled.

Merkrida clenched her jaw, biting into gums swollen with new teeth ready to erupt. She squealed as the ultimate in teething pain began in earnest.

<<Dou'tu'tay! No male but the Warleader is allowed by law and custom to board our warship. Allohindra, you cannot allow even one of them aboard...>>

"I know. I will not allow it. Melkorka will not, and neither will Delwyn. He understands the custom. Yet, I must practice my art freely and without reservation to all those in need."

<<Go to them,>> Merkrida suggested.

"Do you not think I have thought of that? I could take a troop transport and treat them using the transport healer suite. But then what? A troop transport has a short-range FTL jump drive. How can we take them to Elleio or even to Earth from here? We cannot allow the transport to land in the deployment bay filled with males. Melkorka let Delwyn do that with the Ni'zakhonii vessel he and his females captured. That was a technical violation of custom only because Kalinn was dead. Delwyn is not dead, so the custom prohibiting other males from coming aboard stops them."

<<Never, *never*, ever suggest Delwyn's death in my presence again!>> Merkrida signed, raging in a painful snarling fit. <<Why not put them in Delwyn's honor suite?>>

"The Warleader's honor suite is reserved for those rare times when the Warleader must speak face-to-face with another warleader," Allohindra sang at insistence tempo.

<<Mistress of Saga Mirrahindrallin sang once about how Warleader Phalalin brought ten males in his honor suite to Nikkiolo for Kidahin to choose a new warleader from. By the time he arrived, Kidahin had already chosen Delwyn as Warleader. Those males were not warleaders prior to their arrival in Ibeetu orbit nor were they warleaders after our society unanimously agreed to accept Kidahin's choice,>> Merkrida argued.

"That shipwreck contains several thousand humans, half of them males. The honor suite can hold no more than a few hundred all crammed together," Allohindra trilled.

<<Do you really think there are hundreds of human males waiting for you to save aboard that ship?>> Merkrida demanded.

Allohindra sighed, her tail rigid and still. "No," she trilled sadly, "but I cannot help but hope otherwise. All those male lives lost."

* * *

"Tialdrin will be upset with me," Einstika trilled.

"Why?" Jassalin sang. "Because you helped Merkrida almost rip her ear off? No, she will not. Think nothing of it."

"But we are a society! Society members do not fight one another," Einstika keened.

"What you say is true. We do not fight among ourselves. Assault Team-Two social solidarity is strong. Nynava and Zalzadrin ordered us to fight down a false trail. Tialdrin is no more angry with you than Merkrida is angry at Tialdrin for shattering her jaw," Jassalin sang in reassurance.

"Yes," Alfara trilled. "You performed your moral duty. Great honor accrues to you because you did not let your feelings interfere with what must be done. Tialdrin will agree. You are empathically sensitive, as am I. More so, I think, than others in our team. Once you smell Tialdrin's scent you will know she holds no ill will against you."

"What Alfara says is truth, Einstika. You will see once we are together...*Alfara!* Why are you rummaging through that weapon cache?" Jassalin trilled.

Startled, Alfara dropped the knife-heavy bandolier. "Nothing. Why do you ask?"

Jassalin gave Alfara a long, hard, head-to-toe stare. Except when absolutely necessary, Eyloni favored minimal clothing. Their bare breasts were draped by neckwear, a necklace of strings tied on one to three colorful knots anchoring colored beads in place, including the curving left breast adulthood knife and its harness. Waistwear was nothing more than a cloaca-concealing underthong with hip-riding ties and double-wrapped lacings around the waist with a short loincloth looped over those lacings to cover the bare pubis and hide the underthong. Alfara wore a techmistress carry sack over her shoulder stuffed with test equipment.

But unlike Jassalin and Einstika, Alfara also wore a combat harness over her neckwear and diagonally across her chest. Two combat knives were strapped at her hips male-style. Three more knives were tied onto her left waistwear straps and another three knives were tied onto her right waistwear straps.

The dropped bandolier sheathed ten daggers by itself.

"Are you kidding me?" Jassalin keened. "Do you want a bow, too? How about a spear and shield?"

"It took me ten tries to complete my adulthood survival ordeal. Weather, accident, ill-luck, and unintended outside interference invalidated my earlier attempts. What I learned during those previous tries was to always be prepared. I am also taking these forearm bracers. Do you have a problem with that?" Alfara trilled dangerously.

"No. Forearmed is forewarned. As long as you do not encumber yourself or make noise while stalking, I do not care. What else do you have stashed in the combat harness, hmmm?" Jassalin trilled.

"A battlefield combat scanner, a backup commlink, and a thumper," Alfara sang.

"You are worried," Einstika blurted. "I smell it on your scent. Why?"

Alfara picked up the bandolier and snapped it across her chest in a diagonal opposite her combat harness. She logged the items taken from inventory, closed the cache, glided up to Einstika, and looped her tail affectionately around her waist.

"What you mentioned earlier about Delwyn knowing something and the need for emotional control rings true in my heart," Alfara sang.

"What about it?" Einstika trilled. "Obviously Nynava and Zalzadrin laid a false trail for us."

"To teach us discipline," Jassalin trilled, remembering. She turned thoughtful. "Why put us through such an emotionally upsetting ordeal when we were mere hours from jumping into this system?"

"Dou'tu'tay!" Einstika keened. "Nynava and Zalzadrin knew we were jumping into this...mobius fracture...whatever that is...and wanted us on our tails! I am such an a'pea!"

Jassalin twisted her tail, her pons tracing a twisted loop behind her. Still thoughtful, she gave voice to her musing. "No, I do not think they expected these ta'na attacks on our environmental systems. If they had, then our combat test scenario would have concluded before we jumped into the system. No, I think Nynava had Assault Team-Two in mind for a surface assault mission and our conduct during the test was to decide if we would be chosen."

Alfara cinched her tail tightly around Einstika's waist and flicked her ears at Jassalin. "You are Kidahin's second-in-leadership. What do you know about our mission in this system?"

"I know nothing, and I am certain Kidahin knows nothing as well. If Team-Two was already picked for a mission, Kidahin would have been briefed by Nynava, Melkorka, Phelindra, and Delwyn. The mere thought of fighting for him would have seeped into her scent and we would already know by now. This means our involvement was not yet decided," Jassalin growled.

The three Hunters climbed a crimson vine-shrouded steep cliff, reached a narrow trail skirting the edge of the bluff, followed it through heavy jungle until they met a Warrior triad standing in the middle of a trail that seemed to continue into overgrown, comforting rainforest forever.

"Hunter techmistresses returning to the engineering command center," Jassalin sang to the lead Warrior.

The trek down backtrailing and looping jungle trails through the aftstation was without incident. Upon entering the engineering hull, Jassalin led them along familiar jungle paths. She was a competent leader, in some ways she was better at it than Kidahin. "What do you know about this system?" she asked Alfara.

"It has one large gas giant that has one large habitable-zone moon. It took months for us to get here, so we are at the pons-tip of Ni'zakhonii territory. I think we are here to see if the Ni'zakhonii have reached this far and maybe leave some surveillance assets behind. There should be no need for landing assault forces on the moon unless something is there," Alfara sang.

Jassalin flattened her ears. Alfara was extremely knowledgeable and sometimes too smart for her own good. "That is not enough information for us to form an opinion one way or the other," Jassalin growled.

"Kidahin is in the auxiliary command center. Maybe you should have her use the navigation sensors and scan the moon. Find out ahead of time what terrain and environmental conditions we may have to overcome," Einstika trilled.

"That is a wonderful idea, Einstika," Jassalin trilled softly. She twitched an ear to activate her commlink.

"Kidahin? Jassalin. Can you..."

***

An impatient Anailiatha paced in a slow circle around the faux hollow log engineering command center. The engineering test computer was already hours into processing the scan data. Waiting was not an activity she tolerated well. Soon she would know if they were stranded at this star. If they were, they would have to abandon and destroy *Hunter's Moon*. Defects in ship geometry could not be repaired. Nor could another Compact warship tow them back to Elleio. Her warship was a planetary assault battlecruiser and had a mass near the absolute maximum a jump drive could quantum translate. No rescue ship could jump himself and *Hunter's Moon* at the same time.

Anailiatha and her staff watched as the test computer wove an elaborate three-dimensional pattern on the main holographic display. She glared at the growing complex pattern and paced, her ears set wide apart and her tail darting about.

All Eyloni saw data relationships in patterns. The intuitive way they understood patterns let them reach conclusions visually without cranking through monotonous calculations. Anailiatha and her techmistresses were searching for a loss of ship symmetry. An asymmetry anywhere in the pattern meant a shift in jump point origin.

The pattern flashed, completed.

Anailiatha perked her ears forward, wrapped her tail around her waist, and trilled a sigh. "What do you think?" she sang to Hollfara.

Hollfara squinted at the complex pattern. She had been squinting at it since it first began growing in the holodisplay hours ago. She flicked her ears at the pattern.

"I see no asymmetry in ship geometry. The jump point origin appears intact," she sang and then paused, waiting for the contradiction she expected based on the minor but significant symmetrical changes in the pattern.

When neither corrections or congratulations came forth, she continued.

"Mistress Anailiatha, the data presented shows the keel is not misaligned. The hull passes FTL jump drive geometry tests. But I see several spaceframe defects, incredibly minor ones. These errors fall well within tolerances," she sang levelly and then paused again.

Anailiatha pricked her ears at her. "You are correct, Hollfara. The hull was not torqued enough to cause the jump point origin to shift. We can use the jump drive once it recharges. What does the scan pattern reveal about spaceframe structural integrity?"

Hollfara, by far the most junior techmistress and surrounded by experienced techmistresses, studied the fuzzy lines in the complicated pattern.

"I see no structural defects, Mistress. But these fuzzy lines hint at some kind of quantum effect siphoning off random subatomic particles from all the matter in local space, including our warship and even us. This loss of mass over time will eventually degrade the structural integrity of our warship and our bodies. This effect must be what Delwyn calls mobius fracture."

Anailiatha perked her ears forward and gave a slight nod for emphasis. "Correct. The jump point geometry was not affected by the torquing forces we experienced upon jump completion. The ta'na-like swarms are somehow related to the hypercube emission angles. I have no idea how or why they are appearing, why they appear at hypercube vertices, why they appear as ta'na swarms, or why they seem to prefer force field emitters and holographic projectors. Had these ta'na materialized around weapon systems, particle shield generators, or reactor control systems I would have deemed them a weaponization of the fracture phenomenon Delwyn mentioned."

"Did you research Delwyn's suggestion, Mistress?" Hollfara sang.

"I called up from the engineering archives all the data it has on Coalition hyperdrive theory and applied Delwyn's fracture description to it," Anailiatha trilled dryly. "Hyperspace is a mathematical concept that makes a kind of sense to me, but how humans apply the math to a theory of physics and arrive at a means of manipulating it even on a tiny local scale, one barely large enough to open a physical bridge between normal space and h-dimensional space, evades me."

"What about the math?" Hollfara sang. "I tailchased the mobius concept while waiting for profile scans to complete. The physical model is easy enough to grasp. Just take a ribbon, give it a half-twist, and then join the ends. You get a two-dimensional manifold having only one side and only one boundary. It is a chiral object, meaning it can be right-handed or left-handed depending on which way you twist before joining the ends of the ribbon."

"Yes," Anailiatha trilled. "Teachers use it to confound preadolescents in their maths. Draw a line down the middle of the ribbon and it will traverse both sides and return to its starting point. An object having length traversing the band arrives at its starting point inverted."

"How does this have anything to do with human FTL technology?" Hollfara trilled, feeling stupid. She was not the only one, it seemed. Pheromones from the techmistresses told her they were likewise dumbfounded.

"We know mathematically a torus cannot transform into a sphere without ripping. If I join two mobius strips I can make what Delwyn calls a klein bottle. By varying the parameters, this bottle can assume different shapes, including a torus. If local space is spherical and it can be transformed into a torus, it rips. Those rips become wormholes extending into spherical spacetime. Rips on the torus surface make shortcuts between space and time and create a tenth-dimensional hyperspace. The boundaries where dimensions meet resemble cosmic strings of subatomic particle diameters and immense densities."

"This tenth dimension, the hyperspace dimension, must be perpendicular to fourth-dimensional time and parallel but inverted relative to normal space," Hollfara sang thoughtfully. "I can see a twisting mobius band in my head. On the left, before the twist, is normal space. The perpendicular twist is time-dependent and thus, a part of the fourth dimension. Our jump drive theory treats time as quantum-entanglement space. This is where the jump drive singularity breaks the ship into component particles and wraps them around an evaporating event horizon. The event horizon is quantum entangled with the time-shifted jump point light-years away."

"So rather than create a quantum singularity and translate a ship through the present in four-dimensional time, humans somehow follow the twist and create a stable wormhole bridging normal space and hyperspace. Hyperspace must be a compressed quantum inversion of normal space with distances between points drastically reduced. Once in hyperspace, humans must create a second wormhole to exit back into normal space," Anailiatha sang.

"But, Mistress," Hollfara trilled. "Twisting the manifold of space cannot result in an instantaneous angular shift. There must be some lag before and after the shift as local normal space phase shifts perpendicular through the mobius twist. There must be some dimensional fuzziness as the phase angle rotates. In nature there must be third-, fourth-, and tenth-dimensional space existing simultaneously for some small but finite time. The twist must be quantum in nature, virtual, appearing and disappearing."

Anailiatha flicked her ears and snapped her tail, a sign of negation.

"No. If the twist is quantum in nature, then n-dimensional space must be virtual everywhere. It need only be acted upon to phase shift."

Anailiatha made eye contact with everyone in the engineering command center. Up until now she was providing her techmistresses a teaching moment for them generally and for Hollfara specifically. They tailchased human FTL theory and seemed to confirm Delwyn guess, a guess that essentially came down to a sphere of local space collapsing into a torus and causing millions of microfractures to project from hyperspace into normal space.

"To form a multidimensional universe, subuniverses must look like twisted-looped klein bottles," Anailiatha trilled. "Then each subuniverse has two twists, one for each mobius loop forming it. So there are two perpendiculars on the twist, one for time and the second for hyperspace. The first perpendicular causes quantum entanglement and translates space through time. The second perpendicular inverts and translates space into the hyperdimension. I am at a loss how humans phase shift from the first perpendicular to the second to access hyperspace. The phase shift should stop at a quantum singularity and not continue on to make a navigable wormhole."

"We must leave soon," Hollfara sang. She assumed a lecturing pose and continued. "Hyperspace compresses vast distances. It is filled with gravitational anomalies caused by gravity wells in normal space protruding into it. Gravitational anomalies from stars light-years away in normal space must be mere hundreds of astronomical units apart in hyperspace. If two stars are ten light-years apart in normal space, then their hyperspace gravitational anomalies are within the diameter of a star system there. Humans must have a hard time navigating in hyperspace because gravitational eddies flow through it. Hyperspace must be gravitationally dense enough to pull a forming singularity into a wormhole that can bridge dimensions."

"Spirits!" Anailiatha keened. "The hypermass existing there is siphoning particles through the ta'na. They are microscopic wormholes. If the shipwreck drifts closer or we move closer to him the combined tidal forces will degrade ship structure."

"So?" Hollfara trilled. "We stay here and wait for the jump drive to recharge and then jump out of this system."

"We are probably safe here for several days if we only have to worry about random cosmic string wormholes. But if we intersect too many of the hypercube emissions we will not survive more than a few direct exposures," Anailiatha trilled.

"But they siphon electrons... Oh, I see. They could siphon all power away, acting like a short circuit and causing massive power drains and burnouts."

"Mistress Anailiatha?" a senior techmistress trilled. "What happens if we close the distance to the Coalition warship?"

"The hypercube emissions will intersect us more often at stronger levels. We cannot risk even closing to translation range. A troop transport must be sent to him. We still have forty-four hours before the jump drive recharges."

"You should recommend firing a kinetic weapon at that warship and destroy him," the senior techmistress sang.

"Wait, what? No!" Hollfara trilled at imperative tempo. "Sensors cannot discriminate between life signs and background noise. You might kill survivors!"

"Females serving their warships accept the possibility of honorable death risks. Human females certainly accept the same possibility of...," the senior techmistress trilled hotly.

"No!" Anailiatha keened. "Human warships have as many males as females aboard. I will not recommend anything that may threaten the lives of males!"

"Then ask Phelindra to send a boarding party," Hollfara suggested. "They search for survivors, but their main mission is to shut down the warship's hyperdrive coils. That ship is heavily damaged and power control systems are likely destroyed or beyond repair. Someone like Aplilin should set demolition charges on the coil power taps and blow them up."

Anailiatha flipped her ears wide as she stared at Hollfara thoughtfully. She snapped her tail decisively and returned to her station. There, she tapped the console commlink and sang, "Mistress Melkorka, Anailiatha."

"Yes, Mistress Anailiatha?" Melkorka sang.

"We have a problem," Anailiatha began as she sang her report.

* * *

"Kidahin? Nynava," the Mistress of Battle's voice trilled over the combat address system.

"Yes, Mistress?" Kidahin sang.

"You will come with me to a strategy briefing in one hour. Be ready to discuss navigation hazards and solutions for the space we are in."

"Affirm, Mistress," Kidahin sang. "Mistress? Who else is coming to this briefing?"

"Me, Delwyn, Melkorka, Hlinlodyn, Phelindra, Zalzadrin, Anailiatha, and Lo'sutra'est anni. Consider how you might plot an evasive course avoiding these hypercube emissions and through the dust cloud to the shipwreck and back. I expect this information and you in one hour. Get to it."

"Affirm, acting!" Kidahin sang.

# 4
## THE POWER OF TWO, WHEN TO CHASE AND WHEN TO HIDE, THE AGED FEMALE...

"Why are we taking a stealth insertion vehicle instead of a troop transport, Kidahin?" Aplilin trilled. "A troop transport has more equipment space, a short-range jump drive, a heavier weapon system, and a particle shield and some armor. This thing has a single forward-firing medium-power particle cannon and only navigation, counter-EMP, and radiological shields. Spirits, there are places in the hull where I can punch a fist through."

"Quit complaining, my Aplilin," Kidahin sang. "The SIV is small and virtually invisible unless the main engine is at full throttle. He can outmaneuver a transport. I can pitch and yaw quick enough for you to lock onto a target and fire the cannon."

"But these suits, Kidahin. The SIV has no cabin life support. We must wear them and connect to stored oxygen by umbilical cords," Aplilin trilled in complaint.

"For which you will thank the spirits if one of these rocks pierce the hull. We will wear them while exploring *Londiwe Khoza* anyway."

"Seeing warships as female is insulting to male dignity," Aplilin trilled.

Kidahin clenched her teeth and applied full evasive thrusters, avoiding a boulder-sized asteroid. "Did you not pay attention to Delwyn during the mission briefing?" she sang. "He told us why humans consider warships female."

Aplilin fired a particle blast at another small asteroid as it streaked by.

"I always pay attention to Delwyn. I heard what he said. Human tradition calls ships female, but he also said they do not see them as females. His explanation makes no sense. Warships have male personalities, so they are males just as Delwyn is male. How can he call the wrecked ship her while at the same time considering him an 'it'? If he does not see the ship as a female, then why call him a 'she'?" Aplilin growled in confusion.

"I do not understand it myself," Kidahin admitted. "Delwyn tried to explain it to me once. He says humans do not see a personality associated with the ship in the same way we do. Long ago only human males served on warships. The males needed female support. Having none, they resorted to giving their ships the female gender to make up for the loss. Many human warships carry male names, yet they still retain the female gender."

"But Delwyn told us that the name Londiwe Khoza is a female given name. The humans named the wrecked ship after a human female. We do not name warships after a specific male. That is...arrogant. What possessed them to name the ship after a human female? Warships are unique and distinct persons just as much as males are. Naming a warship after someone else, living or dead, commingles the personalities," Aplilin trilled.

"Delwyn told me the person Londiwe Khoza is with the spirits now. Long ago she was an exceptional singer and dancer from a place on Earth called Capetown," Kidahin sang.

"But we all sing and dance," Aplilin snapped. "This Londiwe Khoza person must have been valorous in some way to merit such an honor."

"I do not know," Kidahin sang. "I never pressed the issue with Delwyn and..." Kidahin paused as she took evasive action.

"Hey!" Hollfara trilled. "Pay attention to your flying, Kidahin!"

"I am. I am following my flight plan."

"Following? As in manual flight?" Hollfara keened. "Do not distract her, Aplilin. If she makes a mistake, your cannon is the only thing keeping us from slamming into those asteroids."

"Your confidence in my piloting skill is comforting," Kidahin trilled angrily.

"It is not your skill so much as it is the fragility of an SIV. The A'tayotan hierarchy should remove the stealth insertion vehicle from service. Why did you not demand a transport? The SIV is no better than a sealed hollow log with a fusion engine," Hollfara lectured.

"Worse, actually," Kidahin sang, "if you mean the wood from an elleiu tree males' safe. The first time Delwyn saw males' safe wood he thought he could make nails from it. Zalzadrin told him our earliest rockets used the wood to make booster casings, space capsules, and early satellites. He thought she was joking."

"And your point is?" Hollfara trilled.

"An SIV is light, highly maneuverable, and uses little power. He has no force field or holographic systems, so he is not likely to suffer from the effects of mobius fracture," Kidahin explained.

"Those were not the only reasons," Alfara sang. "Mission planning calls for a vehicle capable of taking us and Aplilin's demolition and breaching equipment. He is also too small for Delwyn to sneak aboard without us seeing or smelling him."

Alfara's comment drew a dry laugh from Healer Mimiran. "The deployment bay mistress would never let him get near a troop transport or an SIV. I do not see what has your tail in a knot, Hollfara. I find manual flight quite stimulating."

"Forget that for a minute," Aplilin sang as she scowled at the Warrior healer. "One problem with a troop transport is where to set him down once we reach the Coalition warship. The SIV has a much smaller landing footprint and can land anywhere on an asteroid's unstable surface. If necessary, he is light enough to land on the Coalition warship near a hull breach. A troop transport must hover at station-keeping above the breach, and hovering means a pilot and copilot must remain behind. Moving equipment from a transport is more work. We would also have to use combat EVA suit thrusters to land on the warship and return to the hovering transport. *Kidahin! Evasive left, now!*"

"Affirm!" Kidahin sang. "Here comes more heavy rubble. Aplilin, blast a hole for me to fly through it!"

"Affirm, firing."

Kidahin shut down the maneuvering system and switched to reaction control thrusters. The RCS lacked the thrust of the maneuvering systems, but Kidahin was flying through clouds of rocky debris so heavy it reminded her of northern La'huaset Tribal continent hailstorms.

"Attitude control systems are active. Thrusting down and evading left."

Loud clattering noises rattled throughout the tiny ship, a clattering that pelted steadily and continuously. The sound was unnerving, as it reminded everyone how thin the hull really was.

"Is it supposed to sound like that?" Seliaha keened.

"This is nothing," Jassalin sang. "Think of hail hitting elleiu tree leaves. Hail hits, makes noise, and bounces off."

"But Aplilin can punch her fist through the hull," Seliaha trilled.

"Well, no. Not really. The skin is thin, but strong. The SIV is designed to make ballistic reentry into atmosphere, land, and make direct surface-to-orbit insertions. He is sturdy, as Hollfara can attest," Jassalin sang.

"Yes, he is sturdy for what he is designed to do. Flying through rocks and boulders is not what he is designed for," Hollfara sang.

"Stop scaring her, Hollfara. You are as bad as Aplilin," Tialdrin growled. "We are not flying against orbital velocity. In fact, Seliaha, you can probably run faster than we are picking our way through this rubble."

"Yes," Merkrida sang. "The rubble orbits its sun. Material seems to fly around us because we are catching up to it. We are also approaching the Coalition ship perpendicular to the motion of the dust cloud. Most of what we are flying through was kicked up when that ship smashed into small asteroids. Take the time to look and really see what is happening. The asteroids and rocky debris are tumbling by and we are evading."

"Warship in sight," Kidahin trilled.

The wrecked Coalition ship listed to his right side, crumpled along an oblong asteroid pockmarked with ancient small craters. He rested against a ridge, as though he rolled into a shallow ravine. The impact inertia compressed the ship to fit along the rim of a shallow crater.

Kidahin opened the commlink. "Mistress Melkorka, we are here," she sang.

"Understood, Kidahin. Go with the spirits. Nynava has something to add."

"Kidahin, proceed as briefed. Do the hull summary first," Nynava sang.

"Affirm," Kidahin trilled in reply. "Hollfara, begin your survey."

"Affirm, scanning," Hollfara sang from the SIV sensor suite station. "Adjust altitude to ten ells above the bow and hold position."

"Affirm," Kidahin sang.

"Scanning for hull breaches. Kidahin, thrust towards the stern at one ell-per-second."

"Affirm, thrusting."

"Probing the hull. Most of the damage is outer hull breaches. One-in-twenty penetrate through the inner hull and into compartments and decks. Several breaches are wide enough for us to enter. However, the between-hulls decks are heavily damaged and likely impassable. I foresee a lot of backtrailing and looping if we do not take the time to scan and map a route," Hollfara sang.

"How many outer hull breaches match inner hull breaches?" Jassalin trilled.

"Thirteen, not counting the heavy broadside rip into the ship. We cannot prowl there. The interior is a mangled wreck, and we might never find passable decks," Hollfara sang.

"Yet that is where Hlinlodyn found low but stable life support signals," Kidahin keened, shuddering. All those male bodies floating there. So many male deaths in one place, at the same time, defined a cultural catastrophe in the Eyloni female worldview.

Eyloni were not superstitious, not exactly. But names were important to them. Kidahin's name literally meant "her strength sings from timeless dedication." Delwyn told her the female Londiwe Khoza was long dead, and messing around with spiritual things invited retribution from the Oyya Web of the spirits.

The close-up view of the smashed ship made Kidahin shudder with sudden dread. She was no longer on her warship, no longer near Delwyn, no longer able to protect him. Doubts assailed her, lying in wait like dry branches ready to snap under her feet.

"See those twenty pods mounted on short pylons on the hull, Kidahin? Those are the hyperdrive coils. Human ship design preserves a maximum utilitarian simplicity. While monotonous from an aesthetics point of view, from an engineering standpoint I think this uniformity will help us. Delwyn says main power runs through chases above what he calls a *broadway* corridor, a centrally located main deck running the length of the ship. If we can reach the amidships broadway deck, Aplilin can set demolition charges in the chases. The engineering spaces, main propulsion reactors, and the sublight drive were destroyed by collapsing wormhole longitudinal elongation. We can easily disconnect the amidships reactors from the coils. Just blow the power distribution nodes and the hyperdrive coils will shut down," Hollfara lectured.

"Why not just blow the pylons off the hull?" Jassalin demanded.

"I guess we could, but it would take more time than...," Hollfara trilled.

"No," Aplilin interrupted. "Hyperdrive pylons are critical structures. They are made of duranium plating several ells thick. I doubt I could breach even one pylon with my entire demolitions inventory. We would need to manually unlock each plate, drop into the recess, and cut into the outer hull and set a charge. Manually unlocking a plate without drydock equipment takes hours, let alone the time it takes to cut into the outer hull."

"A hull plate is a cubic parallelogram that interlocks with surrounding plates. Particle, radiological, plasma, and navigation shield elements run through it. Its outer surface is ablative and kinetic reactive. Ablative armor will resist a plasma torch. Impact hammer strikes may detonate reactive armor," Hollfara lectured.

Kidahin piloted the SIV over the flayed amidships hull. She scanned its depths and tried hard to ignore the male bodies floating there. "We must gain entry here," she sang. "According to Delwyn, the ship has shuttles. That means he must have a deployment bay to launch them from. Where is it?"

"Below the bow and on the ventral hull. It is firmly wedged, if not crushed, against the crater rim. We are not gaining entry through an open shuttle bay door," Hollfara sang.

"We will land on the ship near a breach, drop to a between-hulls deck, and look for an inner hull hatch. On the other side should be a corridor. We make our way to the middle of the ship until we reach the broadway deck. We set charges on the power taps in the maintenance chases, leave, retreat to safe minimum distance, and remote-detonate," Kidahin sang.

"But what about the survivors?" Mimiran trilled. "What about Hlinlodyn's active life support scans?"

"I know," Kidahin snapped, glaring at the Warrior. "The amidships tear is long and wide, but it does not extend into the broadway deck. Hlinlodyn's life support readings suggested intact compartments on the other side of the broadway corridor. Hollfara is right. We cannot EVA into the broadside rip. Gaining entry from there would be as hard as prowling though an endless maze of males' safes."

"Do you see signs of life support now?" the Warrior healer trilled.

Kidahin chose a narrow scanning field and probed the exposed, devastated decks. She ignored the optical pickup, not wishing to see massed male deaths. She concentrated on life support signal strength.

"I cannot tell," Kidahin finally growled. "The sensors are not powerful enough or sophisticated enough to analyze all these signals."

"What kind of signals?" Merkrida trilled.

"I am picking up multiple overlapping signals from all the systems still drawing power. Some noise comes from intermittent system failures, electrical shorts and surges, and field imbalances and overloads. Some signals come from particle emissions. I think the asteroid-facing side of the ship is trying to pull power for the shields. Deciphering life support signals from all these emissions is beyond the capabilities of the SIV sensor suite," Kidahin trilled.

"I agree with Mimiran. We must explore the amidships decks and look for survivors," Merkrida trilled.

"We will check all compartments with life support for survivors," Kidahin reassured her. "Body electrical activity is likewise swamped by all this electromagnetic noise, and that explains why I get no life sign readings."

"It is our moral duty to save males," Tialdrin keened.

"Yes," Merkrida sang, "among other things."

"We should sing for a major consensus," Tialdrin trilled heatedly.

"Why?" Jassalin sang. "We would never abandon a male, any male."

"Correct," Kidahin sang, wincing as doubts sang an ominous dirge in her head. Had she abandoned Delwyn when she became an assaultmistress? She shook her head and snapped her tail against the pilot seat. She ignored her worries and nudged the control yoke back and fired attitude control thrusters. The SIV yawed around to face the warship's bow and skimmed forward and above the wrecked amidships hull.

"This breach looks promising," Kidahin sang.

Hollfara scanned the breach in question. "Confirmed. We can pass through wearing combat EVA suits while carrying breaching equipment. The breach rips through the outer hull to a between-hulls deck, but it does not penetrate beyond the inner hull. I do not see a maintenance hatch from here. Kidahin, how often do these hatches occur?"

"Not very often is my guess. Delwyn said they were used by maintenance and damage control teams. They are not meant for normal access."

"I agree," Jassalin trilled. "You do not want kinetic ordnance penetrating the outer hull and blowing debris through multiple hatches. They must be rare and heavily built, like narrow-trail blast doors. Can you report on hull structural integrity?"

"Affirm," Hollfara sang. "Kidahin can land on the hull thirty ells from the breach. The hull will support our mass easily."

"All these breaches look the same," Jassalin snapped.

"No, they are not. Some fold inward and suggest kinetic impacts. Others blow outward and suggest internal explosions that ruptured the hull. Breaches like this one here are caused by stress deformations. The hull split open like swelling skin splits a scab. Is that not right, Tialdrin?" Hollfara lectured.

"You are not funny," Tialdrin trilled, remembering her torn ear now thankfully healed. "Humor and analysis do not mix well for you, but I get your meaning. What you are trying to say is that rips like these are less likely to cause heavy internal damage."

"Yes!" Hollfara trilled, pleased to hear someone paying attention to her analysis.

"Prepare for landing on the amidships hull. Aplilin, be ready to blast us clear if our mass causes the hull to collapse," Kidahin sang.

"Affirm."

"Hollfara, keep a close watch on those hull stress readings. If they change, abort the landing from your backup controls."

"Affirm. Our mass should not matter in this low gravity," Hollfara sang.

"Descending now. Contact. Hollfara?" Kidahin trilled.

"Hull is stable," Hollfara sang.

"I am shutting down the thrusters. Disconnect life support umbilicals and switch to EVA suit life support. Disembark and report to the exterior weapon and equipment lockers," Kidahin sang.

Twenty minutes later Assault Team-Two and their guest healer fanned out, floating an ell above the hull and drifting toward a long, narrow split.

"I prefer traction boots and walking over drifting and suit-thrusting," Jassalin complained.

"As do I," Kidahin sang. "But a ta'na swarm siphoning power from them will cast any one of us adrift. It is safer to rely on suit thrusters."

"Not once we go inside the ship," Jassalin growled.

"No," Kidahin trilled. "Except for attitude control thrusters to keep us centered in the corridors, we will grab and pull our way along. That reminds me. Not only are human warship pathways bare parallel corridors with intersecting perpendicular corridors, but each corridor has regularly occurring mechanical hatches. These normally open hatches may have closed to maintain life support integrity or isolate damaged areas. If you find a closed hatch, you can open it by touching the override touch plate."

"What if the other side is contaminated?" Einstika sang.

"Touching the override causes it to change color. Remember that humans call green a safe color and red a danger color. Yellow is reserved for cautions and warnings."

"What kind of cautions and warnings?" Seliaha trilled.

"Red means stop. Yellow means that something on the other side is hazardous, such as vacuum, fire, toxic chemicals, no oxygen, radiation leak, or other hazards that are passible with specialized equipment. Green means the area beyond the hatch is safe."

"That is backwards!" Merkrida snarled. "Why do they use a system designed to confuse?"

"It is not confusing to Delwyn," Jassalin sang. "Humans live in a green, dry forest world filled with small trees. Fire threatens dry small trees. No doubt he sees a green forest as safe and red as a fire danger."

"Then why use yellow for cautions rather than blue?" Merkrida trilled.

"I do not know. Small fires burn orange-yellow, maybe?" Jassalin guessed.

"Oh, okay. I can see that," Merkrida sang.

"We are leafchasing. Aplilin, swing a flood lamp down into the breach. Let us see what we are up against," Kidahin sang.

"Affirm, acting," Aplilin trilled. She played the high-intensity beam along the breach. The inner hull was only ten ells from the inside wall of the primary hull.

"I see no between-hull deck below or above the breach," Aplilin sang. She panned the light deeper into the breach. "Ah! I see a corridor thirty ells below me. I think we should drift down through the breach until we hit the secondary hull and slide against it until we reach the between-hulls corridor."

"How hard will we hit that deck?" Kidahin trilled.

"Asteroid gravity is weak. The ship is tipped at an angle. The inner hull surface friction against our EVA suits will slow us down. I calculate we will fall at 1.343 ells per second assuming no one fires suit thrusters or grabs onto anything," Hollfara sang.

"Line up along the breach two ells apart," Kidahin sang. When Team-Two complied, she added, "Drop into the breach and drift down against the inner hull until you reach the between-hulls deck. The inner hull follows the curvature of the outer hull. If you cannot control your speed by drag alone, use suit attitude thrusters to control your rate. For the spirits' sakes remember to thrust parallel to the inner hull or you will strike your head against the outer hull curving up behind you."

"Affirm!" Team-Two sang.

"Jump," Kidahin trilled as she leaped into darkness barely illuminated by the flood lamp above and the much dimmer suit lamp on her helmet.

The inner hull felt smooth through her gloved hands. By the time she noticed it and the light blue walls she felt her knees buckle slightly on hitting the deck.

"Team-Two, status," Kidahin sang.

"Here, Kidahin," each Hunter and the Warrior healer sang in response.

"Form into pairs and move aft. Look for a maintenance hatch," Kidahin sang.

Doubts sang in her head. Hunters preferred prowling in solitary random rotating patterns. Warriors did stalk in small groups, but they also wandered randomly down a trail. This narrow and confining corridor allowed for no random prowling at all, and prowling in straight lines was wrong!

"Would it not make more sense to enter the bow and try to find the command center?" Einstika trilled.

"Delwyn mentioned that we could cut power from the engineering station there, but no one knows how to operate a human engineering console," Kidahin trilled.

"Hollfara can," Einstika trilled. "She is a warship design techmistress. She can make it work."

Hollfara, touched by Einstika's confidence in her skill, smiled a rare smile. "No, I cannot. Not until I first learn how a Coalition warship engineering station works. Delwyn did not know, so I would have to face the console tail-tied. Just as we do not have the time to cut into each hyperdrive pylon, we also do not have the time for me to learn the console, what it controls, and what it is telling me."

"A bulkhead hatch ahead is blocking our path," Jassalin trilled.

Hollfara scowled at the hatch with disgust. "This thing is primitive. Look at it! It has mechanical seals ankle-high all around the bulkhead, hinges, and a mechanical locking mechanism."

"Touch the hatch override, Hollfara," Merkrida sang.

"Affirm. Touching. It glows yellow. A vacuum warning, I think."

"I agree. Press the yellow plate to open it," Kidahin sang.

"Affirm, pressing. No response," Jassalin trilled.

Kidahin frowned. The hatch should have unlocked and swung aside to admit them. What was she missing? She growled at the blue hatch and its chrome seals and locking wheel. For some reason the round spoked chrome wheel drew her into a memory. Sudden sweet, fond images of Delwyn flooded her awareness as she remembered. He brought her aboard his warship on a visit to his special operations command center. On the way there he led her through a hatch similar to this one. After he touched the hatch, he spun the wheel around to close and lock the hatch back into place.

"Grip the wheel and spin it to the left," Kidahin trilled.

"Affirm, twisting left," Jassalin sang. "It moves. A light set in the hub turned green. Should I stop?" she keened, hesitant.

"No. Green means to proceed. Now, push the hatch forward."

"Affirm. Hatch is swinging on its hinges. The corridor looks the same. I can see an inner hull hatch on the left ahead."

"It is a maintenance hatch. Advance to it," Kidahin sang.

They crowded around Jassalin as she pressed the hatch override. It glowed yellow.

"It is not red, just caution yellow. It is probably another vacuum warning," Hollfara sang.

"Open it," Kidahin trilled.

"Affirm, turning the wheel. Hatch is unlocked and swinging inside," Jassalin sang. She stepped through the hatch, saw what her suit lamp revealed, and staggered back retching violently in shock. She vomited into her helmet several times. In near zero-gee, it floated in globs around her head.

"Noooo…," Jassalin keened, retched, inhaled vomitus, and began choking.

"Pull her out! Mimiran!" Kidahin keened.

"Affirm!" the healer trilled. She forced her stronger and heavier Warrior body through the Hunters and yanked Jassalin from the open hatch. She addressed the choking Hunter's helmet. "Healer Mimiran authorizing emergency helmet purge. You will vent for one second on my command. Jassalin, for the spirits' sakes, close your eyes and hold your breath. On three: one, two, three, helmet emergency vent now!"

The momentary decompression vacuumed spew from Jassalin's helmet, popped her eardrums, and ruptured small capillaries in her huge amber eyes. She coughed several times but was no longer retching.

"What happened, Jassalin? What did you see? Mimiran?" Seliaha trilled in panic.

The Warrior surgeon-in-battle, freed from reacting to the emergency, began shaking violently.

"What did you see?" Aplilin trilled at imperative tempo.

"N…n…nothing you ever want to see," Mimiran gasped. Spirits, her teeth were chattering!

"Jassalin, what did you see?" Kidahin keened.

"Dead bodies, a hundred or more, smashed almost flat against the wall. Most of them are males!" Jassalin keened.

"Now what?" Merkrida trilled.

Kidahin wondered the same thing. Assault Team-Two was new, only a few months old, formed from the Hunter females she sponsored to her warship society, the society making up *Hunter's Moon's* all-female crew. Kidahin herself had only twenty months more combat experience than they had. Even then, Kidahin knew that no female in modern history had ever experienced the shock of seeing several hundred dead males at once.

"We must continue no matter how upsetting the dead in this warship is to us," Kidahin sang. She twitched her ear to turn on her suit commlink.

"Mistress Nynava, Kidahin."

"Report, Kidahin," Nynava sang.

"Mistress, we found a breach, entered it, and followed a corridor to a maintenance hatch that opens onto a deck. Jassalin went in first, saw at least a hundred dead males, and vomited into her helmet. She describes the dead as liquefied and frozen. I think inertial dampening must have failed and they slammed into the wall so hard the bodies were crushed into blobs. Mimiran is unsettled from seeing the dead, too. This hatch and the interior deck is our best direct access to the broadway deck. We want Delwyn to sing for us while we move through the casualty areas."

"I should already be doing that," Delwyn said from the background.

"No," Melkorka sang softly. "We may need your songs if combat occurs. You sing well for several hours before losing your pitch, but we can sing continuously for two or three days before losing our pitch."

"I think they need it," he retorted.

"So do I. Well, do what you feel is best. They are in a unique event, one I shudder to think about," Melkorka trilled off-key.

Delwyn began beating at the drum permanently attached to the Warleader's Watch console. Kidahin followed the beat. He would begin singing soon.

"When he begins singing," Kidahin trilled sharply, "we will rush the hatch, turn left, and prowl forward until we find an intersecting corridor leading deeper into the ship. There are bodies eleven ells from the hatch. They appear flash-frozen so there will not be bodily fluids floating in zero-gee. Keep your eyes front and do your best to ignore them."

"Kidahin?" Delwyn said over the commlink.

"Yes, Delwyn?"

"What deck are you on? Scan an image of the maintenance hatch script."

"By your command. Scan taken. I am sending it to you now."

"Hlindredreda?" Kidahin heard Delwyn call to the Mistress of Communications.

"Receiving video from Team-Two talkback telemetry now. I am uploading the image to your console," Hlindredreda sang.

"My thanks, Hlindredreda. Kidahin, you are on deck eighteen, corridor-A, between frame one-eleven and one-twelve. Open the hatch, turn left, and go forward to the first intersection. Turn right and continue to deck eighteen, corridor-C. That puts you above and parallel to the broadway deck. Broadway is deck twenty, corridor-C. You need to go down two decks to reach broadway."

"Delwyn? Why can we not enter the maintenance chases from the overhead parallel deck?" Alfara sang.

"Broadway's much wider than any other deck on a Coalition ship. It's as wide as most pathways on our warship. It's heavily shielded. There are no maintenance hatches accessing the power distribution chases from either deck nineteen or deck twenty-one. You need to go in through broadway and find a maintenance panel to gain access."

"Understood," Alfara sang.

Delwyn started singing about courage and almost immediately the morale boost all Eyloni females felt on hearing a singing male filled Team-Two with confidence and fortitude. It also triggered an instinctive awareness that a male needed their protection.

"Now!" Kidahin keened.

Team-Two rushed the hatch, turned left, and fired suit attitude control thrusters. They flew down a corridor sharply tilted on its side. Ceiling lights flashed on and off at random. Some remained on, but thankfully several long ells of corridor remained dark. On the right at shoulder height a band of red blinking panels followed the entire length of the wall.

Flashing red meant disaster to humans.

"Approaching frame one-eleven intersecting corridor. I see some casualties ahead. Get ready to turn right, but take care," Kidahin sang in warning.

"Affirm, we are ready for the turn," Jassalin sang.

Kidahin saw the bulkhead hatch ahead and the expected intersecting corridor crossing before it. She tapped braking thrusters and slowed to a stop.

"Turn here, and be careful. This corridor is only two ells wide and angles down."

They prowled deeper into the ship. Jassalin and the rest of Team-Two followed close behind Kidahin. She passed the deck eighteen, corridor-B intersection.

"We stop at the next intersection," she trilled in warning.

Kidahin halted when she reached the frame one-eleven, deck eighteen, corridor-C hatch, turned to proceed aft, and her gaze fell upon the unthinkable.

Only Delwyn's singing kept her from crippling shock as she tried to make sense of male bodies crushed and smeared, frozen, against the wall.

"How do we get out of here?" Einstika keened.

"Humans use lifts, ladders, and stairs. Do not trust the lifts. Find a maintenance panel. They open into small landings with spiral stairwells going up and down."

"I found one!" Hollfara trilled.

Kidahin and her team followed Hollfara to an open panel.

"Climb down. Do not use suit thrusters in this tight space. Do not stop at the first landing. Continue down and around to the second one."

Kidahin went first. Climbing down narrow, metal, spiral stairs in combat EVA suits in near-weightlessness became a long exercise in frustration. It was dark but for her helmet lamp. Down did not feel like down, and the tight spiral made it easy to drift off the stairs and ram into the spiral staircase above her.

"I am passing the first landing," Kidahin sang in time with Delwyn's battle song. She pulled herself down the twisting metal staircase, bumped into the stairs above her, and wedged herself in the spiral.

"I am stuck!" she keened. "The staircase is stress-deformed here."

"Do we turn around and return to the landing above us?" Jassalin sang.

"No," Kidahin trilled. She relaxed by immersing her emotions in the calming voice of a singing Delwyn. "Aplilin, pull me out. I think I can crawl down the stairs to the next landing. It is not that far."

"Affirm, pulling," Aplilin sang.

Aplilin found it easier said than done, however. In the near-weightless environment, pulling on an immovable Kidahin resulted in pulling herself into Kidahin. Aplilin anchored herself to the stairway and pulled again.

Kidahin slid backwards into Aplilin's waiting embrace.

"Do not let this happen again, my Kidahin," Aplilin trilled. "I doubt I can find a place for the portable jaws or a jackhammer in here."

"Affirm," Kidahin sang. "Crawl down to the next deck. Follow me."

"Affirm."

Kidahin dropped to hands and knees and drift-bounced down and around the stairway until she reached the next landing. She stepped out of the stairs and reached for the nearby maintenance panel. It opened and she stepped into the wide, brightly lit, broadway deck. Behind her was a closed frame one-eleven hatch.

She looked aft and saw another frame hatch some thirty or forty ells away. There were no dead in this enclosed length of broadway, but the broadway deck ran the entire length of the ship. It was at least twenty-one-hundred ells long, which meant there were twenty-four frame hatches concealing only the spirits knew what behind them.

Einstika stood off to one side staring at the shoulder-level blinking red band running down the wall.

"Red means danger here, Einstika," Kidahin sang. "Do not let the status colors fool you."

"After what I just saw, no blinking lamp of any color can tell me all is well here," Aplilin trilled.

"I agree with you," Mimiran growled.

Kidahin flicked her ears forward and waved her team to her. "Everyone knows how to open the hatches," she sang. "Always look at the seal status colors. Do not open a hatch with a red warning. Use your judgment with the caution yellow ones. Look at these two broadway hatches. What about them takes you by the tail?"

"Windows," Einstika trilled. "This frame one-eleven hatch and the aft-facing frame one-twelve hatch have circular windows set above the shiny wheel locking mechanisms."

"You are right," Kidahin sang. "Look through them before you open a hatch. Hollfara, take detailed scans of this corridor and every intersection. Somewhere on our left as we prowl aft should have areas with minimal life support. Males may need us. You may prowl ahead as you scan for life signs."

"Affirm," Hollfara sang.

"Tialdrin and Kyralin, you are our security prowlers. I doubt there are Ni'zakhonii aboard, but human security prowlers may not know this, so be careful. At minimum, keep our recall path through the stairwell open so we can evacuate if necessary. Stalk through all the hatches we open and rotate through all intersections along the length of broadway."

"We prowl together?" Tialdrin trilled.

"No. Use a staggered pattern. You first and then Kyralin ten minutes later. Meet again at random intervals, report what you find, and separate again."

"Affirm," they sang.

"Merkrida, make a battle damage assessment of the ship's offensive and defensive status. Try to find out if he took battle damage."

"How?" Merkrida trilled. "This is a general access pathway. No human tacticalmistress fought this ship from here."

"I know," Kidahin agreed, "but the corridors intersecting broadway lead to hull-mounted weapon systems. You can access weapons and shield element status from there."

"How do you know this?" Merkrida trilled.

"I saw them when I visited Delwyn's special operations command center on his warship. If offensive and defensive status can be monitored there on his ship, then they should be accessible in the same way here as well."

"Fine," Merkrida trilled, "but I cannot read the human language. How do I know what the combat systems status monitor is telling me?"

"Tactical displays show a schematic of the ship with shield and weapon icons at key points on the hull. Each icon glows with a status color. Depleted weapons will show as red weapon icons and depleted shields will show as red shield icons."

"That sounds simple enough," Merkrida sang.

"Seliaha, look for signs of survivors. Any compartment having life support probably has local inertial dampening fields in operation. You will enter frame hatch one-eleven but move twenty ells forward toward the bow. Find a maintenance ladder going down to the ventral hull. Once there, exit forward. You should see the shuttle bay. Delwyn said this warship is equipped with three of them. Any crew evacuating had to do so in those shuttles."

"Affirm," Seliaha sang.

"Jassalin, take Alfara and Einstika and find the access hatches to the power distribution chases running above and below broadway. Delwyn described broadway as a double-walled tube within a tube. Control electronics, plumbing, main power, and other critical systems route through these chases. We know the distance between hyperdrive pylons, and Anailiatha said that engineering economy requires power taps to run from superconductor busbar directly through the hull to each pylon. Hyperdrive takes a lot of power, so the coupling cannot be mistaken for less-critical power taps."

"Affirm," Jassalin sang. "What about Aplilin? Does she come with us dragging her charges with her? Or does she wait for us to identify the power distribution nodes first?"

Kidahin paused. She wanted the nodes blown as soon as possible, but they had to blow them out at the same time. Should she send Aplilin with Jassalin and set a charge on each node as they found them, or should Jassalin just leave all the hatches open, come back for Aplilin, and help her carry the equipment to the nodes, set the charges all at once, and then leave?

"Find the distribution nodes first and report back. Aplilin can help Seliaha search for survivors and assess the shuttles while you find the power taps."

"Affirm," Jassalin sang.

Hollfara reached the frame one-twelve hatch first. She looked through the round window set in the hatch and staggered back, shuddering. "There are four dead bodies smashed and frozen to where the wall meets the deck. We will drift above them as we move aft. I see three females and.. .a male," she trilled and closed her eyes.

"I understand," Kidahin sang. "Wait for Kyralin and Tialdrin. They will go with you until enough hatches are open for them to separate and begin their prowling loops. Seliaha, you go with them, too. You, too, Aplilin. I will recall you when Jassalin finds the hyperdrive coil power conduits."

"There should be a power chase access panel on the other side of the hatch," Jassalin trilled as she read from a hand-held scanner.

"Good. Hollfara, open hatch one-twelve," Kidahin sang.

"Affirm, acting. The hatch override glows yellow, meaning vacuum. I am turning the locking wheel. The hatch opens and I am moving aft."

Hollfara glided above pools of frozen gore, the partially liquefied remains had slid down the tilted wall to accumulate and freeze where wall met deck.

"Taking internal structural scans," she sang as she drifted slowly toward frame one-thirteen.

Kidahin glanced left and looked down an intersecting corridor and saw nothing but well-lit hallway. "Tialdrin, take this left path. Kyralin, go right. Merkrida, go with her. You should come across hull-mounted weapon systems when you reach corridors adjacent from the inner hull."

"Affirm."

"I found a maintenance panel," Jassalin trilled. "It opens easily. There is a ladder to my right leading up and down. I am climbing."

Alfara and Einstika followed her up the dim and confining tube until they reached a dimly lit maintenance chase filled with plumbing, wire bundles, power conduits, and other frequent and mysterious equipment.

"This superconductor conduit and distribution node diverts power to the left and right hyperdrive pylons above and below us. This is clearly a dedicated system. Aplilin? Do you want to trace conduits aft and blow it up in one place, such as at the power systems junction?"

"No," an out-of-sight Aplilin sang over the commlink. "Cutting power at the node will cause the coil to shut down. If I cut power at the source I can cut power to all coils at once, but I do not know what the open-circuit feedback reflecting into the power plant and reactor will do."

"Why does it matter?" Jassalin sang. "We will be gone when you trigger your explosives. You worry about destroying the ship? Do not. For his own sake he must be given mercy. He will never fight again."

Aplilin flicked her ears in agreement. "Maybe so. Kidahin? Do you want me to remain with Seliaha or recall to Jassalin?"

"Stay with Seliaha. We still need to know if anyone left in the shuttles. Check on them first, then on your return to broadway, pick up your equipment and take the maintenance chase and follow Jassalin's progress."

"Affirm," Aplilin sang.

Twelve hours into their prowling Kidahin's doubts began nibbling at her pons. "This is taking too long," she complained aloud. "This should be a straightforward task and yet we have accomplished nothing."

"Not really," Hollfara trilled. "We opened almost all the frame hatches on broadway. The side corridors to the right do not continue beyond corridor-B because of the amidships broadside damage. We are nearing the aft compartments where longitudinal elongation crumpled the engine complex. I am near frame hatch one-twenty-three and... Kidahin, my radiation and chemical contamination sensors are trilling. There is a radiation hazard on the other side of frame hatch one-twenty-three."

"Are you safe?" Kidahin trilled at interrogative pitch.

"Yes," Hollfara sang. "The hatch is covered by a radiological shield. I am also reading a chemical contaminant. It is either reactor or power plant coolant. Our suits will protect us from the chemical but not from the radiation."

"Jassalin? You heard her?" Kidahin sang.

"I did. We are above you but two frames behind. We are prowling slowly because the chase is narrow and filled with equipment. Some of it was damaged by the impact and hull deformations. We found over twenty high-voltage shorts showering sparks everywhere and live wires pulled from harnesses when the chase bent. Ruptured plumbing is seeping fluids from I do not know where in little floating balls all around us. Thank the spirits no oxygen is here for the sparks to ignite whatever it is."

"Floating?" Hollfara interrupted. "Any leaks should have flash-frozen and self-sealed at absolute zero. What is the temperature?"

Jassalin checked her suit external thermometer. "Tail minus two hundred. There must be a heat exchange system close by."

Kidahin knew that Tail minus two hundred, two hundred degrees below average body temperature, was cold but nowhere near absolute zero. "Hollfara? The heat? Do you think it has anything to do with the coolant release?"

"I do," Hollfara trilled. "The heat comes from one of two possible sources. The safest for us is power plant cooling failure. The hyperdrive coils pull a lot of power and the load on power generation makes heavy demands on plant cooling. If the cooling system fails, the ship will lose all electrical power."

"A gift from the spirits!" Jassalin sang. "Why blow-up power conduits when the power will soon fail? Temperatures are rising at point two-two-four degrees Tail per hour. Let the converters melt down and blow out."

"Power systems are not the only thing needing coolant," Hollfara keened in warning. "Radiation contamination can mean reactor containment failure. Which fails first, power generation or the reactor?"

"Who cares?" Jassalin trilled. "Either one will stop the coils from generating this fracturing effect."

"Does anyone see the flaw in this plan?" Hollfara trilled at derogatory pitch.

"Time," Kidahin sang in a thoughtful melody. "We cannot assess the rate of coolant loss. Reactor or power plant failure may not happen for weeks."

A nearby maintenance panel slid aside as Jassalin swung off the ladder and onto the deck. She drifted in the zero-gee intersection and fired suit thrusters to null her motion. "So how do we proceed?" she sang.

"Purge," Hollfara sang. "The coolant is radiation contaminated. It must be reactor coolant. There is very little leakage given the volume of broadway beyond the hatch. We must find a way to vent the contamination beyond frame hatch one-twenty-three."

"But from where?" Jassalin trilled. "Not from broadway. For safety reasons venting must be done from a damage control station. There should be damage control stations in the chase above as."

"Jassalin, go back and see if...," Kidahin began.

"Jassalin? Alfara. Einstika and I were listening in. We think we found a damage control console. Its screen displays a plumbing system schematic with a flashing yellow symbol."

"What does it look like?" Jassalin trilled.

"A yellow triangle enclosing a black long, vertical line with a dot below it," Alfara sang.

"Sounds like the purge override control to me. Press it!" Jassalin trilled.

Einstika, closest to the console, pressed the icon at the same time Kidahin trilled in warning, "No! Yellow means caution here!"

Nothing seemed to happen.

"I pressed it, Kidahin. The icon stopped blinking but remains on the screen. I am sorry," Einstika trilled.

Jassalin toggled her suit attitude thrusters and spun in a slow circle.

"I do not see anything different," she trilled. "Do you, Kidahin?"

Kidahin flipped her ears wide in the uncomfortable helmet. "No. The damage control system is probably itself damaged. How are we going to proceed without purging the contaminant from the aft compartments?" she sang.

"Kidahin!" Hollfara trilled. "My suit sensors report increasing oxygen and nitrogen levels. There is atmospheric pressure and the temperature is rising as well. I think Einstika restored life support to broadway."

Kidahin heard a noise through her helmet. Sound needed a medium, such as air, to travel through. She heard...what? A bong-bong-bong chime? She once heard such a sound on *Henri Edda,* a warning tone.

"Restoring life support should not set off an alarm," she sang as a voice speaking in the human language became intelligible.

*"Pressure, normal. Airborne contaminate detected. Warning! Amidships decks artificial gravity engaging!"*

Weight returned, and Kidahin fell, striking the steeply tipped deck. She tumbled against the wall as Jassalin keened in surprise.

Kidahin stumbled, clumsy from the return of weight. The tilted walls gave her no flat standing surface. She looked at the spot where Jassalin had been floating.

With gravity restored the gaping intersection where Jassalin was hovering became a pit. It was not a vertical drop but more like a steeply tipped smooth shaft. Jassalin had fallen into the intersecting corridor and bounced and tumbled down the deck.

"Jassalin? Can you hear me?" Kidahin keened.

Hollfara struggled to stand. She crawled up from the lopsided corner where deck met wall and noticed her engineering scanner flashing a brilliant green warning.

"Structural failure imminent!" she keened at warning pitch.

"From what?" Kidahin trilled, "atmospheric pressure?"

"No, from a differential gravitational gradient. The return to full gravity is causing some decks to collapse."

Somewhere far below Hollfara, volatile chemicals, oxygen, and electricity came into contact and exploded. The initial blast triggered multiple chain-reaction explosions that rippled down the asteroid-facing side of *Londiwe Khoza*. Those explosions, powerful ones, were more than strong enough to free the wrecked destroyer from his embracing rocky ridge, were more than powerful enough to launch him above the crater-strewn asteroid.

Hollfara knew what the slight downward pull of acceleration meant. "Kidahin, we are moving!"

"I know this!" Kidahin hissed. "Do we crash back onto the asteroid or did we exceed escape velocity?"

"I am working on that question now," Hollfara trilled. "Sensor accelerometer data says our acceleration is.. wait.  Kidahin, blast-induced acceleration exceeds asteroid escape velocity."

"Everyone, recall to me. Jassalin fell down a corridor when the gravity came on and I cannot get a response from her."

"Kidahin? Aplilin. Seliaha and I are in the shuttle bay. Gravity is not restored here. Delwyn was right. There are support alcoves for three shuttles roughly the size of troop transports. Two shuttles remain but are crushed and pinned into debris. One alcove is empty, and I see evidence of demolitions. I think the survivors cut and blasted wreckage before they could launch the working shuttle. We are backtrailing our prowl, but how do we rejoin you? My sensors read vacuum everywhere except on broadway. Opening the frame one-eleven hatch will cause broadway to explosively decompress."

"You need the portable airlock," Kidahin sang.

"Kidahin? Merkrida. Tialdrin, Kyralin, and Mimiran are with me. We were about to breach a life-support-stable compartment with the portable airlock when the gravity and explosions knocked us flat. We can abandon our effort, meet up with Aplilin and Seliaha, and use the airlock to breach broadway."

Kidahin hesitated. She needed Aplilin to set the charges on all the hyperdrive power nodes found so far. She needed Mimiran if Jassalin was hurt. But male safety came first, even human males.

"No, continue your breaching tasks and then backtrail to hatch one-eleven. Aplilin and Seliaha, wait for Mimiran there," Kidahin trilled at imperative tempo.

"Affirm!"

"Merkrida? What can you tell me about the ship's amidships weapon and shield status?" Kidahin trilled.

"But for impact damage, I cannot find any evidence the shields were fired upon or that the hull-mounted particle and plasma weapons were fired. I conclude that this warship did not engage nor was engaged by the Ni'zakhonii."

"Alfara, Einstika, recall to me!" Kidahin trilled.

"Affirm, acting," they sang.

When the two Hunters arrived, Kidahin perked her ears at them. "We are climbing down the corridor to get Jassalin. With gravity restored, the deck is a steep decline falling into the next hatch..."

Einstika glanced down the tilted corridor. "No lights, but this side of the ship probably has crumple damage from the impact." She looked up. "See? The lights are on for this side of the intersection and... Kidahin, look! The intersecting hatches are all open."

Kidahin stepped beside Einstika and looked into the corridor. "That hatch was closed. I remember looking down and up when I first got here."

"Restored life support?" Hollfara suggested. "It cannot be normal for these hatches to remain closed."

"No, they are not," Kidahin sang.

"Jassalin could have fallen all the way to the inner hull corridor wall," Einstika trilled.

"At least it is not a vertical drop," Alfara sang. "It looks more like she took a tumble down a steep trail."

"It is not the tumble so much as how far she tumbles or if she fell down another intersecting corridor," Kidahin growled.

"But those mechanical seals protruding above the deck should have stopped her from falling more than forty ells," Hollfara objected.

"Maybe not," Alfara sang. "They are not far enough above the deck to stop a tumbling body."

"Can we slide along the deck?" Einstika wondered. "It looks smooth enough. Sliding feet-first we strike the hatch seal and bend knees to take the impact. Then we climb over the seal and slide to the next hatch."

"That may work. Good thinking, Einstika," Kidahin sang.

"I doubt we can climb back up the same way," Alfara grumbled.

"Maybe not, but by then Aplilin and the others will be here. Besides, the floor is smooth, not slippery."

"Maybe Einstika should go turn off the artificial gravity," Alfara growled.

"I was about to suggest that myself," Hollfara sang. "Kidahin, does it strike you odd that Delwyn has not asked about our progress?"

"Spirits!" Kidahin trilled. She twitched her ear to open the suit commlink. "Delwyn? Kidahin," she sang.

She waited a few seconds but heard nothing.

"I get no response from him, Melkorka, or Nynava. Suit commlink relay to our warship is the stealth insertion vehicle comm system. The SIV is either damaged or knocked off the hull."

"Then we are stuck here," Hollfara trilled.

"Kidahin? Merkrida," Kidahin heard over the suit commlink. "We have breached a compartment having breathable air. The corridors and compartments around us have minimal life support as well. We found no survivors, but we have found bodies. These bodies are not collision casualties. They are intact. I do not understand it, but the wounds are consistent and not random like you would expect during combat. I think they are self-inflicted or mercy killings. I also found patchwork repairs and obvious attempts to make the compartment livable long-term. I think the survivors rallied here for some time before reaching the shuttles."

"Mercy killings? Did you find other habitable compartments beside the ones you are in now?" Kidahin trilled.

"No, there are none. All intermittent life support signals come from here. The rest of the ship is uninhabitable," Merkrida sang.

"Recall to Aplilin and Seliaha at frame one-eleven and breach the hatch into broadway."

"Affirm. Kidahin, how is Jassalin?" Merkrida trilled.

"I do not know, but I intend to find out."

***

"*...suit breach detected...pressure forty-one percent...suit breach detected...pressure forty percent...suit breach detected...pressure thirty-four percent...*"

Jassalin groaned. She felt dizzy, nauseous, and cold, very cold.

"What?" she muttered.

"*Three suit breaches found,*" the suit told her. "*Pressure loss critical. Minor breach, left knee. Minor breach, left elbow. Minor breach, helmet seal.*"

Helmet seal? That was bad, very bad. She needed to plug it first before she lost consciousness. "Repair kit...right utility pocket...," Jassalin groaned musically.

She could not move her left leg or left arm. She fumbled at the utility pocket catch, pulled a roll of clear adhesive out and shoved it between her legs. She pushed the dispenser button and a forearm-length, clear strip unwound from the spool. She stretched the strip and ripped it free.

Stretching the strip made it turn sticky. Clumsily, she wrapped it around her neck at the helmet seal. She hurriedly applied three more strips to her neck before going after the suit left knee and left elbow joints.

"*Pressure stabilizing at fourteen percent. Repressurizing...pressure normal.*"

"Kidahin? Jassalin. Can you hear me?"

She got no response, not even static.

"Commlink status?" she asked the suit.

"*Online but at insufficient power to penetrate a local static shield.*"

"Nature of the static shield?" she trilled.

"*Parameters match those used in warship intruder defense systems.*"

Jassalin trilled a curse. Something had triggered the warship's security systems.

"Helmet lamp on," she sang.

The suit lamp blazed from her forehead. Looking around, she found herself atop several frozen bodies smashed against a hatch. The wrong hatch. Broadway was the nickname for corridor-C. This hatch displayed a different string of text, 124 B 21 CC. From Delwyn's explanation of ship locations, Jassalin translated the text to mean frame one-twenty-four, corridor-B, deck twenty-one, lift shaft CC.

How did she get here? She fell. Fell? Yes, fell. She felt the pull of gravity. She fell down the tilted broadway-intersecting corridor.

But she should not have landed on a different deck.

Jassalin shivered, still cold. "Suit temperature?" she sang.

*"Tail minus ten and slowly falling. Suit heating elements offline."*

Cold, and it would get colder. Jassalin looked up at the hole in the ceiling. She was in a cubicle. Did she fall through the ceiling? The hatch across from her was closed and bent in its seal and was blocked by more frozen bodies. It reminded her of a pit, and that reminder summoned the memory of when she led an Environmental Interdiction team across an ice-covered chasm on Elleio's north pole. The ice collapsed under them. She and her EI team fell. Her teammates died in the fall, but she landed in pulverized ice with no serious injury but the wind knocked out of her. She nearly froze to death waiting for Uahua'asee'a Clan Polar Search and Rescue to find her.

Jassalin shuddered and thanked the spirits that Kidahin saw her fall from the broadway deck.

* * *

"Where are they?" Merkrida trilled.

"Have patience," Mimiran sang. "The bow lower decks are wrecked. Aplilin and Seliaha are probably backtrailing and looping several times to reach the shuttles. They need time to retrace the way back..."

"We are climbing into the main deck now," Aplilin snarled over the suit commlink. "You should try it yourself and see how well you do. Seliaha is with me and did well. Is the portable airlock ready?"

"It is, yes. It is in place and we have breached hatch one-eleven. Remember, only two can pass through at the same time," Merkrida sang.

"I know this!" Aplilin snapped. "Seliaha and I go first! I need my equipment so I can set my charges."

"Why?" Tialdrin trilled. "The last two power taps are in contaminated spaces. You cannot disable all of them now."

"I do not care, and it does not matter. Maybe two hyperdrive coils lack the power to sustain a mobius fracture. Get out of my way!"

Aplilin pushed Seliaha into the portable airlock and waited for it to cycle them through the breached broadway hatch. They ran together down broadway to Kidahin. By the time Merkrida caught up Aplilin was above her in the maintenance chase hard at work.

"How do we proceed?" Merkrida trilled.

"We climb down to Jassalin using cable stripped from the wiring harnesses in the chase," Kidahin sang.

"Why not just slide from bulkhead to bulkhead?" Merkrida sang at interrogative tempo.

"I want something to hang onto while climbing back out if Jassalin is injured. We may need to loop a cable around her and pull her out," Kidahin trilled.

# 5

## THE BREAKER OF STICKS, UNTANGLING OYYA, THE STARVED SPIRIT...

"Mistress Melkorka, stealth insertion vehicle talkback telemetry is offline," Mistress of Communications Hlindredreda trilled.

"Caused by the blast?" Melkorka sang.

"Unknown, but likely," Mistress of Tactics Hlinlodyn sang. "The SIV landing pad traction elements can exert an attractive force greater than the structural strength of the landing jacks. But if a ta'na swarm was pulling power from the pads during the blast, then..."

"No," Delwyn interrupted. "SIV sensor readings in the talkback telemetry data would show the pads pulling power but no attractive force generated. Hlinlodyn, what's happening to the *Khoza* now? Is he going to fall back onto the asteroid?"

"No. He is drifting toward our left flank at a negligible velocity and tumbling at 1.141 rotations per minute. The changes in position and roll rate are causing the hypercube emissions to sweep though us more often. We must maintain station-keeping relative to that warship to counteract the increased exposure."

"Trebithia, what do you think?" Melkorka sang.

"Confirmed," the Mistress of Pathwalking trilled. "I am maneuvering us back into station-keeping relative to *Londiwe Khoza.*"

"Mistress Melkorka," Hlinlodyn trilled, "I am picking up several life signs. I can account for all twenty-one, but one of them is separated from the others by more than two hundred ells and is not moving."

"Can you get an interior scan?" Delwyn asked.

Hlinlodyn ran the scan data through signal processing algorithms that produced ghostly afterimages of compartments and corridors blurring into one another. "No, Delwyn. The misfiring hyperdrive coils are distorting the scan data. There is also some data scrambling at work now. All signals are being corrupted by overlapping harmonics. I think maybe shield harmonics. Mistress, I think his shields are up."

"Delwyn? What do you think? An automated defense system?" Melkorka trilled.

"I don't think so," Delwyn said. "Blasting free of the asteroid probably caused enough internal damage to activate the structural integrity fields. They keep the ship from collapsing in on himself and stop atmosphere in intact compartments from outgassing through tiny holes and cracks throughout the hull."

"Hlinlodyn, where is Team-Two exactly?" Melkorka trilled.

"Scanning," the Mistress of Tactics sang. "Signal-to-noise ratio is improving. Mistress, except for the one outlier all team members are near the aft-most two hyperdrive pylons."

"Has the outlier moved yet?" Delwyn asked.

"No," Hlinlodyn growled.

Delwyn called up Hlinlodyn's scan data and transferred it to his Warleader's Watch console. Two hundred ells in the Eyloni base-five number system was only fifty ells in decimal numbers. An ell, the length of a tail, was 1.778 meters.

"About ninety meters as the crow flies," Delwyn muttered aloud.

"As a what flies?" Melkorka sang from her command chair.

"A crow," he muttered absently. "A flying creature. *Damn.*"

"He means 'line-of-sight'," Phelindra trilled as she wrapped her tail around her favorite male. She savored his scent, and her pheromonal empathy rendered the emotional image in his mind. "In this case, Delwyn means the straight-line distance it flies without encountering obstacles."

"What about the crow, Delwyn?" Melkorka keened impatiently.

"She is two hundred ells from the group, but the actual distance is greater. They need to take corridors and companionways through intervening decks. They'll have to leave broadway, drop into the below decks, move forward, and then drop all the way to the ventral inner-hull deck. That's quite a distance. The life sign appears near, or in, a lift shaft. Why would anybody go there?"

"Maybe she was trying to reach the shuttle deployment bay?" Melkorka suggested. "Kidahin was told to find the shuttles."

"Then why is she staying put? She should have left the lift and headed forward by now," Delwyn demanded. "Besides, I told Kidahin to avoid the lifts. Human starships have ladders and stairs just in case of power failure and... Oh, God. She fell down a lift shaft."

"So?" Hlindredreda sang. "It is nothing but a hard bump in near zero-gee."

Delwyn turned to the Mistress of Communications and shook his head. "Not if artificial gravity is working there. Earth-normal gravity would turn a slow, low-gee fall into a treetop plunge."

"I cannot confirm artificial gravity there because of the hypergravity ta'na spikes. Maybe I can learn something from a visual analysis of the before and after blast hull profiles. Yes, I see compression deformations consistent with sporadic gravity restoration on some decks," Hlinlodyn sang.

"Someone probably overrode a life support lockout," Delwyn said. "The structural integrity fields and the artificial gravity fields are bucking one another. That's it, I'm going in after them."

*"No, you will not!"* Phelindra snarled.

"You will remain here where we will protect you," Melkorka trilled at imperative tempo.

Several Hunters wearing a single green web among other multicolored webs in their dreamcatcher military rank earrings stepped out from behind concealing shoulder-length crimson jungle grasses fringing the perimeter of the command center.

"We will not make the same mistake with you that we did with Kalinn," Phelindra sang as she threaded her tail between his legs and around his waist. She tightened her tail and squeezed his abdomen for added emphasis.

Delwyn sighed, leaned back in the chair and against Phelindra's hip, and stared up into beautifully sunlit, diaphanous, yellow-trimmed orange elleiu tree leaves. The sky above the tree was clear blue. He rolled his head across Phelindra's hip to her tail and glanced up at a patiently waiting Lo'sutra'est anni. He frowned at her. The Comari stood in silence and seemed to stare at nothing and was apparently unaware of her surroundings.

But he knew better. She reminded him of a human child with some obscure form of high-order autism. She was incredibly intelligent but seemingly oblivious to many social norms. She never left him, and she got frustrated whenever he didn't act as she thought he should. His voiced intent to go after Kidahin and the real danger to him should make her furious. It didn't, and the shock of that missing outrage left him speechless for several minutes.

"Why are you getting so worked up about it?" he finally asked Phelindra. "Lo'sutra'est anni doesn't care if I go after them."

The Comari blinked her soulful, pale amber eyes at him, canted her head to look down at him, and perked her ears through long, silky pale hair at him. She gave a soft, sibilant sigh. The whisper-quiet sound caused everyone in the command center to pause. Her gaze, her ears, and her sigh told them she was fully engaged in the social drama unfolding around her.

Lo'sutra'est anni's gaze captivated him. She was so much like his long dead daughter Valerie with her ten-year-old looks and towheaded waist-length straight hair. Only her pale-yellow skin and oversized pixielike mobile ears spoiled the likeness.

*Where you go, I will follow,* Delwyn felt in his head. He was nearly nose-blind to Eyloni pheromonal signaling. He relied on an excellent nose and a natural empathy coupled with a soldier's situational awareness to get crude intuitive estimates of their emotions and general ideas of what they were thinking about. Those ideas weren't enough to form the scent-sentences and mental pictures they shared among themselves.

The sole exception was Lo'sutra'est anni. The bond she formed with him let him feel her emotions as streams of consciousness but only when she gave him her full attention and even then only when she was close to him, say within twenty or thirty meters.

"Do not put ideas in his head, Mistress Comari," Melkorka sang, interrupting his musing.

Lo'sutra'est anni snapped her body around behind him and glared down on Melkorka.

<<Males have autonomy and can do what they want subject only to the requirements of privacy and courtesy,>> the Comari signed in battle language.

Melkorka lifted the old cavalry saber from her thighs and jumped out of her command chair, rage consuming her in fiery Warrior fury. "As our Warleader, Delwyn owes us the courtesy of not abandoning us! There is nothing, *nothing*, he can do that an assault team cannot do better."

<<I know, but this is not up for discussion. I will go with Delwyn should he exercise his autonomy.>>

For Delwyn, unable to understand battle language and indeed for a male to attempt to learn it was a death-penalty offense, she shifted her empathy to him.

*We are one, and I permit you this should you decide to go. Yet for you to abandon your occupational association is disrespectful and discourteous behavior.*

Times like these made Delwyn want to beat his head against a bulkhead. For all the autonomy granted males in Eyloni social life, there were times when males had few options or none at all. He couldn't within any liberal reading of Eyloni culture just leave the ship and strike out on his own without defenders.

A warleader was the co-commander of the ship. In fact, the crew considered *Hunter's Moon* his warship. He could countermand any order Melkorka gave at will. And Mistress of the Ship Melkorka was *Hunter's Moon's* commanding mistress by his choice alone.

"Melkorka?" Hlinlodyn interrupted. "I regained contact with the stealth insertion vehicle. Talkback telemetry is up and running. All his systems read nominal and are responding. I transferred his flight control systems to my tactical analysis console. I have full remote-piloting access from here."

"Can you pilot him back to the breach Team-Two used to enter the Coalition ship?" Melkorka trilled.

"Yes, Mistress. I am nulling SIV roll rates and pitching around. I see the breach. I am matching the warship's velocity and roll rates. I am closing to within thirty ells of the hull breach. I am powering up the traction emitters in the landing pads to lock the SIV to the hull plates, otherwise he will drift off the hull."

"Too risky," Delwyn interrupted. "How long can you maintain downward pitch thrust against the *Khoza's* hull?"

"More than long enough for Team-Two to backtrail to the breach. But, Delwyn, what about the outlying life sign?" Hlinlodyn trilled.

"Use both systems," Melkorka sang. "Use pad tractors to hold the SIV to the hull. Set pitch thrusters to fire if the traction emitters lose power."

"Don't monitor power loss," Delwyn added. "Remember, the ta'na effect will draw power. Set the pitch thrusters to fire if physical contact is lost."

"By your command," Hlinlodyn sang. "The SIV continues to close on the warship at one ell-per-second. Team-Two suit talkback telemetry is now available. I see all suit transponders except Jassalin's."

"I bet she's the life sign in the lift shaft," Delwyn said.

"Confirmed," Hlinlodyn trilled. "Suit telemetry matches life sign location. I am landing the SIV on the hull. Contact made, activating landing pad traction fields and maintaining downward thrust on attitude control pitch thrusters."

"Hlindredreda, contact Kidahin," Melkorka sang.

"Affirm, Mistress. Channel open," Hlindredreda sang.

"Talk to me, my Kidahin," Melkorka sang sweetly.

Delwyn smiled and not for the first time at the evocative emotion his fiery-tempered Warrior Mistress of the Ship could summon into her singing voice.

"Mistress Melkorka?" Kidahin sang back instantly. "Artificial gravity came on and Jassalin fell down an intersecting corridor. Can you contact her suit commlink?"

"One moment, Kidahin. Hlindredreda?" Melkorka sang at interrogative pitch.

"Attempting contact, again. Still no reply, Mistress," the Hunter Mistress of Communications sang. "I am switching to signal countermeasures. Negative contact, but I am certain Jassalin can hear me."

"Not enough power in her suit commlink to breach the static shield?" Melkorka trilled.

"Correct," Hlindredreda growled.

"Kidahin? No joy on reaching Jassalin by commlink," Delwyn said. "Status of your team and mission?"

"Everyone is accounted for. Aplilin is setting her demolition charges. She cannot reach the last two hyperdrive coil power distribution nodes because of radiation-contaminated spaces. Will cutting power to all but the last two coils stop this mobius fracturing?"

"I would think so, but I don't know enough physics. The tesseract emissions are beyond me. That's something for Anailiatha to figure out."

"Delwyn, there were survivors here. We found compartments with minimal life support and many dead bodies in them. They were killed by non-combat related fatal wounds. They look self-inflicted to me, but Merkrida thinks maybe they were mercy killings. Females would gladly kill themselves to save males, but most of the dead she found there are males," Kidahin keened.

"What about the shuttles?" Delwyn demanded.

"The shuttles? What about them? How can you care more about them than about the dead males?" Kidahin trilled angrily.

*"What about the shuttles?"* Delwyn roared.

"One is gone. The other two are crushed beyond repair. The survivors spent a lot of time cutting and blasting wreckage clear to free the missing shuttle for launch," Kidahin hissed, livid.

"I wonder if there were too many people to take in the remaining shuttle," Delwyn muttered. "Kidahin, did you scan those bodies?"

"Merkrida did," Kidahin trilled, still outraged.

"I need to see them. It's important."

"I am sending you the raw scan data," Merkrida growled.

Delwyn waited as Hlindredreda relayed the scan images to the Warleader's Watch console. It didn't take her long, and it didn't take him long to assess the casualties.

"A mutiny...," Delwyn cursed.

"A *what?*" Phelindra trilled, pausing a mere instant before her nose translated his emotional meaning of the word. "A betrayal from within a warship society? How is this even possible?"

How could he explain? Eyloni female crews owned their warships outright. The crew of a ship was a society, a social unit having individual familial and clannish customs and traditions enforced by interwoven civil and moral standards. A mutiny just couldn't happen on an Eyloni warship. From an all-female crew point of view a mutiny was a rejection of the occupational association relationship with their warleader. That was nearly impossible, unless he sullied crew honor, given the protective nature females had for the rare male. A mutiny was also impossible because it pitted extended family and interrelated clan members against one another, the moral equivalent of a civil war. War among tribes and clans was outlawed by the Be'atika Senge's global Compact and had been for centuries. Then there were the female hierarchies that regulated moral behavior. They would consider mutiny an honor crime against the male warleader and the male warship. Causing or attempting to cause harm to a male, without honorable justification, was a recognized high honor-point crime in every hierarchy. The penalty was to skin the guilty female alive with her own adulthood knife and leave her to die in the jungle.

"What makes you think this?" Melkorka stammered in shock over the emotional overtones his scent forced on her.

"The uniforms," Delwyn snapped. "The captain is among the dead. So is his executive officer and several command staff officers. There are some common crew ratings and a few noncommissioned officers, too. I don't see any special operations group ARTs members among the dead, and that's strange. SOG ARTs forces would improve the likelihood of post-shipwreck survival."

"All attributable to survivors' luck, maybe?" Phelindra trilled. "As I understand human command structures, the high-ranking humans should cluster in key command sites. The lowest in rank are scattered throughout the ship. When his inertial dampeners and artificial gravity systems failed, only those key sites have the necessary backups to keep key functions and the command staff alive."

"What you say is true, although there are safe zones throughout the ship for crew to duck into," Delwyn admitted. "But collision survival also depends on other factors. If the *Khoza* was at Condition-1, action stations, or at Condition-2, general quarters, then the crew was at battle stations in areas with redundant inertial field generators. The casualties in the corridors Kidahin found aren't consistent with a crew at battle stations. It's as if they didn't even know there was a problem."

"So it was the spirits' own luck, after all," Phelindra trilled sadly.

"No, I don't buy that," Delwyn said. "The survivors, or mutineers, freed a shuttle and left. In the aftermath of a catastrophic hull failure, that takes organization. Leadership matters during any disaster. A Sentry shuttle can get them to the habitable moon, but its limited-use FTL can't take them beyond a star's heliopause. Everyone knew the moon was the only option, and they would look to the captain and his staff for guidance and order."

"Kidahin, what is taking you so long?" Mistress of Battle Nynava trilled over the commlink.

"Jassalin is wedged inside a lift shaft. The commlink does not work on the shaft deck. We are using battle language to talk with her. Her left-side suit powered joints and all heating elements are offline. It is already well below freezing inside of it."

"Cut her out!" Nynava keened.

"We cannot!" Kidahin trilled in fury. "Aplilin is using the breaching equipment to cut spaces for her demolition charges."

"How long until she finishes, Kidahin? It might be better for her to abandon the demolitions mission and get Jassalin out of there. You've confirmed no survivors remain. Get clear so Hlinlodyn can fire a torpedo into that ship," Delwyn said.

"Now you are talking sense," Hlinlodyn sang. "I wanted to do this all along."

"No!" Anailiatha trilled from the engineering command center. She was listening to Delwyn's one-sided conversations broadcasting over the warleader-tracking combat address system. "Loss of power should cause an orderly shutdown of the hyperdrive coils. Torpedoing the ship while the coils are firing may complicate matters."

"Complicate them how?" Melkorka sang at dissonant interrogative pitch.

"The sensor data so far suggests the hypercube may persist after the hyperdrive coils are deactivated."

"I thought the randomly firing coils are what is causing the tesseract to manifest in the first place," Delwyn said.

"I do not think so," Anailiatha growled. "The ta'na effect emits from the hypercube vertices. Shutting the coils down should stop the ta'na effect from appearing within our warship."

"That was the point, was it not?" Melkorka trilled. "The power loss was traced to the ta'na."

"Which is a good thing, right? We can open an FTL scan portal and track down just where on the moon the shuttle landed. We could even jump there directly once we learn whether or not there are any Ni'zakhonii naval assets here," Delwyn said.

"No. *No!*" Anailiatha trilled. "The hypercube is a gravitational artifact, a tenth-dimensional intrusion of hyperspace into normal space."

"What does it matter?" Trebithia sang. "We will be free to navigate."

"No, I do not think so," Anailiatha sang at warning pitch.

"What do you mean?" Melkorka trilled.

"I think the hypercube is a self-sustaining gravitational cage," Anailiatha began.

"Put here by the Ni'zakhonii? Are you serious?" Trebithia trilled. "You cannot barricade an entire star system. We can jump into the inner system and the Ni'zakhonii know this, which makes such an impossible barrier impractical as well."

"Ni'zakhonii FTL technology manipulates a subspace manifold. Hyperspace technology is as foreign to them as it is to us. The hypercube is an artifact caused by whatever affected the Coalition hyperdrive, something that must have happened while the ship was still in hyperspace," Anailiatha trilled.

"Are you saying we've been boxed in by the tesseract?" Delwyn asked.

"I do not know, yet. We are either just outside or just inside of a hyperplane."

"What happens if we pass through one of these hyperplanes?" Melkorka trilled.

"I do not know, Mistress," Anailiatha admitted. "It is ten-dimensional, so it is a cube of hyperspace, and hyperspace has hypermass and hypergravity. It could trap us in a hyperspacial sinkhole, translate us through hyperspace to somewhere else in normal space, or compress us into a singularity."

"I doubt it can send us anywhere," Delwyn said. "There is no open wormhole to admit the ship into the hyperdimension. No wormhole also means no event horizon to cross, so we shouldn't get squashed like a bug, either."

"Anailiatha?" Melkorka trilled.

"Delwyn just summed up intuitively based on no math and pure guessing the same conclusion it took me three hours to arrive at," Anailiatha snarled, piqued at his tendency to reach the right result using the wrong methodology.

"A hyperdimensional cage," Melkorka sang thoughtfully. "And you think the Coalition ship is the means to opening it?"

"Yes, Mistress," Anailiatha sang. "We may need a working hyperdrive to jump us out of the hypercube."

Melkorka gripped Delwyn's saber and glided over to the communications station.

"Hlindredreda, contact Kidahin," Melkorka sang.

"Affirm, channel open, Mistress."

"Kidahin? Status report," Melkorka sang.

"Aplilin has wired all power conduits to the hyperdrive coils except the last two. All decks and corridors further aft remain a radiation hazard. She returned to us ten minutes ago and is busy cutting Jassalin from the lift shaft wreckage. She fell through the ceiling of a lift car and on top of several human casualties."

"I need to speak to Aplilin," Melkorka trilled.

"No commlink works there. I will send someone down with a message delivered by battle language. What should I ask her?" Kidahin trilled.

"Ask her how hard it will be to restore power to the coils if we must," Melkorka sang.

"Restore power? Why do you want to restore...?" Kidahin trilled.

"Do not argue, just ask her!" Melkorka keened impatiently.

Delwyn glanced down from his Watch at Trebithia. His mental image of her somehow altered his scent enough for her to empathize with and realize he was thinking of her.

"Yes, Delwyn?" Trebithia sang.

"A tesseract is not a three-dimensional cube. It encloses a space containing five—well, ten—dimensions. Ta'na effects continue to appear randomly, so are we inside or outside of the cube?" Delwyn asked her.

"Your question is in a sense nonsensical because the hypercube exists in extradimensional space. It is virtual in nature. We are not in a three-dimensional box. A hyperplane is not like the side of a cube, either.

"Hypergravity emits from its vertex points and its edges exist in other dimensions. I am not certain, but I think Anailiatha is right. Engaging the jump drive here would be a mistake."

"Why?" Delwyn asked.

"The hypercube might act like a singularity containment field."

"Meaning?" Delwyn pressed.

"It will exert a pull on our FTL drive jump-point singularity," she sang.

"Wouldn't moving the jump-point singularity do the same thing as altering the ship's jump-point geometry?"

"*A'pea, a'pea, a'pea, a'pea!*" Anailiatha trilled over the combat address system. "That possibility never occurred to me. We cannot use the jump drive!"

"What about sublight propulsion? Anailiatha?" Melkorka trilled.

"It is possible. Yes, in theory we can scan for gravitational eddies and navigate around them. Delwyn made a fair point about event horizons. The ship cannot jump to somewhere else in the universe. Nor can he get crushed in a singularity because no singularity exists. However, the quantum gravity rifts will phase in and out of normal space because they are virtual. Crossing a hyperplane extending into normal space will either translate us into hyperspace with no way of getting back out without the assistance of a Coalition warship, or passing though it will cause the hull to deform under hypergravity to alter our jump-point geometry."

"Which would make using the jump drive fatal," Hlinlodyn growled.

"Mistress Melkorka? Kidahin is calling," Hlindredreda sang.

"Finally," Melkorka trilled. "What did Aplilin tell you, Kidahin?"

"This is Aplilin, Mistress. The coil power taps are superconductor busbar as thick as my neck. The demolition charges will blow out chunks of busbar the size of my head. Anailiatha has superconductor busbar in engineering maintenance stores. Pieces of it can be cut to bridge the blown-out pieces, but there will be huge losses of superconductivity. The patchwork repairs will melt and blowout under full loading, and rather quickly, I think."

"That cannot be helped. They need only work once. Proceed with your demolitions at Kidahin's discretion. Kidahin? Anything on Jassalin yet?" Melkorka sang.

"Mimiran is carrying her out of the lift shaft now. She says Jassalin is unconscious and suffering from hypothermia. Her suit has power, but the heating elements do not work. The stealth insertion vehicle has no cabin life support, so he is not a viable option. Once we got her on the broadway deck, we will have to get her out of the suit."

"We can send a troop transport to you," Delwyn interrupted. "You'll have to put her back in the suit to get her into the SIV. She'll have to endure the cold until you land inside the transport."

Melkorka glared at him. "Do not make promises you cannot keep. What makes you think a troop transport can reach them?"

"The Sentry shuttle is gone, remember? It's no betafortress, but it's still a tough little gunship. It is about the same size and mass as a troop transport, too. There's no sign of the shuttle in local space, not even wreckage. If a Sentry can navigate out of here, then a troop transport can, too," he shot back.

"Kidahin? You heard?" Melkorka sang.

"Stupid question," Kidahin sang under her breath.

"What was that?" Melkorka trilled at imperative tempo.

"What? Oh, ...nothing, Mistress. Aplilin was just asking why you want to restore power to the coils once we shut them down."

"I am sure," Melkorka trilled dryly. "Anailiatha may need to reactivate them to nullify the hypercube manifestation. She thinks it will persist once you cut power to the coils."

"Anailiatha is coming here?" Kidahin sang.

"No, but she will send an engineering maintenance team to restore power in sequence if it is necessary. Once you drop Jassalin off with Allohindra in Health Center, you and your team will take a troop transport to the moon and use the SIV to land on the surface."

"Affirm," Kidahin sang.

"Delwyn? What is the combat capability of the missing shuttle?" Aplilin trilled.

"The Sentry is a light, gunboat-capable shuttle. It has a composite carbon hull with substantial armor belting. The armor and multiple offensive weapons give it poor maneuverability. It masses about seven hundred metric tons and has a standard crew of five."

"Armament?" Hlinlodyn trilled.

"In gunship configuration it carries a rack of fifteen Mark-IV torpedoes, but if they used it to evacuate survivors, then there's no room for the torpedoes. In all configurations the pilot can fire through an arc covering the forward quarter left, dead-ahead, and forward quarter right with two heavy particle cannons. The pilot can launch up to four electronic countermeasure decoys. The Sentry has decent point defenses and damage control systems. The port gunner can fire through an arc covering the forward left quarter and the aft left quarter with a four-barrel duranium kinetic weapon. The starboard gunner can fire through an arc covering the forward right quarter and the aft right quarter with another four-barrel kinetic weapon," Delwyn said.

"What about his weaknesses?" Hlinlodyn pressed.

"Two or three kinetic hits to the same armor plate will cause it to shingle off. Multiple direct hits to the engines sometimes causes the fusion plant to scram and then restart thirty seconds later. Its electronic warfare systems are susceptible to electronic countermeasures. Its shields can take four heavy direct hits. The fifth one always gets through. Port and starboard weapon systems may lose target lock if hit by electromagnetic pulse countermeasures because the Sentry has poor counter-EMP defenses. Sustained weapon hits head-on may interrupt power to the pilot particle weapons, resulting in reduced firepower or possibly even knocking the gun out."

"Can maneuverability be affected?" Melkorka sang.

"The Sentry is not the greatest at maneuvering, but I remember a special operations group briefing on maneuvering thruster vulnerabilities. Sustained evasive action causes the thruster controls to overheat. They reset, and while resetting the Sentry cannot alter course. Maneuvering thruster reset only takes a few seconds, but that few seconds in a straight line can give targeting systems a chance to lock-on."

"What is his FTL flight duration?" Hlinlodyn sang.

"It has about the same duration as a Dart fighter, two jumps into hyperspace and two jumps back into normal space over a maximum normal-space distance of about seventy billion kilometers before its antihydrogen is exhausted," Delwyn said.

"I can guarantee the shuttle did not jump into hyperspace from here," Anailiatha sang over the combat address system.

"Mistress Nynava? Mimiran has just arrived. She is taking Jassalin's suit off and is beginning to administer healer aid," Kidahin trilled over the commlink.

"Understood," Nynava sang. "Mimiran? How is she?"

"I am busy. Go bother someone else," Mimiran growled.

Melkorka trilled a chuckle at Nynava's expense, turned to share the moment with Delwyn, and froze.

Her favorite male, busy with Hlinlodyn, completely missed Mimiran's scathing comment. Now was the time for her to act.

She wandered around and behind him with a complete lack of rhythmic grace so out of character for her that it drew stares from everyone in the command center except their blithely unaware favorite male.

Melkorka issued orders to Nynava and Phelindra in precise battle language. They acknowledged those orders through scent-linked empathy, as did everyone else in the command center.

Nynava nodded, turned, and quietly left.

Delwyn, leaning over Hlinlodyn's shoulder, abruptly stood and walked around behind the busy Warrior. A tingling awareness slowly engulfed him. Warnings like these came from his combat-trained situational awareness. They usually fell out of the blue like an inspiring muse or a haunting specter. Something was wrong.

"What's going on?" he demanded.

"Nothing, why?" Melkorka sang sweetly.

"Don't give me the innocence routine. You're all up to something... Wait, where is Nynava?"

"She went to confer with Zalzadrin about arms selection for the moon reconnaissance mission," Phelindra sang.

"Oh," Delwyn said. That made sense. The Mistress of Battle and the Mistress of Arms planned missions, and sometimes one or the other even took personal command of a mission. "Good. I want to look at that troop transport when Kidahin gets back."

"Of course you do, Delwyn. When Kidahin comes back," Melkorka sang happily.

* * *

"Mimiran, why is Jassalin not responding?" Kidahin trilled.

"Her core body temperature is too low," the Warrior healer trilled. "Everyone, get out of your suits now!"

"We are sharing body heat with Jassalin?" Kidahin sang.

"This is the quickest way to raise her core temperature. Hurry," Mimiran sang.

Kidahin, Merkrida, Tialdrin, and Kyralin stripped their suits and thermal liners. Wearing only their traditional and skimpy neckwear and waistwear, they gathered around the prone Jassalin.

Kidahin and Merkrida lifted Jassalin and pressed her between their bodies and wrapped tails around both her and each other. Kyralin and Tialdrin then wedged themselves into the group and wrapped their tails around Kidahin and Merkrida. Mimiran stepped aside and read from a diagnostic scanner.

"It smells odd in here," Kyralin complained.

Tialdrin snapped her ears wide and locked eyes with Merkrida. "Health Center!" they trilled at the same time.

"Delwyn would say 'jinx' if he heard you," Kyralin sang.

"Why?" Mimiran trilled, curious. "Is jinx the human word for two people yelling the same thing? And what do you mean about Health Center? The air smells stale and has a hint of atomized oil and mild detergent in it."

"Exactly!" Merkrida and Tialdrin sang.

Mimiran glanced up from her scanner. "Another jinx?" she sang. She paused to consider their scents. "No, this air smelled nothing like Health Center."

"It does. We should know. Tialdrin and I were there for hours," Merkrida sang.

"I am the resident surgeon-in-battle," Mimiran trilled heatedly. "I work there all the time, and Health Center does not smell! I am also the Mistress of Inner Strength, and I have several counseling abodes in the Health Center elleiu tree complex. My abodes do not smell!"

"To you because you are always there," Kyralin retorted. "Working there has given you a dead nose!"

"You never learn, do you Kyralin," Tialdrin sang.

"That Warriors are not funny? I know this and have known it for some time," Kyralin sang indifferently.

"You should thank the spirits that I am busy with Jassalin right now, Kyralin," Mimiran trilled softly, almost sweetly. "I do not claim a social debt for your insult, but I will settle with you later."

"Enough," Kidahin sang. "How is Jassalin now?"

"Warming up. She should regain consciousness soon. While we wait, tell me how we are getting her to the SIV," Mimiran sang.

"Put her back in her suit and get her in the SIV swiftly. Turn her oxygen tap temperature up so the circulating air can keep her warm while we return to our warship."

Mimiran flicked her ears back and down against her tight, short ringlets. "Warm air is no substitute for suit heaters."

"Kidahin? Zalzadrin," the Mistress of Arms sang over the commlink.

"Yes, Mistress?" Kidahin replied.

"How is Jassalin?"

"Waking up, Mistress," Kidahin sang.

"Status of demolitions?"

"Aplilin can detonate at any time," Kidahin trilled.

"Get everyone into the SIV now. We are ten minutes out," Zalzadrin trilled.

"Ten minutes out?" Kidahin keened, fearing the worst.

"Yes," Zalzadrin sang happily. "I am piloting a troop transport and Nynava is copiloting."

"And Delwyn?" Kidahin trilled, holding her breath.

"He is busy and safe."

"Thank the spirits!" Kidahin sang.

"Thank the spirits for what?" a groggy Jassalin murmured discordantly.

"Jassalin! Are you feeling better?" Kidahin trilled.

"I am bruised, sore, and cold. Thank the spirits for what?" Jassalin pressed.

"Zalzadrin and Nynava are coming in a troop transport, and Delwyn did not insist on coming or sneak aboard somehow," Kidahin sang.

"Oh," Jassalin murmured.

"You are disappointed. Why?" Kidahin sang.

"Mating, it is all I think about. I cannot get Delwyn out of my head," Jassalin trilled.

"That is normal," Mimiran reassured her. "It is survival instinct. We all feel the drive to mate, but near-death experiences amplify that instinct and fortify the body. How are you feeling, besides the mating urge?"

"Cold, and I am hungry, ravenous in fact."

Mimiran wiggled out of her combat EVA suit and perked her ears at Jassalin. "Good. Eat this. It is high in calories and carbohydrates. It will induce a mild fever. You will be fine in an hour or so. Oh, Kyralin?"

"What?" Kyralin trilled at insolence pitch as the Warrior surgeon-in-battle smashed a fist into her jaw.

Everyone but Jassalin circled the two combatants.

"What did I miss?" Jassalin trilled in puzzlement.

"Kyralin called Mimiran a dead-nose and said Health Center smells like it does here," Tialdrin sang wickedly.

Jassalin watched a willowy and nimble, rhythmic Kyralin circle the heavier and stronger Mimiran. Kyralin leapt, but Mimiran slapped her to the deck.

"Well, Kyralin does have a point about the smell," Jassalin admitted.

"Do you want some of this, too, Jassalin?" Mimiran trilled, twisting her tail, balance-checking. "Come on, Kyralin, face me and admit defeat."

"Never!" Kyralin keened. "The smells in Health Center make my skin creep. How can you not admit it?" she sang as she tumbled into Mimiran's legs, dropping her to the deck.

"Health Center smells like any healing center. It is clean because antiseptics and medications are in constant use. The air is scrubbed by antiviral and antibiotic fields. Ultraviolet light, negative ion fields, and ozone discharges pull contaminants from the air," Mimiran trilled.

"And what contaminants are those?" Kyralin trilled as she chopped the Warrior's muscular neck with a closed fist.

"Dust, odors, biohazards...you know this, Kyralin!" Mimiran sang as she landed a heavy punch to the slender, lean Hunter's solar plexus.

The punch drove the air from Kyralin's lungs. She held up her hands in a sign to wait and not to surrender.

"No...no...odor Mimiran," Kyralin gasped. "What does no odor smell like?"

Mimiran paused, a quizzical look covering her face.

"Well, like nothing, except maybe the wet-metal smell of ozone and... Oh! I concede your point. It does smell something like this here. It smells like bottled air. But that does not mean I have a dead nose!"

"I did not mean it in quite that way," Kyralin sang.

Mimiran paused and considered Kyralin's scent. Kyralin meant it.

"I yield," Mimiran sang.

"As do I," Kyralin trilled.

"Are you two finished?" Kidahin trilled. "Zalzadrin wanted us in the SIV by now. Jassalin, I am sorry but you have to put your suit back on. It will be cold, but you will not freeze by the time we land in the troop transport hold."

Jassalin twitched her ears in acceptance but glared at her combat EVA suit in distaste.

Kidahin twitched her ears, smiled, and turned to Aplilin.

"You should wait until we are in the transport before detonating your charges."

"I agree, my Kidahin. I do not want to stress this ship more than necessary while we are still aboard him."

"My knee and elbow joints do not work," Jassalin complained.

"Be happy I fixed the seals," Aplilin growled. "Kyralin is the smallest, so she will help you through the spiral stairwell. Once we leave this deck, we will be in zero-gee. Be patient and remember the stairwell is stress-deformed. Do not panic and get stuck."

"Everyone, recall back to the hull breach," Kidahin trilled.

Team-Two withdrew, and Kidahin shuddered at the vivid memories of mass dead males smeared into frozen pulp on the intervening corridors between broadway and the breach.

"Mistress Zalzadrin? Why is Delwyn not singing to us?" she trilled.

"He is not in the command center," Zalzadrin sang off-key.

Kidahin flipped her ears back against her head and frowned. Zalzadrin was the premiere sarcastic joker, and the casual seriousness of her remark set Kidahin's doubts to keening.

"So? The combat address system tracks his path throughout our warship. He can sing from anywhere, even from the necessary, and be heard. He is not with you, is he?" Kidahin demanded.

"No," the Hunter Mistress of Arms sang, again at a subtle off-key tone hinting at trouble.

"What happened? You told us he was safe! Nynava?" Kidahin demanded.

"Phelindra and Melkorka tried to keep him occupied in the command center, but you know how he is. His weak nose should not have given him a warning. How he smells out the most obscure things, yet the most obvious scents evade him is annoying."

"What did he do?" Kidahin growled.

"He and Lo'sutra'est anni left the command center together while Phelindra was briefing warleader special security. Ten minutes later, Phelindra froze, snapped her tail so hard she knocked the Huntmistress off the Warleader's Watch, and ran out of the command center," Nynava sang.

"And?" Kidahin growled.

"By the time Phelindra reached the combat staging and deployment bay Delwyn was already in a stealth insertion vehicle and had finished the prelaunch checklist. She jumped into a hovertank and rammed the SIV to stop him from launching."

"And where was the bay mistress the whole time?" Kidahin keened.

"Lo'sutra'est anni told everyone to leave!" Nynava trilled.

"How can that be? Comara females choose the males they feel need their protection and watch them their entire long lives. What was Lo'sutra'est anni thinking?" Kidahin keened, aghast.

"Lo'sutra'est anni is spitting-furious with Phelindra. Melkorka told us about it while we were approaching the Coalition shipwreck. I think Delwyn was trying to intercept us. After all, a transport hold can carry two SIVs, barely," Nynava sang.

"But why did Lo'sutra'est anni help put him in danger?" Kidahin demanded.

"She made it clear through her pheromones that Delwyn was more than up to the task. She told him that leaving our warship without defenders was discourteous. She also told him we needed him..."

Aplilin suddenly trilled a laugh that swamped Nynava's voice. She laughed while Team-Two picked their way over and around crushed male bodies and into the between-hulls deck.

Mimiran, her anger rising again, finally had enough. "You think this is funny?" the surgeon-in-battle keened with pent-up Warrior rage. "Our Warleader must never take unnecessary risks. Mistress Nynava, where is he now?"

"In the recreation center with Lo'sutra'est anni and all warleader special security. The blast doors are engaged, which means open trails and pathways now resemble impassable undergrowth."

"I wonder how long it takes him to realize he is in protective custody?" Kidahin sang over Aplilin's renewed trilling.

"Not long," Nynava growled. "He always figures things out. When he realizes he is detained there and makes an issue of it, they will reopen the trails and pathways. Custom and male autonomy demand it."

"Then what?" Mimiran trilled in fury.

Kidahin stepped onto the Coalition warship's outer hull plates and eyed the thruster-firing SIV warily. "He will figure it out before we return."

"About that," Zalzadrin sang at a much lighter and more humorous melody. "After we recover the SIV and your team, we will maneuver beyond the hypercube anomalies and make an FTL jump to maximum surveillance orbit around the moon. From there, you will deploy to the surface in the SIV while we remain in orbit."

Out of breath from laughter, Aplilin gasped. "Do I still detonate my charges?"

"Oh, yes," Nynava sang. "We detonate, take a few scans, confirm mission status with Melkorka, and off we go. That means if you clear Jassalin for duty you will come along with us, Mimiran."

"I am not sure I want to," Mimiran trilled. "Some of these Hunters are too careless with male safety for my comfort."

"We can leave you here, you know," Kidahin trilled in a deadly tone.

"She is just angry because I am laughing," Aplilin interrupted. "Kyralin is right about Warriors not being funny. Think about it, Mimiran," Aplilin sang with uncommon matter-of-fact patience. "Delwyn cannot be alone now, and you know why," she trilled pointedly.

Mimiran stumbled into the SIV hatch scowling and her anger simmering. "You heard Nynava. Spirits, but you are dense. Once he figures it out, he will follow us when he should remain right where I can find him. The drive to mate with him is overwhelming."

Aplilin tapped Mimiran on the helmet and glared into her eyes.

"And?" she trilled.

"And? And what? What do you mean?" Mimiran trilled at interrogative pitch as she strapped herself into a seat. She plugged a life support umbilical into a teeth-chattering Jassalin's damaged suit before plugging in her own umbilical as well.

"Mating season is upon us. The urge to mate has increased over the past hour or so. You felt it, too," Aplilin growled.

"Mimiran is too old to have mating urges," Kyralin trilled at insolence pitch.

Mimiran secured Jassalin in her seat, turned, and jumped Kyralin.

Tialdrin twisted into Mimiran's path and grappled her while Merkrida shoved her onto the aisle.

"Pitching up," Kidahin sang. "We are thirty ells from the ship and pulling further away. I have the transport in sight." Kidahin paused, hearing scuffling. "What is happening back there?"

"Nothing," Hollfara sang. "Mimiran finds the construction of the aisle interesting."

Kidahin sighed. Mimiran was older than any Team-Two Huntress, much older. Phelindra was called the Eldest Huntress because she was the oldest Hunter female aboard their warship. Zalzadrin was the next oldest, but Mimiran was an early middle-aged Warrior. She had more social, hierarchical, and military rank than anyone aboard the SIV. Kidahin respected Mimiran. That she was a surgeon did not take away from her superior military rank. And, as Mistress of Inner Strength, she held the social supervisory rank of Mistress. Speaking from the point of view of an Eyloni female's deference to male-given military rank, Mimiran had consented to the command of an inferior military-ranked assaultmistress Kidahin. It was Mimiran's social rank of Mistress that gave her a high status within the society of their warship, one on par with Melkorka, Phelindra, and the other supervising mistresses.

"Mistress Zalzadrin? The SIV is in position," Kidahin sang over the commlink.

"I am purging atmosphere and opening the hold hatch. You may proceed, Kidahin."

"Affirm. Thrusting forward. We are in the hold," Kidahin sang.

"Do not hit the hold bulkhead," Nynava trilled. "What is all the grunting and trilling I hear?"

"Mimiran is checking team members," Kidahin sang evasively.

"Oh?" Nynava grunted. "Hold hatch closed. Repressurizing. Mimiran, get Jassalin out of that suit."

"Affirm," Mimiran sang. She released Jassalin's seat restraints and popped the life support umbilical, lifted her and carried her through the open SIV hatch and laid her on the hold deck.

"The healer suite is on the forward bulkhead," Kyralin sang.

"I know where it is!" Mimiran hissed.

"Stop leafchasing," Nynava keened. "Kidahin, we are at a safe distance. Commence demolitions."

"Affirm. Aplilin, do it."

"Affirm, blasting now," Aplilin sang.

"Mistress Melkorka? We have blasted the hyperdrive coil power feeds," Nynava reported via commlink.

"Wait, Nynava," Melkorka sang. "Hlinlodyn is scanning. All but two are offline. The emissions have subsided, but as Anailiatha feared the hypercube manifestation remains. We are still not free to navigate. Continue your mission as briefed."

"Affirm," Nynava sang.

"Well? Now what?" Kidahin trilled.

"We fly clear of the hypercube emissions using the orbital maneuvering thrusters at very slow sublight velocity until we can FTL jump to a surveillance orbit around the moon," Nynava sang.

# 6
## THE POWER OF NAMES, SHARED SLEEP, THE LOSS OF INSTINCT...

"Nynava, why are you flying back to *Hunter's Moon?*" Mimiran trilled.

"The hypercube overlays *Londiwe Khoza.* Kidahin can pilot an SIV right up to him with little difficulty. The transport's mass, however, makes him harder to pilot through the gravitational anomalies. So we must backtrail first," Nynava sang.

"How close to our warship will we pass?" Mimiran trilled.

"Why? Do you want to return to your duties in Health Center?"

"No," Mimiran sang promptly while giving her patient a critical look. "Are you sure you want to continue on, Jassalin? It is no dishonor to withdraw from a mission for health reasons."

"I am fine," Jassalin trilled, shivering.

"You did certify her combat-ready," Kidahin sang.

"Jassalin is physically capable," Mimiran allowed.

"And?" Kidahin persisted.

"And what? She is recovering from severe exposure to cold. Thank the spirits there was no frostbite."

"We are now in translation range of our warship," Zalzadrin sang. "Are you sure you do not want to return to your Health Center treatment abodes, Mimiran?"

"I will stay," Mimiran avowed. "I told you that l find this flying around stimulating."

"Of course you do," Zalzadrin growled. "Anybody else? No? Really? No one wants to go back and stalk Delwyn?"

Nynava stretched in the copilot seat and groaned. Hunter humor tended toward the sarcastic and insulting, but Zalzadrin sometimes took humor to dangerous extremes.

"About Delwyn," Nynava trilled, "let us find out what he is up to."

Nynava opened the hailing channel and sang formally, "Mistress Melkorka, Nynava. We are pursuing our exit loop away from the *Khoza.* Do you have anything further for us?"

"I do," the Mistress of the Ship trilled. "Delwyn, Lo'sutra'est anni, and warleader special security are with the Mistress of Conveyance."

"He is not coming here!" Nynava objected.

"No, he is not, and not by his own choice, either. Akenallin flatly refused his demands to translate him, and them, into your transport."

"I cannot imagine Lo'sutra'est anni, Phelindra, or the Huntmistress even considering it," Kidahin trilled.

"Apparently they knew something he did not. I should have known better myself when Phelindra did not so much as twitch an ear. Anailiatha, Hlinlodyn, and Akenallin are in deep discussions with them now. Do you remember what happened to the navigation sweeps when you tried to scan the moon?"

"What scans?" Kidahin sang innocently.

"The scans Aplilin asked you to take while you were still in auxiliary command center," Nynava interrupted.

"Oh, those scans. I could not get a reliable scan. The FTL scan would not settle down into a stable frame. The aperture jumped around so much I could not get a clear sweep of the gas giant, let alone its moon," Kidahin trilled in disgust.

"And what technology is FTL scanning reliant upon?" Nynava trilled.

"FTL scanners are jump drive derivative technology. So?" Kidahin trilled.

"And translation conveyance technology is based on what?" Melkorka pressed.

"Conveyance translation is quantum teleportation. It is, yet is not, similar to a scaled-down jump drive. Again, so?"

"Think about it, Kidahin," Anailiatha interrupted over the commlink. "The hypercube is essentially a box with edges focusing rays of hypergravity. The hypergravity destabilizes the quantum singularity our jump drive creates to jump the ship. It causes the FTL scan singularity to oscillate, and that gave you scan returns resembling a camera held in shaking hands. The translation singularity also vibrates around its lock-on point. Akenallin, not known for her subtlety, demonstrated her reasons for refusing Delwyn by translating a combat harness from one side of the translation abode to the other side. It arrived several tens of ells outside of the translation abode and not in its original form, either. It was elongated and twisted, as though it had been pulled and twisted into one of Delwyn's mobius bands."

"Well. He is brave. He is fearless, but he is not stupid. Why then is he still with the Mistress of Conveyance?" Kidahin demanded.

"The elongated twist in the combat harness has him by the tail, so to speak. He cannot leave it alone. He had Akenallin translate several items, all with similar results. His compulsive interest in the phenomenon piqued hers, and now they have Hlinlodyn with them. They see something, a pattern. They brought it to my attention, and I see it, too," Anailiatha growled.

"What does it mean?" Nynava trilled.

"I do not know. All these loops and looping... I feel it stalks the trail beside me, but I cannot point my tail at why I have this did-it-before feeling," Anailiatha growled.

Kidahin frowned, distracted by a memory. When Delwyn was taking his adulthood survival ordeal, she had goaded Lo'sutra'est anni into tracking him. Before she sought out the Comari female, she consulted her Oyya Web, what Delwyn called her *we-ge* board. It was a circular multiwebbed image of the Oyya Web of the spirits. It resembled a two-palm wide military rank earring.

"You know," Kidahin trilled softly, "it is a shame the mobius twist is not an Oyya Web. You could ask it a question and trace the twisting threads through the webs until you reach the advice carved on the rim..."

"Spirits!" Anailiatha trilled, "that gives me an idea!"

"What? What did I say?" Kidahin sang.

"I do not know," Melkorka admitted. "Maybe you have that Delwyn guessing knack Anailiatha always complains about."

"Delwyn is not stupid!" Kidahin trilled.

"Did I say he was?" Melkorka demanded, suddenly furious. "He is resourceful and intuitive, and his intuition crosses many disciplines. He is trained in elite combat. That he can empathize with Anailiatha's occupational specialty both pleases and infuriates her."

"It appears you are stuck with us, Mistress Mimiran," Kyralin hummed.

Mimiran whirled on Kyralin. "This pleases you?" she sang.

Kyralin met the Warrior's eyes and nodded.

Mimiran cocked her ears, posturing interest. The Hunter's use of the social rank was far from insulting. Mimiran opened her mind to the scents surrounding her. Her primal and social empathy interpreted the pheromonal emotional chatter rising from Kyralin's body.

"You wish to talk?" Mimiran sang formally.

"Yes, Mistress."

"Then we shall talk," Mimiran promised.

"Nynava? Trebithia," the Mistress of Pathwalking sang over the commlink.

"Yes, Trebithia?"

"I have revised maneuvering plots for your navigation solutions. I am uploading them into your navigational systems now."

"Affirm, course changes received. Implementing navigation updates. Spirits, Trebithia! These changes add hours of normal space flight time. Can we not jump to the moon now?" Nynava keened.

"No. Hlinlodyn just received a tactical maneuvering update warning from Anailiatha. Blame her, not me," Trebithia trilled.

"Do not blame me," Hlinlodyn trilled. "Anailiatha thinks it too risky to jump the transport this close to the hypercube."

"Everyone might as well get comfortable. We have to spiral out and away from *Londiwe Khoza*. At least the transport flight deck and cabin are pressurized, unlike the SIV. Stow your combat EVA suits and equipment in the bulkhead lockers. If you are hungry, use the nutrition niche. If you are not eating, recline in your harnesses and get some sleep," Zalzadrin sang.

Mimiran glided to Kidahin's side. "We are not deployed for the time being," she sang. "I am resuming my place, as befits my military rank and social standing, as Mistress of Inner Strength. Do you consent?" Mimiran trilled formally.

"Of course, Mistress," Kidahin sang. The surgeon-in-battle volunteered to serve under Kidahin's leadership as a precaution if they suffered casualties or found human casualties. Delwyn had likened her role to a 'corpsman', which his scent told her was a healer embedded within a combat unit. When Team-Two reached the moon's surface, Mimiran would again consent to Kidahin's leadership.

Mimiran curled her tail behind her. Its pons, the deep-red ringlet-covered tail tip, twitched mischievously as she glided back into the briefing abode in the hold bulkhead opposite the locker and equipment storage area.

"Kyralin, come with me," Mimiran sang over her shoulder.

"Yes, Mistress."

"With your high empathy rating and social connectivity skills, you could be a mistress of inner strength candidate. You know this, do you not?" Mimiran sang softly.

"I am better suited to security prowling, Mistress," Kyralin sang.

"Why? You exercise self-control, and you use it well when listening to others. You are insightful and clever, confident, and tolerant of others. You have an almost-Warrior sense of humor, but your humor exposes your primary weakness. Do you know what that is?"

"I take honor issues seriously," Kyralin sang.

"No. Your primary strength lies in an impeccable character. Your weakness is the indifference you display for some honor point priorities. You think everything you do is tail-tied to male safety, and you flout honor issues you see as getting in the way of preserving male life. You know this behavior irritates others who rank you?"

"Like you, you mean?" Kyralin trilled.

"Oh, are you being clever and witty now? As I said, you have a Warrior sense of humor, which I can appreciate. Your social self-assurance and tolerant patience is, I think, a strength coming from your moral certitude. Do you know why warleader special security is interested in you?"

Taken aback, Kyralin flicked her ears indifferently. "What makes you think they want me?"

"Phelindra asked if I had reservations considering the Huntmistress's high standards. Do you know why she is interested in you?" Mimiran persisted.

"I am young and retain the juvenile drive to protect males, and my moral views make me qualified to protect our Warleader."

"No, they do not," Mimiran sang. "Any juvenile Hunter having high moral character possesses such traits. What else? And Kyralin, stop masking your pheromones. I cannot guide you when you hide your emotional sendings. Spirits, you mask your scent like a Comari. You still have no idea what has Phelindra so interested in you?"

"No, Mistress."

"Phelindra likes your social cognition. You approach social world mannerisms from a devious and indirect demeanor. It lets you stretch the truth and dissemble well. I smell that your honor prevents you from telling a direct lie, but I am sure you do not correct misunderstanding of intentional misstatements or misrepresentations.

"Your scent tells me you are a proactive planner, are methodical, and are a sly manipulator. You backtrail and loop, always laying layers of false trails in your physical stalking, in your thoughts, and in your actions. These are valuable traits for a warleader special security Huntress. All warleader special security Huntresses are indirect and sneaky. They are also reluctant to share and tend to evade scrutiny."

"Then I should do well as a warleader special security Huntress," Kyralin sang staccato.

"I know why you bait Warrior females," Mimiran sang abruptly. "Do you want to talk about it?"

"No," Kyralin trilled.

"Why not?" Mimiran sang softly.

"What I did in the past is in the past."

"Have you shared your feelings with Tialdrin?"

"No. Tialdrin and I discuss moral issues, but we do not agree on much. Even in moral matters, Tialdrin is too analytical for me to follow."

"Not just you," Mimiran trilled to an exasperated sigh. "Do you know what her societies and the Ok'e'say hierarchy thought of her theorizing?"

"I do, but she does not talk about it much," Kyralin trilled in dismissal.

"You formed strong relationships with Alfara, Hollfara, Aplilin, Kidahin, Jassalin, and Merkrida. You are least like Tialdrin, Seliaha, and Einstika. You are strongly attracted to Alfara, yet you prowl most often with Tialdrin. Why?"

"Tialdrin and I are both assaultstalkers. Our shared skill sets and duties often pair us together."

"Alfara is Team-Two society's Gracious Mistress of the Singing People. Have you spoken to her in her role as ritual leader?"

"No."

"Why not?" Mimiran crooned.

"Alfara is brutally honest. It makes her hard to open up to," Kyralin admitted.

"So let us return to the subject of Warrior females. I consulted with Mistress of Saga Mirrahindrallin before I consented to join this mission. Not only does she know the history of our warship, but she knows the personal histories of every female in the Society of *Hunter's Moon* as well."

"What of it?" Kyralin keened.

Mimiran wrapped her tail around Kyralin's waist and waited patiently.

"I did not mean to kill her," Kyralin finally keened.

"Of course you did not. You did not know Svavaka approached family territory from the direction she did. Your duty was to patrol home territory and repel trespassers. Svavaka was part of your extended family and a Warrior female. Your immediate and your extended families called the death an accident and tied the blame to Svavaka's tail because she approached your position without identifying herself. Uahua'asee'a Clan agreed. Your social debt was forgiven."

"It should not have," Kyralin keened. "I killed my family member, who was also my best friend."

"And now you bait Warriors into anger so they can punish you? Is that what you would have me do? Beat you senseless?"

Kyralin flicked her ears, a shrug.

"Is this why you are pressing so hard to gain Phelindra's attention? Are you prowling with Tialdrin just to take point positions? Are you hoping to get yourself killed?" Mimiran sang gently.

"What? *No!* I have to prowl ahead, identify the enemy and make sure I, we, do not fire on our own teammates."

"We will talk several times over the next few days. I want you to think about self-confidence and what it means to you. For now, I know a song. I want to teach it to you. It will be our song, one we will not share with others. Do you agree?"

"Yes, Mistress," Kyralin sighed musically.

Mimiran entwined her tail with Kyralin's and sang softly, an attentive Kyralin following the notes intently.

Several minutes later Mimiran watched Kyralin glide out of the briefing abode. She sighed, satisfied. She stood and followed Kyralin down the aisle to the forward bulkhead and stepped onto the flight deck.

Zalzadrin glanced up and snapped her tail at the cockpit canopy. "See anything?" she trilled.

Mimiran frowned. "No. Should I?"

"White stars on a black field, maybe?" Zalzadrin goaded.

"Is that supposed to be funny?" Mimiran trilled. She glanced across the cockpit at Nynava. "It must be like a survival ordeal for you, this putting up with Hunter humor."

"Not really," Nynava confessed. "Zalzadrin is my very own personal entertainment."

"I offer insight with a tail-snap of style," Zalzadrin trilled melodiously.

Mimiran shifted her feet and focused her piercing amber gaze onto the horrible black scar running from the middle-aged Hunter's ample left breast to just above her left hip. Puncture marks where Delwyn stapled the wound closed ran down both sides of the scar a fingernail-length apart. The hideous thing marred Zalzadrin's otherwise beautiful orange, red, and yellow-patterned skin.

"You can have the scar tissue removed and regenerated, you know," the surgeon-in-battle sang.

"I won it defending Delwyn," Zalzadrin trilled in challenge.

Mimiran flicked her ears in dismissal but remained silent.

"Did you come here to offer me a cosmetic consultation, or are you bored?" Zalzadrin trilled at the tall Warrior healer.

"Delwyn thinks you have a short-stature complex. What do you think about that, Zalzadrin?"

Busy gauging Zalzadrin's emotional reaction, Mimiran did not see Nynava flatten her ears and mouth *no*.

"Delwyn loves me best," Zalzadrin trilled at declarative tempo.

"Why? Because you are such a tiny little Hunter female?"

Zalzadrin gripped the pilot seat armrests so tight her knuckles turned pale orange. She twisted her tail around the seat, pulled herself into its contoured embrace, and glared forward.

Mimiran knew perfectly well no male loved one female absolutely more than another female. Females had favorite males, just as Delwyn was her favorite male. A male preferred the females in his personal or occupational associations over females outside of those associations. But a male never preferred Warriors over Hunters or Hunters over Warriors, and he absolutely never preferred one female over another within his own associations.

"I am pleased to see you have finally gotten your tail wrapped around your snotty anger issues," Mimiran sang.

"Whatever," Zalzadrin trilled. "Are you looking for something to do?"

"Me? Spirits, no. I am enjoying myself. It has been some time since I prowled in the field," Mimiran sang. She paused to scowl at the cockpit canopy. "No rubble? We have flown clear of the dust ring?"

"We are behind and above it," Nynava sang. "I am backtrailing and looping us around the gravitational extrusions emitting from the hypercube."

"Oh. There is no sense of excitement without the rubble flying by," Mimiran trilled in complaint. She turned, wrapped a friendly tail around Zalzadrin, caressed Nynava with her pons, and left.

"Finally," Zalzadrin growled.

"At least you did not bite her tail off for being head and shoulders taller than you," Nynava sang.

"Whatever," Zalzadrin growled.

Mimiran stepped through the forward bulkhead hatch and looked down the aisle, making casual eye contact with the Hunters seated there.

She drifted down the aisle and stopped when she reached Seliaha. "Come with me," Mimiran sang.

"Yes, Mistress. Have I done something wrong?" Seliaha trilled.

"Of course not," Mimiran sang reassuringly. "Tell me about Team-Two."

"What do you want to know?" Seliaha sang.

"Oh, just how well you are fitting in."

"I like Alfara, Hollfara, and Einstika. We twine tails and talk a lot. Well, they talk and I just listen. Hollfara is really smart. I can keep up with some of the things she talks about more than the others."

"That is because you are very knowledgeable and intuitive. You are thirteen years old, only a few months older than Kidahin. How does that make you feel?"

"I like Kidahin, but she acts much older than me. She has done so much already. She was our warship's huluhar. She chose Delwyn, for all of us, as Warleader. She is already an assaultmistress," Seliaha trilled.

"Kidahin chose Delwyn for our consideration. Remember Mirrahindrallin's lessons? Our society chooses by major consensus, unanimous consent, our Warleader. Had you joined us before Delwyn came to us, then you would have had a voice in our choice."

"I know that, Mistress."

"Your best quality is the respect you give those who rank you. I doubt anyone would ever consider claiming an honor point or a social debt against you. But while healthy respect is one thing, deferring to authority at times can cripple. Do you know why?"

"It helps me cope with others when I let them have their way," Seliaha dodged.

"You did not answer my question. Tell me, are you envious of people who are more socially skilled than yourself?"

"Fitting in is hard, Mistress," Seliaha sang. "It is just easier to follow the group."

"Which is why your nonverbal social reactions give people a sense of befuddlement. Delwyn calls this a *goof-ball* affect. Your social influence radiates feelings of hesitancy, uncertainty, and an inability to commit. Yet your social concern comes through on your pheromones, and I know you care about the welfare of others."

"I give everything I have to those in need," Seliaha sang simply.

"Yes, your social presentation is one of deferential generosity. You are the opposite of Alfara, who hoards items."

"Alfara gives from her hoard to anyone in need," Seliaha objected.

"Good, Seliaha. You just demonstrated social empathy. You capably relate to people's thoughts, feelings, and intentions. What I want to discuss now has more to do with your social cognition. You crave, want, long for, and desire belonging in the social world."

"I am doing better, Mistress. You said as much during our last session."

"Your progress is pleasing," Mimiran sang. "As I told you then, I tell you now. You are a Team-Two assaultstalker, but you were apprenticing with your clan's polar research fleet. Kidahin recommended you for warship duty, and you accepted. That in itself is a bold statement."

"Not really," Seliaha sang. "The opportunity crossed the trail, and I snatched it."

"Tell me, was serving in the Uahua'asee'a Clan polar navy dangerous?"

"Absolutely!" Seliaha trilled.

"It must have made you feel like you were reliving your adulthood survival ordeal," Mimiran sang at insistence tempo.

"Why do you say that?" Seliaha trilled.

"You nearly died from exposure during your adulthood ordeal. The ordeal took place in Uahua'asee'a Clan territory, in the northern polar reaches beyond even the sub-polar rainforests."

"I remember," Seliaha trilled flatly. "I survived by the spirits' own luck and not through any special action I took."

"You question your actions, so you think it better to follow others? Did you happen to hear me harassing Zalzadrin?"

"No, Mistress," Seliaha sang.

"Zalzadrin hates flying, and yet she learned to pilot atmospheric aircraft and troop transports. Do you know why?"

"Kidahin told me that Delwyn expressed an interest in flying on one of La'huaset's lighter-than-air supply ships. Zalzadrin got her pilot certification because he enjoys flying," Seliaha sang.

"Delwyn may have given Zalzadrin the motivation, but her complaint about flying itself has nothing to do with him. Zalzadrin sees an aircraft as a falling leaf held aloft by chance air currents," Mimiran trilled.

"So? We Hunters fight over the high ground. We love climbing trees and high terrain to their highest and most dangerous heights, but we do not like losing contact with some anchor to the ground."

"Yes. We Warriors prefer prowling on low ground, yet we enjoy flying more than you Hunters do. Zalzadrin's complaint is a perceived loss of control, because her fate is tail-tied to a pilot's skill."

"I am not a pilot, so what does Zalzadrin have to do with me?"

"You tend to rely on others so you do not have to trust in your own actions. You succeeded during your survival ordeal. You are worthy of success. Delwyn relies on you."

"Delwyn relies on me? How?" Seliaha trilled plaintively.

"You are a knowledgeable and intuitive naval strategist. You are extremely proactive. And you are risk-averse. Delwyn calls upon you to offer sound tactical and strategic advice when you have it and not sit on your tail and defer to others. I want you to think about this."

"Yes, Mistress."

Mimiran looped her tail snugly around Seliaha's waist. "Good. Now, tell me about Aplilin."

"We paired up when Delwyn declared Battle Status. She told me how a thumper could be used as a weapon against us. Oh, and she thinks Nynava knows more about our mission here than what she told Kidahin."

"What, specifically?" Mimiran trilled sharply.

"Aplilin implied that Nynava knew of some danger to Delwyn here, but she did not know what it was."

"A danger?" Mimiran keened, suddenly tense. "What about Delwyn?"

"Nothing, Mistress. Aplilin was feeling the mating urge. She wants him to see her fight."

"A natural enough reaction during mating season, but this idea about a danger to Delwyn..."

"It may be nothing, Mistress. Zalzadrin said the moon has hazardous terrain. Maybe Aplilin meant conditions on the ground," Seliaha offered.

"An environment hostile to Delwyn? Well, maybe," Mimiran mused aloud. "It may be nothing because Delwyn is not going there. What is your assessment of the human warship?"

"The color codes confused me. They were backwards."

"You went looking for the shuttle deployment bay and any survivors."

"Along with Aplilin, yes," Seliaha trilled in agreement.

"Team-Two did well by giving you the ritual title the 'Stalking One'."

"Mistress?"

"You care for your teammates because you are one with them. You also show independence and commitment. I recommend you spend more time with Aplilin."

"But Mistress, Aplilin and I share no personality traits," Seliaha keened.

"Except those traits normal in Hunter females," Mimiran trilled. "Think about Aplilin when you feel uncertain."

"Yes, Mistress."

"Good. Now, send Hollfara to me."

"Yes, Mistress," Seliaha sang.

Mimiran stood and walked to the flight deck, made a brief comment to Nynava in battle language, tickled Zalzadrin under the chin with her pons, and returned to the briefing abode to find a sullen Hollfara waiting.

"I do not need to talk to you," Hollfara trilled.

"You think not?" Mimiran trilled at insolence tempo. "Your attitude is uncharacteristic for one having such a forgiving nature. Forgiveness is your strength but also your weakness. You obsess over forgiving others."

"Forgiveness does not require a cheery disposition," Hollfara snapped.

"You are correct, and your social attunement is so poor even Delwyn can smell it."

"What is that supposed to mean?" Hollfara keened.

"You are like Seliaha. You both want social involvement. She interacts with others by following their lead, but you compensate by talking down to them."

"I do not talk down to anybody. I tell everyone what I know to be right," Hollfara keened.

"You lecture, you mean. You are one of the brightest Hunters on the La'huaset Tribal continent. You could teach at Uahua'asee'a Clan learning center if you wanted to. Academic honors would follow you everywhere. Why are you an assault team Hunter?"

"I find academic life dry and boring," Hollfara sang at insistence tempo.

"And you find being one of Anailiatha's spaceframe damage control techmistresses exciting? Or is it the lure of being a Team-Two assaultstalker that quickens your heart?" Mimiran sang at interrogative tempo.

Hollfara twitched her ears, a shrugging gesture.

"You do not gossip. In fact, you keep secrets better than anyone I ever met. Assault Team-Two gave you the ritual title 'the One Who Knows' because of your vast learned knowledge and the emotional information you know about your teammates. Do they know you were once a hull quality-control techmistress for the Uahua'asee'a Clan wet navy shipyard?"

"No!" Hollfara keened.

"Nobody is perfect, Hollfara. The Uahua'asee'a engineering peer review found the defect in the hull you passed inspection one your equipment could not detect."

"Everyone aboard that icebreaker died in the frigid farside polar ocean," Hollfara trilled at declaratory tempo.

"Well... Even the icebreaker's warleader died. This was never your fault. Branches break, leaves fall, undergrowth snags the best-placed foot. You cannot exhaustively plan contingency measures for the unknown."

Hollfara glared at Mimiran but said nothing.

"Anailiatha told me your assistance in helping her sound the ship was invaluable. She is considering asking Phelindra to transfer you into her engineering group."

"Really?" Hollfara trilled in shock.

"Indeed. She said your structural defect analysis was exceptional."

"My work was checked by Anailiatha and her senior techmistresses. Nothing I did put anyone in danger," Hollfara trilled.

"You gave excellent engineering analyses to Kidahin. They did have a bearing on our survival. And you did enjoy people listening to your explanations."

"I enjoyed making structural analyses of the human warship," Hollfara confessed. "His construction is primitive! Mechanical hatches? Really? I could have spent hours there..."

Mimiran sat as patient listener while Hollfara gave a passionate three-hour lecture on human engineering. When she finished, Mimiran smiled.

"What?" Hollfara demanded.

"Nothing important, but consider this. Obsession running rampant is the enemy. When you find yourself obsessing over a technicality, break free from it by meditating on Delwyn. He makes Anailiatha want to bite her own tail off."

"But, Mistress, Delwyn is impulsive..."

"Which is an excellent counter to obsession. I want you to think about it over the next few days. Can you do so?"

"Yes, Mistress, I suppose I can," Hollfara conceded.

Mimiran stood, invited Hollfara to stand as well, and wrapped her tail snugly around the Hunter's abdomen. She leaned into Hollfara and whispered, "I have Mirrahindrallin's logs concerning Delwyn's actions from the time Kidahin first met him until Melkorka declared him Warleader on my 'minder. I will download them to your 'minder. You will find them helpful."

"Thank you, Mistress."

Mimiran followed Hollfara from the briefing abode, stopped, and glanced up the aisle. A few Hunters were already asleep. She shrugged and wandered about the cabin for several minutes before stepping onto the flight deck.

She found Nynava asleep as well. Mimiran sat down in the cockpit side-seat, a sideways-mounted, swiveling seat used on the rare occasions when a third pilot sat as backup.

"What happened while I was away?" she asked Zalzadrin.

"No good news," the fiery-tempered, redheaded Hunter trilled. "We tried an FTL scan of the moon, and the scan aperture looked good, but computer modeling showed framing defects. I have to make another sweeping evasion before I can try to scan the moon again. Once I get a clean scan, I can FTL jump us there."

"How much longer, do you think?" Mimiran trilled.

"Another three hours, four at most," Zalzadrin keened.

Mimiran stood, stretched, and padded back down the aisle, noticing only one Hunter awake.

"Merkrida, come with me."

Merkrida looked up, nodded, and followed her into the briefing abode.

"How is your jaw?" Mimiran sang.

"It works great. Allohindra did a fine job. It is hard getting used to the regenerated teeth, though," Merkrida sang.

"They do not feel right against your upper teeth, do they."

"No," Merkrida complained. "They feel like they are misaligned or something."

"They are," Mimiran agreed. "Regenerated teeth are new, which means they grew into place without years of wear. You will have to watch your bite pressure for a few weeks."

"Umm," Merkrida grunted, scowling.

"Tialdrin landed quite a blow to shatter the entire lower left jaw."

"She did. She caught me off-guard," Merkrida sang.

"You forgive her?"

"There is nothing to forgive. Spirits, Mimiran, Tialdrin was defending Delwyn. I told Allohindra I would have done the same in Tialdrin's place."

"You did strike her first," Mimiran pointed out.

"Einstika and I struck her first. It was combat. It happens."

"Your greatest weakness is anger. Are you sure anger had nothing to do with going after Tialdrin?"

"No, it did not. Why?"

"You and Einstika both have anger issues."

"Einstika loses her temper whenever she gets frustrated. I lose mine when people do not reach a consensus on what action should be taken."

"Encouraging social consensus is your strongest trait, but I am more interested in your social concern rating," Mimiran sang.

"Mistress?"

"You are the most altruistic Hunter female I have met. Curiously enough, Einstika scores just below you. She is compassionate. She exudes sympathy and exemplifies kindness. Yet, you put the welfare of Team-Two before your own."

"Yes, Mistress, but I put the welfare of Delwyn before the welfare of Tialdrin," Merkrida pointed out.

"All females put the welfare of a male before their own by nature, but I take your point. To your knowledge at the time, Tialdrin was a danger to Delwyn."

"Correct, Mistress."

"You are an intuitive empath. Others see you as generous and personable. I notice you are a proactive, well-reasoned risk-taker. Your passive-aggression serves you well. You respect danger and make two or three back-up plans."

"Thank you, Mistress," Merkrida sang.

"You are also manners-conscious. You are using your pheromonal empathy to read my emotional state and adjust your mannerisms to those I respond best to. This instinct lets you project a mothering affect to others and help promote their emotional well-being."

"Sometimes they need a little love, Mistress."

"They may at that, and there are times when such emotional aid is helpful. But I warn you that playing with emotion to get your way is discourteous, especially when you call for a consensus not needed under the circumstances or when you influence others emotionally to arrive at a consensus decision you favor."

"I know, Mistress. I pull back when I sense the group is against my counsel," Merkrida sang.

"You have what Delwyn calls survivor guilt," Mimiran sang softly.

"I know," Merkrida trilled softly. "It was the spirits own luck that I reached an ice floe. Everyone aboard the icebreaker drowned or died from exposure. Nobody should be left behind to die in a shipwreck."

"Which is why you agreed to look for human survivors on the Coalition warship?"

"Yes!"

"And yet you wanted to sing for a consensus to save males, when you know all females have a moral imperative to save males? What were you thinking?"

"I thought searching for males should take precedence over Aplilin setting her demolition charges," Merkrida trilled.

"Safeguarding Delwyn and our warship must come first. No living human males remained for you to save in any event."

Merkrida glared at Mimiran but said nothing.

"You could not save them," Mimiran trilled gently. "They were long dead before we arrived in this system. Nothing can be done for them now."

"You are wrong," Merkrida trilled. "They must be sung to the spirits."

"The Death Song ritual? Delwyn is likely considering this as we speak," Mimiran trilled reassuringly.

The reference to Delwyn caused Merkrida to smile.

"What?" Mimiran sang softly, surprised at the sudden change in the Hunter's emotions.

"Delwyn's word for people saying the same thing at the same time."

"What about it?" Mimiran sang, curious. "We did not say the same word at the same time."

"I know, I know," Merkrida sang, frowning suddenly. "He calls the coincidence a *jinx*. He says when you hear two people saying the same thing at the same time, you should say this word."

"I wonder why," Mimiran murmured. "What is the point in drawing attention to a verbal coincidence?"

"He told us it was a joke making fun of the coincidental speech, but his scent associated a sinister taint to the word, a mild one but a taint nevertheless," Merkrida trilled.

"Signifying what, exactly?" Mimiran sang at interrogative tempo. The urge to learn more about their favorite male drawing her in.

"I smelled defense and protection, some kind of ward against bad luck in his scent."

"As if a verbal coincidence can summon the ill-luck of the spirits? Do you think he meant this?"

"I think he intended its use for when there is no expectation of the same word sung by two people at the same time," Merkrida trilled at a slow and droll tempo.

"And that is called giving attitude," Mimiran trilled. "Delwyn's word for giving attitude is 'smartass', but sometimes giving attitude has a point. Team-Two did well in giving you the ritual title the 'Mistress of the High Ground'."

"Thank you, Mistress Mimiran."

"You are welcome. I counsel you to always remember that you cannot save everyone, but save the ones you can save," Mimiran sang softly.

"Yes, Mistress. I will remember."

"Good. Send Aplilin to me, please."

"Affirm, Mistress," Merkrida sang.


"A'pea, Mimiran, what do you want? I have more important things to do than leafchase feelings down a blind trail with you," Aplilin sang at harsh staccato imperative tempo.

"Stop acting like an infant. At the rate Zalzadrin is piloting, you will have hours to prepare. Think of this as a boarding party debriefing," Mimiran suggested. "But first, tell me about your knee."

"My knee? Einstika gave it a good kick, but not bad enough to have a healer trill over it. Why? Do you want to look at it?" Aplilin sang suggestively, flexing her muscular leg in Mimiran's face.

Mimiran watched Aplilin extend the joint with both professional and personal interest. She narrowed her gaze at the faint black bruises surrounding the kneecap. Aplilin was a beautiful female. She was Hunter tall but built like a lean Warrior.

"You shoved Seliaha off a branch. The fall could have killed her," Mimiran sang.

"She was declared ni'zakhon by Zalzadrin and Nynava. I took the most appropriate action."

"You are extremely reactive, reckless, and a risk-taker."

"Thank you, Mimiran."

"Do not take that as a compliment."

"Why not? Seliaha holds no grudge. In fact, we teamed up when Delwyn called us to Battle Status."

"And yet you scared her by implying the stealth insertion vehicle was unsafe," Mimiran sang.

"He is! The SIV is like a brittle branch, and Seliaha should know this. She is tough. She got over her fear, which was my goal. It fortified her, made her strong when we were looking for the shuttles. I like her," Aplilin sang.

"And yet you yank her tail."

"I make a point in my own way. I pull her tail, I shove her, I scare her, and I yell at her. She will remember, she will always be aware, and she will be safe," Aplilin trilled.

"You crave valor. You are brave and selfless. Delwyn is so impressed with you that he calls you his 'G.I. Jane'."

"Which means what?" Aplilin trilled, interested in anything about Delwyn.

"From his scent I deduced he means an exceptional female combatant," Mimiran sang dryly.

"Really?" Aplilin sang, astonished pleasure filling her scent. "All females say males are strange, but I understand Delwyn better than any male I know. He goes off on his own without fear. He likes being alone for hours at a time."

"You are attracted to him," Mimiran sang flatly.

"I want to mate with him. Spirits, just the thought of mating makes my pons tingle."

"You want him all to yourself?" Mimiran keened in outrage.

"No, and calm down. What is wrong with you, anyway? I am sure Delwyn is mating with others aboard our warship right now."

"I understand. You want in his personal association. Have you made the proper overtures to him yet?"

"No," Aplilin admitted. "I am thinking about approaching Phelindra, but I want to discuss it with Kidahin first."

"Why? Because she was the first female to join in personal association with him?"

"No. Listen to me. I tell you no secret but keep my words in confidence anyway," Aplilin sang softly.

"Of course."

"Kidahin doubts she made the right choice when she turned down warleader special security in favor of being assaultmistress for Team-Two."

Mimiran twitched so violently she almost fell out of her seat. She glared at Aplilin in accusation.

"You think she is reconsidering her choice?"

"I think so," Aplilin admitted, "but her mind is unsettled. Her desire is to defend Delwyn. If Kidahin goes to warleader special security, then I will go with her."

"You would join warleader special security for Kidahin? Aplilin, I know Kidahin is your tail-tied lover, and I also know your last lover and stalking partner was killed by an animal during a routine territorial prowl in the Uahua'asee'a Clan southern border jungle."

"Which has nothing to do with Kidahin, me, or Delwyn," Aplilin growled dangerously.

"You admire Delwyn for striking out alone. You took point positions during our assault on the Ni'zakhonii research shipyard at Nikkiolo, and now you want to take point positions with Kidahin wherever she goes?" Mimiran trilled.

"Yes."

"Valor is not the way to find self-worth," Mimiran trilled insistently.

"Did I say anything about self-worth, Mimiran? Listen, I am right and you are not. Leave it alone."

Mimiran parried Aplilin's denial with an emotional feint. "Why did you laugh your head off as we backtrailed from the Coalition warship to the SIV? I thought you were going to pass out from oxygen deprivation."

"The mental image of Delwyn finding himself in protective custody reminded me of a cursing Anailiatha. Delwyn knows similar curses. I hear him sing a few of them over the combat address system from time to time. I would take an SIV if I were in his place, too. He also complains all the time, and so do I. It was funny to me, which means it was funny to the rest of us. You were a real a'pea about it, but as Kyralin is fond of saying, you Warriors have no sense of humor."

"Is that all?" Mimiran growled with ill-concealed menace.

"No. The team needed a distraction from seeing all those dead males. I distracted them with laughter. It worked. I did not hear you offering any emotional support at the time, Mistress of Inner Strength Mimiran."

"Go tell Einstika to come here, and do not let your tail snag that knee on the way out!" Mimiran keened, livid.

* * *

"You are upset," Einstika crooned sympathetically.

"What else does your nonverbal social synchrony tell you?" Mimiran snarled.

"Nothing, Mistress. I am just stating a fact."

"You are ritually named 'the Wild Mistress'," Mimiran scowled. "Your hierarchy reduced you in rank for disrespectful displays of anger during a hierarchy function. What did you do?"

"I will not talk about hierarchy matters but to say they wanted me to take a lead role. I did not want it. I prefer contributing to the whole rather than lead."

"You are not a blind follower. You respectfully oppose a team leader at the possible cost to team cohesion."

"Not in critical situations when it really matters," Einstika objected.

"I smell an undercurrent of leadership in you," Mimiran growled. "You are almost as bad as Zalzadrin when it comes to humor. You are friendly, pleasant, and have true compassion and sympathy for others."

"I love my team members, and I love being involved in Team-Two social activities. I want to contribute to them, and be loved by them."

"Yet you nearly ripped Tialdrin's ear off her head," Mimiran pointed out.

"I was defending Delwyn but I hated being pitted against Team-Two Huntresses. I would rather stick my tail up my a'pea than harm my society members," Einstika keened.

"I expect disgusting curses like that from Aplilin, not you. What did your teammates have to say about your assault on Tialdrin?"

"Alfara said I was worrying for nothing, that Tialdrin would understand."

"And she did, did she not?" Mimiran pressed.

"Yes, Mistress. But I almost killed them all!" Einstika keened.

"When?"

"When I pushed the life support override in the maintenance tunnel."

Mimiran snapped her tail and perked her ears at Einstika. "No. You were told to touch the icon. The human color status meanings are backwards. Imagine how Delwyn must feel every time he sees red nominal status tags on command center consoles."

Einstika smiled shyly.

Mimiran returned the smile, but kept her piercing gaze locked on Einstika until their eyes met. "When not involved with Team-Two and Nynava or Zalzadrin, you are apprenticing in engineering maintenance under Anailiatha. She expects results from her techmistresses. Your desire for social inclusion serves you well within Team-Two, but techmistresses often work alone or with whomever else is available. Your search for group understanding will be stressful there. Anailiatha does not suffer disrespectful displays of anger, although cursing is her natural medium and she is a mistress of it. You yearn for self-control. Command it and you will prosper."

"It is hard, Mistress Mimiran."

"I will teach you a mind song. It will help," Mimiran crooned.

"A new song?" Einstika sang, perking her ears forward. "For me?"

"Just for you," Mimiran promised. She sang a note and focused on the emotions she wanted her words, notes, and pheromones to convey to the anger-frustrated Hunter.

When Mimiran finished the song, she stood and looped her tail around Einstika's stomach. "We will sing this song in counterpoint duet later. For now, ask Alfara to come to me."

"Yes, Mistress," Einstika sang.


"You sent for me, Mimiran?"

Mimiran looked up at Alfara and realized she and Zalzadrin had nearly the same shade of flaming red ringlets.

"No," Alfara sang in response to the emotional thought uppermost on the surgeon-in-battle's scent. "Zalzadrin and I are unrelated. I am Uahua'asee'a Clan and she is O'un Tu Clan."

"I know this! Do you think I know nothing about our warship society's clan affiliations?" Mimiran seethed at the implied insult.

"I know that you know this, which is why your scent surprised me," Alfara sang.

Mimiran looked Alfara up and down before flicking her ears wide. "Spirits, Alfara, what is it with you and knives? Do you not think the bandolier is overdoing it? Spirits, all those knives hanging from your hip ties must make it hard to silent-stalk."

"Never underestimate the value of a blade," Alfara sang.

"It took ten tries before you succeed at your adulthood survival ordeal."

"It was *not* but for the spirits' own luck that I succeeded!" Alfara trilled hotly.

"I did not say it was. To survive the three-month adulthood ordeal naked and alone is the true test of what it means to call yourself an adult female," Mimiran sang. "Even males occasionally fall to the will of bad weather, ill luck, jungle animals, and unintended interference from outsiders during their one-month ordeals."

"I know this," Alfara sang.

"Do you really understand it, though? Delwyn fell, hit his head, suffered a concussion, rolled his ankle, and nearly died during his adulthood ordeal. His survival was not due to the spirits' own luck, and neither was yours. Think about our Warleader when you question yourself."

"I will, Mistress."

Mimiran wrapped her tail about Alfara's waist and sat beside her, humming softly to herself for several minutes before loosening her tail.

"Do you need anything further, Mimiran?" Alfara trilled.

"Send Tialdrin to me, please."

Mimiran watched Tialdrin approach the briefing abode, glance inside, and glide right on in to wait until she was formally recognized. Her behavior was socially perfect. Tialdrin was an intuitive empath, one who acted on the pheromonal chatter of others by instinct and without thinking. She sought consensus often, and her engaging social empathy made her very persuasive.

Tialdrin waited without so much as twitching an ear. Her social demeanor was most correct. Mimiran gave Tialdrin a pheromonal cue, and she slipped silently into the chair.

"Your skills are wasting away following Phelindra around," Mimiran sang.

"Kidahin chose me during her search for crew replacements because my abilities favor reconnaissance and intelligence gathering, Mistress Mimiran."

"True," Mimiran allowed, "but warleader special security does not and, I think, deep down you know this."

"You think I cannot protect Delwyn any better than any other Hunter?" Tialdrin sang flatly.

"Not at all," Mimiran sang reassuringly. "But consider Kidahin. She chose assaultmistress duties over those of warleader special security."

"And she regrets it," Tialdrin sang politely. "She is reconsidering. I smell it on her scent. She has doubts."

"She does, but those doubts leap at her from unique branches. Delwyn is the first human she ever met, the first human male that touched her, the first male she established full empathy with, the first male to select her for intensive one-on-one training, and the only male she favored for us to choose as our Warleader. She is tails-entwined with him and thinks he cannot do for himself without her constant presence."

"Males need minders," Tialdrin sighed musically.

"They need our protection, but Kidahin thinks she can protect him better by stalking his every move. You know what he thinks about this, yes?"

Tialdrin trilled laughter. "He goes off, alone. Sometimes I think he does so just to annoy us. It is unnatural for a male to stray far from female protection for as long as he does."

"The human mind sees things differently. I smelled it once on his scent. He is touched by our care for him, yet at times he feels like we see him as an errant infant."

"But we do not," Tialdrin objected. "Our moral imperative is to protect males. It is morally wrong for Delwyn to wander off alone into danger because any female aid stalking him would by moral duty confront the danger on his behalf."

"There are social customs at play here," Mimiran cautioned. "We grant males autonomy, and they must be allowed the freedom autonomy requires."

"Social customs?" Tialdrin hissed. "You speak of traditions. I am raising moral concerns."

Mimiran snapped her tail behind her and flattened her ears, a sure sign of anger that punctuated the scent radiating from her body. "This idea you have about moral and civil issues and that morality holds the high ground over civility is what almost got you killed. You should sing gratitude daily to the spirits for the hierarchies commuting your honor-point crime to long-term social debt," Mimiran trilled hotly.

"Ok'e'say hierarchy agreed with me in principle," Tialdrin sang.

"Yes, but the societies were furious. Hierarchies govern female moral behavior, but societies govern social cohesion."

"I know this, Mistress," Tialdrin sang. "But I was only making an argument that morality and civility are, in matters of substance, the same thing."

"And you think your theory is unique? You are young, and this notion of yours has been argued before, but not with the fervor in which you did."

"Everyone was impressed with my analysis. I could smell it."

"Yes," Mimiran trilled, "until you suggested the hierarchies dictate social customs directly."

"I meant it so in an ideal universe and not as a practical matter!" Tialdrin trilled in disgust.

"The Assault Team-Two society grants you the title of 'Oyyaess'. You do realize that makes you their wellnessmistress?" Mimiran sang softly.

"You are yanking my tail," Tialdrin trilled lightly. "I am only a month older than Kyralin, and she is only days older than Kidahin, who is the youngest Hunter in Team-Two."

"So? You have a strong drive to fulfill your obligations and you are tenacious. You have a well-rounded, above-average personality. You are an intuitive empath, cooperative, inventive, and rational. Others see you as having an absolute nonverbal synchrony, a sense of humor, a personable demeanor, and a concern for their welfare."

"But a mistress of inner strength is, first and foremost, a healer. You are a surgeon," Tialdrin pointed out.

"Indeed. A mistress of inner strength must be a healer, but not necessarily a surgeon or a physician."

"What are you asking of me?" Tialdrin trilled. "That I leave our society, Delwyn's occupational association, and return to Elleio and study at one of La'huaset's healer learning centers?"

"Of course not. I am only pointing out options. Allohindra can apprentice you in Health Center as an associate healer."

Tialdrin gaped at Mimiran, at a loss for words.

"Once you reach associate healer status, I can apprentice you in wellness counselling," Mimiran trilled.

"Allohindra will apprentice me?" Tialdrin sang doubtfully.

"She will if I recommend it," Mimiran sang. "And you should consider the advantages being an associate healer and wellnessmistress gives."

"Such as?" Tialdrin sang at interrogative pitch.

"The healer occupation concerns itself with moral codes and shoves off the branch those matters of custom conflicting with the Healers' Rede. It lets you push against those who rank you as long as you remain courteous. And it gives you the opportunity to help address Delwyn's wellness issues."

"Delwyn's wellness issues?" Tialdrin sang in hushed tones.

"Yes. You would serve as a kind of warleader special *wellness-security* Huntress."

"Oh! But, Mistress, I love associating with Assault Team-Two."

Mimiran twisted her tail around Tialdrin's thighs and snugged her close.

"It is up to you, but this is something you should think about."

"I will, Mistress Mimiran."

Mimiran nodded. "Go find Jassalin and ask her to come see me."

"Yes, Mistress Mimiran."


"Mimiran?" Jassalin sang.

"Sit down, Jassalin, and be comfortable. Are you feeling better? warmer?"

"Better, yes. Warmer, not so much," Jassalin trilled.

"How are you coping emotionally?" Mimiran sang at interrogative pitch.

"Better. When I fell down the lift shaft, memories of the ice shelf collapsing under my Environmental Interdiction team came back like I was with them again."

"You did well, but I am not speaking about your fall."

"What do you mean, Mistress?" Jassalin sang.

"You know what I mean. What you saw. What I saw in those straight, bare corridors on the Coalition warship."

Jassalin trembled. "I do not want to talk about it," she sang.

"But I do," Mimiran trilled. "I never imagined so many male deaths. I could not stop shaking."

"You?" Jassalin trilled doubtfully.

"Yes, me. I shook like a frightened infant in my EVA suit the whole time we remained aboard that ship. The shakes did not stop until long after we reached the SIV. The shock I felt made it hard for me to control my temper."

"I never want to go in that ship again," Jassalin sang adamantly.

"You had a near-death experience in the past. You had a near-death experience on the human ship. You saw mass male casualties, what no living female has seen in centuries."

"I can handle it," Jassalin sang with tones of certainty.

"'I can handle it' is a Delwyn saying. You are evading the issue."

"Let me work my way through it, Mimiran. Spirits, but I wish Delwyn was here."

"We all do," Mimiran reassured the fluorescent-orange-headed Huntress. "You are the oldest Team-Two assaultstalker and you hold the highest hierarchical rank among them, yet you are subordinate to Kidahin. How do you feel about this?"

"Kidahin holds greater military rank than I," Jassalin pointed out with a tonal shrug.

"Your social attunement is one of a leader. Kidahin leads Team-Two, but when she splits the team into two hands, she always tells you to lead one of them."

"You state the obvious well. Do you have a point, or should I get my Oyya Web and ask the spirits what you are snapping your tail at?"

"Do you not think you can lead Assault Team-Two better than Kidahin?" Mimiran pressed.

"I know I can lead them better than Kidahin, but she is not without skills. I am more disciplined. I have a warfighter's obligation to the mission. All I care about is the mission while it is executing. Kidahin is the better assaultmistress because she is not tail-tied to the mission. She considers events as they happen. Her first strategy is likely the correct one. She dismisses dangers and obstacles to her goals. She plans, and I carry out her plans. She sees my worth. We are much alike."

"Indeed," Mimiran trilled dryly. "You, Kidahin, and Tialdrin are more like close immediate family."

Jassalin perked her ears forward in agreement. "I counsel Kidahin in team cohesion matters when we sing in rituals. My place in Team-Two social ritual as 'the Eldest Hunter' gives me the standing needed to approach Kidahin's military rank without fear of giving offense."

"I thought Merkrida was more the nurturing influence than you."

"I do not nurture anyone. I tell a Hunter what she needs to hear, and she listens."

"So, are you content under Kidahin's leadership?"

"Of course I am," Jassalin sang.

"Do you feel you can support her as her chosen second-in-leadership?"

"Of course I can," Jassalin replied honestly.

"Let us sing the social ritual *The Power of Names* together," Mimiran trilled.

"I am honored," Jassalin sang.

The Hunter and Warrior sat across from each other on the deck, their tails twisted together across their thighs, their ears perked forward, and their eyes locked in a soulful stare. They sang in duet the ritual meaning of names. When finished, they stood up, unwound their tails, and faced each other.

"Tell Kidahin I must see her."

"Affirm, Mistress," Jassalin sang.


Less than a minute passed before Kidahin came stomping into the briefing abode.

"You want to see me now?" Kidahin trilled in annoyance. "I am busy."

"Oh? Doing what, exactly? Pacing the aisle? Bothering Zalzadrin and Nynava?" Mimiran trilled innocently.

"No, although I admit to doing those things, too. Zalzadrin says we are finally clear of the hypercube gravitational anomalies. She has a stable long-range FTL scanning aperture open and she is looking over the gas giant and its moon as we speak."

"Really? Finally," Mimiran sang before changing the subject. "You are a fool to consider prowling with warleader special security," she trilled.

"What? Why do you...? What makes you say that?" Kidahin keened.

"You do not have the mental aptitude required, any more than Zalzadrin does."

"I do not joke around like she does," Kidahin trilled.

"No, you do not. You are duty-driven and single-minded in the pursuit of your duty as you see it. Those qualities and your deep emotional ties to Delwyn are why Phelindra wanted you in warleader special security. I know Melkorka warned you not to get tail-tied to security assignments, and she is right."

"I do not think so," Kidahin snapped. "Doubts wrap their tails around me, and sometimes I leafchase alternative choices so often I end up tailchasing after outcomes that lead me out onto brittle, dead branches."

"You made the right choices when you helped Delwyn take over the Ni'zakhonii light attack craft. You, beyond doubt, made the right choice when you exercised your right as huluhar in presenting Delwyn to us. You made the right choices leading an inexperienced Team-Two in a ground assault at Nikkiolo. You even made the right choice when you goaded Lo'sutra'est anni into shadowing him during his survival ordeal. Tell me, Kidahin, just what are your wrong choices?" Mimiran demanded.

"Doubt kills," Kidahin spat.

"Indeed it does. It kills when it loops like a snagging vine around your foot during combat, but you have never worried about doubt while on-mission, have you?"

"No, Mimiran, at least not until we boarded *Londiwe Khoza*. Something about him smells familiar, but wrong."

"Death, Kidahin. You smelled death."

"No, Mimiran. This smell was different."

"Why? Because you are not shadowing Delwyn every minute of the day?"

"He needs minders, Mimiran. Spirits! He needs minders more than an Eyloni male does."

"What did you just say, Kidahin? Are you saying Delwyn is not Eyloni?" Mimiran demanded, her natural Warrior anger flaring. "Delwyn is Eyloni. He survived his adulthood ordeal, and here you are, sullying our Warleader's honor in this way..."

"*No!* No, I am not. Spirits, Mimiran, I am the last female to suggest such a thing. I meant his human physiology. He cannot smell a flower when his nose is shoved into it," Kidahin trilled.

"I expect wild statements from Zalzadrin, but not from you. He knows more than you think, and you know this. He evades us in the jungle. He figures things out quick enough, but he does not get scent information like we do."

"I know, I know," Kidahin sang, conceding the point. "But doubt still stalks me."

"Why? Because you could not stop Kalinn from dying? You were aboard our warship for what? Four weeks when Kalinn died? You were apprenticing under Trebithia as her helmsmistress, and you were too busy to give him more than the casual empathy you needed to fulfill your duties as huluhar."

"Which I failed!" Kidahin keened. "I am a gifted primal empath. I felt something wrong in Kalinn from the moment I first stepped into the command center. I should have said something," she growled.

"Said what? And said it to whom? Melkorka had misgivings about him personally leading a boarding party. Brelioranda was mistress of battle and should have refused his participation. Our warship society will never let Delwyn do the same thing. He is well protected. You being with warleader special security adds nothing. You can protect Delwyn better as an assaultmistress," Mimiran sang.

"I hope so, Mimiran. I truly hope so," Kidahin sang.

"Kidahin? I have an FTL jump solution ready to implement," Zalzadrin trilled from the flight deck.

Kidahin flicked her ears at the surgeon-in-battle. "Zalzadrin needs me. Was there anything else?"

"I want to discuss Team-Two emotional health, but it can wait until we reach surveillance orbit."

"Anything serious?" Kidahin trilled.

"No, but it may help you with leadership decisions."

"Would you not rather raise those concerns with Nynava?" Kidahin sang.

"Why? You are our assaultmistress, and I consent to your leadership as long as I remain your surgeon-in-battle," Mimiran sang happily.

Kidahin offered the Warrior her tail, and Mimiran wound hers around it in shared intimate empathy.

"Kidahin!" Zalzadrin keened. "I am ready to jump the transport into surveillance orbit!"

"Then jump us there," Kidahin sang.

Mimiran barely had time to notice the loud, explosive bang that deafened her before she and Kidahin flew across the briefing abode. Kidahin tumbled down the aisle, but Mimiran tumbled into a tangle of hanging combat harnesses. She dangled from the ceiling trapped in knotted harnesses as hurricane winds tore at her.

Rapid decompression, she realized. The transport had been hulled. Desperately, she fumbled for the adulthood knife strapped at her left breast and began cutting herself free.

The rushing air abruptly stopped, replaced by silent calm. She took a deep breath. Damage control must have sealed the breach because she certainly was not breathing vacuum.

Mimiran jumped to the deck, ran up the aisle, and froze. A green line ran along the edge of the forward bulkhead, the outward visual warning of a force field seal isolating the flight deck from the cabin. She smelled pheromones, and they painted disaster in her empathic mind.

Kidahin was on the deck, leaning over a prone Zalzadrin.

"Where is Nynava?" Mimiran keened, unable to hear her singing voice.

Kidahin frowned, flipped her ears, and yelled. She frowned and stood. She signed in battle language at Mimiran.

<<The copilot side of the flight deck is gone. Nynava is dead!>>

# 7

## THE TENACIOUS NATURE, THE MEDICINE OF SCENT-MARKING, THE DIVIDED SPIRIT...

"Mimiran! Zalzadrin is not responding to my touch or my voice. The back of her head is staved in," Kidahin keened.

Mimiran jumped to her side in one leap, knelt, and examined the unconscious Hunter.

"What? I can barely hear you!" Mimiran keened. "What happened to Nynava? Are you sure she is dead?"

"I am. There are—body parts—on the deck."

"How did you get Zalzadrin out of the cockpit?" Mimiran trilled.

"I found her hanging halfway through the flight deck hatch. Whatever hit us knocked her out of the pilot seat and onto the deck behind it. When I pulled her clear, the damage control monitor sealed the hatch and put a force field patch across the threshold. It should have put the force field across the open hatch whether her body was there or not. I do not know yet if the damage control system can isolate the cockpit and restore life support."

"Where are we? Did we arrive at the moon?"

"I do not know. Zalzadrin likely programmed the jump for an exit at orbital velocity into orbit to save time by not using the orbital maneuvering system to achieve orbit. We are probably moving at orbital velocity, but to where? Are we diving into the moon? Are we in orbit? Are we flying off in some random direction?" Kidahin trilled.

Mimiran tilted her head and flattened her ears against short orange ringlets. "Zalzadrin has a traumatic brain injury. Tialdrin," she sang, "help us carry her to the healer suite. She needs immediate brain surgery."

"Affirm, Mistress," Tialdrin sang. "Mistress? Alfara has a sprained left shoulder and a broken left foot. Seliaha has a hyperextended right knee and several broken ribs in her right chest. The others have minor cuts and bruises but nothing serious," she sang as she helped Mimiran carry Zalzadrin to the healer suite.

Mimiran opened the clear hood and waited for the surgical pallet to fully extend. When it stopped, they laid Zalzadrin onto the pallet, face up, and it automatically retracted back into the healer suite. Remote surgical probes and scanners extended to just above the unconscious Hunter's fiery red ringlets.

"Engage sterile field, vital sign monitors, and anesthesia. Take a complete skull series," the surgeon-in-battle sang to the suite while looking over her shoulder and down the aisle. "Does anyone need immediate healer aid? Once Zalzadrin's skull scans are complete I will be busy for a few hours."

"My chest hurts...hard to breathe," Seliaha complained. "I can wait. I think my knee is broken. I am not going anywhere. Help Zalzadrin."

"I will fix your knee when I am finished with Zalzadrin," Mimiran sang encouragingly to her. She turned to face Kidahin. "You better get into the pilot seat and find out what happened and where we are."

"Mimiran, I never flew a troop transport before. My clearance certification is for stealth insertion vehicles only."

"A'pea, Kidahin, what difference does it make? You yank a control yoke in a direction and the transport goes there."

"It is not that simple," Kidahin trilled. "A transport does not respond like an SIV. It takes practiced skill to fly a transport into reentry, let alone atmospheric flight."

"Which neither applies here. We are in space. You thrust forward and backward, and you pitch, yaw, and roll, just as you do in an SIV. Go!"

"Affirm," Kidahin sang. She paused and stared at the long battle scar running down Zalzadrin's left side from breast to hip. The sterile field gave the Hunter's beautiful red-and-orange, yellow-variegated skin an unhealthy pall.

Kidahin shuddered away from Zalzadrin and glided along the bulkhead to the flight deck hatch. Across the deck, along the threshold, a green line glowed in warning. An atmospheric force field covered the hatch. The damage control monitor had put it there to stop air flow past Zalzadrin's unconscious body blocking the hatch. The damage control monitor should have placed a structural force field patch on the hull breach itself by now.

Kidahin read the damage control summary on the screen set next to the flight deck hatch. It reported massive damage to the forward and right forward cockpit and flight deck. Several damage control system taglines flashed in warning green. The green VACUUM WARNING alert meant the breach had not sealed. She could open the hatch and step through the atmospheric seal. It arrested air, not solid objects. She could walk through it without causing the transport to decompress. Still, that vacuum warning made it clear she had to wear a combat EVA suit to survive on the flight deck.

"How bad?" Jassalin trilled.

"I do not know. Vacuum on the flight deck means extensive damage control system failures. If flight deck damage control is even partly offline, then several flight avionics systems are probably offline as well. Help me into my EVA suit."

"Affirm."

Kidahin watched Jassalin prowl to the aft bulkhead and the equipment lockers built into it. She counted tails while she waited. Alfara stood on one foot while helping Seliaha find a comfortable resting position. Pain radiated on everyone's pheromones. Those not attending the wounded were busy packing equipment and supplies into combat harnesses, carry sacks, and field packs. They knew, better than she admitted to herself. They knew. Sooner or later they must abandon the troop transport.

Jassalin returned with the EVA suit and helped Kidahin climb into it.

"All seals are set and visually confirmed," Jassalin sang.

"Suit life support confirms airtight seal," Kidahin sang in reply.

"Do you want me to come with you?" Jassalin sang.

"I do not think that is necessary. The flight deck visuals do not work. I do not know how much of it or the cockpit remains intact. I will not risk you. If I am lost, you will assume the leadership of Assault Team-Two."

"Affirm," Jassalin sang at formal pitch.

Kidahin put a gloved hand on the forward bulkhead damage control monitor and tapped the flight deck hatch override.

The hatch slid quietly aside. The cockpit side-seat looked undamaged, as did the instrumentation surrounding it. In front of it was the pilot and copilot blister. The pilot seat was bent to the right and twisted backwards at a sharp angle.

Something big, bright, and light pinkish-blue flashed across her eyes, and she froze.

Stars sped across the clear cockpit canopy. Every four seconds or so an uncomfortably huge moon flashed by.

Kidahin realized that the transport was tumbling, his attitude-control thrusters clearly offline. She thanked the spirits that artificial gravity was working, otherwise centrifugal force would have pinned everyone to the bulkheads by now.

Kidahin stepped over the threshold and through the atmospheric seal and onto the flight deck. Her suit flashed a green vacuum warning, but the insistent warning did not banish the shock surging through her racing heart.

The right forward and right forward quarter sides of the cockpit and flight deck were missing beginning half an ell from the forward bulkhead and extending through the cockpit blister, out the canopy, and on across what remained of the transport's blunt bow.

Star-filled space tumbled past the gaping wound, itself an oval hole cut cleanly from below the deck and through the ceiling, cutting through instrumentation mounted on walls, floor, and ceiling.

Kidahin gasped. The breach was obscenely clean and cut diagonally through the copilot seat. Everything right of the breach was lost to space. Only a corner of the copilot seat, its mounting hardware, and the left armrest remained.

Pieces of Nynava spilled off the seat onto the deck. The left arm and shoulder, left breast and most of the adulthood knife, left hip, knee, foot, and a length of tail to the pons were all that remained of the Mistress of Battle.

Kidahin stared, grief-stricken, at the remains.

"Kidahin?" Jassalin trilled over the commlink.

She ignored Jassalin, struggling to understand what she was seeing. Perversely, she wondered why the explosive decompression did not sweep them into space. The eternal void waited merely a pons-length from her. A hard-green line running along the breach perimeter caught her attention. The hard-green line warned that a structural force field was in operation. Structural patches were solid, meant to reinforce collapsed or missing bulkheads. Unlike the soft-green atmospheric seals, solid objects could not pass through them. Maybe that explained why Nynava's remains had—well—remained behind.

Wait. The damage control monitor reported all structural field emitters offline, yet it was a hard-green line that traced the machine-quality edge. Kidahin carefully reached over the Warrior's remains, hesitated, and pushed a gloved palm forward and across the glowing green line.

And she felt a hard, unyielding surface. It felt like she was pressing against a thick, heavy sheet of glass. Its solid nature confirmed it was a damage control breach-arresting force field, a large and power-draining one at that.

"Kidahin!" Jassalin trilled impatiently.

"Wait, Jassalin. I am checking on something. The damage control monitor is wrong. The cockpit and flight deck breach is sealed with a structural field, and yet the monitor and my suit sensors both read vacuum. Why is the atmospheric seal still on the flight deck hatch? The monitor should read the breach as sealed and pump atmosphere onto the flight deck and then remove the hatch seal."

"Kidahin? Hollfara. Damage control force fields project from local emitters. They use a lot of power, and they overlap damage based on a priority scale. A structural patch draws much more power than an atmospheric seal does. Remember also that in combat conditions the transport must land his passengers."

"Which means what, Hollfara? I do not have time for engineering lectures."

"A ship cannot survive without structural integrity. Damage control prioritizes critical structures. I think several small breaches are venting atmosphere, and not enough power remains to patch them all. If the hatch field fails while the hatch is open the air can vent through small tears, rips, and ruptures throughout the flight deck."

Kidahin returned to the pilot seat, clenched her hands, grabbed a hold of the seat, and pushed and shoved on it with the aid of combat EVA suit muscle-assist joints. It took her a few minutes to bend it back into a semblance of its original shape. She sat in it and eyed the flight control panels and their green status system taglines.

"All main systems are offline," Kidahin trilled. "I see no red system taglines or status lamps anywhere."

"Go to the side-seat," Hollfara sang. "Its systems are independently routed through the forward bulkhead. The side-seat is a performance upgrade and not part of the original design."

"Affirm," Kidahin sang. "Hollfara? All status indicators are dark."

"Of course they are. It is disconnected from the flight avionics systems to prevent someone sitting there leafchasing and hitting flight controls by accident. Sit down and toggle the console override."

"Affirm. I am sitting in the side-seat and tapping the override. It asks for authorization. From whom? Nynava? Zalzadrin? What do I do now?"

"Look at the override panel. Find the 'Flight Systems Overmonitor' tagline and touch it. The override will force the console to interrogate the pilot and copilot systems. If they are both offline, then it will self-override," Hollfara explained.

"Understood, tapping. The backup piloting systems are coming online. Spirits!"

"What is wrong?" Jassalin trilled.

"Several flight control systems remain offline even from this seat. Dou'tu'tay! The antihydrogen tanks read empty."

"That means no FTL jump back to our warship," Hollfara observed.

"Do you have anything better than the obvious to offer?" Kidahin snarled.

"Yes, I do," Hollfara keened. "Force fields pull a lot of power. The draw is insignificant when power comes from the hydrogen-antihydrogen fusion reactor. That reactor is offline, and transport reserve power comes from a boron fusion reactor. Running flight, life support, and damage control systems from that reactor will exhaust the boron supply rather quickly. Reserve power prioritizes demand. More than a couple of structural force fields reinforcing breach damage means load-sharing is trying to power them all and coming up short. That explains why you have no life support."

"I do not think it will matter," Kidahin trilled.

"Why is that?" Jassalin sang over the commlink.

"The navigation system is finally online. We are tumbling uncontrollably and directly toward the moon. We are well within a long-range surveillance orbit. Perimeter sensor data says we collided with a hypergravity point. The collision bled off our jump exit velocity. I cannot boost us back to orbital velocity because the sublight drive is offline."

"What about the orbital maneuvering system?" Hollfara sang.

"The helm fields are offline. Both orbital maneuvering and reaction control systems are also offline. The attitude control system reports thruster controller damage."

"Damaged how?" Jassalin trilled.

"The pitch controller is offline. I can still yaw and roll," Kidahin sang.

"Can you enter a stable orbit using the attitude control thrusters?" Jassalin keened at a doubt-raising descant.

"No, my best effort will give us a suborbital slingshot course that will circumnavigate the moon as it degrades into a meteoric reentry. I need a pitch thruster to make fine reentry corridor adjustments. No combination of roll and yaw thrusting can make up for the needed pitch thrust."

"We must abandon the troop transport. The question is, how long do we have?" Jassalin trilled.

"I do not know, yet. I am working through several maneuvering scenarios. I am hoping to optimize a solution with what I have to work with."

"Kidahin? Mimiran," the Warrior surgeon-in-battle sang over the commlink. "I am in the middle of Zalzadrin's brain right now. I am busy spot-regenerating neural connections and capillaries and will be for another three hours."

"That long?" Kidahin keened in dismay.

"This is no concussion. Properly speaking, Zalzadrin should be regenerating in a chrysalis in Health Center. Using the healer suite means at least a Delwyn-hour of manual surgery and recovery time after surgery before we can move her."

"Affirm. Attitude control thrusters lack the power of the orbital maneuvering kick motor. I will plot for the shallowest possible arc and try skipping us across the upper atmosphere, but doing so makes reentry more dangerous in the long run. I will have to fly the SIV out of the hold at the last possible moment as the transport reenters the atmosphere."

"You are rated as an SIV pilot. You can fly circles around the troop transport as he spirals into reentry!" Hollfara sang with certain confidence.

"We shall see. The SIV is not an endurance vehicle. Flying dodgy maneuvers during reentry will consume fuel I want to use flying over ground obstacles on the surface," Kidahin trilled.

"You will need at least one pitch thruster to properly adjust the reentry angle to hit the upper atmosphere just right to prolong our orbit," Hollfara sang. "You must null out our tumbling component before we skip down into the atmosphere to prevent a tail-first reentry. A tail-first reentry will cause the transport to tumble violently. Violent tumbling will overtax the inertial dampening system and kill the gravity. You could not pilot the SIV out of the hold before he was smashed through the hold bulkhead."

"What do you suggest I do?" Kidahin keened. "Mimiran needs time to complete her work and give Zalzadrin a recovery period before we can move her to the SIV."

"Merkrida and I are damage control techmistresses. We will try to fix the pitch thruster controller. You only need one working pitch thruster."

"I can help, too," Alfara wheezed.

"What do you mean, only one?" Kidahin trilled, ignoring Alfara's plea.

"You need only one thruster to pitch up. Then you fire roll thrusters to invert the transport and fire the same thruster to pitch down," Hollfara sang dryly.

"That will not work!" Kidahin hissed. "I tried to combine yaw and roll thrust vectors but a three-axis adjustment takes too long and I overshoot the reentry corridor."

"That is true using only yaw and roll thrust," Hollfara sang. "But a pitch thruster in combination is more efficient. You can make this sequence work if you optimize your reentry solution."

"Oh!" Kidahin trilled. "The avionics plot agrees with you. I never thought about that combination," she admitted.

"I can help!" Alfara trilled at a bare whisper.

"No, you cannot," Mimiran hissed. "I do not want broken ribs poking holes in your lungs. You will lay still and be quiet."

Kidahin settled into piloting routine. Using the attitude control thrusters, she nulled the roll and yaw components of their tumbling trajectory. The forces involved were familiar enough. She did the same thing all the time when piloting the stealth insertion vehicle. What made this maneuvering difficult was the transport's mass and moment of inertia. The SIV and its smaller profile and lower mass made all the difference, but the much bigger transport's responsiveness to course corrections having fine tolerances and no margins for error was a totally new experience.

It took her what felt like hours to stabilize the transport's tumbling flight. Her efforts were not perfect, either. The transport still tumbled, but now he tumbled head over tail at a placid three a minute.

"Hollfara? Where is my pitch thruster?" Kidahin keened.

"We found one still intact. It is stuck in stand-by mode. Its control electronics are burned out. Alfara is rewriting the software in one of the yaw thruster controllers to function as a pitch thruster controller."

"I want a reactionless helm field right now," Kidahin snapped wistfully.

"I am sure, but the controller is all we have. It will work," Hollfara trilled in reassurance.

"Thank you. How long before I can use it?" Kidahin sang.

"Alfara says within the hour, maybe less."

"We will hit the upper atmosphere in one hour and thirty-four minutes," Kidahin sang at warning tempo. "How is Zalzadrin?"

"I do not know!" Hollfara keened in anguish. "Mimiran and Tialdrin are working nonstop. Spirits, Kidahin, she looks worse now with a quarter of her skull peeled back. Watching Mimiran apply her skill is amazing. She and Tialdrin are in complete pheromonal harmony and have not spoken for some time now."

"That can only be a good thing," Kidahin sang.

"You should send a status update to Melkorka," Hollfara trilled abruptly.

"We have no antihydrogen," Kidahin reminded her. "There is not enough power for FTL scans or FTL hyperlink..."

"Forget the FTL technology," Hollfara interrupted dryly. "Use the radio."

"Radio?" Kidahin keened. "Spirits, Hollfara, radio is limited to the speed of light. Do you know just how far away Melkorka is right now?"

"Thirty-one EST hours one-way radio traffic and double that, one hundred and thirteen hours round trip if Melkorka replies right away," Hollfara sang concisely.

Kidahin snorted and clenched her jaw, gritting her teeth, and tried her best to suppress a trilling giggle.

"What is so funny about that?" Hollfara sang, genuinely curious. "Your memories of Delwyn and his counting problems?"

"A memory of how Delwyn screams about how we count leapt at me. He would double your one-way estimate and arrive at a different number," Kidahin trilled in laughter.

"So?" Hollfara sang, adding a note of perplexity as she missed the point. "He counts his fingers. We count our arms, legs, and tails. What does it matter? Time is still time. The duration is the same no matter what base you count in. Even if you counted in binary numbers the duration is the same. Really, Kidahin what is so..."

"You are missing the humor," Kidahin complained.

"What about the humor? Oh, you should use a tight-beam transmission. The hypergravity surrounding our warship may pull a radio beam off target. Remember that you cannot put enough power into a broad unidirectional signal," Hollfara lectured.

"I should not need much power," Kidahin growled. "Hlindredreda is likely listening for my on-site report. But your caution is warranted. I will alternate between unidirectional and tight-beam transmissions."

"That sounds prudent," Hollfara sang, satisfied that her advice was taken seriously.

"Thank you," Kidahin trilled into a descant as she fed *Hunter's Moon's* coordinates into the radio transmitter. She switched in the high-gain antenna, paused to gather her thoughts, and began singing her report.

"Mistress Melkorka, Kidahin. We have suffered a jump arrival mishap. Nynava is dead and Zalzadrin is undergoing emergency in-the-field brain surgery. Our situation is grave. We plan to..."

"Kidahin? Kidahin? *Kidahin!*" Jassalin's voice keened from the EVA suit speakers.

"Hmmm? What?" Kidahin snarled sleepily.

"Wake up. Zalzadrin is out of surgery. Finally," Jassalin sang joyfully.

"I was thinking, not sleeping," Kidahin objected defensively.

"Noted. I understand. I have good news."

"I hope so. The moon dominates my forward view now. I will begin making reentry maneuvers in twenty-two minutes," Kidahin sang.

"Alfara completed and tested her thruster controller software changes while you were...thinking. The aft dorsal pitch thruster works. Hollfara, Merkrida, and I tried to reroute fuel and thrust control systems for the fusion engine. We did not succeed. There was just too much damage."

"What good is the engine to me?" Kidahin trilled.

"Engine thrust would let you enter a stable orbit and give us the time to leave in the SIV. Abandoning the transport at our leisure is safer than leaving during a rough suborbital reentry trajectory. We were hoping it might even let you land the transport on the surface intact," Jassalin sang in a dispirited melody. "Do you have enough time to revise our reentry?"

"I am working on it now," Kidahin trilled. "Executing final update plot. Pitching into new reentry track for slingshot into the upper atmosphere and skipping around the moon to degrade into an unstable reentry. Reentry window is shifting. I am trying to give us as much time as I can."

"Why not fly at a tangent to the atmosphere and skip on by?" Jassalin trilled. "The SIV certainly has the range for a return to orbit and safe reentry."

"We are too close for attitude control thrusters alone to make a difference. Atmospheric reentry is unavoidable. I am plotting for maximum orbit but cannot evade the upper atmosphere. Our choices are diving into the atmosphere and burning up immediately or skipping around and down into the atmosphere until we burn and break up. Every possible orbital plot ends with us burning up. The only difference, the important difference, is how long until we burn up."

"Understood. Do not miss a course correction window. I do not want to get incinerated," Jassalin sang dryly. "Come back as soon as you can. You need enough time to preflight check the SIV."

"Wait, the reentry corridor is shifting. Time to reenter atmosphere is increasing. Final maneuver completed. We have thirty-two minutes before the transport breaks up."

"Get back here now!" Jassalin keened.

"I am scanning the surface," Kidahin sang calmly.

"No!" Jassalin trilled in fury. "Do not waste the time. The SIV has his own scanners and...," she paused, remembering that compared to the troop transport the SIV scanners were only one branch above the quality of hand-held scanners. "Just download a sensor sweep to the SIV and look at it later!"

"I plan to, but I need to see enough now to know where to land."

"See anything?" Jassalin snapped.

"Not really. It is a third smaller than Elleio with a thin oxygen-nitrogen atmosphere at low atmospheric pressure. Think about breathing while prowling across the stratospheric impact crater ridges on Elleio. The atmosphere has more carbon dioxide than Elleio, too. I am getting an anoxia alert. We will need to wear rebreathers, I think. Humans definitely will need them. The average surface temperature is Tail minus twenty, cool but livable. I see no oceans, lakes, or rivers. It looks dry, but I see evidence of flooding."

"It gets rare, violent, and long storms?" Jassalin suggested.

"I think so. You should see the foliage I am looking at."

"Such as?" Jassalin sang, curious.

"The surface is relatively flat everywhere and covered with sand one to three ells deep over bedrock. The ground is covered with massive, elleiu-tree thick, vines. They grow to the horizon having stems some two hundred ells thick and covered with gray-black, rough bark. The stems sprout leaf stalks, one about every hundred ells, and each stalk is ten ells thick, grows about a hundred and forty ells tall, and supports a single cobalt-blue leaf bigger than a sail. That makes the ground-to-leaf height about three hundred to four hundred ells."

"They grow to the horizon? That means they must crisscross often," Jassalin sang.

"They do," Kidahin sang in agreement. "I see clumps of them, three or four atop one another, growing in tangled masses some thousand ells above ground—tall enough to reach the lower main branches of an elleiu tree."

"Mimiran will love that," Jassalin trilled.

"I will love what?" Mimiran's voice trilled over the suit speakers.

"It looks like we have a lot of climbing ahead of us on the surface," Kidahin sang.

"And? I can climb like any female can. Why? What is wrong with the ground?" Mimiran trilled.

"Nothing. It is covered in sand," Jassalin sang.

"It sounds boring," Mimiran sang. "What about the sand, Kidahin?"

"Nothing I can point my tail at. The vines are the dominant plant life. The leaf stalks have parasitic vines and lianas growing from them and some epiphytic bromeliads. Oh, the vine stems have spiral tentacles, tendril-like suckers, growing out of them at ground level—a lot of them.

"Not for anchoring the vine to the ground, surely. From what you describe, their own mass is sufficient to keep them in place," Jassalin sang. "The leaves are cobalt-blue? If those tendrils were bright green, they would remind me of the parasitic vines back home."

"Not these. I am transferring a scan to the bulkhead screen," Kidahin sang. "See them?"

"I do," Jassalin sang. She studied the image a moment. "Parasitic vines on Elleio use their tendrils to bore into photosynthesizing plants and steal their nutrients. These are barely longer than an SIV and no thicker than I am tall. They taper down to a point. They look like horizontal wooden stalactites. Some are coiled up like springs. I wonder why."

"I do not know. Maybe they are...wait a minute. Jassalin, did you see that?"

"See what? More sand?" Jassalin keened, growing impatient. She felt a subtle vibration through the deck. They were running out of time.

"No," Kidahin snapped. "Is that dark object a rock or a structure of some kind?"

"I do not see anything. What is it? The Coalition shuttle?" Jassalin sang.

"No, not a shuttle, this is rocky-looking. There, see it in the center of the screen?"

"That large oval boulder in those gigantic vines? It is only a rock. Hurry, Kidahin. We are running out of time."

"Surface scans found no rocks on this hemisphere poking out of the sand at all."

"You think it may be something the Ni'zakhonii put here? As a structure, it could barely serve as a hanger for four troop transports. It is about the size of a field command bunker. How much of it goes below the sand?"

"Not much," Kidahin admitted. "It is about half the size of the light attack craft I helped Delwyn take from them, except..."

"Except what?" Jassalin trilled.

"Some of the scans are being deflected, but I am reading a lot of solid mass throughout with occasional small voids inside."

"One of those geodes they were mining in the Nikkiolo system," Jassalin sang with certainty.

"Kidahin? Zalzadrin is out of recovery. Her condition is guarded, but stable. I am putting her into an EVA combat suit and strapping her into a seat in the SIV. How long before we must leave?" Mimiran sang at insistence pitch.

"Thirteen minutes, Mimiran. We are in the suborbital entry corridor now. I am trying to find the missing Sentry shuttle so I can land near him."

"Would the humans not land near the geode? The only way out of the system for them is to capture an Ni'zakhonii FTL-capable ship," Mimiran sang.

"They can call for help. The Coalition will send a ship to investigate what happened to *Londiwe Khoza.*"

"But they are not calling for help, are they?" Mimiran trilled.

Kidahin twitched her tail in surprise. "I never thought about that!" she confessed.

"What does it matter?" Jassalin demanded. "We cannot receive FTL hyperlink transmissions, and they would not use radio to contact Earth."

"No, but certainly Hlindredreda would have picked up an FTL distress call well before we even left our warship," Mimiran sang.

"I found him!" Kidahin keened triumphantly.

"The shuttle?" Jassalin trilled.

"What else? I am scanning him now. He has heavy damage to the spaceframe. His profile does not suggest a crash. I think they made a hard landing. I read no life signs. He landed in sand between two huge vine stems twenty-three khnells southeast of the geode."

"What is your plan? Land near the shuttle?" Jassalin sang in suggestion.

"I think so. I will land a few kanells north of the shuttle so we can prowl to him and see what he can tell us," Kidahin sang.

"I hope your plan includes flying us to the geode. It will take two weeks to reach it on foot in clear terrain at stalking speed," Jassalin sang.

"I think we will fly about a hundred kneells, land, and prowl a security sweep. Then we make khnell-long jumps, twenty of them, until we reach the geode. We will prowl at each stop. Maybe we will find signs of survivors," Kidahin sang.

"Try contacting them by commlink," Merkrida's voice chimed over the suit speakers.

"No. I do not think attempting contact is a good idea," Kidahin trilled.

"Why not?" Mimiran sang at interrogative tempo.

"Delwyn warned that those killed on *Londiwe Khoza* made him think about mutiny. This concept of society members turning against one another troubles me. His tone made it clear that those guilty of mutiny are ni'zakhon, beyond the law. Our presence here may not be welcomed."

"We should discuss this at length," Merkrida trilled.

"I know, but wait until we land. I am skipping along the atmosphere now, in case you have not noticed the increasing vibration through the deck plates. It is time to abandon the transport."

"Affirm," Merkrida sang.

Kidahin made a few more timed thruster final adjustments meant to pitch the transport at the equator. The updated reentry angle insured the transport would disintegrate and burn up in the atmosphere, a fitting end to his service and guarantee that Compact technology did not survive for the Ni'zakhonii to salvage.

It would also give Nynava's remains a spectacular send off to the spirits in the Oyya Web.

She stood, glided to the bulkhead, opened the hatch, and stepped through the atmosphere-arresting force field.

"Everyone take your seats in the SIV. We have four minutes. Mimiran? A word?"

"Yes?"

"Give me a report on Team-Two health status."

"Affirm. Zalzadrin remains in guarded condition. She is no longer critical and I expect her to make a full recovery. She is strapped into a seat and fully reclined. I repaired Alfara's broken foot and sprained left shoulder. Her foot is fine, but her shoulder will cramp and tighten over the next few hours. I mended Seliaha's broken ribs and spent an hour repairing her hyperextended knee. That knee took nearly a third of the time I was in Zalzadrin's head. She will limp without pain for the better part of the day. Everyone has some minor abrasions and bruises but nothing serious."

"Thank the spirits," Kidahin sang.

"Now you must listen to me in my role as Mistress of Inner Strength," Mimiran sang formally.

"Yes, Mistress?" Kidahin replied just as formally.

"What you said to Merkrida, about not contacting the Coalition shuttle, is sensible," Mimiran sang softly. "I spoke with Team-Two members earlier. They all think, and I am convinced they may be right, that the A'tayotan sent us here for a specific reason. There is something here that requires Delwyn's unique knowledge and skill, but this something also poses a danger to him."

"A danger?" Kidahin trilled. "What danger?"

"I do not know, but I think Melkorka and Phelindra do. It has not occurred to them, but subconsciously they think, and I think so, too, that Nynava definitely knew something and Zalzadrin does, too," Mimiran growled.

Kidahin ground her teeth as she followed the surgeon-in-battle and Mistress of Inner Strength through the hold hatch and into the waiting stealth insertion vehicle.

"We will discuss this after we land. I do not have time now."

"Of course," Mimiran sang, formally resuming her subordinate role as healer support for Team-Two.

"Aplilin, take the gunner seat and prepare for departure."

"Affirm," Aplilin trilled huskily.

"Everyone, strap in and attach your suit umbilicals to SIV life support," Kidahin sang.

A steady vibration shook the transport. It got worse by the second as Kidahin rushed through the preflight checklist. She purged the air from the hold and opened the exterior hold hatch. Gripping the yoke with a steady hand, Kidahin fired bow thrusters and backed the SIV out of the doomed transport.

Once clear, she shot off at an angle, too busy to watch the falling transport glow in the friction of reentry.

*"A'lumal na ka me na nako nabi,"* Kidahin sang defiantly, echoed by her team: with you or with the spirits we wish you well and hope to meet you again.

"We are clear. I am moving us into a stealth reentry track and landing one hundred and thirty-four kneells north of the shuttle."

The SIV sliced through faint, misty, insubstantial clouds. The sky was pinkish-blue, but below, a jungle of giant vines stretched to the horizon in all directions.

"They look like some kind of weird jungle from here," Jassalin trilled. over the suit speakers. "Remember our training in the combat deployment bay? The simulated landing in Ah'vou'ree Clan rainforest?"

"What about it?" Kidahin sang.

"You should take the time to find a place where we can avoid those long climbs and longer prowls we did during the training scenario."

"I like your thinking," Kidahin sang softly. Louder, she added sibilantly, "You must also take into account that humans generally do not climb if the ground ahead is clear. They will walk on the sand."

"But we do not have to!" Seliaha keened. "We can climb the vines and prowl down the stems."

"And I think we will," Kidahin sang. "But we must find a sandy path going north from the shuttle. The survivors will follow a ground path north."

"What about this one, my Kidahin?" Aplilin sang, pointing at a screen with her tail. "It is very wide, and it follows a winding path passing within a hundred kneells of the shuttle."

Kidahin twitched her tail at the screen in agreement. "It looks good to me. Prepare for landing."

The SIV spiraled down toward the sandy ground. On both sides vine stems soared two hundred ells above him.

"We are thirty ells and descending slowly. Brace for landing," Kidahin trilled softly.

At ten ells above ground the SIV hovered uncertainly.

"My Kidahin?" Aplilin trilled. "What is wrong?"

"I am just looking around. Maybe it is better if we land on the vine stem itself."

"I agree. Why climb up the side of the stem when we can land on it? Think of the time and effort that saves us."

"You are thinking about sabotage?" Jassalin sang.

"That was not my first thought, no. But I think we should keep our presence hidden. Humans would never think of a vehicle landing on a vine stem."

"Delwyn would," Aplilin trilled pointedly.

"He would indeed think of it," Kidahin sang affectionately, "but only because he knows how big elleiu trees grow. I do not think these humans have that knowledge."

Ascent thrusters fired until the SIV hovered above the vine stem. Kidahin pushed the yoke left until she hovered over the center of the stem. Descent thrusters fired gently until the landing jacks absorbed the touchdown jolt.

"I am taking an air sample and sending it through biofilter analysis," Kidahin sang to her team.

The SIV biohazard analysis systems passed the air sample through a series of microscopic filters and found—remarkably little.

"Mimiran, look at these bioscans," Kidahin sang.

The Warrior surgeon-in-battle read the biohazard summary. When finished, she pulled up scans of the biofilters themselves and manually scanned what they had filtered out of the air.

"This atmosphere is remarkably clean," Mimiran trilled. "There are no viruses or bacteria inimical to mammalian life. They are, however, hazardous to botanical life. This vine we are sitting on must be highly evolved."

"How can you tell that from these samples?" Kidahin sang, curious.

"What the biofilters caught are complex arboreal pathogens—plant versions of colds, viral influences, and pneumonia."

"Pneumonia? How can a plant get pneumonia?" Aplilin trilled.

"Water surrounds the cells and prevents transpiration, just like fluid filling the lungs but on a microscopic scale," Mimiran sang enthusiastically.

"Is the air safe for us?" Kidahin trilled impatiently.

"What?" Mimiran keened in flat disappointment. "Oh, yes, but Allohindra will want us to decontaminate when we return to our warship. She will insist on this even if the biohazard scan found the atmosphere sterile," she sang in usual Warrior dry humor.

"So we can breathe the air?" Kidahin keened in annoyed persistence.

"Of course. Did I not just say so? Oh, you were wrong about the rebreathers—well, incomplete, anyway. We will not need them over short periods, but hours of normal activity or doing strenuous work will make them an occasional necessity to prevent light-headedness. We will need them the most when we go more than three hundred ells above ground. Humans must wear them all the time, more because of the high atmospheric carbon dioxide than the thin air, but any continuous physical exertion, even walking, will put them into oxygen debt. I classify the atmosphere as a low-risk anoxia hazard."

"At least we need not wear the EVA suits," Jassalin trilled in relief.

"Do not sing joy to the spirits yet," Aplilin trilled in warning. "If what Delwyn suspects about these humans is true, we may need them. They are called *combat* EVA suits for a reason."

"EVA means *extra*vehicular activity, as in outside of a vehicle in vacuum or in air you cannot breathe. We can breathe this air," Jassalin sang pointedly.

Kidahin and Aplilin stood up in their seats together, left the cockpit, and walked down the passenger cabin aisle.

"Do you have other suggestions?" Kidahin sang. "We should backtrail from here to the shuttle and investigate him. I still think the survivors are heading for the geode, but we should not ignore that shuttle. There were no life signs there when I scanned him, but we may find something."

"You scanned the area surrounding the geode for life signs, did you not?" Tialdrin trilled.

"I did, but I found only trace readings, as though a very few of them had reached it, but then abandoned it. They were puzzling readings, too. As though those few slept or were in comas."

"Maybe they are suffocating from lack of oxygen," Mimiran sang doubtfully.

"Or they fell from a vine stem and are dying," Einstika suggested.

Mimiran flicked her ears in the negative. "I doubt it. Even in this low gravity a fall from a vine stem is as fatal for us as it is for them. There are no branches or wide leaves for us to ride the fall down to the ground."

"Mimiran? Do you think Nynava really knew why we are in this system?" Kidahin trilled.

"It is possible," Mimiran admitted dryly. "The A'tayotan asked us to come here, to the tail-tip of Ni'zakhonii territory. They wanted surveillance assets placed here. I think Delwyn believes this is the mission, too. If the A'tayotan added a mission stipulation, then the Mistress of the Hunt would have briefed Melkorka on A'lon'aloop naval station prior to our departure."

"She kept it a secret from Delwyn?" Kyralin trilled, aghast.

Kidahin grimaced in dismay. "That would not be hard. He cannot smell pheromones at all and would have no idea of her emotional state."

"No," Tialdrin sang clearly. "Kyralin and I were in command center with Delwyn and Melkorka. We would have smelled her agitation if she was keeping something from him."

"But wait, Tialdrin," Kyralin interrupted sharply. "Melkorka and Phelindra were both aggravated. Anything mission-related Melkorka discusses with Phelindra is because she is Delwyn's Protectress. They would have told Lo'sutra'est anni. Melkorka would have briefed...Nynava...because she was the Mistress of Battle."

"And Nynava would have briefed Zalzadrin because as Mistress of Arms, she has a need to know," Kidahin keened in fury. "Mimiran, can you wake Zalzadrin?"

"What? *No!* Absolutely not! Even when she wakes naturally, her mental faculties will be—doubtful—for a day or better, maybe longer…maybe much longer."

Kidahin turned to Merkrida. "Do you have a proposal you wish to discuss?"

"No, not yet." Merkrida sang. "I am in agreement that we should investigate the Coalition shuttle. If we find nothing, then maybe."

"Let us go," Jassalin sang. "Who is staying in the SIV to care for Zalzadrin?"

"I am," Kidahin replied. "You will lead Team-Two. Tialdrin will stay with me. You will take Mimiran in case her surgical skills are needed."

"Affirm," Jassalin sang. "I am ready."

"Go then. I will follow your progress on the commlink. Trill the alert if you need assistance, and we will fly air support for you."

"Affirm. Team-Two, exit the SIV and go to the external weapon lockers."

Kidahin and Tialdrin walked down the aisle to a reclining Zalzadrin.

"How is she doing?" Kidahin trilled.

"Resting and in no distress," Tialdrin trilled. "Help me remove her suit."

"Affirm."

They stripped the combat EVA suit from the comatose Hunter. Tialdrin placed a rebreather over Zalzadrin's face to supplement the oxygen in the thin atmosphere.

"Mimiran is a true mistress of surgery," Tialdrin keened wildly. "Her skills surpass those of a few mistresses of trauma I know. Look at her head. You cannot tell her skull was wide open only a few hours ago!"

"Mimiran should have used sutures to sew up her scalp," Kidahin trilled in a chuckle.

"Why?" Tialdrin sang.

"Zalzadrin is fond of her scars," Kidahin sang, pointing to the long scar running down the redheaded Hunter's side. "She will not have one to memorialize this mission."

***

"Aplilin, do you really think you need that thing?" Jassalin trilled, pointing her tail at the plasma cannon harness Aplilin was strapping herself into.

"This cannon is my infant. I would go nowhere without him if I had my way."

"You say so now, but let me hear you say so and mean it after climbing up and down the sides of these vines."

"You will, Jassalin. Believe me, you will."

"If you say so," Jassalin conceded. "I name you leader of Kidahin's hand."

"I am honored. But by doing so, your hand will be a Huntress short."

"More than just one with Tialdrin staying behind. Alfara and Kyralin, follow me, Merkrida and Einstika, stalk point positions for Aplilin."

"Hey! Wait one minute...," Aplilin trilled heatedly.

"No, you listen!" Jassalin trilled. "We will backtrail to the shuttle. I doubt any survivors remained behind. All of them should be well north of us by now, but they may return to the shuttle if the geode is nothing to them. That geode is a Ni'zakhonii device. It can fall upon us at any time. You are our weaponmistress, and I want you watching our tails."

"Well, when you put it that way...," Aplilin sang roughly.

"Merkrida, Hollfara, Einstika, and Seliaha, come with me," Jassalin sang.

"Where do you want me?" Mimiran trilled eagerly.

"You will prowl between our two hands. Keep watch constantly. You do not know who may need healer aid first."

"Affirm."

"Merkrida and Einstika, you work well together. Take point forty ells ahead of Aplilin," Jassalin sang, watching Seliaha as she tested the pull of her bow. Jassalin smiled her approval. They carried traditional weapons. Even Aplilin carried them. She was not stupid. Electronic countermeasures could kill her cannon, but no electromagnetic pulse could harm bows and arrows or knives—well, make that most arrows.

"Seliaha, what arrows did you put in your bow quiver?"

"Twelve sheaf and twelve antipersonnel arrows, why?"

"Just asking, is all," Jassalin sang.

She turned through a slow circle as they prowled along the stem. Everyone had their bows nocked and ready, everyone except Mimiran. She wore a Warrior's combat harness with two long knives in their sheathes. Bracers covered both arms, and a short sword hung from her hip.

Jassalin glared at Alfara, who was easy enough to find with a knife-stuffed bandolier and a few extras hanging from her waistwear underthong ties.

"Do not let me hear even one metallic jingle coming from you, Alfara."

"You will not," Alfara growled.

Jassalin spied Aplilin behind them and smiled.

"Team-Two, comm check," she sang over the commlink.

"Merkrida, here."

"Alfara, ready."

"Seliaha, I am ready."

"Aplilin, I hear you."

"Kyralin, I hear you."

"Hollfara, my commlink works."

"Mimiran, ready."

"Einstika, I am ready."

"Kidahin? Comm check."

"Jassalin? Comm clear. All comms linking to Team-Two commlink are online and stable," Kidahin confirmed. "I am receiving talkback telemetry sensor and visual data as well. *Meh nati ka meh.*"

Go with the spirits.

*"Meh nati ka meh,"* Jassalin sang, completing the formal leave-taking ritual.

Jassalin looked forward. Einstika and Merkrida, in point position, prowled slowly down the seemingly endless vine stem. Kidahin was right to compare the vine to a felled elleiu tree trunk stripped of all its branches. It was wide enough for heavy tanks to drive four side-by-side at standard armor spacing and remain an ell or three from the curving edge. Their only obstacles were the regularly spaced leaf stalks sprouting from the middle of the stem.

The bark was rough, too. They had no trouble obtaining purchase with bare feet and hands while climbing down or up its tall sides.

"Jassalin?"

"Yes, Merkrida."

"Two vines ahead are grown over this stem. Do you want to climb over them, or do you want to climb down to the ground and walk under them?"

"Climb over them. I do not trust the sand," Jassalin growled.

"What about the sand?" Hollfara trilled.

"Nothing I can point my tail at," Jassalin confessed. "But I can see what is on the stems. I have no idea what lies beneath the sand."

"I thought the scans reported bedrock," Seliaha sang.

"They did, but you cannot tell me the whole hemisphere is solid bedrock. Vines as big as these must have roots piercing it, just as elleiu tree roots do. I can imagine cracks in the bedrock filled with sand, and I do not trust the sand."

"Quicksand?" Hollfara trilled sharply.

"We did not have time to check, but probably not. No, I worry more about hollow spaces that subside when the ground is walked upon. Animals waiting in ambush under the sand is a possibility as well."

"I do not like how the air smells," Aplilin trilled from her rear position.

"What smell?" Kyralin sang in a disgusted tone. "I smell almost nothing in the air, but I should be smelling molding leaves and rotting wood. The ground is not covered with broken leaf stalks or dead leaves. Leaves fall from trees for various reasons and branches sometimes break, but I see nothing but sand below."

"Another reason to stay where we are," Jassalin sang. "Kidahin thought rain was rare here, but when it rains, it rains long and hard. These stems channel rainwater into temporary raging rivers that sweep the ground free of forest litter. Currents strong enough to wash a leaf stalk away should also take sand with it. There may be subsurface water just below the sand."

Merkrida and Einstika climbed halfway up a vine stem growing across this one. Both Hunters climbed side-by-side with bows slung across their backs.

Jassalin, watching their progress, keened to them. "Wait! Einstika, what do you see?"

"Nothing but more vine stems. The one we are on is fused to another one. They grow across your path and dip down slightly before climbing up the vine stem growing next to this one. We can cross over to the other stem or we can continue climbing over and down this tangle to the original stem."

"Merkrida? What do you think?" Jassalin trilled.

"I see no reason in preferring one stem over the other. Stay on this one," Merkrida sang.

"I agree with you," Jassalin sang. "Team-Two, there is a climbing obstacle ahead. Now you will regret carrying that infant of yours, Aplilin."

"You think so? Just watch and see," Aplilin sang in retort.

Jassalin debated holding back just for the joy of seeing Aplilin climb with the unwieldy cannon. While she waited, she saw Mimiran's head snap around and down toward the sandy ground far below.

"Mimiran? Have you thoughts you want to share?"

The Warrior surgeon-in-battle flexed her ears wide and held her tail rigid behind her. "Come here," she trilled.

Jassalin glided up beside the Warrior female and looked where she was gazing so intently. On the ground below, seemingly impaled by one of the vine's spiral tentacles, rested the desiccated remains of an animal, an animal better than three times her size.

"I thought Kidahin found no significant animal life here," Jassalin sang softly.

"She did not have time to scan the entire hemisphere. Maybe they are rare."

"It has been dead for some time," Jassalin observed.

"A very long time," Mimiran agreed. "It likely died in a flash flood and got tangled in the tentacle. The climate is cool and dry most of the time. The curious rarity of bacteria in the atmosphere prevented it from rot. That is why it is a dried-out husk and not a bone pile."

"Do you wish to examine it?" Jassalin trilled solicitously.

Mimiran flicked her ears sideways, a dismissal. "No," she added. "It is clearly not human."

"Are you ready for a good climb?" Jassalin trilled wickedly.

"Of course."

Jassalin flicked her ears before resuming her place in the prowling order.

Climbing up, over, up again, over and then down the other side of the magnificent, twisting, impossibly huge vine stems was exhilarating for everyone.

That is, everyone but Aplilin. True to her word, the plasma cannon did not encumber her or otherwise slow her climbing, although it did require clever placement on her body. When she reached the bottommost stem, she paused to field-assemble it.

Assembling the cannon was easy for Aplilin. Intimately familiar with the weapon, she could assemble it with eyes closed. The rote work her hands were doing did not distract her eyes from watching the hoarder Alfara step lightly and adjusting what remained of her knife hoard.

Something else moved. Aplilin stood, twisted the barrel home, thumbed the trigger guard up, aimed, and fired.

The cannon belched a plasma bolt at supersonic speed into the side of the overlapping stem at the same time a deafening *chua* echoed down the living canyon walls.

The ionizing blast took a three-ell-deep chunk out of the vine stem where it grew over the stem she stood on, pulverizing a tentacle in the process and knocking Alfara twenty ells across the stem. Had the blast angle been more acute, it would have blown her off the vine stem to her death below.

Alfara bounced up from the rough bark pulling knives from her bandolier and looking about wildly.

"Everyone keep clear of those tentacles!" Aplilin keened at alert tempo.

"Aplilin, what are you firing at?" Jassalin trilled.

"At a tendril, tentacle, whatever it is. I saw one move. It coiled like a spring as Alfara was passing it."

While she examined Alfara, Mimiran looked up into Jassalin's eyes.

"The dead animal?" Jassalin sang.

"Precisely. These tentacles must be opportunistic carnivores," Mimiran sang.

"These vines cannot live solely on animal flesh. Spirits! Look at the size of them. All the animals in this hemisphere cannot feed more than one vine."

"They are not part of the vines," Mimiran sang. "They are independent plants, just as the lianas and small vines growing in the leaf stalks are."

"Another parasitic plant?" Alfara trilled as she wrapped a length of tail around her waist and examined it closely.

"I need to examine them to tell if the tentacles are parasitic or symbiotic," Mimiran sang eagerly.

"I do not care what they are. Just avoid them," Jassalin trilled.

"Jassalin, another vine crosses up ahead," Merkrida trilled.

"Climb it and we will follow."

"Are you going to complain about my infant now?" Aplilin sang with a note of curiosity.

"No," Jassalin trilled, annoyed. "I doubt an antipersonnel arrow can kill a tentacle, let alone slow it down."

Aplilin flipped her ears wide and then perked them forward, a nod, and began field-stripping the cannon for the next climb.

Team-Two climbed up and down several overlapping stems uneventfully as they followed the broad stem north. Jassalin was preoccupied with just how much their prowling down the vine stem made her think she was on felled elleiu tree trunk. Team-Two prowled another three hours before Merkrida and Einstika paused and stuck their tails in the air, holding them rigid.

"We have arrived," Merkrida sang over the commlink. "The shuttle lies below us."

Jassalin joined them. Mimiran, Hollfara, and the rest of Team-Two followed Jassalin to the stem's edge.

As one they looked down onto a long broad sandy path spanning their stem and the one next to them. The Coalition of Earth Colonies shuttle was dug an ell or two into the sand. Behind him a fresh ditch trailed for a hundred ells or more.

"He came down hard," Aplilin sang.

"Yes, he did," Jassalin agreed. "Kidahin, do you see this?"

"I do," Kidahin sang over the commlink. "How I want to send out ears and tails to overfly that shuttle."

"I am sure you do, my Kidahin," Aplilin agreed. "The remote surveillance probes can cover a lot of ground. Too bad they went the way of the troop transport."

"The SIV is not equipped to support autonomous probes. There was no place to put them even if we had time to remove the necessary support equipment and install it into the SIV," Kidahin sang.

"How should I proceed?" Jassalin trilled.

"He looks abandoned. Anyone remaining behind would have come running after hearing Aplilin's cannon. Climb down and prowl the immediate area. Set up ambush prowlers. Try to board the shuttle if possible. If you can board him, post stalkers outside and out of sight."

"Affirm," Jassalin sang. She turned to include the others with her. "You heard our assaultmistress. Climb down well out of range of those tentacles and spread out. I do not expect hostile fire from allies, but if Delwyn is right about this mutiny concept then I do not want to lose all of you in one blast. Go!"

They climbed down the side of the vine stem, one at a time, Jassalin going first. When she reached the sandy ground, she danced a light pattern, paused, pulled her bow, and nocked an antipersonnel arrow.

Aplilin, the last Huntress waiting to climb down, spent the time waiting by aiming her plasma cannon at the shuttle. Delwyn had likened the survivors as tailcutters and tailcutters deserved no mercy.

"You are waiting for us to climb down before you field strip your weapon?" Seliaha sang.

"I am," Aplilin trilled sourly. "I do not like this. It smells of slippery bark and blind trails."

"I brought you something," Seliaha blurted.

"Oh?" Aplilin sang melodiously, her ears swiveling on Seliaha, but her eyes remained glued to the targeting screen, her tail twisting gently.

"Yes. I knew Alfara hoarded one of them, I asked her if I could have it and she gave it to me. You are a good archer. Maybe you can use it."

"Look at my back, Seliaha. I have a bow. Go on, it is your turn to climb down."

"I did not bring you a bow."

Aplilin glanced at the device in Seliaha's hand.

"A thumper? What does a thumper have to do with my archery skills?" Aplilin sang at a curious pitch.

"Your bow pulls harder than any other. You can remove the antipersonnel explosive from one of your AP arrows and replace it with the thumper and fire it into a target."

Aplilin kept her gaze locked on the targeting scanner, but she flipped her ears, intrigued.

"Maybe," she sang. "It is heavy. It is not aerodynamic. It uses more power than an AP charge. It will also reduce arrow range."

"Oh," Seliaha keened in disappointment.

Aplilin smelled the dismay on Seliaha's pheromones.

"Do not feel sad. I can make it work. Thank you, Seliaha."

"You are welcome," Seliaha trilled happily, turned, and began climbing down the side of the vine stem.

Ten minutes later everyone was spreading out across the sandy ground and waiting for Aplilin to disassemble her weapon and climb down to them. While they waited, Jassalin planned aloud.

"We will approach at assault prowling speed. The shuttle looks damaged, but I see no breaks in the hull. Once we get close, fan out around him. Look for open hatches. Sing out if you find one, and we will converge on you. Go!"

Team-Two scattered, each Hunter charging across the sand while watching her spacing to prevent a single shot from killing them all.

Jassalin ran slightly ahead in sand up to her ankles. Her four-jointed toes and opposable big toes dug into the sand, flinging it behind her and propelling her body steadily forward at a speed their favorite male could never hope to match.

She flanked the shuttle on his right, turned, and ran for his bow. She looked for an open hatch near the flight deck and found none.

"Jassalin?" Merkrida sang over the commlink.

"Yes, Merkrida?"

"The aft troop bay door is open and extended as a ramp. The interior is illuminated. No sign of humans."

"I am circling around the bow and will meet you there. Do not go inside," Jassalin sang.

"Affirm."

"This shuttle will never fly again," Hollfara sang with certainty. "I scanned the fuselage and found hundreds of minute fractures and heavy engine damage. I will know more once I take some inside scans. I can confirm his power systems are active but at a low level."

"Do you think he is capable of atmospheric flight?" Jassalin sang.

"No," Hollfara sang promptly. "But if there are no contamination hazards or reactor problems, he is an ideal emergency shelter. I do not understand why they abandoned him. Shipwreck doctrine says to remain with your ship."

"Not if they try to capture a Ni'zakhonii FTL-capable ship," Jassalin growled to herself. "Aplilin, where are you?"

"Seliaha and I are behind the shuttle. She is covering me with antipersonnel arrows, and I am covering you with my infant."

"Jassalin? Einstika. I am walking from the stern around the left flank. I found something...strange."

"Strange? What do you mean by strange?" Jassalin trilled.

"Sand dunes, a hundred and ten of them. They are no taller than my ankles, are oblong, and maybe a bit longer than I am tall."

"Sand dunes? They cannot be wind driven. These stems are like cliffs. Those dunes are likely sand bar remnants from flash flooding."

"I do not think so," Einstika objected. "They are in a line along the shuttle's left flank."

Jassalin frowned, thinking hard.

"Stay away from them. They may be concealed ordnance. Aplilin, I need your demolitions and weaponmistress skills. Come in and take a look at what Einstika found."

"Affirm," Aplilin sang over the commlink and turned on Seliaha. "Come here and put this on. Keep an eye on the targeting scanner. If you feel you must fire, touch here, flip the trigger lock up, brace yourself, and pull the trigger."

"But Aplilin," Seliaha trilled in protest. "I cannot wear that thing. I am too small. The harness will not fit properly and the back blast will knock me on my tail."

"You will probably not have to fire. You will do well." She flicked her ear to open the commlink. "Jassalin! I am running to Einstika."

"Mimiran? Where are you?" Jassalin keened.

"Near the aft ramp and walking left. I can see Einstika. She is correct. There is a row of sand dunes here."

Mimiran hesitated a moment to look across the wide, sandy path. "They are indeed artificial dunes. The surrounding sand looks nothing like them."

Alfara ran toward Einstika, her hoard of items bouncing against her smooth, velour-soft, crimson and orangey yellow dappled skin. She felt around in her combat harness while she ran, struggling to pull a battlefield scanner clear.

"Stand still," Alfara keened. "You may have walked into a line of antipersonnel pop-up mines. Let me take a scan."

"Affirm!" Einstika trilled, eyes wide.

Alfara held the palm-sized battlefield scanner and turned in a slow circle near Einstika. She stopped, read the results, and twitched her ear.

"Jassalin? Alfara. I just did a scanner sweep and found no ordnance."

"Affirm, I see you," Jassalin sang in relief.

Aplilin, standing beside Einstika, turned her gaze from the hoarder Huntress to Kyralin and keened, "Kyralin! What are you doing?"

"Digging into one of these dunes. I think these are survival caches. Yes! I am right. I just found a long blue bag with the Coalition of Earth Colonies seal on it."

"That was stupid, Kyralin!" Aplilin trilled violently. "You might have gotten yourself killed!"

"I always make sure nothing harms our society," Kyralin snapped.

Jassalin and a few others gathered around Kyralin and her partially unearthed prize.

"Step away, Kyralin," Mimiran keened at imperative tempo.

"Mistress?"

"Step back now. It is human. Can you not smell it?" Mimiran sang sadly.

"Smell it? Of course I smell it. The shuttle is a human ship."

"No, I do not mean the scent of humans. I mean this bag contains a human body," Mimiran sang gently.

Kyralin recoiled from the Coalition duffel bag as though it burned her.

"All of these dunes contain dead humans?" Jassalin trilled in a hushed tone.

"I am certain of it," Mimiran keened softly.

"Victims of the crash?" Jassalin trilled.

"Perhaps so," Mimiran agreed. "I would need to conduct an autopsy to know for certain."

"Can you do them here?"

"I can perform basic autopsy scans and give you an initial assessment, but I am not a cause-of-death specialist. Allohindra would have to review the scans and make the final determination."

"On behalf of any males buried here, I give you consent to act as their postmortem healer. Although they are human, I cannot give consent to disturb any dead females you unearth."

"Of course," Mimiran trilled. Males are terrible patients, which was why any female could give consent for any healer treatment a male might need, whether he wanted it or not and regardless of his customary autonomy. But females had the right of refusal once they understood their disorder and its proposed treatment.

"Aplilin, strap your cannon back on. You will lead a prowler group into the shuttle. Make a stalking sweep and report what you find," Jassalin trilled.

"Affirm! Hollfara and Seliaha, come with me."

"Me?" Hollfara trilled. "Why me?"

"The shuttle is wrecked and alien, and you are a spacecraft designer. Seliaha comes because she is an ordnance specialist and has good ideas. Come on, we are wasting time."

"Affirm!" Hollfara sang, excited at the prospect of seeing more human engineering.

"Kidahin? Mimiran," the surgeon-in-battle called over the commlink.

"I hear you," Kidahin sang.

"Have you looked at our talkback telemetry video?"

"I have," Kidahin sang. "Delwyn told me once that humans cremate or bury their dead."

"Cremate I understand if pathogens are involved," Mimiran sang. "But burying them? The point of leaving the dead in the jungle is to give back to the rainforest what it gave us in life. To what purpose is burial?"

"I do not know. He said there was ritual involved, something like the Death Song ritual."

"Oh, I will have to ask him about it when we get back," Mimiran sang.

"So, will you do the autopsy scans?" Kidahin trilled.

"Yes, I have to. Anything about these burials strike you as odd?"

"The number of them, you mean?" Kidahin trilled in distress.

"Precisely," Mimiran agreed. "There are too many of them. You cannot convince me the shuttle crashed, without exploding or smashing himself to pieces, and yet all these people died as a result of a hard landing."

"Do you need anything in the SIV? I can fly to you in minutes."

"No, I have all I need in my healer's harness. I will scan the bodies and make initial virtual autopsy assessments. I will send them and the scans to you. You will upload the files to our warship with a priority notice to Allohindra."

"By radio?" Kidahin trilled discordantly. "It will take a signal the better part of two days to relay Allohindra's conclusions back to you. What does Jassalin propose we do in the meantime? Wait in the shuttle?"

"No," Jassalin cut in. "We continue as planned. We explore the shuttle and gain intelligence, and then we fly a khnell, prowl the area, fly another khnell, and so on until we reach the geode."

"Maybe I should overfly the route using active scans. That would be faster, and we will find any humans remaining," Kidahin grumbled.

"And if that geode is an active Ni'zakhonii asset, it will shoot you out of the sky as easily as I swat salt flies with my tail," Mimiran sang.

"Probably true enough," Kidahin admitted. "But I can skim over the sand to you in minutes. The plan was for me to pick you up once you secured the shuttle."

"You can come now," Mimiran suggested. "Tialdrin can help me with the autopsies. How is Zalzadrin?"

"Resting. She woke up, asked Tialdrin if she had a nice scar, and fell back asleep."

"Good, *good!*" Mimiran sang happily. "You should ask Jassalin about flying here, though. It is her place to make the request, not mine."

"Affirm. Jassalin, what do you think?"

"Not yet. We have not secured the area. Aplilin is in the shuttle right now. Give her an hour before you lift off," Jassalin suggested.

"Affirm," Kidahin sang.

# 8

## THE STALKING APPETITE, THE DANCE OF BODY AND SPIRIT, THE SHADOW REBELLION...

"Kidahin?" Mimiran trilled softly from her seat behind the cockpit bulkhead.

No reply answered from the pilot seat.

"Kidahin?" Mimiran trilled again.

"Leave her alone," Aplilin growled.

"Melkorka kept mission-critical information from us!" Einstika snarled.

"She put Delwyn at risk!" Merkrida and Kyralin sang simultaneously.

"Did you two just invoke a jinx ward against ill-luck?" Mimiran sang flatly.

"You think putting our Warleader at risk is funny?" Aplilin trilled at challenge pitch.

Mimiran immediately pulled her knapped flint adulthood knife from its sheath curving around and under her lean left breast and growled a challenge at the insult Aplilin was implying.

"Calm down, Mimiran. You, too, Aplilin. I think Melkorka thought she was protecting Delwyn by keeping worrisome chords from finding his ears. Males *do* need minders," Jassalin sang humorously to lighten the sudden deadly mood. Male safety was never a topic females joked about. "He is safe with Lo'sutra'est anni, the Huntmistress, and Phelindra tangling his every move with their tails. The radio message was clear. Melkorka wanted Nynava to brief us after we landed here."

"But we received Melkorka's first message over eleven hours ago, and Kidahin has not sang a note since," Kyralin complained.

"Not a coherent one, anyway," Hollfara sang. "She keened long and loud enough soon after Melkorka began speaking, though. I thought she was going to smash the cockpit to pieces."

"She would have if not for me holding her back," Aplilin sang at a contralto dissonant trill from the gunner seat.

"She does not need to sing to fly the SIV," Jassalin pointed out.

"But she is tail-tied to her anger," Kyralin trilled. "Her pheromones reek with anger and blinding hatred."

"Melkorka sent a second message barely an hour ago, remember? She sent Allohindra's autopsy results. We need to discuss them, because they make no sense," Hollfara trilled.

"Allohindra confirmed Mimiran's cause-of-death conclusions for every dead male she examined. They all died from asphyxiation caused by rapid decompression. None died during the hard landing itself or from some structural or system failure before or during reentry," Tialdrin sang.

"I do not understand how they could have died from rapid decompression," Hollfara keened. "I took detailed scans of the shuttle. I found no fuselage breaches, not one. The cockpit, flight deck, gunner station, passenger cabin, combat bay, and the cargo hold were intact. I closed the aft deployment ramp and ran a pressure test. The fuselage, hatches, and all seals held. The inertial dampening system was online and the artificial gravity generator was producing Earth-normal gravity. No breach-arresting force fields were in operation. No in-flight damage control measures were taken."

"How is that possible?" Seliaha trilled. "The *Khoza's* shuttle deployment bay was smashed and barely habitable. Two shuttles were smashed beyond repair given what resources were available to the survivors. They freed the remaining shuttle using demolitions, plasma torches, hydraulic jacks, jackhammers, and even manual pushing and prying. Is this not so, Aplilin?"

"It is," Aplilin sang in agreement. "You probably missed a damaged seal that failed during reentry, Hollfara."

"I did not!" Hollfara keened in outrage at the tail slap to her competency. "The fuselage was heavily scarred with superficial, cosmetic damage. Exterior armor belting was intact, and I determined that belting like this can flake off the fuselage if it takes moderate kinetic impacts."

"We are missing something," Jassalin sang. "Aplilin, tell us again what you and Seliaha found inside the shuttle."

"What more is there to tell?" Aplilin trilled at interrogative tempo. "The shuttle is a moderate gunship-capable craft. Seliaha and I prowled everywhere we could fit and found nothing remarkable. The reactor defaulted to stand-by mode. The fusion engine was heavily damaged. Structural damage was not bad enough to breach the fuselage. His limited-range hyperdrive coils seemed intact, but the hydrogen-antihydrogen reactor was offline due to the loss of antihydrogen containment. The cockpit, flight deck, passenger cabin, combat bay, and hold were clear, clean, well-illuminated, and well-stocked. What more can I say?"

"Anything you want to add, Seliaha?" Jassalin prompted.

"Me? No, nothing more than what Aplilin just reported. It was foolish for them to abandon the shuttle. His internal systems were online, including a small healer suite and a nutrition niche. I accessed all menu items," Seliaha sang, "including—meat—items," she trilled into a discordant gag and blanched at the nauseous idea of eating animal flesh.

"Anything more to add?" Jassalin persisted.

"No," Seliaha sang, "except that..."

"Except what?" Jassalin pounced.

"Oh, well...the obvious. They left a lot of equipment behind including knives, grenades, and a full inventory of cowardly small arms and hand-held heavy infantry weapons."

"Of course not," Jassalin trilled. "They are stalking the Ni'zakhonii geode. If the geode is FTL-capable, they will not take encumbering equipment along and..."

"No!" Aplilin keened from her place at the gunner seat. "Not if they must fight for it. They need supplies and ordnance nearby, not days away from a combat zone. Combat doctrine calls for breaking out supplies and bringing them forward. The shuttle and his health suite and nutrition niche guarantee shelter while they move supplies forward to an operations base. From the base they go back and move more supplies forward. Once the moves are completed, they advance and establish a new operations base and transfer the supplies from the old base to the new one. They continue making northward incremental moves until all supplies are cached near the geode for immediate access during combat."

"Taking no supplies forward suggests they are expecting a happy welcome," Jassalin sang. "They would need the entire shuttle complement to capture the geode. Why then are all those males dead?"

"They were spaced!" Kidahin keened from the pilot seat.

"What does 'spaced' mean?" Hollfara sang at interrogative pitch.

"It is a Delwyn word," Mimiran sang. "Allohindra discussed it in her report. Delwyn spat this word as she briefed him and Melkorka. He told them that to space someone is to put her in an airlock and blow the outer hatch, expelling her into the void to die in the vacuum of space."

"They were killed? Just as the *Londiwe Khoza's* warleader and his society were killed? Why?" Hollfara keened. "There are no more than thirty or forty survivors left. The pilot and copilot seats, left and right flank gunner seats, and the electronic countermeasure and electronic warfare seats account for thirteen. They put another twenty or so on the flight deck. Everyone in the passenger cabin and combat bay died. They were all spaced?" she trilled, horrified.

"Yes!" Kidahin keened.

"The number thirty agrees with the stalking pattern we see in the sand heading northwest every time we land and make a security prowl," Alfara sang.

"They lost one, the male we found dead a few hours ago," Mimiran added. "That vine stem tendril, tentacle, whatever it is, speared him, wound up inside of him and sucked the bodily fluids from him until he was a dry husk."

"They stripped the gear from his body, too," Alfara sang in approval. "They are conserving their resources, and that confirms they do not intend on returning to their shuttle."

"I wonder how Anailiatha can use the Coalition warship hyperdrive coils to...," Hollfara sang.

"How the Mistress of Sails goes about freeing our warship from the hypercube is not tactically relevant to our goals," Jassalin interrupted.

"But it is," Hollfara trilled. "Melkorka sent Anailiatha's engineering report along with the autopsy findings. She concludes that part of the hypercube has extended into hyperspace and is transmitting an FTL beacon to the Coalition star Mu Arae. She speculates that *Londiwe Khoza* came from there to this system."

"And apparently collided with the hypercube artifact, killing all but a fraction of his crew."

"Which brings us back to what special knowledge Kidahin knows," Mimiran sang.

"What knowledge, Mimiran?" Jassalin trilled, curious.

Mimiran stood and glanced into the cockpit. "The humans Melkorka mentioned in the first radio message. Kidahin, who is this tailcutter Harrison?"

Kidahin snarled in black rage.

"My Kidahin?" Aplilin sang, concerned, smelling waves of fury radiating from her lover. Aplilin held a primal empathy rating near the average norm, but Kidahin's pheromonal sending drew pictures in Aplilin's mind that not even the empathically blind could miss. Images of a human male representing a danger to Delwyn flooded her awareness, images not even closed eyes could banish. Aplilin also smelled an aura-like scent surrounding Kidahin, an undercurrent of indignant outrage aimed at, surprisingly, the Huntmistress.

"What about warleader special security and this Harrison?" Aplilin trilled.

"They were supposed to kill him before we left Ibeetu!" Kidahin snapped, her singsong voice trilling outrage. "After Melkorka named Delwyn our Warleader, Phelindra sent a small group to Delwyn's Coalition warship. They packed his personal items so we could put them in his abode on our warship. While packing, two warship special security Huntresses prowled off and abducted Harrison and his aide. Phelindra said nothing about it aloud, but her pheromones told all of us that the hierarchy representatives on our ship knew Harrison meant Delwyn lethal harm. He even tried to convince Warleader Phalalin to order Melkorka to arrest Delwyn..."

"Order?" Tialdrin growled musically. "Phalalin is warleader of *Fearless*. Only a ship's warleader can give an order to that ship's mistress of the ship. If Phalalin were to give Melkorka an order, he would violate the male autonomy rights held by our warship."

"Correct," Kidahin spat-grimaced in distaste at the very idea. "Melkorka raised the issue with Phelindra. She sought and received a Major Consensus that Harrison planned lethal harm to Delwyn should he return to *Henri Edda*. The intent to harm a male without honorable justification is a death penalty honor point crime, so warleader special security acted. The humans never found Harrison or his aide. Delwyn learned of Phelindra's involvement during a warleader-to-warleader visit aboard *Fearless*."

"How did Phalalin find out what the hierarchy representatives on our warship ordered?" Tialdrin trilled in fury over the apparent trespass into both warship and hierarchy matters.

"His protectress smelled it on Phelindra and laughed about it aloud. Delwyn was not so amused," Kidahin trilled, smiling wickedly in spite of her anger.

"Why not?" Aplilin sang. "But that is not the point since hierarchy matters are no male's business. Warleader special security protects a warleader as they see fit. They do not require his leave to act in his best interests. The greater concern, as I see it, is their apparent failure. Harming or attempting to harm a male without honorable justification calls for the death of the person wielding the intent. She must be skinned alive with her own adulthood knife. How did warleader special security go about passing judgment on human males for such a high honor crime?"

"Females intervene whenever we think males may harm one another," Alfara sang. "When it is clear a male becomes a danger to another male and has the specific intent to harm that male, then he is guilty of intending lethal harm and must be, regretfully, killed. But for a male the killing cannot be demeaning, as it must be for any female guilty of the same crime."

"Quit making speeches, Alfara. You sound like Hollfara. We all know a male is held by a triad of females while they strangle him with his own tail. The two Huntresses should have strangled Harrison and his aide. Why did they not do so?" Aplilin trilled.

"Humans have no tails," Seliaha blurted flatly. "The Huntresses could not strangle the tailcutters in the traditional manner, but strangulation is the required penalty."

"I thought the Huntresses spaced them," Kidahin confessed. "Melkorka is furious and rightly so. If our FTL comms were working, her communications avatar would still be keening about it. She said the A'tayotan discovered Harrison's FTL distress call and briefed her and Phelindra immediately. Phelindra called warleader special security to account for Harrison's continued breathing. The Huntmistress launched an immediate investigation and learned that the two Huntresses decided to let Harrison suffocate on an Ibeetu heading into its broiling summer, a summer with heat and humidity far beyond our, let alone human, tolerances. They do not understand how Harrison could survive long enough to leave Ibeetu.

"The Ni'zakhonii," Kyralin trilled. "That sneaky tailcutter somehow stole an FTL-capable ship. The Ni'zakhonii were transforming those geodes into small, combat-capable ships in the Nikkiolo system."

"I doubt it," Jassalin sang. "Harrison would flee into Coalition of Earth Colonies territory. Why would he flee into Ni'zakhonii territory, through it, and come this far opposite of Coalition territory? The geode reached this system, so he could just as easily have reached Earth before exhausting his antihydrogen. No, I think he was captured by the Ni'zakhonii while still on Ibeetu."

"Ni'zakhonii eat Eyloni and humans alive. That is a far more fitting end to him as far as I am concerned. Either way, he should be dead. How is he still alive?" Kidahin trilled derisively.

"Did Harrison have allies plotting against Delwyn?" Mimiran sang at interrogative pitch.

"Yes, he did," Kidahin sang with certainty. "He had a small staff with him while he was on Ibeetu. I remember some of them."

"Well, you said that you recognized a scent while we were on the *Khoza*. Did that scent belong to a Harrison supporter?" Mimiran sang sharply.

"No, I do not think so," Kidahin growled. "But I am certain it was the scent of someone I met on Delwyn's ship while he was showing me his command center there."

"You never went into the shuttle, did you," Mimiran sang.

"No. I saw no need to," Kidahin admitted.

"You should have. You might have recognized the scents lingering there."

"Do you want to fly back and check, my Kidahin? It will not take long. We could fly directly there and return here without landing because there is no reason to stop and prowl ground already prowled," Aplilin sang persuasively.

"We are approaching our next prowling stop," Kidahin snapped. "Prepare for landing," she growled.

The SIV spiraled down from vine stem height to a wide, sandy path as Kidahin growled to herself. Except for finding the dead human male, this fourteenth landing since leaving the Sentry crash site was the same. Her Huntresses found signs confirming a force numbering thirty-four. Of those thirty-four, fourteen staggered across the sand oblivious to the otherwise well-managed prowling pattern the remaining twenty maintained. The clumsy footwork perplexed Kidahin, making her ears dip.

"My Kidahin?" Aplilin trilled, smelling puzzlement on her lover's scent. "These fourteen who cannot follow a simple prowling pattern..."

"What about them?" Jassalin trilled while preparing Team-Two for a perimeter sweep.

"They are a surface assault team liability. Their footprints say they have no idea how to prowl on sand."

"Maybe that fourteen had a twentieth? The one sucked dry by the vine tentacle?" Einstika suggested. "They knew about them, and yet he stumbled into one anyway."

"One of Harrison's tailcutters, no doubt," Kidahin growled in satisfaction. "Remember the clothing the dead wore on the *Khoza*? What was the tentacle-speared human male wearing?"

"He wore different clothing. Does clothing reflect rank in human culture?" Kyralin trilled.

"It does," Kidahin sang in approval. "Humans always wear clothing to excess. Warship crews wear uniform-looking clothing with varying colors and symbols showing rank. Humans permit the rare guest aboard their warships, and they do not, and I believe cannot, wear this uniform clothing without incurring an honor debt. Harrison and his staff did not wear warship uniform clothing."

"Does this mean the tailcutters are not combat trained?" Jassalin trilled over the commlink. "What about the others with them?"

"I think they are an elite combat force similar to what Delwyn trained and led. Be wary. Human elite combat teams, what Delwyn calls special operations groups, wear special uniform clothing covered with pixelated patterns of random blacks, dark greens, greens, and light greens."

"I do not understand how they can prowl effectively while wearing tightfitting clothing," Merkrida trilled. "They are staying on the sand and keeping close to the vine stem. They should take advantage of the landscape and wear sand and bark-colored clothing."

"I know," Kidahin sighed musically. "Delwyn often wore camouflage clothing during security sweeps on Ibeetu designed to blend into the surrounding foliage. He called it a 'kill suit.' We should anticipate this force wearing similar suits as well."

"Random green shades are no help against dark bark and tan sand," Jassalin sang.

"Do not mistake kill suits for pixelated uniform clothing. They are not the same," Kidahin trilled. "I examined Delwyn's kill suit once. It is made from three-dimensional mesh material impregnated with holographic lensing film. It scans the immediate area and alters the mesh to reflect the colors surrounding its wearer. A kill-suited human, as long as he remains still, has an advantage. Our skin with its varying red, orange, and yellow shades and patterns will not hide us against dark bark and tan sand. Be wary and remember that humans see red as a warning color. They will see us before we see them."

"Affirm," Jassalin sang.

"Aplilin, go with Jassalin," Kidahin sang.

"Why?" Aplilin trilled. "We are more than two million ells, two khnells, from the geode. The shuttle survivors are probably reconnoitering a perimeter around it while we tailchase time away approaching from their rear."

"I know, but soon we must advance on foot," Kidahin sang.

"But not yet!" Aplilin keened. "Two khnells on foot at stalking speed is two days of nonstop prowling without sleep."

"I know," Kidahin repeated. "But we will not begin sustained ground prowling until we are within a hundred thirty-thousand ells or so from the geode. Once there, I will fly air support while you prowl to the geode."

"That sounds better," Aplilin sang happily. "I can carry my infant on a hundred thirty kamell, eleven-and-a-half hour prowl."

"I never doubted it," Kidahin sang.

Aplilin climbed out of her seat and jumped from the open cockpit exterior hatch to chase down Jassalin. Mimiran glided into the vacated gunner seat and wrapped her tail around Kidahin's waist.

"Zalzadrin ate," Mimiran trilled happily.

"Really? Did she say anything to you?"

"She did," Mimiran trilled, perking her ears at Kidahin. "She said, 'Dizzy, tastes bland, thank you' in flat, rhythmless notes and fell back asleep."

"You are pleased with her progress," Kidahin sang with a hopeful lilt.

"I am," Mimiran sang in the same lilting melody. Pure pleasure radiated from the surgeon-in-battle. Her pheromonal flavor seized Kidahin's nose savagely and her own insensate fury dissolved.

"You are enjoying yourself!" Kidahin trilled accusingly.

"I am," Mimiran sang in three-part harmony. "Being tail-tied to the Society of Assault Team-Two is exciting. It gave me an opportunity to explore a human warship and perform my occupational specialty in the field. Why, just think of it! I am in the field and protecting Delwyn at the same time. I will consent to your leadership and remain with Team-Two, subject to your approval of course. If only I can convince Allohindra, Phelindra, and Melkorka to let me remain with you."

"Let you remain? With us?" Kidahin trilled. "You want to join Assault Team-Two society permanently? Why would you do that? You hold mistress social rank and you are our warship's Mistress of Inner Strength!"

"And you are our warship's auxiliary command center navigator and Team-Two assaultmistress. Secondary occupational specialties are necessary since surface assault or boarding action teams are infrequently deployed. Why? Do you object?"

"Of course not," Kidahin sang. "But you can look out for Delwyn every time he comes to Health Center."

Mimiran trilled musical laughter at that. "Allohindra is the Mistress of Healers. She will trip over her own tail in haste to climb to any emergency involving Delwyn. But what can really happen to him on our warship? The same is true for warleader special security Huntresses. They always make sure to smell danger before he does, but just how often does this kind of danger happen on our warship?"

"I never thought much about it," Kidahin trilled thoughtfully.

"No? Then consider this. At Nikkiolo you led Team-Two against a Ni'zakhonii research shipyard. You were actively protecting him."

"I was not," Kidahin denied, her voice musically flat. "I led a mission to recover research and development materials related to how the Ni'zakhonii were making warship hulls out of geode crystal elements. Delwyn was in orbit above me leading the battle group as Warpact Warleader."

"Yes, while Team-Two and other assault teams breached the research facility and kept them from taking offensive action against Delwyn," Mimiran sang harmoniously.

"A one-time instance," Kidahin trilled discordantly.

"Do you really think so? What are we doing now?" Mimiran sang slyly. "Aplilin blew up *Londiwe Khoza* hyperdrive coil power taps to protect him. We are here because of Harrison, so we are protecting him again. How many more times will we be called upon to protect him while we are here? Do you not realize that warleader special security Huntresses envy you?"

"That is...that is nonsense, Mimiran," Kidahin spluttered discordantly. "Warleader special security Huntresses are feared!"

"They are indeed," Mimiran agreed. "They are feared because anybody they suspect comes under their scrutiny. They can go anywhere on Elleio in pursuit of a danger to Delwyn. Just how often is anyone ever considered a threat to a male, let alone a warleader?"

"On Elleio?" Kidahin replied in counterpoint melody. "In theory? Rarely. In practical day-to-day life? Never. Warleader special security Huntresses today are poised to act if, say, a Ni'zakhonii somehow gained a foothold aboard our warship or if something happened to our warship like what happened to *Londiwe Khoza.*"

"And how often do you think either possibility can happen?" Mimiran pressed in staccato voice.

Kidahin watched Team-Two transponder blips crawl across a perimeter scan and frowned, her tail darting behind her.

"Well?" Mimiran demanded.

"Practically never," Kidahin sang softly. "But *Londiwe Khoza* is proof it can happen."

"Which is why warleader special security Huntresses are dour and no-nonsense. They sacrifice their time stalking after the one instance that changes theory into practice. This was why Melkorka warned you to avoid warleader special security occupational options. But for the one extremely rare practical security threat, our society—Delwyn's occupational association—protects him always. But here, in the field, you have already protected Delwyn more than the Huntmistress herself has. What is more satisfying to your young Hunter mind when you know above all else that males need minders?"

"Prowling with Team-Two," Kidahin sang at low dissonant pitch. "But I keep having doubts..."

"You have?" Mimiran interrupted sharply, hearing a chance to pounce. "When was the last time you felt doubt creeping up your tail?"

Kidahin thought hard for several minutes as she watched transponder blips backtrailing across the perimeter scan toward the SIV.

"I do not remember," she trilled, exasperated. "Not that long ago."

Mimiran flicked her ears aside and then pricked them forward, snapping her tail as she did so. "You have not entertained a single doubt since we talked just before the jump drive mishap that crippled our troop transport. How long ago was that?"

"Two days. But, Mimiran, two days means nothing. I have been too busy to think about doubt!"

"Which is the point, I think," Mimiran sang softly. "You know what to do, what duty requires. Here, as assaultmistress, you are protecting Delwyn. But right now, on our warship, Delwyn and his warleader special security Huntresses are at the mercy of Anailiatha and her techmistresses."

"Oh! I never thought about that. Each Huntress is probably pulling hairs out of her pons by now," Kidahin sang in delight, knowing she was doing important work. She paused and thought about Delwyn, her special relationship with him, and their shared adventures.

"Do you really want to formally join Assault Team-Two?" she trilled.

"I do," Mimiran sang. "I rank Zalzadrin, but Phelindra's opinion matters in this. She and Allohindra will discuss it, but my going on occasional surface action missions will not inconvenience Health Center surgical readiness nor interfere with my obligations as Mistress of Inner Strength."

"We must agree as a society," Kidahin pointed out. "It will require a Major Consensus and Merkrida would insist on one even if it did not."

"I understand, and in this case she is correct to insist on a unanimous consent," Mimiran sang.

"Kidahin? Jassalin. We are in sight of you," Jassalin sang over the commlink.

"Affirm. My local scan shows nothing but sand and vines. What did you find?"

"More sand and vines," Aplilin grunted.

"The same as before," Jassalin sang in counterpoint to Aplilin's annoying complaint. "I found one obvious difference. Tracks of fourteen stumblefeet are showing signs of joint and muscle fatigue. Their foot placements are excessively sloppy. They cannot even pull their feet clear of the sand, preferring to drag them through it instead."

"That makes sense," Kidahin sang, turning thoughtful. "Neither Harrison or his aides have the training or the endurance needed for sustained forced prowling. Jassalin, you called them an elite combat force and I suspect they are Coalition special operation group combat forces. Did you find anything that would confirm their elite status?"

"I think so. I accidently noticed scrapes on stem bark. I think they are regularly climbing the vine stem for a high-ground view and then climb back down before proceeding forward. An assault team would do so since leaving the shuttle, but I did not think to look down ells and ells of vine stem," Jassalin keened.

"It is not your fault. It is mine," Kidahin trilled. "I made an issue of humans preferring ground prowling to climbing. Delwyn showed me on Ibeetu how wrong I was to think he could not climb. He commanded elite forces, and I knew human elite training was not unique to him alone."

"But then why are they not walking atop the vine stem?" Alfara trilled at interrogative tempo.

"Falling hazard?" Seliaha guessed. "We live in trees but humans do not, so why would they risk falling when a high ground view of the sand ahead appears clear?"

"I think our concern for male survivors is misplaced," Merkrida growled. "There is no one here worthy of rescue."

"If every survivor is in league with Harrison then I agree," Seliaha trilled in disgust.

"Good for you, Seliaha," Mimiran sang softly.

"You agree with her?" Kidahin keened in surprise.

"No, not with her sentiment," Mimiran sang. "But I am very pleased that Seliaha is asserting herself rather than falling in line with the group."

"I agree with Merkrida, too," Aplilin trilled. "They are all tailcutters, and they are a danger to Delwyn."

"What do you suggest we do? Retreat? Sit idly by? Leafchase the time away waiting for Anailiatha to free our warship and jump into orbit above us?" Jassalin keened.

"But we are tailchasing time away following them!" Aplilin snarled impatiently.

"Leafchasing means wandering in your mind to no purpose. Tailchasing means performing an action to no purpose. We are doing neither," Kidahin trilled angrily. "The SIV cannot take us back to Delwyn. The geode is clearly a Ni'zakhonii military asset. We must capture or destroy it. My nose tells me we came here to help people who it turns out are tailcutters. While giving them aid they did not deserve, Nynava was killed. They owe us a social debt. Do not forget Harrison. He tried to capture and kill Delwyn and is guilty of a high honor crime. I will not let him evade hierarchy justice again."

"We must consider that some of those humans are not allied with Harrison and his forces," Kyralin keened. "We cannot leave honorable males behind. Those buried in the sand clearly did not prowl with the tailcutters. What if, say, the pilot is no tailcutter? If he is not, then he is in need of female protection."

Kidahin flexed her ears wide while twisting her tail in lazy loops and stared intently at Merkrida. "I call the question. Do we continue as planned? Do we have a minor consensus?" she trilled formally. By ancient custom, no group of females undertook an action whenever a contrary minority view existed. Majorities never wielded power in Eyloni culture.

"We do," Merkrida sang. "All those agreeing with the question will sing until a Major Consensus is reached."

Each Hunter sat in ritual order on the flight deck between the cockpit and passenger cabin bulkheads and looped her tail against the thigh of a neighbor. Alfara the Gracious Mistress of the Singing People sang about female unity. Her melody wove the twenty Hunters into a pheromonal metamind.

Kidahin, aware of a missing melody, altered her pheromones to form a scent-based name with a subtle questioning stress.

Mimiran, standing behind the ritual branching pattern, twitched a tail in surprise as she took meaning from Kidahin's scent. She considered the surgeon-in-battle a part of Team-Two and welcomed her to sing her opinion of how they should proceed.

Emotions raged through the metamind as they sang. Objection to helping tailcutters, even male tailcutters, gradually subsided in favor of protecting Delwyn and innocent males, including the honor and dignity of those killed in the furtherance of tailcutter treachery.

Alfara brought the song to a close when she smelled that everyone had reached an agreement.

"I call the question," Kidahin sang ritually.

"We have reached a Major Consensus," Alfara confirmed. "We shall continue as planned."

"Affirm," Kidahin sang, confident. The society of Assault Team-Two agreed with her plans. Mimiran was right to point out that Kidahin had felt no doubts since the transport accident. Mimiran was also right about warleader special security. They could not act against this threat to Delwyn while stuck on *Hunter's Moon,* but she could.

"You changed your mind about warleader special security, my Kidahin?" Aplilin trilled, her ears twitching.

"I have. You can smell it?"

"Your pheromones reek of it," Aplilin trilled softly. "I am glad. I was ready to go with you had you decided to leave, but I would have missed my infant."

"Zalzadrin would never let you keep a plasma cannon. That weapon is for assaulting mechanized infantry forces, barriers, and defilades. It is not meant for antipersonnel use against individuals. To use a modern weapon against a person is cowardly and shameful," Kidahin reminded her.

"I know that!" Aplilin growled.

"What about me?" a weak and tottering Zalzadrin trilled unsteadily from the cabin aisle.

"Nothing. Go back to your seat before you fall down!" Mimiran sang as she rushed to the fiery redhead's side.

Zalzadrin staggered and froze, afraid to move least she fall face-first onto the deck.

"Kidahin, Harrison is here," Zalzadrin trilled in a descant, biting her tongue to stop the dry heaves she felt rolling in her stomach.

"I know that," Kidahin keened. "So we have discovered no thanks to you," she added tersely.

"This is not my fault!" Zalzadrin trilled, gagging several times. Afterimages flashed before her eyes. She swayed, unable to find her balance, a note of shame for any Eyloni, let alone a Hunter female. "Melkorka, Phelindra, Nynava, and I came to a Major Consensus on how to keep the knowledge from Delwyn until we were beyond recall and his ability to somehow join us."

"What did you think he was going to do?" Kidahin trilled, "recklessly jump our warship here?"

"N...n...noo," Zalzadrin gagged. "Melkorka was afraid he would order Hlinlodyn to fire torpedoes at the surface."

"My favorite male is truly a male of the same mind as I," Aplilin sang in appreciation.

"I think Hlinlodyn agrees with you," Kidahin sang. "She wanted to fire on the wrecked Coalition warship and remove the threat from the beginning."

Mimiran wrapped her tail around Zalzadrin and carefully walked the Hunter back to her reclined seat.

"I can help," Zalzadrin protested weakly.

"No, you cannot. Your memory will fade in and out and your strength will fade much faster. You will eat, relax, and go back to sleep, healer's orders."

"Affirm," Zalzadrin stammered.

"Tialdrin, Zalzadrin may eat, liquid diet only," Mimiran sang, turned, and glared at Zalzadrin. "You behave yourself, or Tialdrin will strap you down. That means the catheter and not assisted trips to the necessary. Do you understand me?"

"Affirm," Zalzadrin squeaked.

"Now, about strategy," Kidahin began. "I think we..."

"Kidahin," Zalzadrin trilled around the straw Tialdrin was trying to put into her mouth.

Mimiran's Warrior aggression surged as she spun on Tialdrin. "I told her to eat and relax. Strap her down and feed her intravenously."

"No...*No!*" Zalzadrin keened, a towering force of anger in her own right as she struggled to assert herself. "This is important! Kidahin, the A'tayotan analyzed the Harrison distress calls coming from this system. Several mistresses of inner strength spent days reviewing them. They concluded that Harrison was...insane. He called for help from the closest Coalition colony world, yet his words and delivery were chaotic, disjointed, even hysterical. The A'tayotan asked Ambassador Alan Dean Winters to listen and give the Be'atika Senge his counsel. He told them Harrison sounded like the ravings of a mad-male, crazy."

"I understand. Drink your meal and get some sleep," Kidahin insisted. She turned to Mimiran. "I am surprised Melkorka did not offer you a chance to listen to these words. Your counsel would be mission-critical."

"As am I!" Mimiran snarled.

"You did not pick up any human radio traffic, did you?" Einstika demanded.

"If I had, you would have heard it yourself by now," Kidahin snapped. "Maybe we are going about this all wrong."

"What do you mean?" Jassalin sang.

"At first we thought the shuttle crashed here, and the humans were planning to capture a Ni'zakhonii FTL-capable geode ship. If our guessing is correct and Harrison somehow stole the geode ship from Ibeetu and got this far before running out of antihydrogen, then these tailcutters cannot be trying to capture the geode."

"I said this already," Aplilin scolded. "They would not leave ordnance and supplies behind they would need to take the geode ship. They are expecting to leave with Harrison in that geode."

"But they are not carrying antihydrogen to him," Hollfara trilled. "And they have nothing Harrison could need to help him leave this moon."

"Maybe he needs food," Einstika suggested.

"No," Kidahin sang thoughtfully. "He called out to a Coalition system. If he had control over the geode, then he would have gone there directly. I think he sabotaged the geode and forced it to land here. He expects *Londiwe Khoza* in orbit above waiting to rescue him. If the shuttle contacted him before crashing, he knows the warship is destroyed. If he contacted the shuttle after he crashed, then he has to know the shuttle is beyond repair. If he is mad, then he will not believe the bad news."

"What do you want to do?" Jassalin sang.

"I think we will land about one hundred kamells, a fourteen Delwyn-hour prowl, from the geode. You will lead Team-Two and prowl ahead while I fly close air support."

"The SIV is not a close air support asset," Hollfara objected. "He is a stealth reconnaissance proxy. If the geode does not blow him out of the sky, then human hand-held heavy infantry weapons will blast holes in him."

"I agree with Hollfara," Jassalin sang. "Our branch-hops north are merely hovers ells above sand, skimming over sand, landing on sand, prowling on sand, and then skimming over sand to the next stop. We cannot use the active scanners without alerting the geode to our presence. Flying close-in air support means flying above leaf stalks at over eleven hundred ells above ground!"

"The SIV is virtually invisible to Ni'zakhonii sensors," Kidahin sang.

"But he is *not* invisible! Passive visual scans cannot miss him at close range!" Merkrida keened.

"I will climb out on that branch when I reach it," Kidahin sang.

"What do you know about these humans?" Aplilin trilled. "I know they do not fight with traditional weapons in melee, which is cowardly in itself. Are they capable of shooting the SIV down?"

"I watched a training session involving Delwyn's special operations forces while I was aboard *Henri Edda*. They regularly carry one hundred and thirty-ell range particle weapon sidearms and ten thousand-ell range particle weapon long guns. Some of his forces are heavy-weapons trained and carry either kinetic railguns that fire magnetized ceramic slivers at supersonic speed or grenade launchers that fire AI-controlled smart grenades. I assess these two weapons as their hand-held heavy infantry alternatives to your plasma cannon, Aplilin."

"Can the SIV take sustained fire from those weapons?" Merkrida trilled.

"No," Aplilin keened insistently.

"Yes and no," Seliaha trilled at the same time.

Aplilin flattened her ears against her orangey ringlets and spun on Seliaha.

"No!" Aplilin repeated, trilling menacingly.

"Yes and no!" Seliaha trilled louder. "He can take their particle weapon fire. They are merely antipersonnel weapons, coward weapons in the truest sense of our traditions. The SIV has minimal particle shielding meant to take incidental fire from even Ni'zakhonii mechanized heavy infantry."

"Seliaha is correct," Hollfara sang. "He can take concentrated hand-held heavy infantry particle weapon fire for a short time, but they would need sustained and prolonged contact to cause any damage."

"I do not care about the small arms," Aplilin trilled. "I care about the railguns and the grenade launchers. The SIV is not shielded against kinetic attacks. Hard, metallic slivers fired at thousands-per-second rates will slice through the fuselage like a band saw. The grenades, be they contact or proximity-triggered, can blow gaping holes in the SIV. You have nothing but a small cannon to fire back with!"

"I will direct your advance from the high ground while Tialdrin gives you covering fire," Kidahin pointed out.

Aplilin, whipping her tail madly behind her, was unwilling to back down. "No. Tialdrin cannot hit an elleiu tree with computer-assisted targeting."

"Hey!" Tialdrin snapped. "I can put a reticule on a target and pull a trigger. It is not like I am shooting at a shielded mechanized armor piece."

"Yes, Tialdrin," Kidahin sang, "but your task is not antipersonnel. You may not fire on them unless they use heavy weapons against us first."

"Yes, Tialdrin," Aplilin trilled. "Do not deprive me of an opportunity for personal combat honor. Do not shoot me in your haste to give us covering fire. And," she added ominously, "if anything happens to my Kidahin, do not bother returning."

"Kidahin, what is our fuel status?" Hollfara sang at interrogative pitch.

Kidahin checked flight status and scowled. "Well below half if I conserve for fusion engine boost, but more than enough if we never need to reach orbit again."

"The stealth insertion vehicle is not an excursion vehicle. Hovering against gravity over the distance to the geode consumes hydrogen just as main engine boost does. Once Melkorka arrives, the Mistress of Conveyance can quantum translate us aboard our warship. But if you get into aerial combat with the geode, we will not have enough fuel for sustained aerial combat," Hollfara lectured.

"And that is another branch I will climb out onto when I reach it. Jassalin, deploy Team-Two when we land. Mimiran, go with her. Tialdrin, stay here and watch Zalzadrin and fire the cannon if Jassalin needs covering fire."

"Affirm," Tialdrin and Jassalin sang out together.

"Is that another jinx ward?" Mimiran trilled drolly, twisting her pons in slow, tight circles.

"No. Delwyn said the simultaneous utterance from both people must be unexpected. Their responses are expected, so no jinx happens," Kidahin trilled in laughter.

Kidahin engaged pitch thrusters and the SIV lifted off and flew thirty ells above sandy ground fast enough for the canopy view ahead to remind her of the adolescent years she served in the Uahua'asee'a Clan polar fleet. She often piloted a high-speed hydrofoil supply ship between ice cliffs. The SIV aft viewer showed a trail of sand racing behind, reminding her of the ocean mist wake raised by the hydrofoil. Unlike the mist, the heavier grit never rose more than thirty or forty ells above ground and well below the living vine stem cliffs.

An hour later Kidahin throttled back to stationary hover and, this time, landed atop the vine stem.

"We are one hundred and thirty thousand ells from the geode," Kidahin sang.

"What do the passive scans report?" Jassalin sang.

"The same thing as the other stops. Nothing," Kidahin sang.

Jassalin flicked her ears at the expected answer. "We should make contact soon," she trilled in warning. "Everybody but Tialdrin get into your combat EVA suits!"

"Why now?" Hollfara demanded. "Rebreathers are sufficient for endurance prowling. They have worked well enough so far."

"Aplilin, Merkrida, and I discussed this on our way here. Aplilin pointed out, again, that combat EVA suits are called that for a reason, and they give you a choice between rebreather air and suit bottled air," Jassalin sang.

"But, Jassalin, combat EVA suits ruin stealth prowling," Kyralin keened in objection.

"And if we were going up against only tailcutters, I would agree with you. But we also face that geode, and I am not taking any chances."

"Affirm," Kyralin trilled.

"Team-Two, deploy," Kidahin sang. "Tialdrin and I are moving level with the leaf stalks and will weave above and below the leaves and take occasional dips to the ground and then up a hundred ells above the leaves and back again. Go!"

Kidahin lifted the SIV off the stem as soon as the last of Team-Two cleared the hatch. She climbed to leaf level and nudged the maneuvering thrusters forward at a slow prowling pace.

"All this near-stationary hovering will burn through our fuel supply," Tialdrin trilled.

"Let me worry about fuel status. You keep an eye on your targeting scanner. Let us hope Zalzadrin gives us no problems."

"She will not. Mimiran gave her a mild sedative," Tialdrin sang.

"Good," Kidahin trilled. She opened the commlink. "Jassalin?"

"Advancing," Jassalin commed back. "Alfara, prowl with Aplilin and Seliaha. Use that battlefield scanner of yours but for the spirits' sakes do not take active scans."

"I already know this!" Alfara snapped.

An hour of prowling over stem bark passed uneventfully.

"Are you sure they even made it this far?" Seliaha trilled in frustration.

"Quite sure," Alfara sang. "Their footprints register on my scanner."

"Have patience," Kidahin encouraged them. "We are closing on them."

Two more hours on the bark passed, again uneventfully.

"We are nearly halfway there," Jassalin trilled. "We should run into them at any time now."

Kidahin dropped the SIV down to just above the sandy ground, hovered stationary, and panned a simple camera in a full sweep around the immediate area.

"They were here. See the disturbances in those sandy ripples? Their prowling pattern is disorganized. I think they are spending more time helping those fourteen numbfeet than before. They are carrying or dragging them along, and I do not see any signs of backtrailing and looping, no signs of flanking prowls, and no signs of point prowlers venturing ahead and returning. They are clustered in a tight group and... Spirits!"

"What, Kidahin?" Jassalin trilled over the open commlink, suddenly tense and alert.

"Their footprints end here. They are not circling or backtrailing, either. They climbed. Jassalin, beware. You may encounter hostiles on the vine stem you are prowling."

"Affirm," Jassalin sang. "Alfara, scan the area ahead."

"Affirm, acting. No trip wires, antipersonnel ordnance, or powered weaponry in scanning range found. No life signs found in range, either... Wait...I am detecting something...Scanner reports slight bark damage resembling scuffs from specialized footwear abrasions. Kidahin, does human combat camouflage clothing include footwear?"

"It does, but while we rarely use footwear humans wear footwear all the time...," Kidahin trilled into a long pause. "Jassalin, I am reading thirty-four low-level life signs three thousand ells ahead. They are stationary and resemble readings associated with coma. There are no life signs at conscious levels in the area."

"Affirm. Team-Two, hold position. Merkrida, what do you think?" Jassalin trilled.

"This close to Harrison? Some of them went on ahead to get him," Merkrida sang.

"Without leaving at least one stalker triad behind to watch over unconscious team members?" Aplilin keened.

"They killed males on their warship and they killed males on their shuttle, so what stops them from killing males here when they are so close to their goal?" Kyralin trilled.

Kidahin twitched her tail, lost in thought. What Kyralin said made sense, yet the life sign numbers did not match the footprints followed here. So who was continuing ahead?

"Tialdrin, this smells wrong. Unsafe your cannon. You may have to fire at an instant."

"Affirm," Tialdrin sang from the gunner seat. "Cannon is unsafe and ready to fire."

Mimiran pulled a medical scanner from her healer's harness and held it out as she glided across the bark to Alfara and Aplilin.

"We are getting close to them. They are registering on my medical scans. The scanner suggests possible coma... No...I think they are more consistent with sleepwalker levels."

"Injured by vine tentacles?" Aplilin sang doubtfully.

"This many, so close together, and all at once? No. Besides, four of them are suffering critical injuries resulting from blunt-force trauma. Ten more are suffering from simple exhaustion. All fourteen are in various stages of shock and may die soon without healer aide. The remainder are simply inactive, but I cannot find a medical reason why."

Aplilin and Alfara nodded to her and glided back to confer with Seliaha. "What now?" Aplilin trilled.

"Anything more definite coming from your scanner, Alfara?" Jassalin trilled as she joined them.

"Nothing helpful, but remember that battlefield scanners find hidden hazards like pits, berms, defilades, ordnance, and personnel. The life signs are scattered in clumps up ahead, but I do not see signs of the usual mines or other antipersonnel surprises I would expect on a perimeter..."

*"Ambush...Oh, spirits!"* Mimiran's voice keened over the commlink.

Jassalin and Aplilin spun on their heels and found the Warrior surgeon-in-battle missing.

"Mimiran?" Aplilin keened.

"Movement forward...all low-level life signs are advancing," Kidahin sang in denial as she spun the SIV down across the vine stem and out over the ground below.

"I see her!" she trilled on the commlink. "She is on the ground about a thousand ells ahead and below Aplilin. I am going down for her!"

Kidahin slammed the control yoke forward into a dive and skimmed the SIV over sandy ground as she rapidly approaching the prone Warrior. Halfway there a terrific blast struck the SIV from the left and behind the cockpit. The blast inertia slammed Kidahin into the pilot seat restraints.

"Jassalin, I am taking fire. Tialdrin, lock-up on that incoming and return fire!"

"Affirm, acting!" Tialdrin trilled. "Targeting is blinded by electronic countermeasures. I am returning fire manually." What was she firing at, Tialdrin wondered. This was Aplilin's seat, not hers. She was no gunner. Yes, she knew how to fire the weapon in theory: scan for targets, lock onto them, and pull the trigger. The fire control system prioritized targets, but hostile ECM prevented the cannon from receiving firing solutions. She could only fire line-of-sight into the towering tangle of vine stems and hope to the spirits she hit something. She pulled the trigger, holding it down, spraying the area ahead with random cannon fire.

"Down!" Aplilin warned as cannon fire spat wildly down vine stem bark at the same time as hostile incoming fire flashed all around her.

Aplilin raced ahead two hundred ells to the cover of another leaf stalk, set up her plasma cannon, and braced it against the stalk. She flipped up the targeting scanner tripod and saw the telltale static of electronic countermeasures. She ignored the blinded scanner, flipped up the manual sighting reticule, spun on bare feet around the stalk, and fired off several plasma bursts before darting back behind the safety of thick, dense wood.

Concussive blasts answered her plasma fire. Antipersonnel grenades struck the stalk with a fury no match for the leaf stalk's sheer mass.

"Jassalin, I have good cover, but no targeting. I suspect ECM activity."

"Set up a thumper and let the EMP short out their electronic countermeasures and weapons before you advance," Jassalin sang.

"We do not have the range, yet," Aplilin trilled in fury.

Heavy fire erupted again from the mountainous tangle ahead, firing into the sand too close to Jassalin and her right flank.

"Covering fire!" Kidahin keened. "I am taking heavy fire!"

"Returning fire, Kidahin," Tialdrin trilled. "Without targeting I can only strafe their positions. I cannot even tell if I am hitting anything!"

"Keep firing," Kidahin panted. "I will land on top of Mimiran," she keened as railgun fire grazed them from cockpit to main engine bell.

Aplilin gripped the rough stem bark with her bare, opposable toes, held on to stalk bark with her left hand, leaned into the stalk, braced the plasma cannon barrel against it, and fired.

"Jassalin! I can cover you while you advance two more leaf stalks and into the third. It will put you within two hundred ells of the merged vine stem high-ground defilade."

"Affirm. Alfara, Seliaha, stay with Aplilin. Everyone else head for the third leaf stalk."

Merkrida charged past Jassalin and the others at a run meant to overbear any opponent she happened to slam into. She could not see individual targets, but from cover ahead they kept pouring fire onto the SIV.

"Jassalin, Merkrida," Merkrida sang over the commlink. "I see tracer fire from at least ten points of origin on the stem climbing over ours. I cannot see anyone, and I suspect kill suits in use."

"Aplilin. Do you see them?" Jassalin trilled.

"Not from here, not with my targeting optics jammed. I cannot stop and look around without giving them an easy target—*me!*"

Tialdrin lurched downward in the gunner seat as Kidahin smacked into the sandy ground hard enough to drive the landing jacks into their stops. She bolted from the gunner seat down the fuselage to the main hatch and froze.

"Spirits!" she trilled. "There are holes bigger than my head in the fuselage!"

"Ignore them, and do not use the main hatch. I landed on top of her. Use the belly hatch!" Kidahin keened. "Is Zalzadrin safe?" she added.

Tialdrin glanced at the unconscious Hunter female reclined in a seat near the aft bulkhead.

"She is fine. I am through the deck hatch and next to the life support mixing tanks. I am opening the belly hatch now," she sang as high-pitched whining slashed diagonally through the deck above her, through the open deck hatch, just missing her and the oxygen-nitrogen mixing tank.

"We are taking railgun fire. Given enough time, they will compromise fuselage airworthiness. When I keen, get vertical fast!"

"Affirm," Kidahin sang.

Multiple grenade blasts shook the SIV. Kidahin watched the damage control monitor register particle weapon fire raking the fuselage. It was small arms fire mostly ineffective against the fuselage, but it was not designed to take extended concentrated fire from even small infantry weapons.

"Kidahin! Belly hatch closed! Go!" Tialdrin keened.

"Affirm! Firing ascent thrusters. Jassalin, we have Mimiran and are heading for altitude beyond their weapon range."

"Affirm. Merkrida is in effective thumper range now," Jassalin sang. "Thumpers are being deployed with full EMP coverage directed into opposing forces. Thumpers are firing... All their unshielded or moderately shielded electronics are probably inert by now. Aplilin, advance to me."

"Affirm, acting!" Aplilin sang. "Alfara and Seliaha, grab your bows and AP arrows and advance to me!"

"I see one, four, twelve...twelve, I think, on the vine stem doubling over ours. Merkrida, Hollfara, and Einstika are climbing after them," Jassalin trilled. "Kidahin, I hear loud popping sounds. They cannot be grenades," she added.

"Dou'tu'tay!" Kidahin swore as she leveled out ten thousand ells above the fray. "Firearms. I forgot about them. Delwyn's forces always carried them as backups against Ni'zakhonii EMP countermeasures."

"Firearms?" Jassalin trilled curiously. "As in slugs thrown by chemical explosion or magnetic action?"

"Yes, the chemical ones. They can be deadly at close range," Kidahin warned.

"I have been shot!" Merkrida hissed in surprised astonishment, "in the arm. It burns. A'pea!"

"Dou'tu'tay!" Aplilin cursed as she reached Jassalin's side. "My infant's targeting is completely burned out. They have fired an EMP blast at us."

Kidahin growled at seeing twenty strong life signs taking cover along a row of massive leaf stalks.

"Tialdrin, help Mimiran strap into a seat and get up here now. I am lining up for a strafing run on a row of leaf stalks."

"I cannot," Tialdrin keened. "Mimiran is unconscious and critical. She has massive internal injuries, fractures, and broken bones."

"Can you help her?" Kidahin keened, grief-stricken.

"I can make her comfortable, but I am no healer. The SIV has no healer suite even if I was one. I have her healer's harness and its equipment, but the only thing I know how to use is the vascular regenerator. I may be able to stop some minor internal bleeding, but I lack the skill to regenerate large bleeds. I might cut off blood flow to a major organ!"

"Do what you can and hope she will live long enough for Allohindra to get here," Kidahin sang. What should she do? She could not fire the cannon from the pilot seat. The SIV was not an assault craft. Besides, honor and tradition demanded they fall on the hostiles with nothing but knives, swords, and bows and arrows.

"Jassalin, prepare to advance," Kidahin trilled. "I will hover above them and beyond firearm range. They cannot know we are forbidden by custom from firing on them. I will hold the high ground. They may surrender."

"Affirm," Jassalin sang.

*"Eyloni! Kill them, Deering! Kill them now! Rend their flesh! Eat them alive. Kill them! Kill…kill kill kill them!"* A male voice jeered maniacally in the droning human language from the SIV communications surveillance monitor.

"Deering!" Kidahin spat.

"Who?" Jassalin trilled at interrogative pitch.

"Delwyn's mistress of battle aboard *Henri Edda*. Her scent is the familiar one I smelled on *Londiwe Khoza*."

"She was allied with Harrison?" Merkrida trilled.

"I am…not sure. She disagreed with Delwyn on key matters. She supported the charge of piracy against Delwyn for capturing the Ni'zakhonii prototype light attack craft on Ibeetu. She despised me, thinking I was manipulating Delwyn. Her scent betrayed a…discomfort with…a condescending view, of Eyloni in general. Dou'tu'tay!"

"My Kidahin?" Aplilin trilled.

"Weapon lock coming from the geode. I am diving to ground cover and going evasive!"

Aplilin watched as the SIV contrail looped across the sky and dodged down as a missile streaked by, exploding with enough force to blow a troop transport out of the sky.

"Get to ground, my Kidahin. Missile tracking will not work in ground clutter. But go to ground at some distance and skim back to us before he can fire his intercepts."

"Affirm!"

"Kidahin, how is Mimiran?" Jassalin keened over the commlink.

"Bad, very bad," Kidahin trilled.

"Jassalin? Merkrida. The hostile force has withdrawn further into the high ground. We found ten humans shot by the same type of slug-throwing firearm I was shot with. They are all recently shot, within the last twenty minutes or so. Three are dead and two are critical."

"About the same time Mimiran keened for help," Kidahin mused. "What are they wearing?" she sang as the SIV reached safe ground. She immediately fired forward maneuvering thrusters and sped across the sand.

"Two are wearing the uniform clothing you described, the pixelated clothing. Three others are wearing tight-fitting clothing of a delicate material unsuitable in combat environments."

"Are they males?"

"Males and a female," Merkrida confirmed.

"Save them if you can," Kidahin sang. "They might be unwilling or unknowing Harrison allies. Delwyn can tell us later if they are guilty."

A full rack of missiles rained down on the spot Kidahin vacated mere seconds ago. Over the Coalition Tactical Channel came a shrill, insanely howling voice.

*"Deering? Deering! Don't you dare retreat. Kill those Eyloni now, before they can get to me. I can't seem to find a way out of this Lizard piece-of-shit ship."*

"We're coming, Mister Ambassador, but I told you when we landed that the Sentry's FTL is offline. We have to capture the ship, rescue you, and figure out how to fly it out of here."

"No! No! No!" Harrison screamed. *"I want out of this thing! You will escort me back to your shuttle and take me to the Coalition Government on Earth. The Eyloni are food...are the enemy. They aren't really people. Only we are people. Kill Melkorka, too. That bitch didn't listen to Phalalin. She made Marsch her warleader. Treason...traitor! Marsch must be torn to pieces and his flesh savored!"*

# 9

## USING FIERCENESS, THE DANCE OF DEATH, THE NORMALIZING OF THE ABNORMAL...

"Kidahin? Did you hear that?" Merkrida growled over the commlink.

"I did!" Kidahin snarled. "He threatens Delwyn in our hearing!"

"Einstika, Hollfara, and I are tracking eleven people carrying grenade launchers, railguns, and various small arms. They are holding the high ground four hundred ells above and ahead of us but are falling back and behind the first force," Merkrida sang.

"Can you advance?" Kidahin trilled.

"No, not while the first force holds the high ground. The three vine stems crossing ours look like three knots tied one atop the other resembling a four-hundred-ell tall thicket. I see leaf stalks sprouting everywhere around the knotted vine stems. Some of them are barely forty ells apart. Each stalk is ten ells thick, which gives them some very suitable cover."

"And the smoke will add a bit to what cover they do have," Kidahin keened.

"Smoke?" Merkrida trilled at interrogative pitch.

"Yes, smoke," Kidahin sang. "I smell it coming from the south. Those missile strikes hit the ground where I dove for cover and ignited some vine stems. We are too far north to see any fires, but I can already see hints of smoke from those smoldering stems."

"Smoke will not hinder them," Aplilin snarled over the commlink. "Their rebreathers can filter it from the air."

"We may be able to use this smoke to our advantage," Merkrida sang thoughtfully.

"Oh?" Kidahin trilled.

"Yes," Merkrida replied. "You said it may improve their cover. If the SIV were a light armored vehicle, I could drive it through these smoke-shrouded leaf stalks while dropping off Huntresses in the retreating force's rear."

"An LAV is twenty ells long and four ells wide. The SIV is thirty-three ells long and fourteen ells wide. You cannot make tight turns around those leaf stalks."

"I can steer around anything," Merkrida trilled.

"Oh, you can, can you?" Kidahin snarled. "I am skimming over the sand below and behind you. Climb down and get in. I will fly you to the knotted crossover vine stems, and from there you can drive the SIV into their rear."

"Drive?" Merkrida spluttered. "You mean fly, do you not? I have no flight certification, and you know this!"

"The SIV pilot controls mirror LAV driver controls," Kidahin baited. "The leg and joint control collective works something like the SIV control yoke. The only difference is that the collective controls mechanical limbs and the yoke controls attitude thrusters. You do not need the flight or engine systems to hover an SIV at LAV leg level."

"The response times are different!" Merkrida keened. "Mechanical legs are slow compared to thruster responsiveness. Legs give feedback through the collective that tells the driver what or where she is stepping on or into."

"So?" Kidahin sang. "The yoke provides pitch and trim feedback that feels something like collective surface feature feedback."

"Well, roughly speaking maybe...," Merkrida trilled softly.

"Kidahin! You cannot risk losing the SIV," Tialdrin trilled. "He shelters the critically wounded human males, Zalzadrin, and Mimiran. He is not a gunship. Their antipersonnel EMP electronic warfare cannot defeat his EM shielding, but EMP EW from the geode can."

"Merkrida, I am below you now. Bring Hollfara and Einstika down with you and climb in," Kidahin sang over the commlink, ignoring Tialdrin.

"Affirm," Merkrida sang.

"But Kidahin, I...," Tialdrin trilled.

"The males are unconscious and Zalzadrin is sedated and strapped into her seat. How is Mimiran?" Kidahin interrupted.

"Critical but stable, for now. She fell feet-first. I cannot understand why. No one falls feet-first," Tialdrin trilled angrily.

"Pushed?" Kidahin snarled.

"No. I think she was shot by a kinetic round, a slug from a firearm or magnetic launcher," Tialdrin growled. "I used a medical scanner on Mimiran. It targeted internal bleeding so I could use the vascular regenerator to heal them. It diagnosed her injuries at the same time. Dou'tu'tay! I do not know most of the anatomical terms it uses."

"Such as?" Kidahin prompted.

"The scanner took Mimiran's prone landing position, distance she fell, her likely position before she fell, and the injuries themselves into account when arriving at a diagnosis."

"And?" Kidahin growled, impatient with both Tialdrin stalling and Merkrida taking her time climbing down the vine stem.

"When Mimiran fell, she landed feet-first while twisting to the right, causing a Nilop fracture, a tibial plateau fracture, and a spiral shaft fracture of the right tibia."

"Those are ankle and lower leg fractures," Kidahin trilled.

"Yes, I know what a tibia is," Tialdrin growled as she continued reading. "The impact hyperextended the left knee and drove the distal femoral epiphysis into the distal shaft, fracturing the femoral neck, the acetabulum, the sacrum, and the lumbar vertebra."

"A femur is an upper leg bone and vertebrae are backbones," Kidahin muttered.

"Yes," Tialdrin agreed. "Most of these words are beyond me. According to the diagnostic report, the knee impact drove the patella into the center anterodistal surface of the femoral shaft while at the same time the impact to the right hip drove the right innominate into the sacrum, and the sacrum into the left innominate, dislocating and fracturing the sacrum and the left innominate, and elevating the retroauricular surface."

"Which means what?" Kidahin growled in frustration. "A patella is a kneecap, and I know what a hip is. Too bad Mimiran is not conscious. You could read the diagnostic to her and smell the meaning in her scent."

"Yes, assuming she was rational enough to understand what I was reading to her," Tialdrin sang. "The report concludes that Mimiran was conscious when she stretched her arms out in an attempt to break the fall and fractured both proximal humeri on impact, the right one more severely than the left, with spiral fractures near the midshaft, an Aniculin fracture of the right radius, and several other fractures of the radii and ulnae. The impact depressed and retracted the right scapula, which depressed the clavicle into the first rib, fracturing both."

"That sounds wrong to me," Kidahin trilled. "No one uses her hands to break a fall. We instinctively tuck into a tumble because we are more likely than not to hit branches or leaves on the way down and roll onto a wide branch or into a bole itself."

"But these vines are hometree-trunk wide, over two hundred ells thick! No vines or lianas hang from them and no leaves or branches sprout from the sides for her to roll onto. What choice did she have but to put her arms out?" Tialdrin sang rhetorically. "Mimiran also has a frontal impact fracture at the left pubis which drove a portion of the anterior inferior pubic ramus posterolaterally, and the hole in the left pubis is clearly a bullet hole."

"Are you certain it is not a railgun projectile?" Kidahin trilled.

"Yes, I am," Tialdrin sang. "The railgun fires projectiles at a rate that would cut her in two. This is likely a firearm bullet wound from a silenced weapon."

"Kidahin?" Merkrida sang over the commlink. "We are outside. Open the hatch."

"Affirm, about time, too," Kidahin commed. "Does the diagnostic say anything else, Tialdrin?"

"Yes, the worst of it. The impact slammed Mimiran's thorax into the ground, fracturing every rib and three thoracic vertebrae. The ground struck her skull slightly left of center, creating a tripartite punchpoint fracture of the mandible and several cranial fractures as well."

"So she has a lot of fractured bones. Are broken bone punctures what caused all the internal bleeding?" Kidahin trilled as Merkrida, Einstika, and Hollfara joined them at the cockpit bulkhead.

"No," Tialdrin growled, snapping her tail madly. "Falls like these cause severe damage to internal organs when they decelerate upon impact. Some bleeding comes from broken bone piercing, but most of Mimiran's critical internal injuries come from compression pressure between the sternum and spine. This hydraulic-ram effect caused cardiac injuries as the abdominal organs were thrust into the diaphragm."

"And all these injuries were initially caused by a bullet?" Kidahin growled in fury.

"Ultimately, yes," Tialdrin sang. "The diagnostic report posits her facing the shooter while being shot at close range. Bullet hole orientation relative to the pubic bone supports a shot likely fired from vine stem level at an acute angle. The impact spun her body nearly vertical and around as it propelled her over the vine stem."

"Close range prone shooter," Einstika growled, "from someone lying in ambush wearing one of those kill suits?"

"Probably," Merkrida agreed as she turned to Kidahin. "About this plan of yours, the three of us are not enough to assault a force on the high ground. You and Tialdrin cannot abandon the SIV and join us."

"I know," Kidahin growled. "We will swing around and pick up a few others. Have Tialdrin dress your wounds," Kidahin added as she addressed her commlink. "Aplilin?"

"My Kidahin?" Aplilin trilled promptly.

"Report your status."

"Alfara, Seliaha, and I are under cover. My infant's targeting scanner is burned out but he can still fire. Their forces are moving over the far side of the knotted vine stems and beyond the arc of weapon fire."

"We will be flying under tangled leaf stalks and into their rear. If you cannot fire on them, then they cannot fire on us. Climb down and meet us. Merkrida is going to try something," Kidahin trilled.

"Affirm. We are breaking cover and are approaching the stem edge. I see you below us. We are on our way down to you now," Aplilin sang.

"Affirm," Kidahin sang. "Jassalin, where are you?"

"Kyralin and I are swinging around their left flank, on overlapping vine stems, and two hundred ells below them. We are near the topmost vine stem, behind the tallest leaf stalk in the area, and not more than forty ells from their rear. Are you recalling us?" Jassalin sang at interrogative pitch.

"No. We are heading for the second crossover stem. From there, Merkrida will fly the SIV around and under the leaf stalks at stem level, dropping off Huntresses as we pass through them. Keep your bows ready."

"But, Kidahin," Jassalin keened, "that force has grenade launchers and railguns. They were well beyond Merkrida's initial thumper attack. Any weapon surviving those EMP bursts can fire on you!"

"I doubt it," Kidahin sang. "It takes little EMP to short out unshielded weapons. It was your suggestion during the Ah'vou'ree combat simulation that we should not remain on low ground prowling for hours but rather fly to a higher insertion point and save both time and effort."

"This is no training simulation. They have modern personal heavy weapons," Jassalin trilled.

"Our thumper EMP burned out their weapon electronics," Kidahin sang.

"Do not count on it, my Kidahin," Aplilin trilled as she, Alfara, and Seliaha climbed through the fuselage hatch. "The targeting scanner on my infant was burned out by electronic countermeasures, but his plasma force chamber and power supply are shielded from the EMP generated by plasma ignition. Otherwise they would burn out the first time he was fired. Force chamber EMP has no range, which is why the back-blast shield prevents nearby electronics from burning out when the cannon fires."

"They do not have plasma cannons, Aplilin. I doubt any of their self-guiding AI grenades survived Merkrida's thumpers, and I know their particle weapons should not have."

"But not the railguns," Tialdrin interrupted. "They chewed a three-ell gash through the fuselage. Railguns employ tail-temperature superconductor magnetics, and they generate high EMP over an ell or so. Those railguns should still fire."

"You are right about that," Kidahin sang. "But they fire fine metallic-ceramic slivers. As Aplilin pointed out, they did not bring caches of ordnance forward. They cannot have a large stockpile of railgun ammunition on hand."

"If they use those railguns as cowardly antipersonnel weapons, it will not matter," Tialdrin spluttered. "I saw a railgun burst cut through the fuselage, two seats, and the deck like they were leaves. It can cut you in half so fast you will see yourself in two pieces before you even feel the pain."

"It does not matter," Kidahin sang. "Remember that combat doctrine says 'battle on the low ground is folly while the high ground remains. unsecured'."

"Now you sound like an assaultmistress," Jassalin sang over the commlink.

"Yes," Kidahin trilled, "I am an assaultmistress. Any thoughts I had otherwise were specious, as Mimiran was right to point out. Jassalin, how long before you reach your leaf stalk watch point?"

"We are atop the third vine stem and running to it right now…We are here. I wish I had Alfara's battlefield scanner," Jassalin keened.

"You had a chance to grab one from a weapon cache before we left our warship," Alfara trilled haughtily.

"Kidahin, the smoke is getting heavier and the wind is right. If Merkrida is going to hover over the vine stem and between leaf stalks, then now is the time to do it," Jassalin trilled.

"Affirm," Kidahin sang as she fired pitch-up thrusters. The stealth insertion vehicle drifted slowly and silently up the side of the vine stem.

"Tialdrin, did you send Mimiran's medical scans to Allohindra?" Hollfara sang.

"I did, for all the good they will do. Simple radio traffic from here to her and back again takes hours. Mimiran will probably die before I receive Allohindra's guidance," Tialdrin trilled sadly.

"The tailcutter Harrison used the hypercube to send an FTL distress call. If we capture the geode, I can use it to contact our warship," Hollfara sang. "Aplilin? Maybe you should plug your cannon into its charging unit," she added.

"I was about to," Aplilin snapped.

"Temper, temper," Hollfara sang. "What is pulling your tail, hmmm?"

"Mating urges," Merkrida sang flatly. "Be wary of them. Without Delwyn singing to us for focus, we are easily blinded by the emotions a male in danger provokes. Our being in season will magnify those feelings."

"Oh, I am so stupid!" Kidahin spat.

"My Kidahin?" Aplilin trilled.

Kidahin snapped her tail against the pilot seat while adjusting the ascent rate before carefully nudging the SIV into the looming triple-knotted crossover vines up ahead.

"I have several battle songs Delwyn sang for me on Ibeetu stored in my 'minder," she trilled excitedly.

"You have personal Delwyn songs?" Aplilin keened in accusation.

"Wait," Jassalin trilled over the commlink. "I am hiding behind a leaf stalk with only Kyralin for company, and you have a collection of our Warleader's songs all to yourself?"

"Yes, yes, I am sorry," Kidahin sang, meaning every word of it. Females drew strength from the male singing voice. She paused the hover maneuver just long enough to download the music from her 'minder into the SIV communications system and set it to broadcast the music as commlink background audio.

Kidahin flew between two leaf stalks and landed on the bark-covered stem a few minutes later. She vacated the pilot seat and invited Merkrida to take her place with the flick of her tail.

"This is going to get interesting," Merkrida murmured in a musical drawl. "I cannot use active scans because doing so will attract geode countermeasures. Passive scans can tell me only so much, though. Aplilin? You, Seliaha, and Alfara go out and prowl ahead. I need your eyes."

"Affirm," Aplilin sang. "So much for getting a full charge," she keened, directing her annoyance at Hollfara, who spun her pons in a lazy circle under Aplilin's nose in reply.

Aplilin shoved open the hatch with more force than necessary, jumped out, and waited irritably for Alfara and Seliaha to join her.

"Move in watch triad formation," Aplilin trilled. "Alfara, scan ahead. It looks like the best way forward is up the left side of the stem. Up ahead and over the next vine stem is where the second force retreated. Let us go."

"Affirm," Alfara sang as she glided next to Aplilin.

"The smoke is getting thicker. Are you sure there is no fire?" Seliaha trilled.

"No flames," Alfara reassured her. "Thermal scans say the temperature is too low for complete combustion. The wood smolders, and the reason there is so much smoke is because the missile strikes blanketed a wide area."

"It smells like burning cloth," Seliaha complained.

Kidahin trilled laughter over the commlink. "Delwyn thinks wood fires on Elleio smell like scorched cloth."

"Really? This is what wood smoke smells like to him on Elleio?" Seliaha keened, shuddering.

"Stop leafchasing and guide me around those two leaf stalks up ahead," Merkrida snapped.

"Affirm," Aplilin sang.

"He will not fit between them," Alfara trilled in warning.

"He will fit!" Aplilin growled. "Merkrida, make a hard right turn."

"Affirm, thrusting right... Dou'tu'tay, Aplilin!" Merkrida keened as the aft left landing jack housing smacked into a leaf stalk.

"Gently, Merkrida, gently. He is not an LAV with slow mechanical limbs," Aplilin sang.

"I know that! The yoke is touchy compared to a collective. Gripping it makes my gunshot arm cramp and spasm, which is not helping."

"I am sorry," Aplilin sang, pausing a moment to control her rising anger. "Do your best," she added helpfully.

"What do you think I am doing? I am shifting clear of the stem and swinging back around and thrusting up and forward. Passive scan visual enhancement is filtering out the smoke. Too bad it cannot filter out the leaf stalks as well."

"Use the active scanners," Alfara sang.

"And provoke another missile strike? No," Merkrida sang. "Hold on a minute, Aplilin. I see two more leaf stalks ahead. I think I can fit between them, but the hanging vines may cause problems."

"Affirm," Aplilin sang. "You have a two-ell clearance on each side. When you pass between them you will brush clumps of vines, lianas, and thick patches of bromeliads."

"I do not care about vines or bromeliad aerial roots. Just do not let me snag the lianas," Merkrida trilled.

"Then listen to me," Aplilin keened. "Turn left, now! Stop! I said stop, a'pea! Now, fire aft left and bow right thrusters until you swing parallel to the stalks. Good...good, now yaw right twenty ells. Stop. You snagged two lianas. They are draped about the cockpit, and they are about to foul the bow landing jack housings. Fire longitudinal bow thrusters and back up slowly. Good. Stop."

"Am I clear now?" Merkrida trilled.

"Yes, and you are lined up for a steep climb... Merkrida, carnivorous tendrils are tracking your movement."

"What do they matter? The SIV is not alive. They will ignore him."

"No," Aplilin growled. "They are tracking you. They are coiling to strike. I do not think they can tell the living from the non-living."

Aplilin watched ten spiral tentacles strike the fuselage and coil about the left aft and left bow landing jack housings. They knocked the SIV out of trim before retracting, pulling the SIV rapidly toward a tangle of leaf stalks.

"Fire left jack housing yaw thrusters full power and prepare for sudden breakaway!" Aplilin keened.

"Affirm!" Merkrida sang. The thruster plasma burned through the tentacles in seconds. Free, the SIV lurched right thirty ells before Merkrida could null her sideways plunge.

"Beautifully done," Aplilin sang, impressed. "Readjust your heading to parallel the stalks and continue up the incline."

"Affirm," Merkrida sang.

"Aplilin! I have an ordnance alert!" Alfara keened. "My scanner is detecting explosive devices nearby."

"Merkrida, hold position!" Aplilin trilled.

"Affirm!"

Aplilin ran to Alfara and glanced over her shoulder at the scanner.

"What are they? Mines? Merkrida cannot trigger mines while in hover," Aplilin keened.

"No. They are improvised explosive devices. Some kind of contact-triggered antipersonnel explosives…Yes, they are reworked AI-grenades. There are several of them scattered all around us. They are tied to trip wires."

"Jassalin? Kidahin," Kidahin trilled over the commlink. "Alfara found improvised mines. Look for trip wires."

"Affirm," Jassalin sang. "These are AI-equipped grenades. Now we know the grenade launchers do not work."

"Thank the spirits!" Merkrida sang. "Kidahin, what is our range-to-target?"

Kidahin took a passive scan reading from the gunner seat. "We are moving up the steep side of the third merged stem near the top knotted vines. I see a leaf stalk twenty ells ahead. The first force should be thirty ells behind that stalk, with Jassalin and Kyralin forty ells behind them."

"Aplilin," Merkrida interrupted, "recall to the SIV. I will hover over the mines and land nose-on to the stalk ahead for a ground assault deployment."

"You cannot land!" Seliaha keened.

"Why not?" Aplilin trilled.

"Look how steep the incline is here. The SIV's mass will cause him to slide along the bark and off the stem. Merkrida cannot use the attractor plates in the landing jacks because tractor elements make a subsonic, teeth-jarring hum powerful enough to give the humans notice that something is wrong."

"She is right," Kidahin sang. "I will hover while Team-Two deploys around the base of the leaf stalk. Once you are in place, I will fly over them as a distraction while you advance into them."

"Affirm," Jassalin sang.

Minutes later eleven Huntresses prowled barefooted over bark, leaving Kidahin back in the pilot seat and Tialdrin in the gunner seat, their desperately ill passengers strapped helplessly into their seats.

"Jassalin? You and Kyralin fire AP arrows as soon as you see targets. They should give themselves away as I fly over them."

"Affirm!" Jassalin sang.

"Merkrida, you have the leadership until Jassalin rejoins you. Advance when Tialdrin fires the SIV cannon over their heads."

"Affirm."

Kidahin fired ascent thrusters, and the SIV lifted slowly, level and nose-on to the leaf stalk. She stopped just below the single, huge, cobalt-blue leaf and yawed right before pushing the yoke forward.

"Fire," Kidahin sang to Tialdrin.

"Affirm, firing forward over their position."

"Vi e'ta ka nabi!" Aplilin sang. It was time to part the branches.

"Trip wires!" Alfara keened over the commlink.

"Where?" Merkrida demanded as the SIV cannon fired above them.

Faint, buzzing whines filled the air from somewhere up ahead, just behind the closest leaf stalk.

"That is railgun fire directed at the SIV," Aplilin keened, pointing at barely visible tracer fire.

"Alfara, where are those improvised mines?" Merkrida keened.

"Wait while I pulse a countermeasure strobe," Alfara trilled. "See? The green strobe makes the trip wires glow slightly in the smoke, just as fine aerial roots on epiphytic plants sparkle at dawn when coated by morning mist. Smoke particles settle on the trip wires. Can you see them?" she trilled at imperative tempo while pointing at the dark bark with her tail.

"Of course I can," Merkrida sang. "Everyone look at the bark and watch for faint fluorescing green lines. They will fade the closer you get to them, so be careful where you step or you will trip a grenade. Go!"

Delwyn's singing voice whispered over the commlink. Soft, like an exaggerated mutter, his voice nevertheless threatened to overtake its Team-Two listeners. Eyloni females evolved on a world where males were rare, precious, and valued. This male voice, singing a martial beat, carried words and music unique to him. Delwyn was their favorite male. That he was not with them, that they were in mating season, and that he was in potential danger poured adrenaline on a fiery, ancient protective aggression. Every Hunter's mental awareness shrank to pinpoints, narrowing their focus as Delwyn's voice heightened their senses and emotional fortitude.

Merkrida charged forward, deftly stepping over grenade-triggering trip wires. Seliaha followed close behind, so close she got a face full of Merkrida's pons.

"Merkrida, flank them on the left! Aplilin, flank them on the right! Jassalin, approach from behind and fire AP arrows, but for the spirits' sakes watch those trip wires!" Kidahin keened over the commlink in counterpoint melody with Delwyn's insistent voice.

Kidahin flew northwest, around the gargantuan overlapping vine stems knot for a few hundred ells before swinging back around to the southwest.

"Jassalin, Merkrida, the second force is retreating down to the original vine stem and heading north at a staggered withdrawal pace. Jassalin, one force is directly ahead of you and moving to your right. If they continue, they will reach the second vine..." A buzzing chatter whined over the commlink. "Spirits! I am taking railgun fire. I have lost trim thruster control!"

"Land!" Jassalin keened over the commlink.

"No, not yet!" Kidahin snarled. "I still have yaw and pitch thrusters."

The SIV cannon belched plasma continuously, strafing wildly into opposing-force positions.

Several popping sounds, like those of snapping tails, drifted on the smoke, very close.

"Antipersonnel arrows," Merkrida growled. "Dou'tu'tay! That a'pea Jassalin!"

"Now, while their backs are turned!" Seliaha keened. She sped forward, around Merkrida, and disappeared into heavy smoke.

"Seliaha!" Merkrida keened. "You will run into Jassalin's AP fire! Get back here!"

"I have an idea!" Seliaha trilled insistently.

"Aplilin, where is Einstika?" Hollfara sang.

"I do not know!" Aplilin snarled. "She was running with you," she snapped.

"She did not cross my path, and I know she did not fall behind. She must have drifted left."

"If she did, then she is following Seliaha."

"But why?" Hollfara trilled.

"Backing Seliaha up, maybe? Never mind. Stop here. I have a clear field of fire, but I see nothing without the targeting scanner. We have no cover here, so get ready to duck," Aplilin warned.

"Affirm."

"Kyralin?" Jassalin sang over the commlink.

"What?" Kyralin sang under her breath.

"Where are you?" Jassalin trilled.

"About twenty ells ahead of you and moving to your right."

"Affirm," Jassalin sang. "Listen to your nose…Those kill suits Kidahin mentioned…"

"I found them!" Seliaha keened in triumph. "Ha! One down…Two down…Three down…Four down…Tumbling and evading…"

"What are you doing?" Merkrida trilled.

"I danced up behind them and pulled the rebreathers off four of them and threw them over the stem. I am backtrailing and looping, toward... Oh, spirits! I am surrounded!"

"Seliaha, jump right and tumble!" Einstika keened as she slammed into the two humans aiming at Seliaha.

Gunshots answered Einstika's fading keen.

"AP arrows! Fire from behind," Kyralin trilled as she drew back her bowstring.

"No!" Jassalin countermanded. "Help Seliaha carry Einstika. I will give you AP arrow cover."

"Affirm," Kyralin sang.

"Aplilin, can you give Kyralin and Seliaha covering fire?" Kidahin trilled.

"Not with my infant, I cannot," Aplilin snarled. "Without a target lock, the plasma bolt will pass through them rather than through the force ahead. Hollfara and I are advancing with AP arrows drawn."

"Affirm," Kidahin sang.

"Kidahin? Einstika has been shot at least ten times. By the spirits' own luck all of them look like flesh wounds to me," Seliaha trilled. "Her combat EVA suit wound pressor fields are stanching the bleeding. I think Tialdrin should take a look at them."

"Me?" Tialdrin keened over the commlink.

"Yes, you," Kidahin sang in approval. "You know how the vascular regenerator works. You can stop the bleeding and field dress her wounds."

"Kidahin? Jassalin. I see Kyralin. She and Seliaha are with Einstika."

"Is she conscious?" Kidahin trilled with concern.

"Yes. She was hit in the left shoulder, the left upper arm, the left buttock, and both thighs. Her commlink is broken, but what she is signing in battle language would impress Anailiatha."

"Oh, well...wait a minute... Jassalin? The force ahead is falling back and retreating down the vine stem to the one below it. They are following after the more-distant second force. I will land near you. Everyone! Recall to Jassalin!"

"Seliaha? Where are the humans you killed?" Merkrida trilled.

"I killed no one. They were all males! I pulled the rebreathers off their faces and threw them over the edge."

"What good does that do us?" Merkrida keened. "They can put on new ones!"

"No, they cannot," Aplilin sang as she and Hollfara rejoined them. "Rebreathers are sturdy and not likely to fail in battle conditions. This force would not encumber itself by carrying spares. By letting them live, Seliaha is forcing them to share rebreathers. Sharing will slow their retreat to the second force."

"This is true. Well done, Seliaha," Jassalin trilled.

Hollfara and Aplilin both scowled at the battle-scarred SIV as he spiraled down and landed near them.

"The A'tayotan really should pull the stealth insertion vehicle from service," Hollfara spat, eying the gaping hole where the missing left bow landing jack had once been. Its attractor plate, hydraulics and suspension, and housing were gone. A clean cut from a railgun burst had separated the assembly from the fuselage like a sharp knife slicing a bud off a stem.

Aplilin growled her agreement as the SIV touched down and dipped slightly leftward.

"Get in," Kidahin trilled.

Aplilin leaped through the open hatch and shoved her way down the aisle toward the cockpit as Tialdrin sprinted aft to help Einstika and slid into the cockpit gunner seat.

"You cannot keep using the SIV as a spotter and air-cover asset," she trilled at Kidahin.

"Do you have a better idea?" Kidahin keened in frustration. She was tired. A war of attrition was, according to combat doctrine, no way to win a battle. "We are down two, and both Tialdrin and I must remain aboard to secure the SIV and tend to our wounded. That leaves us with an effective force of ten against the group-one force of what, twenty-four?"

"I think more like thirteen or fourteen," Aplilin sang. "And we have an advantage besides the SIV."

"What advantage is that?" Kidahin trilled. "Seliaha's clever trick slows the first force down, but it is not as if she threw their railguns over the vine stem."

"She did something even better. She slowed their advance," Aplilin snarled as she struggled to contain her aggressive nature.

Jassalin poked her head into the cockpit. "We should bypass this force with the railguns and assault the second force," she asserted.

"Yes!" Aplilin trilled. "At least Jassalin sees the pons twitching in her face! We take out the second group, destroy the geode, and then reengage the group-one force on our terms."

While Aplilin was finishing her point, the music playing softly over the commlink paused a moment before Delwyn's voice began singing the song Kidahin loved best. This battle song honored males locked in mortal combat without female support. They kept firing their cannons until the barrels began to melt. The desperate males captured water reptiles and forced cannon shot down their throats and packed their a'peas with gunpowder and fired again. Doing so frightened their enemies so much they fled through jungle so dense not even a ke'nah could pass through it.

Aplilin joined Kidahin unsure what was arousing her the most, Kidahin's intense expression or the idea her favorite male really could fight using a reptile's body for a cannon.

The song ended, and Kidahin returned to normal breathing as her pinpoint pupils dilated to normal size.

"My Kidahin?" Aplilin trilled reverently.

"Hmmm?" Kidahin murmured absently, lost in thought.

"Delwyn sang a battle song, yes?"

Kidahin twitched her ears in the affirmative. "That he did, the first one I learned from him while on Ibeetu. Spirits, Aplilin," she trilled. "If he were here singing that song, I would already be prowling into their midst and killing them all!"

"And not just you alone," Aplilin sang softly, barely restraining herself.

"Jassalin, your idea of bypassing the first force makes good sense," Kidahin admitted. "We will fly over them and engage the second group."

"Affirm," Jassalin trilled.

"Tialdrin, how is Einstika?" Kidahin sang.

"In pain but otherwise fine," Tialdrin sang.

"Good, change of plan, we are going after the second force."

"S-two, this is S-one Actual," Deering said over the SOG TAC channel. "Enemy is overflying us and heading your way. Take cover and safeguard your supercargo."

"Acknowledged, S-one Actual. We are currently about three klicks north of your position..."

*"No! Shoot them down, Deering! Do it now!"* Harrison screamed over the TAC channel.

"Please, Mr. Ambassador, get off the air!" Deering yelled.

Railgun fire chewed into the SIV, goring the fuselage underside. An explosion rocked the cockpit. Alarms keened in warning.

"Fire in the cabin life support bay!" Kidahin trilled. She flipped several safety switches off and armed the explosive bolts surrounding the nitrogen and oxygen tanks feeding the SIV life support system.

"Jettisoning tanks!" she keened before slapping a green toggle.

Tiny explosives fired below the passenger cabin. The life support storage and mixing tanks blasted away from the fuselage and tumbled into the sandy ground.

"We have no life support but EVA suit bottled air," Hollfara muttered. "We cannot fly at altitude now."

"We should not need to," Kidahin sang. "The second force has no heavy infantry weapons."

"S-two, S-one Actual. That puddle-jumper is still incoming. We hit it pretty good, but it's still flying. Expect it to drop a force of two squads, a commander, and her second-in-command," the TAC channel blared.

"Eighteen troops incoming, aye-aye, S-one Actual," the second force replied.

*"No! No! I told you to shoot them down, Deering. Can't you do anything right? Forget them! I want out of this ship. Where's the second SOG force you mentioned, anyway?"*

"Mr. Ambassador, please, Sir, get off the air. You're compromising my troops just by talking…"

*"Compromising your troops? With whom? The Eyloni? Is Marsch with them? I want him dead, Deering! Dead dead dead dead…You were supposed to kill him on Ibeetu, damn you!"*

"He never came back to the ship, Mr. Ambassador. Melkorka made him warleader on her ship. Don't you remember, Sir?"

Silence filled the cockpit for several long seconds before hysterical laughter screamed from the speakers. The hoarse, insanely modulated chortle screamed from impossible highs through choking lows and back again in a single exhaling breath Kidahin knew was flatly impossible for a human to maintain.

"I never heard Delwyn sing a note this long without pausing for breath," Alfara trilled, her ears folded against her short, frizzy orange ringlets.

"He cannot," Kidahin sang. "And Harrison cannot, either. I remember his voice. He yelled, threatened, and turned evasively engaging at need. He said whatever he thought others wanted to hear. He droned words contrary to his body language and his scent. He is elderly, unfit, and has no moral difficulty with outright lying to reach an end."

"But, my Kidahin?" Aplilin trilled.

"His anger prowled topmost in his voice. His anger and his arrogance betrayed a certainty that his view of the world was right. He was always calculating... But what we just heard sounds nothing like what I remember on Ibeetu."

"Are you certain this is the same male?" Jassalin trilled.

"Of course I am!" Kidahin snarled, insulted at the thought she could not identify a male by his voice. "I remember the tonal qualities in his voice. It is him, and yet..."

"*I see them!*" Harrison cackled inanely over the TAC channel. "*I see them, Deering! They're flying low, heading right for me! There's got to be something here I can use to kill Marsch and that parasite Kidahin!*"

"Mr. Ambassador! You'd be better off spending time looking for a way out of the Lizard ship and not screwing up our communications!" Deering yelled.

"*I told you I can't find a way out of here, you idiot! Eyloni! I want to rend their flesh, eat them whole...Wait! I found something!*" Harrison cackled with glee.

"Found what, Mr. Ambassador? A way out?" Deering asked, sounding hopeful.

"*A weapon! A weapon a weapon a weapon a weapon!*" Harrison jeered.

"Mr. Ambassador?" Deering asked apprehensively.

"*A weapon! And you are wrong, Master Chief. There are two Eyloni troop ships out there, not one. One of them is ten kilometers away and on the ground. The second one, the one you let escape, is flying low just under two kilometers from me!*"

"Mr. Ambassador, it sounds like you're describing a ship weapon system and not small arms. Are you on the Lizard's bridge?" Deering asked.

"*No! I'm in a dark room filled with panoramic holographic displays. I see the fire controls right in front of me and the two Eyloni ships in the display. I can reach into it...I got the trigger!*" He laughed, laughed, and laughed. "*They're both so close. I'm shooting them down, something your inept advance squads can't seem to do...*"

"Another ship? One of our troop transports?" Merkrida trilled.

"It is not likely while the hypercube remains," Hollfara sang. "Otherwise, Melkorka's communications avatar would be singing to us by now if the FTL comms were online."

"Incoming fire!" Kidahin keened. "Going evasive. Two torpedoes on track to us and two more heading southwest."

Kidahin broke right and accelerated above crisscrossing vine stems, flying between leaf stalks, throttling up the ascent engine but trying her best to stay in level flight as the SIV streaked away from the grounded geode.

"There is no doubt now. That geode is a ship. He fired four torpedoes, probably his entire inventory," she sang.

"You cannot run to orbit, Kidahin! We have no life support!" Hollfara trilled.

"I know, but torpedoes are not missiles. They do not have the range of even small missiles."

"But they are closing!" Hollfara keened.

"I know!" Kidahin sang as Delwyn began singing, *"This is it, boys. This is war..."*

"Do something!" Hollfara keened.

"I am firing countermeasures. Strap in and brace for high-gee turns."

"The railgun damage, my Kidahin. Proximity torpedo explosions or high-gee turns will rip the SIV apart!" Aplilin sang.

*"I got one! I got one!"* Harrison cackled in triumph.

"You got one what, Mr. Ambassador?" Deering demanded.

*"The one on the ground!"* Harrison giggled hysterically.

"S-one Actual, this is Recon," a feminine voice said over the TAC channel.

"Go ahead, Recon," Deering said.

"Actual? I've lost talkback telemetry from the Sentry."

"Harrison, you idiot! You blew up our shuttle!" Deering screamed.

*"Don't take that tone with me, Deering, or I'll rip your head off..."*

"Threaten the Eyloni all you like, Mr. Ambassador," Deering interrupted. "But let me remind you that I can break your neck with one hand tied behind my back. The Sentry, damn you, had assets we need to get out of here."

*"You said the Sentry lost antihydrogen containment!"* Harrison howled. *"So what? The* Khoza *is in mobius teleport range..."*

"The *Khoza* is an abandoned hulk, Mr. Ambassador, remember? I told you that!"

*"I don't give a damn if it's wrecked! Once we get there, I can use the FTL communications network to call for reinforcements!"*

"We have no antihydrogen to FTL jump us back!" Deering screamed.

*"This Lizard ship has residual antihydrogen in its sump tanks. It's not enough to jump it into FTL, but it must be enough to jump a shuttle back to the* Khoza."

"Not the Sentry. Not anymore. We'll have to use the gig, so for the love of God don't fire on the gig!"

*"I didn't...didn't...didn't,"* Harrison laughed and cried inanely.

The two torpedoes tracking Kidahin abruptly flamed out and fell into the vine stems below.

"What besides us and the Sentry is Harrison shooting at?" Jassalin wondered.

"Some Ni'zakhonii asset?" Hollfara suggested. "Maybe a fragment of our troop transport survived reentry and hard-landed?"

Kidahin snapped her tail in a 'no' gesture. She overflew the mountainous tangle of vine stems concealing the second force. "No," she sang. "The female named Recon reported losing telemetry with the Sentry shortly after Harrison fired his torpedoes."

Hollfara spun her red-ringleted pons in the slow circles Delwyn called "eye-rolling," because it conveyed the same feelings he did whenever he rolled his eyes at them.

"My Kidahin? I am reading life signs below," Aplilin sang. "They are low-level ones, the ones Mimiran called sleepwalker levels."

"Kill suits," Kidahin growled. "Your battlefield scanner has problems picking them up?" she asked Alfara.

"It does," Alfara snarled. "At least while the wearers remain still. When on the move, I get anomalous readings. You are better off using the SIV scanners and vectoring us into them on the ground via commlink."

"Maybe I should jump out and let them shoot at me again," Einstika trilled in wry self-deprecation.

"Spirits, but you truly are not yourself," Tialdrin, the social sophisticate, trilled while Aplilin and Jassalin trilled hysterically.

"Forgive me, Einstika, for I do not say this lightly," Tialdrin sang over Aplilin and Jassalin's crude trills, "but you always wear anger like a second pair of waistwear. You just got shot. Why are you not screaming in insensate fury?"

"I figured out what Mimiran meant about emotional control. The song she taught me celebrates anger in control as a useful weapon, but I did not fully grasp her meaning until I heard Delwyn's battle songs."

"Yes. He is with us in his music just as he is when we are together," Kidahin agreed, recognizing the truth in Einstika's words and reflected in her scent.

As if on cue, another song began playing over the commlink, and Kidahin followed the singing male voice with single-minded intensity. She realized she never abandoned Delwyn, for she fought with him in her mind just as she had always fought for him.

"Kidahin...Kidahin? My Kidahin!" Aplilin trilled. "I have a lock on the geode ship."

"Scan him for life signs while you can," Kidahin trilled.

"Affirm. Scanning," Aplilin sang. "No readings possible on passive scans."

"Switch to active scans. Everyone brace for possible evasive maneuvers!" Kidahin keened.

"Affirm," Aplilin sang. "Taking active scans...thirty percent of the scan is being reflected by geode hull geometries."

"Just like the LAC I helped Delwyn capture on Ibeetu," Kidahin muttered.

"Scans completed. No life signs found," Aplilin reported.

"None?" Kidahin trilled.

"Not one," Aplilin confirmed. "No Ni'zakhonii, no human, and no Eyloni. Nothing!"

"Could Harrison be shielded somehow? Wearing a kill suit, maybe?" Kidahin wondered.

"I do not think so," Hollfara sang. "Even the kill suits leak life sign signatures, the sleepwalker signals."

"What?" Kidahin trilled. "Then how is he..."

"Weapon lock detected from geode point defenses. Kidahin, go evasive now!" Aplilin keened.

"Affirm!" Kidahin trilled as she slammed the yoke forward and then yanked it hard right as she fired the main engine.

"Geode point defense pods firing," Aplilin trilled. "Plasma bolts and particle bursts incoming. Continual firing, Kidahin. He will exhaust his point-defense reserves soon at this rate of fire. It makes no sense."

"When we captured the Ni'zakhonii LAC for Delwyn, we barely figured out how to turn things on and off. Maybe Harrison can only turn the point defense system on but not off."

"Brace for aft impact on the engine bell," Aplilin keened. "My countermeasure efforts are ineffective!"

Kidahin slammed into her seat as the proximity blast drove her into its restraints.

"Engine bell and gimbals are damaged. The fusion engine has scrammed," Kidahin trilled. "Maneuvering and attitude control thrusters still work, but our best velocity is only the maximum that the orbital maneuvering system can maintain."

"Which is no substitute for an engine but more than enough for horizontal travel at a hover. What are we going to do now?" Hollfara sang.

"Continue toward the geode," Kidahin sang. "Harrison fired everything he had at us. I want to know why we cannot pick up his life signs!"

The SIV turned left as Kidahin throttled the OMS thrusters to full power. Even at maximum thrust it took several long minutes to retrace their evasive flight back to the geode.

"There he is," Alfara sang. "Aplilin should use the cannon and fire on him while she can..."

*"Deering! I hear Marsch! I remember that awful singing on Ibeetu. He sang some kind of wake ritual for those filthy Eyloni there! He's here! You were supposed to kill him!"* Harrison screamed.

"And I would have, Mr. Ambassador, had Melkorka returned him to the ship. She didn't, and I never got the chance! We are on a forced march now and should reach Recon and her squads in under an hour. That puts us less than ninety minutes away."

*"Too long,"* Harrison howled. *"I've got to do something. Wait…this blinking blue crystal…? EMP perimeter defenses? Yes, that's it!"* Harrison giggled.

"He has tapped into the commlink," Merkrida trilled. "Comm silence!"

"EMP electronic warfare warning! ECM countermeasures!" Kidahin keened.

"Ineffective! We are too close and his EW is too strong," Aplilin trilled.

"I am going for ground cover," Kidahin sang. "Descending through one thousand ells…"

The SIV went dead in mid-air.

"…No power!" Kidahin keened. "Reactor offline, auxiliary power offline, battery power is insufficient to maintain attitude control. Assume crash positions!"

The SIV swooped low like an aircraft on a recklessly fast runway approach, plowed into the sandy ground, and slid to a stop mere ells from a massive vine stem.

"Visual examination!" Kidahin trilled. "Look for fire and contamination caution and hazard warnings."

"No fires and no radiation leaks," Hollfara trilled. "We did not break up, thank the spirits. Dou'tu'tay, Kidahin. Every powered-up circuit is burned out."

"Which means every circuit," Jassalin growled in disgust.

"Most of them, yes," Hollfara agreed. "My damage control scanner and my 'minder still work!"

"My 'minder works, too!" Tialdrin sang. "So does Mimiran's medical scanner and the vascular regenerator."

"My 'minder does not," Kidahin trilled sadly.

"Nor does mine," Aplilin growled, livid at losing Delwyn's music.

"What can we do now, Kidahin?" Merkrida trilled. "We cannot move the males, Mimiran, and Zalzadrin. Einstika cannot travel far on foot."

"I can hold a knife and fight!" Einstika snarled.

"Good," Jassalin sang, "because you will defend the SIV and his wounded while we advance on the second group."

"I said I can fight, not act the healer!" Einstika keened.

"You will help Zalzadrin to the necessary and to eat," Tialdrin sang. "Mimiran is critical and not going anywhere. You cannot feed her. The most you can do is keep her clean. I must go and fight for the honor of our Warleader."

"I am going with you!" Kyralin snarled impatiently, her tail snapping behind her.

"And I am going with both of you!" Aplilin trilled. "You will do what I tell you to do, when I tell you to do it. The geode's EMP blast, this close, was powerful enough to burn out the weapons the second force carries."

Aplilin stopped short and glared at Alfara. "We will need weapons and backups for them," Aplilin continued, staring pointedly at the multitude of knives hanging from the hoarder Hunter's underthong ties, hanging from her hip-riding waistwear ties, and stuffing her bandolier.

"Of course," Alfara sang with a vocal wince at the thought of losing her surplus.

"What about thumpers, Alfara?" Merkrida trilled. "How many do you have, and do they still work?"

Alfara pulled four thumpers from her combat harness and glanced at the red power indicators set in their triggers.

"I have four working ones, but they must be thrown," she sang.

"Give them to me," Kidahin sang. "Pass your knife collection out so everyone has one and a spare or two. You keep a knife, a bow, and two quivers of AP arrows. Stay with Einstika and help her hold the SIV against counterattacks."

"No!" Alfara keened.

"Yes," Kidahin insisted. "You are trying to hide it, but you re-injured your left shoulder when we crashed."

"But...but...," Alfara spluttered, indignant.

"Listen!" Kidahin keened. "You are a good AP arrow shot, and the group one force is rushing to get here. Seliaha pulled and tossed rebreathers from four of them, but twenty or so more are coming up behind us and will have railguns. Set up a watch in a leaf stalk above the SIV and keep a watch for them!"

"Affirm!" Alfara sang.

Kidahin gave Jassalin, Aplilin, and Merkrida each a thumper. "Use them wisely," she sang. "They will disable comms and small arms but not anything with moderate shielding within twenty ells. They fire when they hit the ground, so for the spirits' sakes do not throw them over the vine stem."

"How far are they from us?" Jassalin trilled.

"SIV sensors put them at some four hundred ells northwest of us along a direct line of sight," Kidahin sang.

"What are we waiting for? I want to end this!" Aplilin sang, her triad flanking Jassalin and pulling ahead of her. They reached the vine stem growing over the one they stood on and started their climb.

"No, you do not! We climb together, reach the high ground together, and hold it together while the rest climb up. You will not advance on your own," Jassalin growled as she climbed parallel to Aplilin and then climbed ahead of her, reaching the topmost vine stem and its nearby leaf stalk.

"I wish you had Alfara's battlefield scanner," Merkrida sang under her breath as she reached the leaf stalk.

Kidahin flicked her ears in negation. "Alfara can use it to detect the magnetic action of those railguns, but if the geode fires an EM blast, it will destroy the scanner. I cannot believe it still works after EMP hit the SIV."

"Alfara was smart enough to turn it off and ground the circuits," Hollfara sang.

"Enough talking," Kidahin snapped. "Climb down the other side to the stem below and move out at prowler speed. From this height you can see the stem below winding around other stems two hundred ells ahead. I do not see any leaf stalks there, so remember to drop and crawl to the top of the stem. Go!"

"When does it get dark here?" Seliaha wondered aloud.

"Not for several more days," Kidahin trilled reassuringly. "This moon is similar to Elleio. It has days-long sunlight periods followed by days-long nights."

Jassalin reached the lower stem and extended her lead to point position with Aplilin, Kyralin, and Tialdrin barely a tail-length behind her.

Jassalin increased her lead as the stem angle steepened its climb over another obstructing stem. She glided up to the highest point and looked over the edge into the face of certain death.

"Jassalin! Down!" Aplilin keened from behind, refusing to duck and crawl herself.

"Force on the vine above, identify yourself!" a male speaking in the monotonous human tongue demanded.

Jassalin stood frozen and thought about mating of all things as she waited for death from cowardly personal particle weapons.

"I am Kidahin from the Compact warship *Hunter's Moon!*" Kidahin sang loud and clear from behind Jassalin.

"Kidahin? I know you! All hands, stand down!" the male yelled.

"No! Treason! Mr. Ambassador! Gunnery Sergeant Watkins is surrendering to the Eyloni! That means Marsch is here!"

"Keep 'em quiet!" Watkins bellowed at his men. "Kidahin, we're glad to see you. Is Senior Chief Marsch with you?"

"He is not. Warleader Delwyn is aboard our warship. Gunnery Sergeant William Watkins, I remember you. You were in Delwyn's command center when I visited your warship."

"Yeah, that's right. Kidahin, we came to this system in response to a distress call."

"I am going down to them. Cover me with AP arrows," Kidahin sang softly to Aplilin.

"Do you know this human?" Aplilin sang aggressively, ignoring her and fighting the instinct telling her that males were inherently safe.

"I remember him, yes. He was once subordinate to Delwyn's command."

"Males commanding males without a Warpact?" Aplilin trilled in astonishment.

"It is true. I do not understand it, either. Delwyn tried explaining it to me more than once. Come with me. Hollfara, Seliaha, cover us!"

"Affirm," Aplilin trilled, clearly unhappy with Kidahin's bold move.

"I am coming down to you, Gunnery Sergeant William Watkins."

"Right!" Watkins replied.

Kidahin climbed down easily barehanded and barefooted until she reached the next vine stem and a group of thirteen humans standing on it. Three of them cowered in the rear. They were watched casually, or was it contemptuously, by two other humans. Watkins and two more walked unarmed to her and stopped just outside of tail reach, respecting her tail-radius personal space.

"You came here to rescue Harrison?" Kidahin trilled, intentionally omitting Harrison's rank, a vulgar display of disrespect in her culture.

Watkins nodded. "Our ship came here, pressed into service by the influence these three had on somebody in the Defense Directorate. My troops and I are part of our ship's special operations group. The troopers with Master Chief Deering are her own picked force. None of them are *Londiwe Khoza* crew. God, the *Khoza!* She hit something in hyperspace and the next thing I knew we were trapped in the SOG Operations Center. Deering and her troops found us and got us to the shuttle bay. They told us that whatever hit us drove most of the surviving crew mad and they killed each other."

"I do not believe the hypercube caused this madness," Kidahin trilled, smelling the pheromones radiating from Watkins and understanding he related the truth as he knew it.

"No?" Watkins asked. "Did you hear what Harrison's been screaming? He's nuts!"

"More 'n nuts, Gunny," an SOG trooper added. "He's talkin' about eatin' folks, 'specially Senior Chief Marsch. If I didn't know no better, I'd say he's a Lizard himself!"

"Kidahin? Alfara," Alfara commed. "My scanner is picking up powered personal infantry weapons. It must be the force we overflew earlier."

"Are they in your AP arrow range?" Kidahin sang.

"No, but I am in the extreme range of their railguns."

"Get into cover behind a leaf stalk. It is too thick for even railguns to shoot through. But take a shot if the opportunity arises."

"Of course," Alfara trilled, insulted.

"I think he's a fake-out!" Watkins blurted.

Kidahin smelled the emotional meaning behind Watkins's words and snapped her tail in agreement.

"Yes," she sang. "I scanned the geode before his EMP countermeasures disabled our stealth insertion vehicle and found no life signs, human or otherwise."

"You lie!" one of the three huddling behind Watkins shouted. "Ambassador Harrison is held prisoner by the Lizards. He caused their ship to crash here!"

Without turning from Kidahin's direct gaze, Watkins shook his head. "I don't buy it, Mr. James. How can the Ambassador, with no technical ability whatsoever, disable a Lizard ship?"

"I don't know, Gunnery Sergeant, but he did," James yelled.

"Something is wrong here," Jassalin trilled suddenly, her nose catching a scent that smelled wrong.

"Wrong, mistress?" Watkins asked.

Jassalin swept her ears back on hearing the rank applied to her but shook the human's ignorance aside. "There are only thirteen of you...?"

"Eight," Watkins corrected. "But James, Quist, and Hennesy don't count. Master Chief Deering has nine with her, and Lance Corporal Lyons has four squads in the captain's gig."

"Captain's gig?" Jassalin trilled, smelling his scent for an emotional translation. "Do you mean a pinnace? A small ship attached to a warship, some kind of proxy?"

"Uh-huh. It's the captain's pretty shuttle. It has no arms or shields. Hell, it doesn't even have armor," Watkins sneered.

"What are they doing with him? Why not use him to drop your force near the Ni'zakhonii geode?" Kidahin trilled.

"Lyons's using the gig to transfer supplies from the Sentry to a perimeter near the Lizard ship."

"I told you they needed to move their supplies forward sooner or later!" Aplilin keened.

"How many people make up a squad?" Merkrida trilled.

"Eight," Watkins said. "That's thirty-two troops. If what you say about no life signs coming from that ship is right, then this is a trap. Lyons's squads carry only particle weapons and not much else. I'd better warn them..."

"Treason! Traitor!" one of the three watched humans screamed. He drew a pistol from behind his back and fired. His two cohorts immediately followed suit.

Watkins and two soldiers died instantly.

Merkrida ran forward, overbearing a surviving soldier and knocking him to the ground, saving him from scattered wild shots.

Kidahin and Jassalin charged the second surviving soldier and knocked him onto vine bark and covered him with their bodies. That gave Aplilin, Tialdrin, and Kyralin an opening to fire.

Antipersonnel arrows rained down from above as Hollfara and Seliaha fired into the vine stem behind the shooters, distracting them.

The three humans returned fire, clearly unable to hit anything beyond point-blank range.

Aplilin ran into the shooters, overbearing all three, and grappled the one called James.

Tialdrin and Kyralin separated, each charging into and easily taking the other two down onto the bark.

"This one seeks to kill Delwyn!" Aplilin keened. "I smell it on his scent."

"So does this one!" Kyralin interrupted.

"As does this one as well!" Tialdrin snarled.

"Mr. Ambassador," James yelled over the SOG TAC channel. "Gunny Watkins is a traitor. We've been captured by Eyloni forces and *gakk...*"

Aplilin squeezed powerful fingers around his neck, choking him, as she ripped the comms unit off his head.

"Any injuries?" Kidahin sang.

"None of us, and I saved a male!" Merkrida trilled in triumph.

"Kidahin? Incoming reinforcements," Alfara sang over the commlink.

"Type and number?" Kidahin trilled.

"A vehicle of some kind is vectoring in on Deering's force. He is some kind of pinnace. He is unshielded, and my scanner reads one hundred twelve individuals armed with particle pistols and long guns. I think the pinnace is about the size of an SIV but has no combat capability whatsoever."

"That said, AP arrows will do little more than blow holes in what I think is an unarmed shuttle," Kidahin sang. "Be wary all the same. He can climb to your watch point and fire."

"I have an idea," Aplilin trilled.

"*We* have a better idea," Seliaha interrupted as she and Hollfara climbed down and joined Aplilin. Each Hunter carried a length of liana as long as her tail.

Kidahin looked at them, slowly blinked her eyes several times, smelling their intent. She turned to Jassalin.

"You hold the superior hierarchy rank among us. What do you say about this?" Kidahin sang formally.

"Me?" Jassalin asked, shocked.

"The scent of their conviction is overwhelming evidence," Kidahin sang. "And honor crime adjudication is a hierarchy function."

Jassalin, Kidahin's second-in-leadership, faced another kind of life-and-death event. She was the oldest Hunter. She was called the Eldest Huntress in all Team-Two social rituals. She was confronted by ni'zakhon, outlawry, from males clearly guilty by their own emotion-reeking body odors. Both the Ta'lauek and the Ok'e'say hierarchies would support her decree should she make a life-and-death judgment.

Jassalin began singing the "Power of Names" song she had so recently sung with Mimiran. She sang the meanings of the names of every Team-Two Huntress, the meaning of Mimiran's name, of Zalzadrin's name, of Nynava's name, and the meaning their warship society attributed to Delwyn's name.

When she finished, she turned to the three captives and spoke while Kidahin translated.

"We smell the emotions in the minds of others. Your body odors, although weak, paint pictures in our minds of your intent. On the Coalition warship *Henri Edda* you conspired with Harrison and Deering to kill Warleader Delwyn before he could advise the Be'atika Senge hierarchy sitting as the Compact Counsel of the Ten Tribes of Elleio to refuse further talks with Harrison and negotiate only through Captain Winters.

"We females centuries ago deemed the intent to fatally harm a male without honorable justification an honor crime punishable by death. In the names of the Ta'lauek and the Ok'e'say hierarchies, I smell the guilt on your scent and decree your deaths."

Jassalin turned to Aplilin, Tialdrin, and Kyralin. "I ask you to assist me by taking the appropriate action in the traditional manner," she trilled sadly.

Aplilin glided up to Seliaha, accepted the tail-length of liana, and returned to Tialdrin and Kyralin. Together, they advanced on the ni'zakhon known as James.

"I knew something was wrong with those guys!" a surviving SOG soldier muttered.

"No! No! Wait! You can't do this," James screamed hysterically at the approaching muscular Hunter female.

"Be calm," Aplilin sang softly, her gentle singing harmony at odds with her usually coarse and frightening demeanor. "It will soon be over," she added as Tialdrin and Kyralin gently but firmly gripped James by the hips and shoulders and stood rock-steady.

# 10
## THE FEMALE INSIDE, THE DEATH SONG, THE OBSESSION OF ADDICTION...

As the third tailcutter succumbed to the liana garrote, Aplilin lost all semblance of soothing comfort as she reverted to her harsh, aggressive self. Her dilated pupils, black pools surrounded by amber iris haloes, contracted to pinpoints in a sea of amber. Her muscles trembling, her chest heaving, she slung the plasma cannon over a shoulder, spun on bare feet, and fled down the bark-covered vine stem at pursuit speed.

"Aplilin, where are you going?" Kidahin demanded.

Aplilin ignored her and flicked an ear to activate the commlink feeler attached there.

"Alfara!" she trilled. "Return to the SIV and back-up Einstika."

"Affirm!" Alfara replied.

"Get off the commlink, Aplilin. Harrison can hear you," Kidahin keened as she ran up to and alongside of her muscular lover.

"I know that," Aplilin spat. "I have an idea! Fall back and stay well behind me in case I am wrong. Head for the point where the second vine stem climbs over this one. If what I have in mind works, you will know soon enough."

Kidahin slowed. "But what are you going to do?" she trilled.

"Something stupid," Aplilin sang.

"Aplilin?" Alfara commed. "I am off the leaf stalk and near its base. I can see the pinnace hovering above this stem a good distance away. I think he is going to pick up Deering and her stragglers. I am climbing down the vine stem now."

"Good," Aplilin sang. "I am running to your leaf stalk now..."

"Then why are you sending me back to the SIV?" Alfara interrupted as she dropped the final four ells to the sandy ground. "I have the battlefield scanner, and two of us firing AP arrows at the pinnace are better than one."

"Not for what I have in mind. The pinnace cannot help but overfly the SIV. If he lands, you must fire on the combatants he drops off. We are too far back to support you!"

"Affirm. I see Einstika," Alfara sang.

"Aplilin, shut up!" Jassalin keened. "What is wrong with you? You sound like Harrison..."

"My Aplilin! Think about this," Kidahin implored. "You cannot engage the pinnace by yourself. What if he opens his hatches and strafes you as he flies by?"

"He cannot," Aplilin sang with certainty. "His combatants cannot forward-fire from a fuselage hatch. Deering must approach side-on to me if she wants to fire at me from open hatches," she laughed.

"What is she doing?" Jassalin demanded, catching up with Kidahin. "Is she trying to draw the pinnace away from the SIV?"

Kidahin, certain Jassalin was right, staggered as the empathic force of Aplilin's lingering scent triggered in her mind.

"No, wait!" Kidahin trilled, shaking. The certainty in her lover's body odor brought with it absolute confidence.

"She will fire AP arrows at the pinnace, for all the good that will do. Team-Two, split into hands. Jassalin, go after Aplilin. Take Kyralin and Tialdrin with you. Merkrida, Hollfara, and Seliaha, come with me."

Kidahin turned on the two humans.

"Stay back," she said. "You do not fight with us. Our combat ethics tell us to use traditional weapons—knives, bows, spears, and hand-to-hand skills—once we destroy an enemy's modern weapon capability. Using modern weapons against individuals having none is cowardly. You train in hand-to-hand and knife combat, but my time with Delwyn tells me you use them as a last resort."

Kidahin paused, shaking her head vigorously to stress the point she made in the cumbersome monotonic Coalition tongue.

"You do not fight as we do," she said. "Different forces and tactics cannot combine without ruining the unity of both forces."

"Kidahin!" Einstika sang. "Alfara and I are together under cover near the SIV. The pinnace landed on the vine stem. Um..., he is taking off now and listing into a slow approach toward us. He is closing the distance but remains level with the leaf stalks. He sees us! We are digging in."

"What is he doing now?" Kidahin asked. "Alfara?"

"Slowing down," Alfara replied, "but staying well above us. He is beyond AP sheaf arrow range. Dou'tu'tay! He stopped. He is about to land. Yes, he is descending..."

*"Deering!"* Harrison's voice screamed over the TAC channel. *"Stop screwing around and get your ass to this ship and get me the hell out of here!"*

"Mr. Ambassador," Deering sighed, her tone of voice betraying exhausted impatience. "The Eyloni scoutship crashed. I'm dropping a squad off to take out the survivors."

*"No, you don't!"* Harrison thundered. *"I took 'em out myself. Me! Me! Me! I did what you can't seem to do. I see only six survivors in the wreckage and another ten scattered across six hundred meters northwest of you. Fly over them and get me out of*

*this ship! Once I'm out, we'll pick up some heavy weapons and hunt them down like foxes, shred them to pieces, and gorge ourselves on their flesh!"*

"Yessir, Mr. Ambassador," Deering snapped.

"Aplilin? The pinnace is climbing back to leaf height and drifting slightly east. No, he is correcting now. You a'pea! My battlefield scanner says he will pass within a hundred ells of you but beyond AP arrow range if he keeps going," Alfara sang.

"I am pressed up against a sail-sized leaf and braced on the stalk against it," Aplilin sang. "And I have something better than an AP arrow!"

"Your cannon?" Alfara keened. "Impossible! Without targeting, you must hold the cannon away from the leaf stalk and aim through the manual sighting reticule. You cannot hold onto both the cannon and the stalk and still fire."

"I am not firing my infant. I am firing my bow."

Aplilin gripped the rough stalk bark with her four-jointed toes and opposable big toes, embraced the living wood sensuously, and balance-checked her body with her twisting tail. She nocked an ungainly looking arrow, drew the heavy short bow, and watched the Coalition pinnace drift slowly overhead, edging ever so slightly into extreme sheaf arrow range.

Aplilin held the bowstring rock-steady and waited. She wanted an overhead shot with its shorter flight path than what firing at an angle could give. Aplilin was strong, stronger than most Hunter females, but still on the lower average for any Warrior female. She watched the pinnace through pin-prick eyes, her vision naturally adapted to judging changes in patterns. Even from this distance she could see the tiny ship creep toward her until he drew no closer. Indeed, he seemed to begin drifting away from her.

"Vi e'ta ka nabi!" she yelled and loosed the arrow.

Amazingly enough, given the range, her precarious perch on the leaf stalk, and the dubious aerodynamics of the shaft itself, the arrow struck the fuselage a glancing blow, penetrated the outer skin, and hung there.

And nothing happened.

"Aplilin? What is going on? Are you firing on him yet?" Kidahin trilled.

Aplilin, counting to herself, ignored her. The pinnace fired his engines and cruised on, gaining the altitude needed to fly over the tangled, knotted vine stems where she had so recently left Kidahin and the bulk of Team-Two.

Aplilin reached zero and squinted at the pinnace. A momentary aura shimmered across the fuselage, so brief it was that she thought it nothing more than a figment of her hopeful imagination.

Kidahin saw the pinnace coming, watched him fly over the leaf stalk Aplilin was certainly hiding on. The pinnace flew on, climbing higher as he topped the piled heap of vines. As he soared above her, he gracefully rolled to the left and fell nose-first fourteen hundred ells into the sandy ground below and behind the vine stem.

The impact rammed the cockpit and flight deck deep into the fuselage. Its skin rippled with impact compression waves, concentric rings, rushing aft. Unable to support the engine mass, the fuselage folded in on itself and ruptured, spilling passengers across the ground seconds before slamming upside-down onto them.

"My Aplilin! You did it!" Kidahin sang. "But what did you do?"

"Seliaha is a small-arms genius," Aplilin sang over the commlink.

"Seliaha is a what?" Kidahin wondered. "She is here with us. What are you talking about?"

"I shot the pinnace down with an improvised thumper arrow!" Aplilin trilled in triumph. "It was Seliaha's idea."

"An improvised what?" Kidahin trilled.

"I mounted a heavy thumper onto an AP arrow and shot the pinnace with it. His control systems burned out from the EMP, and he crashed."

"Aplilin?" Jassalin said over the commlink. "Look down."

Aplilin glanced down from her precarious hold on the cobalt sail-leaf. Far below, Jassalin, Kyralin, and Tialdrin stood on the stem, waiting.

"Get down here," Jassalin trilled, "and from now on, keep off the commlink!"

"Why?" Aplilin demanded while climbing down. "The pinnace threat is neutralized."

"The geode can still fire on us!" Jassalin seethed. "What if..."

"Jassalin?" Kidahin sang over the commlink. "Forked assault on the crash site. Commlink silence during the engagement!"

"Now you have a reason to keep off the comms! Just what were you thinking, running off like that?" Jassalin trilled.

"I told you I had an idea," Aplilin trilled at arrogance pitch.

"Leave the cannon behind, you will not need it," Jassalin snapped. She turned to her hand. "Strip your combat EVA suits. Battle beckons us to fight for the honor of our Warleader!" she sang.

Jassalin stripped off her suit. Dressed only in flimsy beaded neckwear with the adulthood knife curving around her left breast, hip-riding underthong and loincloth, and her rank earring, she picked up a bow and combat knives and led her hand back down the stems they had just climbed, complaining aloud that climbing was not fighting.

* * *

"What now?" Merkrida asked Kidahin as they stood together overlooking the smoking wreckage.

"We climb down and wait for Jassalin to reach her place. Strip your combat suits," Kidahin sang, certain that now was the time to act.

"Kidahin?" Zalzadrin sang unsteadily over the commlink.

"Zalzadrin! Get off the commlink!" Kidahin trilled at imperative tempo.

"You do not sing orders to me. I am Mistress of Arms here. I am sending Einstika and Alfara back to you."

"No!" Kidahin seethed. "They stay to protect you and the injured."

"I do not need them. The two males died; from shock I think. Mimiran has an irregular heartbeat. I shocked her twice, and she is in regular rhythm now, but her injuries are well beyond my battlefield-aid training."

"I cannot count on you remaining conscious, Zalzadrin, let alone capable. Einstika and Alfara, go back and help Zalzadrin," Kidahin snapped.

"Too late," Jassalin's voice sang in her ear. "Alfara and Einstika just joined my hand."

"Fine," Kidahin growled through clenched teeth. "What is your status?"

"We are on the bottom vine stem. Alfara has you pinpointed on her battlefield scanner. We are two hundred ells south of you. I am sending Einstika to join you. Wait for her," Jassalin sang over the commlink.

"Fine," Kidahin repeated, "and if nobody has any more speeches, then stop talking over the commlink!"

Kidahin glanced at her own hand of Huntresses.

"Who has a working 'minder?" she demanded.

"I do," Hollfara sang.

"Good. Use it to play Delwyn's songs for us."

"About time," Hollfara grumbled.

"What was that?" Kidahin snapped.

"Affirm, I mean...," Hollfara sang, drawing out the final note as Delwyn drummed up a strong, aggressive beat.

The male music provoked them as Kidahin expected it to. Everyone would now draw upon the fight response reserves cued by the rhythmic martial beat and the insistent singing voice. The male singing voice directly affected the female mind. It banished sorrow and worry, it soothed wounds, it encouraged craftiness, it summoned strength, it urged them into graceful determination, it quickened reflexes, it gave them hammer-fists, but it also roused a terrible wrath.

Einstika dropped the final few ells to the sand behind Kidahin.

Kidahin whirled on her. "What kept you?" she demanded.

"Running here and climbing down kept me," Einstika growled with menace. "What did you want me to do, jump off the vine stem?"

Kidahin bit her tongue and twisted her pons in slow circles under Einstika's nose, a "whatever" gesture.

Einstika glared at Kidahin, indignantly, not from the twisting pons, but from the suggestion in Kidahin's pheromones hinting where Einstika could stick her tail.

* * *

Jassalin, her hand in place, likewise goaded by male music, led them over the side of the vine stem. They climbed down the near-vertical rough bark barehanded and barefooted.

Halfway through their descent Jassalin paused to count her Huntresses and came up one short.

"Aplilin? Where are you?" she keened.

"She went after her cannon," Alfara sang back with annoying unconcern.

"When?" Jassalin trilled.

"When I was climbing over the side, she told me she was getting her infant."

Jassalin growled to herself until her bare feet touched sand. Several shots rapidly popped off behind her.

"Firearms!" she yelled. "Dig into the sand!"

Dropping to the ground herself, Jassalin peered at the smoking pinnace crumpled on the sandy open field. A group of thirty-one combatants led by a tall, willowy human charged around the wreckage barely a hundred ells away.

"AP arrows, return fire!" Jassalin sang at insistence pitch.

* * *

Kidahin spun on hearing distant small-arms fire.

"Look!" she said, pointing south. "They are firing on Jassalin using the wreckage for cover. We will flank them from this side and come in behind them. Bows ready. Advance!"

Merkrida and Kidahin ran together, with the rest of her hand following close behind with arrows nocked and bows slung under armpits as they flew across the sand toward the crash site. Kidahin saw human bodies littering the ground. Some likely fell from open hatches when the pinnace pitched over, but most were mangled by the collapsing fuselage when they were ejected from the wreckage.

"It is the spirits' own luck anyone survived the crash," Merkrida trilled.

"I know. How many of them do you think there are?" Kidahin asked.

"At least forty," Merkrida sang. "The sound and number of shots tell me there are more than just a few of them firing."

"I do not hear the whine of railgun fire," Kidahin sang, perplexed. "I wonder why?"

"High-yield, single-pulse EMP," Seliaha sang. "I gave Aplilin an infantry vehicle countermeasure thumper. It fires one huge pulse, one powerful enough to knock out an armored personnel carrier or a light armored vehicle. APCs and LAVs are lightly shielded against EMP, and the one I gave her was designed to overcome such shielding. Gunnery Sergeant William Watkins called the pinnace a ceremonial noncombatant vehicle. Even moderately shielded personal heavy infantry weapons like Aplilin's plasma cannon or Deering's railguns will fry in the wake of this electromagnetic pulse."

"What do they have besides firearms?" Merkrida wondered.

"Mechanically initiated chemical explosive devices," Hollfara sang. "Impact-to-primer triggered ones. You know, firearm bullets, concussion and fragmentation grenades, and the like."

"The grenades are likely hand-thrown ones, right?" Kidahin asked as they swung up and around the smashed fuselage.

"They used all their smart grenades to make improvised explosive devices after we took out their grenade launchers. The grenades they have now are dumb as rocks and hand-thrown, just as our remaining four thumpers are," Hollfara sang.

*"Deering? Deering! Marsch is singing again! I told you to kill him! Where are you? Where are your advance squads and their shuttle?"* Harrison screamed over the Coalition tactical channel.

"My shuttle is grounded," Deering said grimly. "I've got hostiles on my six and on my left flank!"

*"I don't give a rat shit about your left flank or your ass. My aides are with Watkins, and he's also on your left. Slash though Marsch and his Eyloni. Soak the ground with their blood. Eat your fill of them, and meet up with Watkins."*

"But, Mr. Ambassador, didn't you hear what Edwin said on TAC? Watkins surrendered to the Eyloni. He's either dead or actively working with them!"

*"Edwin wouldn't let him. Wouldn't let him!"* Harrison laughed hideously. *"Edwin James is a true believer. Quist and Hennesy are soft, but easily led. They'll do whatever Edwin tells 'em to do. Break their ranks, overrun them, get my aides, and get me out of this damn ship!"*

"Why is Harrison not taking the warning about Gunnery Sergeant William Watkins seriously?" Einstika wondered aloud.

"Driven insane by captivity in a Ni'zakhonii ship, maybe?" Kidahin replied cautiously. "I was a captive in a Ni'zakhonii light attack craft until Delwyn rescued me. I told you about it many times. Harrison is a weak-minded person with a pale constitution, no endurance in him at all. Maybe the Ni'zakhonii ate his cultural attaché alive before his eyes. Mimiran could tell us if she was in any condition to hear him."

"Kidahin!" Merkrida interrupted. "An armed group is advancing toward us!"

"Arrows, ready!" Kidahin sang.

"James, Quist, and Hennesy are traitors!" a gruff, monotonic human voice rasped over the Coalition TAC channel. "They're tryin' to undermine the Coalition-Compact alliance we got with the Eyloni. Harrison wants the Eyloni gone, an' Deerin's workin' with 'im."

"That's a lie, S-two. You've been fed disinformation by that traitor Marsch and his Eyloni handler, Kidahin," Deering shouted.

"No way," S-two replied. "Gunny told us you said Captain Bhari an' the senior staff went crazy from exposure to gravaton flux comin' from the gravity field we hit in hyperspace. But Deputy James said before he was killed that they died in a structural collapse in one of the ship's shelter zones. The Eyloni went to the *Khoza* an' told us the captain an' the others were executed. I may be a dumb grunt, but even I know all three stories can't be true. Then there's this here Eyloni engineer who says there's nothin' wrong with the Sentry's hull..."

"The people on the Sentry mutinied during reentry!" Deering screamed. "They went mad, just as most of the survivors on the ship went mad. I popped the cabin seals before they could storm the flight deck. You know that, S-two, because you were there!"

"Kidahin, what are they arguing about?" Merkrida asked, aghast.

"Mental warfare," Kidahin sang. "The two we saved are telling anyone who will listen these inconsistent facts to foment doubt."

"I don't know about the shuttle, S-one Actual, because them people was beatin' away on the bulkhead, but them Eyloni are pretty convincin' about Captain Romesh Bhari bein' executed, an' what Gunny said about..."

"I don't care what Gunny Watkins told you. It's all Eyloni disinformation! And... S-two..? What was that about Deputy Ambassador James being killed?"

"Yeah, he's dead. Hennesy and Quist, too. But so what, S-one Actual? Ain't you been listenin' to Ambassador Harrison? He's talkin' about eatin' people! An' that laugh of his? We think he's really a Lizard agent, one who lured the ship to her death! He's tryin' to capture us and turn us into what that thing claimin' to be the ambassador is!"

"That's crazy talk," Deering said in dismissal. "You screw your head on straight right now! That's an order! You're a victim of a disinformation campaign run by that traitor Marsch!"

"Uh, I don't think so, Master Chief," S-two replied uncertainly.

"Yes, you do," Deering yelled. "I hear it in your voice. Now, act on your instincts..."

"S-two, this is Recon. Authenticate your sitrep," a high-pitched feminine voice interrupted.

"Aye, aye, Recon. Sitrep is Nocturne Slumber, repeat: Nocturne Slumber."

"Very well, S-two. Master Chief, S-two believes..."

"I know what the code word means, and it means nothing! Eyloni women use their body odors to control men. That's how they compromised Senior Chief Marsch! Now, you hold the line. Those Eyloni don't have an infinite supply of exploding arrows!"

"But, Master Chief...," Recon managed to get out before the TAC channel abruptly cut off.

"There they are," Seliaha said. "Dug in next to the fuselage at its rupture point. I see two groups, Kidahin. Can you see them?"

Kidahin flicked her ears in the affirmative and leaned against Merkrida. She said nothing, but let her pheromones do the talking.

"Deering is right about Jassalin's arrows, and AP arrows are the only thing holding those cowardly firearms at bay," Merkrida sang. "I can see what looks like two of their squads plus a few individuals. Do you think the others died in the crash?"

"I do not know, but right now all their attention is focused on Jassalin. Advance to their blind side along the fuselage, now!" Kidahin sang.

*"Deering! Stop Marsch's awful singing! It's setting my teeth on edge!"* Harrison screeched over the TAC channel. The scream dropped to a bloodcurdling chuckle before becoming intelligible again. *"Marsch is coming to kill me! Where are you? I order you to abandon the Eyloni for now and help me...Help me! Help me! I can't leave the Lizard ship! I'm connected to it some..someho...somehowwww,"* he shrieked.

Kidahin and her hand reached the safe cover alongside the downed pinnace. They danced on light feet around it until they faced the enemy's rear.

"If Alfara is paying any attention to her battlefield scanner, she should know we are here. Jassalin should rush them, just like she rushed us in the arberi tree stronghold on our warship. The humans should try to hold the pinnace and what cover and supplies he affords them, just as we held our tree against Jassalin," Kidahin sang at a thoughtful beat.

"Let us hope Alfara is paying attention and not scrounging every stray knife she finds in the wreckage," Hollfara sang.

* * *

"Where is Kidahin?" Jassalin asked Alfara.

"She circled around the pinnace at some distance and waited while the humans argued over their tactical comm channel. Then she swung back behind the pinnace and continued the advance. They are hugging the fuselage now."

"Jassalin, I am out of AP arrows," Aplilin sang.

"I am as well," Kyralin sang.

"Get ready for a charge," Jassalin sang as Delwyn's voice began to sing a battle song called, ironically, "Battle Hymn." He sang about glory marching onward.

Aplilin, Kyralin, and Tialdrin reformed their stalker triad and surged forward.

"Aplilin! Stop!" Jassalin keened. "You will wait until I tell you to go!"

"What are you waiting for, then? Say 'go,'" Aplilin growled, well under the influence of the battle song.

"Not until Alfara pinpoints soft targets. She said that Kidahin put her hand in a flanking posture... No, a'pea that! We will rush into them, keeping them off-balance, while Kidahin sweeps into their flank and pushes them into the fuselage and us."

"You are provoking direct action," Aplilin sang, pleased.

"I am," Jassalin replied.

"You should coordinate hand-movement with Kidahin," Alfara warned.

"No," Jassalin said. "Our hands are in position for an open field direct charge and a flanking fork attack. Combat is fluid, and this opportunity will not last long."

"All soft targets located, Jassalin. Wait! Kidahin is starting her flanking assault now!"

"She knows me better than I know myself," Jassalin trilled in deep admiration. "Aplilin, take your triad and break through them. Take out the female fighters. Try to withhold lethal force against the males but for self-defense," she sang, her female nature unwilling to kill any male unless absolutely necessary.

"Affirm. Kyralin, Tialdrin, go!"

One drawback of firearms was the need to reload. Aplilin and her triad glided across the sand and in seconds felled two human females with graceful, lethal blows to the neck.

"Alfara? Find any modern weapons?" Jassalin asked as she ran behind Aplilin.

"No," Alfara sang from her right. "On your left! Grenades!" she yelled.

Jassalin twisted left, drew her bow, and fired a sheaf arrow as she ran. The arrow, not an AP arrow, pierced the human in mid-throw. She fell, and three seconds later the grenade exploded beneath her.

Moving into point well ahead of her hand, Aplilin crashed into a volley of pistol fire. She staggered but did not fall.

Kyralin and Tialdrin split around her and daintily danced into two female shooters. They each picked one shooter up and slammed her into the ground, lifted her vertical, grabbed her by the neck, and twisted her head completely around with all the strength a double-jointed, muscular arboreal tree-dweller could muster.

"Jassalin, we should join Kidahin and come against them as one," Alfara trilled.

"No! Keep assaulting their line," Jassalin sang.

"But Aplilin was shot! I think Kyralin was, too."

"So what! There is a bullet in my hip. You do not hear me keening to the spirits about it, do you?" Jassalin snapped.

Aplilin, driven by shock from gunshot wounds, by fear she felt for her favorite male's safety, by his insistent music, by her strong fixation on him, by the need to survive and mate, by the act of strangling three tailcutters, and by worry for Kidahin, she fell into a murderous berserker frenzy as she charged into thirteen humans.

Kyralin and Tialdrin rejoined Aplilin, and together they formed triad-of-death.

"Kidahin has entered melee. The second group is turning to meet her advance," Alfara sang as she clipped the battlefield scanner to her underthong ties. Ready to enter melee herself, she did not need it.

Jassalin shouldered her bow, pulled a heavy knife and ran behind Tialdrin, Alfara right beside her.

Kyralin, holding the apex of their triad, broke through the human line and into Deering's rear, which had turned to meet Kidahin's advancing hand. Kyralin separated from her triad and charged.

Aplilin punched a male in the throat and turned in time to see Kyralin's tail flitting as she ran into melee combat.

Aplilin flipped her ears back and growled, wary. What did Kyralin see? Male hyperprotectiveness turned adolescent females into adrenaline-soaked, instinct-driven, heedless rage engines, but it did not make them stupid. Aplilin blinked, trying to drive the rage from her own male-loving mind. She was no thinker even with a clear head. What was Kyralin doing?

"What, Aplilin?" Jassalin sang as she drew up alongside her.

"Hurry!" Aplilin keened. "Kyralin is charging into them without us, but I cannot smell why!"

Jassalin listened to the battle as she ran alongside Aplilin and Tialdrin. Aplilin's graceful gait faltered as they ran, and an odd gurgling wheeze began to whistle in Tialdrin's heavy breathing.

Wait...the gunfire. Deering's forces were firing differently, more measured, more organized, and with a more methodical determination.

And the air was turning foggy. It was not smoke from the geode missile strike in the south, which was too far away and the breezes blew wrong.

"Smoke canisters!" Jassalin keened. "Alfara, scan the field ahead."

"Affirm, but Jassalin, Kidahin does not have a battlefield scanner!"

Aplilin surged ahead of her fellow Hunters and ran, trilling madly, into the enemy force.

A line of humans stood—their backs to her—in the thick smoke. At least ten of them were firing into Kidahin's advancing hand. They did not see Aplilin, but she could not shoot arrows into the smoky cover and risk hitting Kidahin!

Aplilin dropped the arrow and swung her bow like a club, smacking the helmets of all ten and breaking the bow with the force of her follow-through.

She would not lose another lover.

The first two humans she hit dropped to the ground. Jassalin and Tialdrin killed the third. But the last two swung pistols around in time to shoot Aplilin point blank, and she fell face-first into the sand.

"Jassalin! I am shot in the back. I cannot feel or move my tail or legs!"

"Tialdrin, battlefield aide, you know enough about it," Jassalin sang.

"Affirm. What about Kyralin?"

"I will get her. Alfara, help Tialdrin with Aplilin."

"Affirm, acting!" Alfara sang.

* * *

"Dou'tu'tay! Smoke canisters!" Merkrida swore.

"Cowardly to hide behind clouds of smoke!" Einstika growled angrily.

Kidahin listened, one ear cocked forward at Einstika, the other cocked back in Jassalin's direction. The sound of gunfire changed. Her sensitive ears picked up two important facts. Jassalin's hand was taking fire, and…

"Kidahin, I am out of AP arrows," Merkrida sang.

"And I have only two left," Seliaha added.

"Quiet!" Kidahin snapped. "Do you hear…less firing?"

"Yes," Hollfara sang excitedly. "Jassalin is attacking their rear, and they must be running low on ammunition."

"Shoulder bows and advance into them," Kidahin ordered, knowing with absolute certainty now was the time to press the attack.

Someone charged at Kidahin from out of the smoke. She ran toward that someone, a heavy knife at the ready. She dropped her shoulder and rammed, overbore, took down, and stabbed at that someone in defense of her Huntresses.

And barely missed Kyralin's chest.

"Hold!" Kyralin trilled as she landed flat on her back and twisted away from Kidahin's blade. "You will hit Jassalin's hand! Do not hurt them. I think Aplilin was shot in the back!"

"Kyralin?" Kidahin keened as her blade stabbed into the sand a mere fingernail from Kyralin's neck. "Where is Jassalin relative to Deering's forces?"

"Aplilin charged their line and knocked out most of the gunners before getting shot. The remainder folded into the body facing you and retreated into the smoke. I stopped you from firing AP arrows at us or from charging into us."

"Use your head!" Merkrida trilled. "You have a commlink."

"Mine does not work!" Kyralin growled.

Kidahin twitched her ear to key open the commlink attached there and sang, "Jassalin? Kidahin."

There was no reply.

"My commlink is burned out," Kidahin sang. "Merkrida, yours?"

"Mine is dead, too," Merkrida trilled in disgust.

"Mine does not work," Seliaha snarled.

"Mine does not, either," Hollfara snapped, depressed at the loss of Delwyn's comforting music.

"A low-yield EMP strike," Hollfara trilled thoughtfully. "Deering must have fired it while we were caught up in the charge because I…I did not notice when Delwyn's music stopped," she added guiltily.

"I did not, either," Kidahin admitted, deeply ashamed that her mind was so occupied as to not miss his music. She felt humiliated.

"Kidahin!" Jassalin keened as she ran up to her. "Deering is retreating northwest."

"How is your hand?" Kidahin trilled.

"Shot up," Jassalin growled. "Aplilin got hit in the back and is paralyzed. Tialdrin got hit in the chest and has a collapsed lung. I got hit in the hip. Alfara is fine, but I think Kyralin got hit, too. She ran off on us!"

"I stopped Kidahin from firing AP arrows at you," Kyralin sang, holding a bloody hand to her shoulder.

"Assault Team-Two, recall to me!" Kidahin trilled at imperative tempo. "We are in an attrition situation. Deering is heading for the vine stem and high ground. From there, she can fire on us as her forces retreat to the geode ship."

Tialdrin glided up to Kidahin. "Alfara and Merkrida are carrying Aplilin. How do we climb the vine stem with her?" she asked.

"I will stay with her. Jassalin will assume the leadership. What about you? Can you use the vascular regenerator on your lung?" Kidahin asked.

"No," Tialdrin sang, blood staining her brilliant white teeth. "They fired their equivalent of a thumper. Everything operating when the EMP charge fired blew out our minders, Alfara's battlefield scanner, and the commlinks. The only things working are the four thumpers. Even the firing circuits in Aplilin's plasma cannon are burned out."

"Then why is she still carrying it around?" Kidahin wondered aloud as a fondness for Aplilin shuddered through her.

"She told me she can short circuit its force chamber and cause it to fire a massive plasma burst. She can only do it once because the cannon will melt to slag," Tialdrin sang with a wheezing note in her voice.

Merkrida and Alfara carried Aplilin to Kidahin.

"Leave me," Aplilin sang.

"Never!" Kidahin hissed.

"I cannot climb. We have no rope. You are pursuing people who are a danger to our Warleader. You have no choice!" Aplilin sang at insistence pitch.

"Delwyn often says there are always choices. I must find them and then consider them," Kidahin trilled reassuringly before turning to her second-in-leadership. "Jassalin, pursue and destroy them. Humans cannot climb like us. Catch them climbing and shoot them with sheaf arrows. Go!"

The smoke screen, until now contained by the surrounding hillside tall vine stems, began to disperse as Team-Two chased after Deering's force.

"What are her numbers?" Kidahin asked.

"Somewhere around fourteen, I think," Merkrida sang.

"Fourteen? Fourteen is nothing," Seliaha trilled.

"Fourteen plus one is twenty, the number of people in an able-bodied assault team, and we are not able-bodied. Do not underestimate their numbers," Aplilin snapped. "The force facing Kidahin was the Deering-led force. Gunnery Sergeant William Watkins said her forces are loyal to her and not to her warship."

"Yes," Kidahin sang. "She is allied with Harrison and must...," she hesitated at the sound of distant gunfire.

"Firearms! They are shooting...at what? They do not have the range to hit us," Jassalin sang.

Seliaha cocked her ears. "I hear two groups of shooters, Kidahin. The shots echo off the vine stem. I can hear the difference between shots fired on the ground and shots fired above it."

"The above-ground fire comes from the males we saved," Aplilin trilled happily.

"Flanking run!" Kidahin sang. "Now is our chance to catch them in a crossfire!"

Team-Two closed the distance to the enemy. Kidahin saw ten of Deering's fourteen fighters shot dead on the ground. The remaining four had already dropped their weapons. She recognized one of them.

"Deering!" she spat.

"Kidahin?" a human voice yelled from atop the vine stem. "D'ya need any help?"

"Yes," she keened back. "I need guards and help with the wounded."

"We got climbin' gear. Ya want us to come down or are ya comin' up?"

Kidahin turned to Jassalin.

"What do you think?" Kidahin asked her.

Jassalin glanced around. The ground surrounding the crash site was bracketed by crisscrossing vine stems, every one of them an easy enough climb for an able-bodied barefooted and barehanded Eyloni, but a nearly impossible one for humans without climbing equipment.

"Walk with me," Jassalin sang softly. "Smell them and tell me what you think."

Kidahin twined her tail around Jassalin's as they walked among and around the prisoners sitting on the sand. The two Hunters danced a pattern around and among the prisoners for several minutes before withdrawing.

"Well?" Jassalin sang at a stiff interrogative tempo.

"The three with Deering, a female and two males, are loyal to her. Deering herself is dedicated to Harrison, but I do not smell anything coming from the three regarding Harrison," Kidahin sang flatly.

"What do you want to do with them?" Jassalin pressed.

"We pull them up onto the vine stem. From there someone has to take Tialdrin and Aplilin back to the SIV."

"No, we are not going back!" Tialdrin and Aplilin sang together.

"I can hear Mimiran saying 'jinx' right now," Kidahin trilled with a faint smile.

"Kidahin, we cannot separate now!" Merkrida trilled. "I know what you have in mind. I smell it on your scent. Do it here. This is the appropriate place."

Kidahin thrashed her tail from side-to-side for less than a minute before turning her back on Jassalin and Merkrida and gliding resolutely up to the prisoners.

"I am Kidahin Uahua'asee'a La'huaset Eyloni," she announced in the awkward, flat human tongue. "I take you prisoner. I charge you with acts of war you may, or may not, have committed against the Compact of the Ten Tribes of Elleio. Coalition Ambassador Alan Dean Winters will decide whether you face the A'tayotan hierarchy or Coalition outlawry sanctions."

Kidahin returned to Merkrida's side.

"Bind them hand and foot. Jassalin will take everyone able and climb onto the vine stem. Help them hoist the prisoners onto the stem, then return to me."

"Affirm," Merkrida sang and turned to do her assaultmistress's bidding.

Kidahin looped her tail at Kyralin and Tialdrin, a summons, and they left Aplilin's side and glided up to her at once.

"Walk with me," Kidahin trilled.

"Yes, assaultmistress," they sang in reply.

The three Hunters surrounded Deering.

"Pick her up," Kidahin sang pleasantly.

"Get your hands off of me, alien filth!" Deering spat.

Master Chief Deering was a powerfully built human female. Kidahin remembered thinking long ago that Deering was Delwyn's mistress of battle, an honored position chosen by a mistress of the ship and always held by a Warrior female. That thought reminded her of Nynava, and

Kidahin flipped her ears against her short crimson ringlets and tried to restrain her latent juvenile adolescent temper.

As heavily built as Deering was, either Kyralin or Tialdrin, by herself, could lift Deering over her head. Having the two Hunters hold her off the ground was to make a demeaning point.

"You do not smell the same as the last time we met," Kidahin sang to Deering. "Back then you smelled of superiority and hated for my personal association with Delwyn, but I never smelled the desire to harm him on you. But now you smell different. You smell like Harrison did then. The hatred riding his scent stung my nose, as did his need to harm Delwyn."

"Ambassador Harrison saw through you, all of you," Deering shouted. "You infected Senior Chief Marsch! He's not himself. Hell, he's not even human anymore. I tried to convince Ambassador Harrison to take Marsch into his confidence, but he foresaw Marsch opposing him. Harrison was right. You women bewitch men. How else could Marsch give up commanding SOG-444? How else could the men in my own team turn against me!"

Kidahin listened patiently, but her eyes watched as the first prisoner was pulled up the vine stem.

She focused her eyes back onto Deering.

"Harrison sought personal glory," she sang evenly. "He saw making an Eyloni-human alliance as an opportunity for personal glory. He wanted to tie the Be'atika Senge's honor into using the Compact fleet to blockade Ni'zakhonii worlds. He saw the fosterage oath Delwyn made with Phelindra to train me on Ibeetu as a threat to those plans. When co-Ambassador Anlann told Captain Winters he would surrender Warpact command to Delwyn and recommend all future talks between Earth and Elleio take place between them, Harrison plotted to kill Delwyn to prevent him from recommending anything to the Be'atika Senge hierarchy sitting as the Compact Counsel."

Deering glared pure hatred, but Kidahin glanced at the second roped and tied prisoner rising off the sand.

Huntresses began gathering in a circle around Kidahin and Deering.

"What?" Deering sneered at them. "Ambassador Harrison has powerful friends in the Coalition Government. When they hear his report, they'll..."

"This voice you hear over your TAC channel is not Harrison," Kidahin interrupted.

"That's a lie," Deering said. "He knows operational codes, codes only he could know. He used them to divert the *Khoza* from Mu Arae picket duty and have us transferred aboard."

"He doomed that warship, and you killed his survivors," Kidahin accused.

"We couldn't tell Captain Bhari about the hypergravity lens the Ambassador was using to call Mu Arae. I didn't know we could actually ram into it, for God's sake. After the damage control assessment, Bhari wanted to jump the ship back into hyperspace and break out of the hypergravity box to send a distress call. He had to be eliminated. Some survivors fought us at first, but soon figured the Ambassador was the safer bet. They changed their minds during reentry, and I had to pop the seals before they took over the Sentry."

"You act no different than Harrison sounds," Kidahin trilled as she watched the third prisoner rise on taught ropes.

"Your plotting was all for nothing. What called out to Mu Arae, what shrieks at you now, is not Harrison. I will demonstrate the truth of my words."

Kidahin grabbed Deering's comms unit and keyed open the TAC channel. "Harrison, this is Kidahin Uahua'asee'a La'huaset Eyloni. Warleader Delwyn comes to kill you!"

*"Kidahin! Marsch! Kill you! Kill you all! Make you suffer and diiiie!"* Harrison squealed joyfully and nonstop as more Hunters climbed down to join the circle around Kidahin and Deering.

"You see?" Kidahin said. "No human can sustain such laughter. This is the sound of a mechanism, a Ni'zakhonii device. There is no living person inside the geode ship."

"No! No! That's not true!" Deering gibbered.

"But it is! Warleader special security went aboard Delwyn's warship to pack his personal items and bring them to our warship. They captured Harrison and his aide and left them on Ibeetu. Harrison could not have left that moon!"

"But he did," Deering crowed, certain now. "He stole a Lizard ship, but it crashed here."

"Have you heard a word from Cultural Attaché Parakh?" Kidahin asked.

"Well, no... but it doesn't matter!"

Kidahin turned around and perked questioning ears at Jassalin.

"I polled scent while you were talking. We are in agreement," Jassalin sang in a cacophony of pure disgust.

"Can you do this? The ranking hierarchy female must be the one who acts."

"I know. I am ready," Jassalin keened.

Kidahin nodded. Jassalin stepped around her and up to Deering. She pulled Deering's long, metal blade from its hip sheath.

"Strip her," she told Kyralin and Tialdrin.

"Hey, what're you doing? I don't have any more weapons!"

The two Hunters deftly ripped Deering's clothing off and forced her, face down and naked, onto the sand.

Jassalin returned to Deering's side, grabbed her by the foot, and drew the sharp blade across her ankle.

"For the crime of intending harm to a male, I hope this knife of yours is dull," Jassalin spat with blinding hatred as she began filleting Deering's left foot.

Deering shrieked, sounding much like Harrison, Jassalin thought.

***

"Keep them under guard next to the stealth insertion vehicle. Do not go inside unless invited. Stay here until we return," Kidahin told the two Gunny Watkins troopers in their cumbersome speech.

"Yep, we kin do that fer ya," the one said. "Won't have no trouble with 'em, not after they saw what ya did to Deerin'."

Kidahin smelled both revulsion and satisfaction on the male's scent and felt a need to reassure him, his teammate, and his prisoners.

"It is a high honor crime for any female to consider harming a male. You heard both Harrison and Deering talk about killing Warleader Delwyn."

"Yeah, ya told us so when ya killed James an' his two buddies. Ya killed 'em peaceful-like, too, yet ya tortured Deering fer it. Why?"

"We females protect males," Kidahin sang. "But males are not obligated to protect other males beyond what civil custom requires. When a male intends actual harm toward another male and takes steps to cause that harm, we regretfully take his life to preserve the life of the male he intends to harm. Both our survival instinct and our culture drives us to protect males over other females, even our own female infants. Any female who considers malekilling without honorable justification must be removed from her hierarchies, societies, and associations by the most demeaning and ruthless way possible."

"Deering wasn't one of your kind. How could you do that to her?" one of the prisoners stammered.

"Once we learn of an intent to harm a male, we act to protect that male. Delwyn is our male, our territorial possession, and we protect our territory."

"Uh-huh. Well, these three ain't gonna cause no trouble. We're low on field rations, though. How long do ya reckon we'll be on this rock, anyway?"

"That," Kidahin paused, "depends on what we find in the geode ship."

"Ambassador Harrison, ya think?" he asked.

"I do not think so," Kidahin said, flicking her ears in dismissal.

"I am leaving Kyralin behind to help Zalzadrin," Jassalin trilled softly.

"To 'manage' Zalzadrin, you mean?" Kidahin trilled a giggle as they shared a pheromonal joke.

"Maybe Zalzadrin and Aplilin can scream at one another just to entertain Kyralin," Merkrida sang, smelling the humor in her assaultmistress's body odor.

"Maybe so, but we need everybody else to assault the geode. According to Aplilin, Seliaha is a small arms genius. Einstika and Alfara can trace geode power systems. Hollfara is a hull designer and can find a weakness in the geode hull. If there is one. You, me and Merkrida are their combat support."

"What are we waiting for?" Hollfara trilled. "I told you I may be able to contact our warship using Harrison's hypercube generator. Tialdrin says Mimiran is near total systemic failure, the point where no accelerated healing technology can make a difference because of the system shock regeneration causes."

The Hunters ran from the SIV, across the sand, up to the vine stem, and climbed up the side. Once atop, they jogged down the wide bark-covered stem, heading northwest. They ran for nearly two hours and covered twenty-thousand ells before reaching the geode ship crash site.

The geode laid sideways, tipped in the sand, a glittery dark chunk of slag big enough to fill a third of a warship's combat deployment bay. It looked harmless enough, which made it seem all the more menacing.

Harrison's continuous, literally breathless, hysterical laughter sent shivers down Kidahin's tail. The male voice was a comfort to all females, but this gibbering travesty made a mockery of that comfort. She could not imagine any male ever making such an emotional attack on female ears.

She killed their commlink tap into the SOG TAC channel feed, unwilling to further expose herself or her teammates to the demoralizing screams.

"If Melkorka thought Delwyn wanted to torpedo the moon, then I think he is right to do so. We cannot allow this thing to continue existing," Merkrida growled.

"Hlinlodyn would second that course of action," Kidahin sang as they reached the sandy ground. They surveyed the geode ship and the surrounding area, seeking any hint of an occupying force.

"I do not think the humans got this far. At least there are no Ni'zakhonii garrisoning the geode," Seliaha trilled in relief.

"There is that," Kidahin agreed. "Well, Hollfara, what do you think?"

Hollfara stood, her tail held rigid behind her, her ears set wide apart, her eyes narrowing.

"I see some loss of symmetry. See this crumple zone? It looks like impact damage," Hollfara sang, her tail whipping side-to-side. She looked around, growling to herself before continuing. "An impact like this should have made a crater," she keened in outrage.

"Hollfara? Look at this crease in the hull. What is it? A compression fold?" Einstika sang at interrogative pitch pointing at a long, wedge-shaped indentation in the hull.

"What?" Hollfara snapped. "No! A crystalline hull cannot compress like that. It must be a design flaw."

"But how?" Einstika persisted. "We saw these things being grown on the asteroid research base we raided in the Nikkiolo system. This looks post-production to me, some kind of damage."

Hollfara glared at Einstika for long moments before continuing her assessment.

Several minutes passed before Merkrida gave voice to her impatience. "Well?" she trilled.

"Einstika is correct," Hollfara grudgingly allowed. "This is a post-production defect, but I cannot grasp how it was made. It looks like someone took a pile driver and rammed a wedge into the length of the hull. It is clearly not crash damage."

"It looks something like how the flight deck was cleaved off our troop transport," Kidahin trilled.

"Does it?" Hollfara sang her interest piqued. "No, a hypergravity wave cleaved our transport. This is not hull material cleaved away. This is hull material compressed into a groove by possible momentary exposure to hypergravitational stress."

"Are you saying the geode hit the same gravitational anomaly *Londiwe Khoza* did?" Kidahin asked.

"No. He hit the anomaly in hyperspace, but the Ni'zakhonii use a dimensional drive for FTL travel. No, I think this groove was made by accident when Harrison created the hypercube."

"This crease, or whatever it is, is several ells long, but only as wide as my thigh. Are you sure it is not a seam?" Jassalin keened in doubt.

"No seam," Hollfara trilled, pausing to twist her pons under Jassalin's nose. "This is a compression fold, and the hull is weakest along its length."

"Can you breach it?" Kidahin asked.

"I could with a plasma torch, given enough time. But we do not have one."

"What about Aplilin's cannon?" Alfara asked. "Set the force chamber to explode. The blast will be spectacular!"

"It might breach the hull," Hollfara allowed, "but I do not think the breach will be wide enough to squeeze through. We left our breaching equipment behind when we abandoned the troop transport."

"I do not care if we can enter or not," Jassalin trilled. "What I need is a hole big enough to expose circuits I can throw the thumpers at," she added, tossing a thumper up and down in her hand.

"It is a question of shorting out the chamber plasma induction cathode to dump the full charge into the plasma pump," Alfara sang.

"Can you do it?" Hollfara asked.

"I think so. Aplilin already did most of the work and showed me how to finish the job. But I cannot build in a delay. Once power dumps into the chamber, plasma ignition begins and the weapon fires. This much plasma, all at once, will vaporize the weapon."

"How long before the weapon fires?" Jassalin asked.

"About the time it takes for me to snap my fingers," Alfara trilled, demonstrating with a snap.

"Blast radius?" Kidahin asked.

"The barrel will direct most of the blast into the hull, but plasma weapons generate back-blast plumes deflected by magnetic shields to protect the gunner. The shield will not matter much against this much discharge, but then again back blast is not barrel-focused plasma. Still...maybe three or four ells?"

"Spirits, I can jump four ells at the snap of my fingers!" Seliaha sang, full of confidence.

"No," Kidahin sang. "I will fire the weapon."

"No!" Seliaha objected vehemently. "I can do this!"

"I know you can," Kidahin reassured her, "but I am assaultmistress. The duty is mine. How long before it is ready to fire?"

"Not long," Alfara sang. "Aplilin did all the hard work because as weaponmistress she knows the cannon inside and out. I need an hour or so to remove her safeties and short-circuit the ignition cathode to the fuel cell."

"How do I trigger the blast?" Kidahin asked.

"The same way you fire the weapon, by pulling the trigger," Alfara sang.

"Hollfara? What do we look for once the hull is breached?" Kidahin sang at interrogative pitch.

"A power distribution nexus. If the prototypes we found at Nikkiolo are any guide, a nexus will look like fractured ice or glass. Give me the thumpers. It will take all four of them firing at once to crash the ship's systems, if they can crash them."

Alfara, Jassalin, and Merkrida passed their thumpers to Kidahin, and she passed them and her own thumper on to Hollfara.

"We have only one chance, so be certain," Kidahin cautioned.

"Affirm," Hollfara sang.

"I am ready," Alfara keened.

"Already?" Jassalin trilled.

"Yes," Alfara growled, scowling. "Aplilin removed the safeties and modified the force chamber while the plasma ignition system was still powered up. I will kill her! I do not care if the firing circuits are burned out! I am surprised it did not explode while we were climbing."

"You are wasting time. Set it up," Merkrida sang.

"Affirm," Alfara sang. "Hollfara, where do you want the cannon to fire?"

"Here," Hollfara pointed. "How will you stabilize the weapon? Kidahin cannot hold it while pulling the trigger."

"Use the mounting clamp," Alfara sang. "The clamp secures the targeting scanner to the cannon. EMP burned out the scanner, so Aplilin removed it. She left the clamp attached. You can clamp the weapon to any edge or lip that will fit."

"What about the crease deformation? Is there an edge it can bite into?"

"Maybe," Alfara sang. She tried, swearing, as the clamp slipping several times off the crease before it held.

"She got it!" Hollfara sang. "Kidahin, pull the trigger gently, or you will yank the clamp off the hull."

"Understood. Stand back!"

Kidahin looked around, tensed as she dropped into a crouch, ready to spring away at the last moment.

"Firing!" Kidahin keened as she touched the trigger and jumped away from the geode, using her momentum to pull the trigger.

The cannon exploded half a second later, firing most of its plasma energy into the geode and catapulting Kidahin forty ells across the sand.

Merkrida rushed to Kidahin's side as Jassalin and Hollfara approached the white-hot breach.

"I see internal lighting!" Jassalin called out. "We are in!"

"Kidahin is unconscious!" Merkrida keened.

"What?" Jassalin trilled. "How bad?"

"I see nothing wrong with her. I think she has a blast-induced concussion."

"Stay with her," Jassalin sang. "How long before the breach is cool enough to squeeze through?" she asked Hollfara.

"Twenty or thirty minutes," Hollfara keened impatiently.

*"Deering! Is that you?"* Harrison's voice shrieked from within the geode.

"That sounds like a voice screaming over a combat address system, does it not?" Seliaha asked.

"Indeed," Jassalin sang. "Merkrida? How is Kidahin?"

"Still unconscious."

Jassalin waited for the breach to cool before giving it a cautious touch. It was hot and would singe the fine waterproof keratin fuzz—what Delwyn called their "velour"—on their skin, but otherwise would cause no serious injury.

"Hollfara, come with me. We are going in."

"Affirm. Einstika and Alfara, come with us. Seliaha, stay with Merkrida and Kidahin."

Jassalin squeezed between the searing breach edges and stumbled onto the deck. Dim, yellow light colored the compartment. She saw no corridors. Random sheets of glowing shattered blue glass covered floor to ceiling. It reminded her of the twisting wooden males' safe mazes in elleiu trees.

Hollfara dropped down next to Jassalin. "Crystal," she trilled. "This is no deck. This is geode crystal reworked by Ni'zakhonii crystal programming."

"Meaning what?" Jassalin trilled.

"This is all circuit elements, and it is not part of the original design, either," Hollfara sang.

"No? It looks all the same to me," Jassalin keened.

"No. These blue crystalline shrouds are new. Think of this as some kind of crystal tumor. See the original geode crystal making up this compartment? It is darker blue and more organized. This new stuff grew out of the original crystal."

*"Get out! Get out of my head! Get out! Get out! Get out!"* Harrison's voice screamed around them.

"This is Harrison!" Hollfara trilled.

"What is? This thing?" Jassalin sang incredulously.

"Yes, this must be an AI avatar-like simulation of Harrison. Gunnery Sergeant William Watkins was right. This is trickery!" Hollfara keened.

"Where is the maze circuit nexus?" Jassalin demanded.

Hollfara raced through twists and turns between crystal curtains until she found a device she recognized.

"Here, this looks like one of the crystal programming units we captured at Nikkiolo. Someone programmed a piece of geode to replicate Harrison's mind, and it grew beyond its original mass and into the ship. I think..."

"I want less thinking and more doing," Jassalin keened. "Throw all the thumpers at the nexus. Do it now!"

"Affirm, acting!" Hollfara trilled and threw all four thumpers at the crystal programmer.

All four electromagnetic pulse electronic countermeasure devices hit the deck at the same time and fired. EMP static fields crackled across crystal surfaces for a moment before dissipating.

Hollfara, Jassalin, Einstika, and Alfara, caught in the stunning electrical storm, fell to the deck, writhing as every muscle twitched convulsively as if hit by antipersonnel shock grenades.

Harrison's continuous giggling screams abruptly cut off as the fractured blue crystal maze turned clear as glass.

Einstika, the furthest from the EMP blast, was the first to recover. Then Alfara and Jassalin stood and went to Hollfara's side as she, too, regained control of her limbs.

"Remind me to never be near a thumper when it goes off," Hollfara growled, tasting blood from involuntarily biting the inside of her mouth, tongue, and lips.

"Did we kill the ship?" Einstika asked, awed.

"I do not think so," Hollfara sang. "See the original crystal? It still glows deep blue. The Harrison simulation was an adjunct to the geode."

"Hollfara?" Kidahin's voice trilled from the breach.

"Yes, assaultmistress?" Hollfara sang respectfully.

"You said you could use Harrison's FTL distress hypercube to act as a hyperlink transmitter. Can you use it to contact Melkorka?"

"I do not know!" Hollfara keened. "With the Harrison AI network offline, the ship should be drawing minimal power. He's not doing anything but sitting here."

Hollfara looked around, gesturing for Einstika and Alfara to follow.

"You are both power systems techmistresses," she trilled. "Maintaining a tap into the hypercube for FTL comms must take a lot of power. The bluer the crystal turns, the more power it draws. Look for deep blue crystals!"

"Affirm," Alfara sang and ran off.

Einstika remained. "Even if we find it, what can we do about it?" she asked.

"Turn it on and off to send Melkorka a message in drum language," Hollfara sang.

The geode, crammed full of crystal components, had few voids and none of them very large. It took no time for the Hunters to prowl through twisting turns of colored glass and find a bank of crystals glowing in black light.

"Assaultmistress! I think we found the hypercube tap!" Hollfara sang.

"Can you turn it on and off?" Kidahin asked.

"I think so..."

"Then do it!" Kidahin sang.

"Affirm, acting," Hollfara trilled. She held her breath, reached out, and touched the obvious blinking control crystal.

"The bank glows diamond-white. I think it is off."

Hollfara touched the crystal again, and the bank glowed in black light again.

"Confirmed, assaultmistress. I can turn the hypercube tap on and off."

"Send a message to Melkorka!"

"Affirm, coding..."

Hollfara got as far as the second sentence before the crystal bank turned red. No amount of touching coaxed it to change back to its operating color.

"Assaultmistress! The hypercube tap is offline!"

"What? Why?" Kidahin demanded.

"I do not know!" Hollfara keened, frantic.

It took Hollfara and the two techmistresses four hours to find the reason why, but not the cause of, the hypercube FTL relay shutdown.

"It is no longer receiving talkback telemetry?" Kidahin sang. "Talkback from what? The Coalition warship?"

"It is the only conclusion I can think of," Hollfara sang. "The change to red must mean the transmitter is ready, but there is nothing for it to transmit to."

"Hlinlodyn fired on the derelict," Merkrida snarled.

Hollfara snapped her ears in negation. "No. Anailiatha was planning on using the derelict human warship to jump our warship out of the hypercube. Maybe she tried it."

"I did, and it worked!" a familiar voice sang from behind them.

Kidahin turned as Anailiatha, Melkorka, and Phelindra glided up and wrapped their tails around her.

"Mistress Melkorka," Kidahin began, "Mimiran is in critical..."

"I know. We jumped into orbit, found the SIV, and translated there first. Allohindra took Mimiran, Zalzadrin, Aplilin, and Tialdrin to Health Center. Kyralin and the honorable human males are guarding your three prisoners. What happens to them is up to Delwyn, but I am certain I will not like his decision."

"We are, on the other hand, pleased with your performance," Phelindra trilled.

"The Harrison distress call was a trick," Kidahin keened. "It was a simulation. Hollfara destroyed it."

"Mistress Anailiatha?" Hollfara interrupted. "How did you get out of the hypercube?"

"I sealed the mobius fracture by repairing the derelict's hyperdrive coils and jumping him into hyperspace, causing the hypercube to fold in on itself and cancel out. Our warship was being pulled into hyperspace when Delwyn ordered full sublight velocity to evade the collapsing quantum singularity. It kicked us halfway across the system as we fell back into normal space. Delwyn then ordered an FTL jump into orbit above us."

"So we remain here another day while the jump drive recharges," Jassalin trilled in disappointment.

"Correct," Anailiatha sang.

"What will happen to *Londiwe Khoza* now?" Seliaha asked.

"He will drift forever in hyperspace. I do not think even the Coalition can find a ship adrift there," Anailiatha trilled sadly.

"What are we supposed to do while the jump drive recharges?" Kidahin trilled impatiently.

"Delwyn will sing the Death Song ritual for Nynava," Melkorka sang. "He will sing a tribute to the society of *Londiwe Khoza* at the same time."

"Now?" Jassalin growled in surprise.

"Of course not now!" Melkorka trilled. "Preparing for a Death Song ritual takes time, longer than the time it takes for the jump drive to recharge."

"Which means you can spend some time dissecting this thing," Phelindra trilled at Anailiatha." She paused to flick her ears at Kidahin before continuing. "Take your Huntresses to Health Center and get healer clearance from Allohindra before reporting to your secondary occupational duties. Remain there until end-of-watch." Phelindra trilled, pausing a moment before adding, "I strongly suggest you get some sleep. I want no cacophonies of dissonant harmonies from you while Delwyn is singing!" she warned, her scent suggesting a dire threat.

"Affirm, Mistress," Kidahin sang.

***

Kidahin and her remaining Huntresses quantum translated aboard their ship, paused to sing formal greeting to the Mistress of Conveyance, and ran out into deep, heavily overgrown rainforest.

Overcome by rainforest beauty, Kidahin paused. Orange grasses fringed narrow trails running through crimson bushes and golden brush. Trees taller than the vine stems they left below cloaked in red and orange leaves variegated with yellows seemed to go on forever.

Above, turquoise-blue sky and brilliant yellow sun gleamed down on them through those diaphanous pastel leaves. No clouds marred the bright view.

*"Sa lau a'hei ti elleio,"* Jassalin trilled softly.

"Yes, it is good to be home," Kidahin agreed.

"I never thought I could miss the environmental home option simulations so much," Hollfara keened. "I know they are holograms sculptured by force fields, but I would not trade them for anything right now!"

"Come on," Kidahin urged. "We cannot put Allohindra off for long. She will come looking for us if we do not report to her soon."

"Yes," Jassalin agreed. "And I want to see how Mimiran is doing."

Kidahin flicked her ears in agreement and snapped her tail for emphasis. She reluctantly led them down a narrow trail in the general direction of Health Center. The path to Allohindra took them far from the command center and from Delwyn.

"Kidahin!" a baritone voice trilled as the Mistress of the Forestation glided up next to her.

"Mistress?" Kidahin asked.

"Phelindra called me from the surface. You and the rest of Assault Team-Two will present yourselves to the hierarchy representatives at end-of-watch!"

What did we do wrong, Kidahin wondered. "Affirm, Mistress. Mistress? Have we done something wrong?"

"Wrong? Wrong? Spirits, Kidahin, your teammates saved male lives. You are all being advanced in hierarchy rank!"

Kidahin stared at the Warrior female, mesmerized by her idly swaying tail.

"Mistress? When will this happen?" Jassalin asked, brushing Kidahin with her tail and wondering when they would find time to sleep.

"Before Delwyn sings the Death Song ritual for Nynava," the Mistress of the Forestation sang. "And before he decides who is worthy of honor knots, mission beads, and accomplishment webs for your rank earrings," she added.

Kidahin paused on hearing the Warrior's news. Hierarchy rank was important in female daily life. Social ranking was important as well, but military rank reflected an unbiased male honoring of female bravery and was highly coveted.

"Mistress? May I prowl with you?" Kyralin trilled.

The Warrior's ears perked forward in surprise. She narrowed her eyes as she sniffed the air around Kyralin.

"You wish to prowl with me?" the Forestation Mistress sang.

"Yes, Mistress," Kyralin sang sincerely. "I want to know you."

"Then come and prowl with me," the Mistress sang.

"Maybe we should follow them," Jassalin trilled under her breath. "Kyralin's mouth always gets her into trouble with Warriors."

Kidahin stood on the simulated dirt path and twisted her pons in slow circles while considering both Kyralin's scent and Jassalin's concern. "I think not," she said. "I remember Kyralin singing in counterpoint to Delwyn's songs as they played over the commlink. Her song was the one Mimiran taught her about self-confidence. Did you happen to hear any of it?"

"No, not really," Jassalin sang. "She sang to herself, and I do not intentionally break customs of courtesy and privacy."

"Nor I, not on purpose," Kidahin admitted, "yet I heard her singing Nynava's name and something about Hunter-Warrior female rivalry and unity. I think Mimiran helped her make peace with the death of her Warrior family member. I think Kyralin is now a strong Warrior female ally."

"I thought she wanted to check on Tialdrin. They are quite close," Merkrida sang slyly.

"Oh, I do not think Kyralin and the Mistress of the Forestation will be long. She will not want Allohindra hunting her down," Kidahin trilled.

"Forget healer clearance!" Jassalin keened. "I want this bullet out of my hip. I am sure everyone with bullet wounds cannot wait to see one of Allohindra's healers."

Kidahin trilled sympathetically as they continued their prowl among tall crimson trees and through flame-orange brush.

Once in sight of the Health Center elleiu tree, Kidahin picked up the pace and led her Huntresses around and up through ascending fused aerial root tiers surrounding the massive hometree until they finally reached the long-term regeneration chrysalis abodes.

In one of them Kidahin found Mimiran suspended in a transparent oval bubble, floating in clear fluid. Mistress of Healers Allohindra was hovering over the chrysalis control console. Standing, her tail twitching madly behind her, Allohindra watched vital signs while making rapid adjustments.

"Mistress? How is she?" Kidahin sang.

"Bad, very bad," Allohindra trilled. "The regeneration process begins, but I must go about it slowly or the rapid healing will trigger fatal shock. She may die from her injuries before I can stabilize her."

"How long?" Jassalin asked, awed by the medical technology she hoped never to find herself trapped in.

"I need two or three days of constant monitoring just to stabilize her," Allohindra growled in disgust, her pheromones slapping at their noses. "She needs about a month to reverse all the damage. After regeneration she will need another ten or twelve months of physical therapy."

"Why?" Kyralin asked as she glided up to the bubble and its critical patient. "Her body will be like new."

"But not the same," Merkrida sang, rubbing her jaw. "My new teeth do not fit against the ones in my upper jaw. Regenerated muscle tissue is infant-new. It has no muscle-memory, having never been flexed before. Chewing is still a chore for me, because my jaw jumps sideways and I bite my tongue or lip all the time. Mimiran's muscles, healing in that posture, will resist any other position when she is removed from the chrysalis. She will leave her first several physical therapy sessions singing words Anailiatha will faint at."

"Kyralin!" Tialdrin trilled from an adjacent examination abode. "It is about time you came to see me!"

"Tialdrin? Your chest? How is it?" Kidahin asked.

"It is as good as new!" she trilled.

"She was shot in the lung," Allohindra trilled, unconcerned. "It was nothing critical."

"Kidahin, we want to talk to you," Tialdrin sang as she wrapped her tail around Kyralin's waist.

"We have time now, unless you are invoking privacy," Kidahin sang.

"No, this concerns our team. We no longer want warleader special security assignments. Prowling with our team on the surface was more exciting than ship security prowling."

"Talk to Phelindra about it," Kidahin suggested. "You need mistress approval to change secondary duty assignments."

Tialdrin twitched her tail at Allohindra, brushing the healer's pons momentarily, and flicked her ears at Kidahin.

"Mistress Allohindra has accepted Mimiran's recommendation that I apprentice with her as an associate healer."

"When did Mimiran do this?" Kidahin trilled.

"When she sent the human virtual autopsy scans to me," Allohindra sang, growling lightly at the distraction. "And, Tialdrin, if you think prowling our warship is boring after surface action duty, then you will positively hate the boredom healer studies will bring to you."

"What about you, Kyralin?" Kidahin asked.

"The Mistress of the Forestation asked me to join the combat hull forestation Hunter liaison force."

"Really? That is about as close as you can get to duty into and out of the forestation, considering only Warrior females work there. They will grant you forestation special access privileges. But if you abuse their courtesy they have dire ways of making you wish you had never been born," Kidahin trilled.

"She made that quite clear to me," Kyralin trilled steadily.

"Both of you should tell the Huntmistress your plans. She expressed an initial interest in both of you. You do not want her feeling insulted or manipulated," Kidahin trilled in warning.

"We are going to her after we get approval from Phelindra," Tialdrin sang.

"Yes, Kyralin, you cannot just step up to the Huntmistress and say 'thank you, but no thank you'," Jassalin trilled derisively.

"Where is Hollfara?" Merkrida asked, changing the subject.

"She left right after healer clearance," Tialdrin sang. "I think she ran to Power Systems and Propulsion to find Anailiatha. She sang something about ideas the Mistress of Sails should hear about the geode ship and how the Harrison neural network was made. She thinks the Ni'zakhonii put them here as a test. She also wants to tell Anailiatha something about human engineering."

"Oh," Merkrida grimaced. "Boring engineering lectures. Anailiatha will be ecstatic."

"She will not," Allohindra sang with a chuckle. "She was too busy figuring out how to free our warship from the hypercube for mating time with Delwyn. I am absolutely certain she is pursuing him with a single-minded intent."

The Hunters snapped their ears forward and twisted their tails sensuously. They gave one another furtive glances. Kidahin and her Huntresses were all adolescents, barely out of juvenile age. None had ever mated before, and Allohindra's mean casual remark shoved it into their noses.

"That is not funny!" Aplilin keened from a corner treatment abode.

Kidahin and Jassalin forced themselves to walk away from a floating Mimiran and follow Aplilin's growling.

They found her strapped onto a table with a metal torus mounted in its center. Aplilin laid there, the torus covering her from hip to breasts, humming lightly.

"How is your back feeling?" Kyralin sang softly.

"Painless and slow," Aplilin sang in mild dissonance. "It tickles, it feels warm, and I can wiggle my toes! I want out of here so I can tell Delwyn how I shot down a pinnace with an arrow!"

"Mate with him, you mean," Jassalin trilled, trying hard not to laugh.

"That, too," Aplilin agreed, aggressively ignoring Jassalin's pheromonal odor.

"You should all thank the spirits that we are in the grip of mating season!" Allohindra trilled from Mimiran's bubble.

"Why? Being in season is distracting!" Seliaha complained.

"Mating was all I could think about after I got shot," Einstika sang.

"My point exactly!" Allohindra sang. "None of you paid much attention to your flesh wounds, some of them quite serious, too. The need to survive and mate gave you all physiological fortitude. Mimiran certainly would have died without it, Tialdrin could not have pressed on with a collapsed lung without it, and... Oh, spirits!"

"Allohindra? Is it Mimiran?" Kidahin keened as she bolted from Aplilin's side ... and ran face-to-face into Lo'sutra'est anni!

The pale, petite Comari's long, yellow hair rustled as her ears perked at Kidahin.

Kidahin stepped back. Lo'sutra'est anni rarely left Delwyn for long. What was this deadly package of rage doing in Health Center, anyway?

Lo'sutra'est anni considered Kidahin and her pheromonal scent. She tipped her head, much like Delwyn often did, because neither possessed a tail to convey mood.

<<Delwyn is mating with Aheila and her three lovers,>> the Comari signed in battle language. <<He is safe and well-protected,>> she added as a casual afterthought.

"You!" Kidahin hissed angrily. "You told everyone to leave the deployment bay so he could commandeer a vehicle and try to catch up with our troop transport? What were you thinking?" she added, disregarding the very real threat the Comari posed to anyone interfering with her absolute prerogatives regarding Delwyn and his safety.

<<I helped him secure the craft. I also sent word to Phelindra to stop us. She did not get to us in time to stop us. She rammed us with another vehicle. I told her that if Delwyn had taken injury from her carelessness I would have killed her. >>

"Why did you help him just to frustrate his plans?" Kidahin keened, the urge to mate and her youth making her loud, angry, and reckless.

<<Delwyn needs to feel useful protecting us. It is an endearing part of him that must be addressed with some tact. You know this firsthand, because he once went on his own to rescue you and other females.>>

As the Comari signed, Kidahin smelled an aggrieved emotion on the Comari's scent.

"What about the other human males?" Kidahin keened.

<<Delwyn says the innocent must be accommodated in his honor suite and taken back to Elleio,>> Lo'sutra'est anni signed savagely.

Kidahin trilled a sigh. She expected as much. Tradition and custom stronger than law all but prohibited any male but the warleader aboard a Compact warship. The honor suite was meant for rare warleader-to-warleader visits and not for accommodating unwanted male travel companions.

"We took a few humans prisoner. What about them?" Kidahin asked.

<<Delwyn decrees they be given supplies and abandoned for a Coalition ship to pick up. He wanted to bring them back for trial, but our society refused to reach a Major Consensus allowing it.>>

"What did Delwyn think about that?" Kidahin asked.

<< Nothing. He understands. And his scent told us he really did not want them here.>>

Kidahin twitched her ears in relief. Still, having other males aboard, even quarantined in the honor suite, during mating season would make everyone aboard dangerously testy.

"About Delwyn's need to fight with us..." Kidahin began.

<<He wants to share the risk with us, as all males do. But no Eyloni male ventures far from overwhelming female support and protection. Delwyn, his human mind, thinks about safety differently. I will make sure he feels useful while keeping him far from actual danger. I take you into confidence in this matter,>> the Comari signed expressively.

"Entiki. You have it, always," Kidahin affirmed upon her honor.

"Kidahin?" Jassalin interrupted. "Allohindra wants us with Mimiran."

Kidahin excused herself and rushed to Allohindra's side.

"Mistress?" she keened, breathless.

"Melkorka called. She wants you back at the auxiliary command center navigation console. All of you must report to your secondary apprenticeship duties, except you Tialdrin."

"Me?" she sang, worried.

"Yes, you. You are familiar with the Healer's Rede, are you not?"

"I am, Mistress. I memorized it while doing the autopsies with Mimiran."

"Well, we are here and Mimiran is here. Sing the Healer's Rede!"

"Yes, Mistress!" Tialdrin keened. She took several deep breaths, turned to face Mimiran, and sang.

"I, Tialdrin Uahua'asee'a La'huaset Eyloni, upon my honor, declare in memory of Aniculin the Healer who taught females the healing arts, to Didora, the first female healer, and to her daughters Eirlodyn and Menglodyn, that I will freely teach my art to all who ask without seeking recompense, I will do all I can to relieve sorrow, worry, and sickness, and above all I will do no harm.

"I declare I will never seek favors for treatment, nor will I give a harmful substance or a false diagnosis. I will never treat a female without first gaining her or her guardian's consent after telling her the nature of her illness, its cause, and its proposed treatment.

"Further, I declare I will preserve male lives at all costs, and I say to the spirits that I will allow no male to refuse my treatment once female consent is given on his behalf. Entiki."

Allohindra ordered everyone out of regeneration but Tialdrin and Kidahin. The Mistress of Healers swiftly returned to Mimiran and made several rapid adjustments.

"Will she get well?" Kidahin keened at Tialdrin.

"I do not know, but I will feel better once the bubble turns opaque and full regeneration begins."

Kidahin smiled at a memory.

"Mimiran thought surface actions were exciting," she sang. "I wonder if she changes her mind when she comes out of the chrysalis."

"Ha!" Tialdrin trilled. "Allohindra is furious with her. She will not allow her to take a permanent place with us. She says if we ever get a mission that needs a surgeon-in-battle, Mimiran may come with us—if she wants anything to do with us after all the injuries she suffered."

"Um," Kidahin trilled. "I hear the Mistress of Fortifications is making a place for the Death Song ritual on the surface."

"Yes," Tialdrin agreed. "I hope Delwyn can muster the strength needed to sing through the ritual."

"Why would he not? Mating is restful, nothing more than laying tail-twined to establish an empathic connection for emotional sharing while the soft male organ rests against the cloaca. It takes no effort, and Delwyn can stay awake longer than we can."

"And he sleeps twice as long as we do, too," Tialdrin trilled.

"I guess we will find out soon enough ourselves...," Kidahin began as Melkorka's voice trilled over the combat address system.

"Kidahin, where are you?" she keened, sounding put out.

"Leaving Health Center, Mistress," Kidahin sang, which was technically true.

"You are late. Report to auxiliary command center navigation, now!"

"Affirm, acting," Kidahin sang. She wrapped her tail around Tialdrin's tail in farewell before heading down the winding, hollow, spiraling Health Center elleiu tree trunk and out onto the heavy yellow-trimmed, orange and red rainforest trail that led off in the direction of the auxiliary command center.

# ABOUT THE AUTHOR

David Michael Martin graduated from the Ohio Institute of Technology in 1982 and designed PC-integrated laboratory analyzers until 1987. An avid science fiction and fantasy reader, Mr. Martin successfully wrote and told engaging and entertaining stories as a games master for several of the popular fantasy roleplaying game systems appearing today.

Mr. Martin returned to college and pursued his interests in English and the humanities at Ohio University, earning cum laude honors. Mr. Martin continued his English education, taking graduate English courses at Adams State University.

Mr. Martin has over twenty years' experience tutoring adult basic education classes for adult students seeking their G.E.D. diplomas. Mr. Martin currently lives in western Michigan and trains puppies using Karen Pryor clicker training techniques to become guide dogs for the blind.

Assaultmistress Kidahin is his fourth book in the Hunter's Universe saga and begins the second trilogy of the series. The first trilogy features Warleader Delwyn. The second trilogy features the Eyloni Hunter female Kidahin.